P9-DCF-647

Lc ✓

THE SENSATIONAL KISS

Lord Norwood took a step closer to Hyacinthe. He pulled her cap off, placing it in her hands, then ran his fingers through her tumbled curls.

She found it impossible to retreat. She cleared her throat, knowing that if she had any sense at all she would march away from this rake. Yet she could not move.

"I must thank you for all you have done," he whispered, hovering over her, his lazy grin teasing her.

Her lips parted to give her consent, for he leaned down to place a warm kiss on her lips.

She had never been kissed like this. This melting sensation was entirely different from past experience. When she opened her eyes, she gave him a confused look.

"You are welcome," she whispered back. . . .

SIGNET REGENCY ROMANCE
COMING IN FEBRUARY 1994

Mary Balogh
Dancing with Clara

Dawn Lindsey
An Independent Woman

Sandra Heath
Highland Conquest

AT YOUR LOCAL BOOKSTORE
OR ORDER DIRECTLY
FROM THE PUBLISHER
WITH VISA OR MASTERCARD
1-800-253-6476

THE RAKE AND THE REDHEAD

by

Emily Hendrickson

A SIGNET BOOK

SIGNET
Published by the Penguin Group
Penguin Books USA Inc., 375 Hudson Street,
New York, New York 10014, U.S.A.
Penguin Books Ltd, 27 Wrights Lane,
London W8 5TZ, England
Penguin Books Australia Ltd, Ringwood,
Victoria, Australia
Penguin Books Canada Ltd, 10 Alcorn Avenue,
Toronto, Ontario, Canada M4V 3B2
Penguin Books (N.Z.) Ltd, 182–190 Wairau Road,
Auckland 10, New Zealand

Penguin Books Ltd, Registered Offices:
Harmondsworth, Middlesex, England

First published by Signet,
an imprint of Dutton Signet,
a division of Penguin Books USA Inc.

First Printing, January, 1994
10 9 8 7 6 5 4 3 2 1

Copyright © Doris Emily Hendrickson, 1994
All rights reserved

 REGISTERED TRADEMARK—MARCA REGISTRADA

Printed in the United States of America

Without limiting the rights under copyright reserved above, no part of this publication
may be reproduced, stored in or introduced into a retrieval system, or transmitted, in any
form, or by any means (electronic, mechanical, photocopying, recording, or otherwise),
without the prior written permission of both the copyright owner and the above publisher
of this book.

BOOKS ARE AVAILABLE AT QUANTITY DISCOUNTS WHEN USED TO PROMOTE PRODUCTS OR SERVICES.
FOR INFORMATION PLEASE WRITE TO PREMIUM MARKETING DIVISION, PENGUIN BOOKS USA INC., 375
HUDSON STREET, NEW YORK, NEW YORK 10014.

If you purchased this book without a cover you should be aware that this book is stolen
property. It was reported as "unsold and destroyed" to the publisher and neither the
author nor the publisher has received any payment for this "stripped book."

*Dedicated to Jennifer Enderlin
with deep appreciation
for her enthusiastic support
and unfailing understanding.*

1

Hyacinthe clutched the letter tightly in her left hand as her right reached out to pull the window curtain of the swaying coach to one side to peer outside. Tom Coachman had slowed the traveling coach, no doubt approaching the inn where they were to spend the night. They were entering a pretty village set in the gently rolling landscape of Oxfordshire not too terribly far from her destination.

The brightly colored sign of the Black Lion Inn hung from above the door to a neat white building. Pink snapdragons bloomed with perky white daisies and orange wallflowers alongside the highly presentable hostelry. The innkeeper could be justly proud of his establishment, she decided when she observed the neat yard and fast-moving ostlers.

She let the curtain drop and turned her attention to her companion and maid, Fosdick. If a more respectable soul existed, Hyacinthe couldn't imagine who it might be. To have Fosdick at her side was the only way dear Aunt Bel had permitted Hyacinthe to dash off to Cousin Jane on an errand of mercy. At the moment the neatly garbed Fosdick looked to have been sucking a lemon from what she termed the havey-cavey scramble across country into the wilds of Oxfordshire.

Which thought brought Hyacinthe's eyes back to the letter again. She had read and reread the missive, horrified to learn her dearest Jane was about to be dispossessed of her precious little cottage, turned out by some heartless man just to improve his *garden*! The village in which Jane lived spoiled his lordship's view, she wrote, so it must go.

"Dreadful man," Hyacinthe declared under her breath. She had no high opinion of gardeners in general and male gentry who toyed with gardening in particular. Her pride still smarted from her previous encounters with his eminence, the rakish and lofty Lord Norwood, while visiting her aunt.

The handsome and dashing gentleman had preferred discussing fertilizer and lawns with Lord Leighton to a pleasant flirtation with Hyacinthe. She could tolerate being ignored for another woman. But fertilizer? Shocking!

It hadn't been their first encounter. She had met his rakish lordship during her brief stay in London, an insult she had kept to herself. Accustomed to flattering attentions from smitten swains, Hyacinthe was mortified to find herself studied through Lord Norwood's quizzing glass and then dismissed. He had as much as declared her to be unworthy of a word, much less a flirtation. It had caused a deep wound, one she could not dismiss no matter how hard she tried.

He must have suspected he had captured her interest, the dratted man. But to depress her attraction in such a heartless manner consigned him to the depths of the most rakish . . . beyond all that was proper. What a pity he was so handsome, such an exquisite dancer, and dressed to the nines upon every occasion. That blond rascal had flirted with every presentable miss and matron in town. All but herself, that was. Oh, the ignominy of it all.

Her only consolation was that the beautiful and accomplished Lady Olivia Everard had chased him quite shamelessly and been given her comeuppance as well.

Heartless, unfeeling man, just like the man who intended to toss Jane from her home. Well, he had Miss Hyacinthe Dancy to reckon with now. She narrowed a pair of fine green eyes and fingered a red curl that had escaped her bonnet while she considered what she would like to do to the gentleman gardener who threatened her cousin.

The traveling coach drew to a halt. Shortly the door opened and the steps were let down by Warton, her groom. Fosdick busied herself collecting the bits and pieces scattered about the interior of the coach.

Hyacinthe gathered the skirts of her dark green traveling dress in one hand and took her reticule with her as she prepared to descend. Her fashionable cottage bonnet caught on the coach door and tumbled down her back, held only by the ribands. Vexed at this disarray to her usually neat person, Hyacinthe paused on the step, intending to push the bonnet into place.

The landlord bustled up, then paused at the sight offered in the door of the coach. Later—when she had peered in a looking glass—Hyacinthe could understand his reaction. At the moment she fumed when the man began to shake his head.

"This be a respectable place, madam. We have no room in this inn for the likes of you." He squared his shoulders with a righteous sniff while motioning her back into her coach.

Seething, more furious than she could recall ever being before—no doubt aggravated by her recollections of Lord Norwood—Hyacinthe stepped down to confront the man. "I am Miss Hyacinthe Dancy, my good man. I require rooms for myself and my abigail plus accommodations for my coachman and groom for the night."

She was insulted at the way his eyes took on a knowing look and roved her slim person. Then the respectable Fosdick materialized at her side and Tom Coachman rounded the coach from where he had been instructing the ostler as to what was required for his employer's equipage.

Just as the innkeeper appeared to be thinking he had made an error, a gentleman Hyacinthe had not noticed before turned to stroll across the inn yard to also confront the innkeeper. And Hyacinthe.

She met his gaze with a fearless tilt of her heart-shaped face, her eyes the frozen green of a northern fjord.

"Well, if it isn't Miss Hyacinthe Dancy," the elegantly dressed and perfectly polished Lord Norwood drawled. "How charming to see you again. I trust you are on your way to Blenheim for the festivities?"

Hyacinthe wasn't sure she could unlock her jaw to give a civil reply. She was not on her way to Blenheim but he couldn't possibly know it. Nor could the innkeeper. Rather than tell an outright lie, Hyacinthe smiled, the brilliant smile for which she and all the Dancy girls were famous.

The innkeeper took a step back, bowed most humbly, then said with a sweep of one arm, "I do beg your pardon, Miss

Dancy. Please to follow me and you shall have the very best rooms I have to offer."

Hyacinthe suspected that Lord Norwood had already claimed the best, but remained silent lest she be labeled a harpy. She bestowed what she hoped was a regal nod on Lord Norwood, then swept past him toward the door of the inn.

She found the infamous lord at her side, placing her gloved hand upon his arm, and behaving as though they were marching in to dinner at Blenheim rather than entering a humble inn.

"I shall lend you consequence, you see," he whispered with a lazy wink from one of his remarkable blue eyes.

Hyacinthe wondered if she could be pardoned for shooting him.

"A male member of the nobility carries a deal of *ton*, you recall. More than a green girl could possibly command. My attentions will insure you a decent supper and a prompt breakfast come morning." He smiled down at her with his well-known and decidedly devilish grin. His astonishing blue eyes held a glimmer of amusement; they crinkled up at the corners, revealing the time he had spent out of doors. Gardening, no doubt, she thought wryly. Or possibly he acquired that attractive tan while at the racetrack, betting on all the winners, for he was known to possess uncanny luck.

She maintained a seething, icy silence until they paused at the bottom of the stairs leading up to the bedrooms. Then she turned to give him a falsely sweet smile and said in a voice dripping with propriety, "You are too kind, Lord Norwood. What a pity we shan't be meeting at Blenheim after all. I understand there usually are a considerable number of gentlemen in attendance at the parties there."

The amusement left his eyes and he gave her a rather thoughtful look. Then with a shake that seemed to say he must have misunderstood what might be concealed in her words, he bowed, relinquishing her hand only after placing a lingering kiss on the delicate glove covering her right hand.

"Until later, dear lady."

"Until later," she echoed. And to herself she added, "Much later; with any luck, never." Once a girl's heart had been wounded, only a fool would seek further injury.

Not until she entered the lovely room on the next floor of the inn and surveyed herself in the looking glass did she gasp with dismay. "Oh!" she exclaimed to Fosdick, who had entered the room directly behind her.

"Oh, indeed, miss," the abigail said in her most reproving tone. "What his lordship must have thought is beyond consideration."

The girl in the looking glass had blushing cheeks and indignant green eyes beneath tumbled red curls. Her green traveling dress clung to her slender frame just a shade too familiarly. What Hyacinthe had considered reasonably proper now seemed a trifle forward in looks, the cut of the dress appearing indiscreet.

Hyacinthe allowed Fosdick to untangle the ribands of her bonnet, then watched as it was placed on the dresser. The pelisse she had worn, only to remove when she became overly warm, was placed on the high four-poster bed. If only she had been wearing that respectable garment with its buttons that marched up to her chin none of this would have occurred. She would have been spared the confrontation with the innkeeper and the interference of Lord Norwood.

Yet she had to admit that she hadn't felt so exhilarated in ages.

It must have been the battle between two of the opposite sex. Hyacinthe—like any true redhead—loved a good clash. Oh, the audacity of the man. His very look had taunted her, bringing back that moment of humiliation when she had been rejected as unworthy of a flirtation by the premier rake in London. Not that she was a flirt. It was the challenge that enticed her. Like any woman worth her mettle, she wondered if she might be the one to turn his head, lure him from his bold ways.

"I trust we shall not see his lordship again," Fosdick said, a question lurking in her voice, a reproach ready to be administered if necessary.

"I hope not, dear Fosdick," Hyacinthe said in a little voice quite unlike her earlier tone of anger and contempt. "I have met the gentleman before, as you may have gathered. We did not precisely agree with one another. In fact, I would be foolish beyond permission to think he intended anything more than his own amusement."

"I see," the maid replied. Indeed, Fosdick probably saw more than her mistress intended, for the maid was wise beyond her years—which put her in the category of Methuselah, most likely.

"His lordship changes his attentions as often as a weathercock alters direction," Hyacinthe mused aloud while she drifted to the window to look down upon the very same inn yard where she had suffered his rescue. "I would have been quite fine had he minded his own business. Once the innkeeper caught sight of you and Tom Coachman, not to mention that dour-faced groom Aunt Bel bestowed upon me, not a soul in the world would judge me improper." She whirled about to give the maid a defiant stare as though to convince both of them of the fact.

"Warton is most amiable for a groom. It would not be seemly for him to be otherwise, miss," Fosdick said, removing the gown intended for the following day from Hyacinthe's traveling portmanteau. "However I have no doubt but that you would have prevailed in the end."

"Indeed." Hyacinthe sighed and returned her attention to the view from the window. While she watched Lord Norwood crossed the yard to chat with Warton and Tom Coachman. With his hat removed, the sun blessed his blond curls with more than radiance. He looked positively angelic. And Hyacinthe knew him to be the opposite. Wretched man.

She leaned forward as though she might catch what was said. Of course she couldn't detect a word of the conversation, but she thought it most strange. Another oddity was that his eminence did not appear the rake she knew from London. But that was silly. The man was the same one she had watched in Town, flirting, dancing, cutting a yard-wide dash through society.

Hyacinthe decided that she quite detested him. He might be heartbreakingly handsome and have manners so polished that young men looked to him as an example to emulate, but he was not a caring person. Beneath that elegant exterior was nothing . . . no heart, no substance. Just when she'd decided that she required those particular qualities in a gentleman she couldn't say, but she did. And Blase Montague, the charming Marquess of Norwood, failed on both counts.

Her heart soothed by this new knowledge, she faced the remainder of her day with more confidence. A rather feline smile crossed her lips. "I wonder if the man who seeks to oust my cousin is like Lord Norwood. I rather believe he must be."

"Then he'd be a gentleman and make no mistake," Fosdick said with a snap. A rap on the door prevented her from continuing in her observations on his lordship.

"Yes?" she said, peering around the door with sharp-eyed suspicion.

A country-fresh maid, her snowy mob cap properly covering brown curls, sidled into the room with a hesitant step, a tray in her hands. Tantalizing aromas drifted from the tray to tease Hyacinthe's nose.

"If you please, miss, his lordship says as how you might like a cup of tea before your dinner. He begs you to join him in the best parlor later." She pressed her lips together in anxious silence after delivering what was undoubtedly a memorized message. It was not every day that a country miss had a chance to make contact with nobility.

"Extend my thanks, but I shall dine in my room." Hyacinthe smiled at the girl, for it wasn't her fault that Lord Norwood offered yet another insult to Hyacinthe.

Once the girl had placed the tray on a table and departed, Hyacinthe turned to give Fosdick a fulminating look.

"It would not be proper for me to join him and he knows it. Why, it could compromise me beyond redemption," Hyacinthe declared indignantly. That that very compromise could place him in the danger of having to offer for her lurked in the recesses of her mind. What a stupid thing for him to do.

"Quite true." The abigail frowned thoughtfully while she poured out fragrant cups of steaming Bohea for them both, for her employer was never one to deny her maid a restoring cup of hot tea. "Since he does know better, one wonders why he did such a thing."

Hyacinthe exchanged a speculative look with her maid. It was indeed a conundrum of the first order.

There was also a plate of fresh-from-the-oven lemon biscuits on the tray. Hyacinthe and Fosdick proceeded to restore their nerves, then Hyacinthe urged her maid to take a rest. The older woman was not quite as stout as she pretended to be and Hyacinthe's tender heart worried about her health.

Besides, Hyacinthe intended to question Tom Coachman about whatever his lofty lordship had wanted with them. Once Fosdick snored genteelly away while stretched out on her comfortable bed, Hyacinthe slipped silently from her room and down the stairs.

She had not made the mistake of leaving without her pelisse buttoned to her chin and her bonnet snugly tied below same. First glancing furtively about, she ventured across the inn yard until she espied Tom and Warton conversing near the doors to the stables. Their talk ceased as she came near.

"Is all well, Tom? Nothing is wrong with the horses, is there?" She clasped her hands before her in genuine concern. Nothing could go wrong here. She felt a need to prove her independence to everyone, particularly Lord Norwood.

"Nay, miss. Just chewing the fat with Warton, here."

Hyacinthe chatted briefly about the day's journey, commented on what might be expected on the morrow; then, as she appeared about to leave, she paused.

"Oh . . . by the bye, I noted that Lord Norwood spoke with you earlier. What did he say?"

"Why, ma'am, he inquired of our cattle and asked if we had far to travel tomorrow. Kindly gentleman, I believe," Tom declared with a genteel smile. It seemed that he had approved of the gallantry displayed when his lordship came to the rescue of Tom's employer.

"You revealed our destination to him?" Hyacinthe asked in a rather quiet voice.

Alarmed, Tom replied, "I hope I didna' do wrong, Miss Dancy."

"No, no," she hastily assured him. "But perhaps you might be less forthcoming should anyone else inquire." Then she turned to slowly make her way back to the inn, deep in thought. So deep, in fact, that she failed to note that Lord Norwood waited for her in the entry hall of the inn.

"Miss Dancy, what a pleasure to see you again."

"Really, my lord?" Hyacinthe answered with a cool look. She had the man's measure. He thought that with no one else suitable available he might indulge in a bit of flirtation with her now. Well, he could take a running leap for all she cared. There would be no flirtation.

He had been leaning against the entry, looking secure with his position in life in general and well-pleased with himself. When Hyacinthe came closer, he stood straighter, bowing elegantly.

"Save your beautiful manners for one who appreciates them, sirrah. And do not bother my servants again, although why you might wish to know my destination is beyond me," she said in a considering way. She continued. "The maid may have informed you that I shall dine with my abigail in my room."

For good measure Hyacinthe drew herself up and flashed a reproving look at him, "Although you must have known that I would not agree to such a shocking suggestion. Your manners are not all they ought to be, are they?" she concluded in a soft voice.

"Blase, confound it, I've been hunting all over the place for you." A good-looking young man with shining dark hair, dark flashing eyes, and a tall, slender form came sauntering up to join the two who confronted each other in the entry. "I might have known you would find the only presentable woman—"

Before he could finish whatever he intended to say, Lord Norwood broke into his speech. "Val, may I suggest you allow me to present you to this lovely lady." He then proceeded to correctly introduce the newcomer.

Hyacinthe inspected the man presented as Valentine, Lord Latham. She had seen the baron about London. He possessed the same reputation as did Lord Norwood. Birds of a feather did indeed travel together.

"Good afternoon, sir," she murmured with just barely the correct amount of propriety.

"Indeed," the good-looking baron replied, bowing over her hand with excessive—to her way of thinking—flair.

Hyacinthe suspected that he might be a shade piqued that she didn't appear bowled over by him or his title. She offered a chilly nod, then marched up the stairs with a well-bred air and measured tread, not to mention a stiffened spine.

"I believe we have been well and truly put in our place, ol' chum," Val said in a reflective voice as he caught sight of a well-turned ankle when Miss Dancy took the last step at the top of the stairs.

"Sorry to interrupt you, but I feared you'd offer her further insult with some comment on her many charms. Miss Dancy is as prickly as a hedgehog." Blase looked up the stairs, catching the same glimpse of that ankle as Val, thinking that Miss Dancy was not quite as he had remembered.

"Much prettier, though. I always did think redheads a challenge. They say they make fiery bed partners. Do you recall that one we met while at Oxford?" He gave his friend a cynical grin, then nudged him along the hall.

The chuckles that followed brought forth a good many shared memories as the two handsome young men adjourned to the common room to enjoy a pint of excellent home brewed.

It was some time later while they applied knives and forks to an excellent roast beef that Val raised the subject of Miss Dancy again.

"Is she someone you knew from Town?"

"I met her once, saw her about frequently. Her brother wasn't in London then, but he's reputed to be one of the finest swordsmen around. And she has a flock of highly protective cousins. I decided it wasn't worth my life to flirt with the girl, even if she is a delectable piece."

"Her brother being . . . ?"

"Sir Peter Dancy. Odd fellow, taken to strange things like mummies and all that Egyptian rot. Began with some treasures brought back from the Egyptian campaign by his father in 1802. But don't be fooled, he's a dashed fine swordsman, as I said. As to Miss Dancy, we may see her again, for she travels on tomorrow."

"Not Worthington?"

"Precisely," came the smug reply. "Miss Dancy does not know what is in store for her." His chuckle bordered on the sinister, but his angelic smile took away any evil from his intent.

* * *

"I hope their lordships have departed by the time we leave in the morning," Hyacinthe said, her manner somewhat distracted from the fine meal their host and the maid had brought to her room.

"You would never deign to speak with them at any rate, would you?" Fosdick nibbled daintily at a roast potato. Her perfect manners would put many of the gentry to shame.

Hyacinthe gave her abigail a cross look. Why was it that Fosdick always had the knack of sounding like a governess, or at the very least a conscience?

"I should never do such a thing, Fosdick. My dear mama taught me better than that before she went aloft." A shimmer of moisture gleamed in her eyes for a moment, then Hyacinthe returned subdued attention to her meal.

All was as she hoped when, after completing a lovely and restoring breakfast in her room, she came downstairs in the morning. It wasn't necessary to make discreet inquiry about his lordship, for all around her she could hear snatches of conversation about the elegant Lord Norwood and his friend, Lord Latham. They had driven from the yard with an amazing flourish that every man around envied, it seemed.

Hyacinthe insisted to herself that she was quite pleased not to have seen them when they left, never admitting that she had peeped from her window—briefly, mind you—when she heard the commotion in the yard below. It was all of a piece—their dashing good looks and that curricle that appeared so rakish and probably bounced unmercifully. A secret smile curved her lips when she considered the uncomfortable drive they must make to wherever they were going.

Perhaps her entourage was not as elegant, nor as dashing, but admiring glances were many when Hyacinthe—garbed today in a neat Nile green pelisse and chip bonnet—stepped into her carriage. Tom Coachman sprung the horses as Hyacinthe had politely requested and they were off.

The miles to Worthington dragged by with seeming tedium. Hyacinthe reviewed all the words she had exchanged with Lord Norwood, debating whether or not she had acquitted herself well.

When at last they entered the pretty village tucked away in a green vale, Hyacinthe drew a breath of pleasure. Granted it was a tiny village, barely qualifying for the name, yet it was exceedingly charming. Some of the old thatched-roof cottages were covered with roses or ivy, tiny yards filled with an abundance of flowers and an occasional cat.

When Hyacinthe viewed her cousin's cottage, it seemed to her that the upper windows peered out from beneath the roof like sparkling eyes from under a shaggy mane. She fell in love with the place all over again.

Tom and Warton busied themselves removing the luggage from the boot and tending the horses, all the while fending off a number of curious children who were drawn by the unexpected sight. Traveling coaches were as rare as a warm day in January around here.

The white-painted door flew open and Jane came rushing down the flagstone path to the neat little gate. A soft gray shawl couldn't hide the thinness of her figure, nor could her smile quite conceal the lines of worry around her eyes. Her pretty auburn hair escaped in wisps from beneath her white cornette.

Hyacinthe absorbed all this in seconds as she hurried to wrap her dearest cousin in an enveloping hug. "It is so good to see you again," Hyacinthe whispered in a voice clogged with happy tears. She was utterly loyal to what family she had, and the thought that some monster would dare to oust her precious cousin from her hearth made her furious all over again.

Once settled in the sitting room located at the front of the ground floor with a pot of tea and cakes, they talked.

Jane Pennington lived as quietly as she pleased, far from the autocratic grandmother she quite feared. The notion that she might have to give up her peaceful existence and wait upon this dragon upset her nerves to the point where she could scarcely discuss the matter.

Rather, she inquired about the journey from Wiltshire and marveled at Hyacinthe's speed of travel, considering the deplorable state of the country roads.

At long last they turned, not without some reluctance on Jane's part, to the matter at hand.

"Where do things stand at the moment, Jane?" Hyacinthe inquired after placing her teacup back on its saucer. "How do the others in the village feel about having to leave the place they have called home for so long?"

"Well . . ." Jane said reflectively, "most are unhappy about being ousted, but a few—those with roofs that need patching and those whose families are too numerous to fit in the space they have—are amenable to the scheme."

"When does his lordship contemplate beginning this dastardly plan? I wish to know how much time we have." Hyacinthe brushed off a few crumbs from her gown, then eased back in her chair.

"I truly do not know. His bailiff came here the day I wrote to you. He informed us that we would be moved, but not when or how or where. As well, the rent is to be raised. Oh, dear," Jane said with a sob, pulling a crumpled handkerchief from where it had been tucked into her sleeve. "What shall become of me?" Then she dried a tear to give Hyacinthe a defiant look. "For I absolutely refuse to go to Grandmama Dancy. The woman would drive me mad in a day."

"Who is this man we must deal with? You never mentioned his name in your letter. At least, I do not think that you did," Hyacinthe reconsidered, recalling the missive that had been crossed with lines in both directions, making it difficult to read.

Jane frowned. "I thought I did. He is Lord Norwood. I hear he is expected to arrive any day now. And then his scheme will be set in motion." She dabbed at her eyes once again, then gave Hyacinthe a startled look when that young woman jumped to her feet and began to pace back and forth across the tiny sitting room, fists clenched, face angry.

"Infamous! Outside of enough! That man . . . just wait until I can fix his hide." She ought to have anticipated this, given his gardening lordship's proximity when last seen.

"You *know* Lord Norwood?" Jane asked in a breathless voice, clutching the arms of her chair in excitement.

"Indeed. And I shall take the greatest of pleasures in seeing that he receives his just desserts!"

2

"What is to be done?" Jane said anxiously, her hand rising to touch her throat in apprehension. "His lordship owns the entire village, the very ground upon which we trod. He is entitled to do anything he pleases with what is his own."

Hyacinthe cast her a frustrated glance, then looked out of the sitting-room bay window at the pretty village green. It was an irregular shape with neat cottages in a line around its edge. In the center of the green a lovely pond was fringed here and there with reeds, enhanced by stately oaks and elms. In ragged order along the far end of the green ranged the Cock and Bull, a century-old inn, then not far away a blacksmith and the usual small village shop that sold practically everything necessary. The ancient stone church, its spire thrusting toward the clouds, occupied a splendid spot on the opposite side, with a tidy little graveyard beyond an old lych-gate.

True, many of the roofs badly needed rethatching and one cottage looked ready to tumble down—witness to bad management on his lordship's part—or his bailiff's. But all in all, it was a charming place. Climbing roses and late-blooming hollyhocks peeking over the hedges that lined the street increased the appeal of the mellowed brick cottages. The village ought not disappear from the face of the earth just to please a whim.

"How does your cleric feel about this? Surely he must protest the destruction of his edifice, one that has sat in that spot for a good many years?" Hyacinthe clasped her hands before her while she contemplated the scene from the bow window of Jane's small cottage.

"Ambrose Clark is such a quiet man, I doubt he would say boo to a goose much less his lordship."

"Oh, dear." Moving closer to the window, Hyacinthe peered out more intently at a figure she noticed. "And who is that man going about as if he intended to buy all the village?"

"That is Mr. Wayland." Jane rose to join Hyacinthe by the window. "While at church last Sunday I heard that he is an architect hired by Lord Norwood to inspect the cottages to see if any are worth moving."

"I doubt he would wish to save anything in that event. It would profit him more to build new. Perhaps he is to design new homes for you all?" Then Hyacinthe considered the rake she knew and shook her head. "I doubt that, for Lord Norwood does not appear the type to be overly concerned with his estate—or, at least, the people living on it." She exchanged a disgusted look with her cousin.

"He has not held the title very long," Jane replied, perhaps in an attempt to justify the young lord's lack of achievement. "He was abroad for some while. Then, after his father died— from a dreadful cold, you know—he returned. He did not spend much time here before he left for London," Jane admitted.

"No doubt he has been cavorting about Town all the while," Hyacinthe replied with a sniff, then added, "when he wasn't out at the racetrack betting on the horses." When she saw Jane's dismayed expression, Hyacinthe felt compelled to note, "He is marvelously lucky, winning large sums with astounding frequency. All that lovely money enables him to cut quite a dash in Society." She turned aside from the depressing view of the angular Mr. Wayland, his legs reminding her of a crane perched at the water's edge.

A look at Jane's hopeful face prompted Hyacinthe to try anew. "Is there no one at all of influence in this area? Someone who might try to reason with Lord Norwood?"

Hyacinthe plumped herself back on a chair, poured a cup of tea, then settled back, waiting.

Jane appeared to consider the matter at length while she reseated herself, then turned an interesting shade of pink when she replied, "Well, there is Sir Charles Ridgeway. He lives on the edge of the village in an old manor house of Tudor vintage. I expect he also must relocate, but I do not know how he feels about it." Jane began pleating the apron she had put on over her dull green gown to protect it while she made tea.

Hyacinthe noted the flush of color and the nervous movement of those spinster fingers. Jane must be all of thirty summers, definitely on the shelf and past her prayers. But Hyacinthe's romantic heart saw no problem, unless Sir Charles was married.

"I fancy his wife and children must be up in arms? It would be difficult to move from a house you like."

"Oh," replied Jane in a flustered manner, "he is not married, although his sister visits from time to time." Since her neatly capped head was now bent, it was impossible to discover what her eyes might reveal.

"I see," Hyacinthe said with a sage nod. Indeed, she thought she saw a great deal. "Well, I had best change out of my traveling clothes and see if Fosdick is able to find a place for our things."

"I hope you will be comfortable in your rooms. I fear Fosdick will have to be content with the small chamber behind yours." Jane rose to walk to the entry hall with her guest, fussing with her shawl as she did.

"She will be," Hyacinthe assured Jane kindly. "And I have instructed Tom Coachman and Warton to settle in at the Cock and Bull. I fancy we might have need of transportation, and I know that you do not keep a coach of any sort."

Appearing cheered at the very thought of having a coach and four at her beck and call, Jane smiled delightedly.

"Mind you, it might be the height of comfort in coaches, but it cannot compare in looks to the dashing elegance of his lordship's curricle. I wonder if we shall see him?" Hyacinthe tipped her head to one side in a considering way while she observed the frightened look that crept over her cousin's face.

"Oh, my. Whatever would we do in that event?" Jane walked with Hyacinthe to the bottom of the stairs where she stood with hands clasped and a worried look in her eyes.

"I shall do something, you may be certain." With those unsettling words, Hyacinthe hurried up the circular staircase to her room at the left of the landing.

Jane decided she had best send for the Widow Smith's girl to help out while her cousin was here. It was easy to see that Hyacinthe would require more than the simple life Jane endured while alone. Although she was *not* unhappy. Reluctant to socialize, the peace of her cottage and the simplicity of village life where everyone knew everyone else appealed to her. She abhorred upheaval. And she very much feared that having Hyacinthe come to stay was like inviting a storm to dinner.

Upstairs Hyacinthe quickly changed into a pretty green sprigged muslin, high-necked and tucked across the bosom, and donned green gloves and her favorite leghorn hat bedecked with an enormous green satin riband. The tips of her green morocco slippers could be seen when she walked.

Before she left she instructed Fosdick to take out the gowns that Hyacinthe had brought along, fearing to find precisely what she did—that her cousin Jane dressed like a country mouse in dull colors and styles. These were new dresses from London, not yet worn. And Hyacinthe's tender heart had decided them a perfect present for her cousin.

"I believe I shall stroll about the village, perhaps check on Tom Coachman and Warton. Would it be unseemly for me to look at the church, since I shan't have my maid with me?" Hyacinthe paused at the bottom of the stairs while her cousin looked on in silent admiration of the fashion plate that had materialized in her humble home.

At last Jane recalled herself. "Of course you may go anywhere. Dressed as you are, there's not a lad around who would dare approach you, nor anyone who might offer insult."

Hyacinthe reflected that she obviously didn't expect Lord Norwood to come around.

She turned to leave the cottage, then paused again. "I forgot to tell you that I bought you a present. Fosdick has placed it on your bed." With a gay wave of her hand, Hyacinthe flitted from the house, drifting across the road to skirt the edge of the village green.

Jane forgot propriety and dashed up the stairs that curved around like those of a church bell tower. Presents rarely came her way, and when she saw the lovely collection of gowns spread out for her eyes to feast on, she burst into tears. Her flurry of emotion didn't last long. Within minutes Fosdick was assisting the slender young woman from her drab green dress into one of pale blue lutestring trimmed in the prettiest lace Jane had ever seen. As she and her cousin were nearly the same size, it required little adjustment to fit nicely.

"If you please, miss, perhaps I might try a different style for your pretty hair." When Jane silently agreed with a nod of her head, the abigail removed the dainty cornette Jane had embroidered in white thread on white muslin. "Ah," said Fosdick in a pleased exclamation, "so soft and silky it is, and the color of a nightingale." Fosdick beguiled Jane into the chair before her seldom-used dressing table and set to work.

Putting thoughts of her cousin aside, Hyacinthe explored the village. It hadn't grown much since she was last here some years before. She thought she recognized a few faces. At the Cock and Bull, Tom Coachman and Warton were pleased to see her, accounting for their time by the high polish on the burgundy coach with delicate gold lines trimming it. Hyacinthe suggested that when not occupied with the coach and horses they might lend a hand at her cousin's house. She was certain there were a few tasks where a man's strength would be an asset.

From the inn, Hyacinthe strolled along the green, crossing to the church. Upon closer inspection she could see that the building could use a new roof. Moss and age had not been kind to it. That was a minus, while surely the antiquity of the building would be a plus in any argument to preserve the edifice.

Within the churchyard she studied the gravestones, noting the dates. Most were from long ago, with a cluster of newer graves to the far side of the building. Inside the church she considered the memorial tablets; shiny brass, softly painted plaster, and two exquisitely carved in marble. How could any man be so heartless as to disturb these relics of the past?

The pews of heavy oak most likely had seen all the people who ever lived in the village. She had a vision of people garbed in the dress of a century past filing into their pews to hear much the same service as served today.

"I say, miss, could I be of assistance?" A high-pitched, beautifully accented voice penetrated her reflections.

Startled and feeling as if she had been hurled through time in seconds, Hyacinthe whirled about to confront a man who had to be the curate, Ambrose Clark. He was a man of moderate height with a thin, intelligent face, bespectacled eyes, and hair that receded to either side of a central portion, resulting in a hairline shaped like the letter *W* upside down.

"I do beg your pardon, for it seems I have surprised you," he said, nervously putting his hands together before him almost in supplication. "That happens quite often, I fear. People come and fall into retrospection."

Hyacinthe informed him of her identity, then looked about her. "It is a very lovely old building," she said, proceeding cautiously.

"Aye," he replied, then sighed. "And that is a problem, for we need a new roof and there is no way we shall receive one. Our only hope is to have the church moved. Lord Norwood has promised to replace all the roof tiles. It would be lovely to work in my office on a rainy day and not have water dripping into buckets all over the room." He tapped his fingers together in a sort of rhythm. "Yes, indeed. However, I suspect there are some among us who do not wish this move."

"Are you not shocked to think my dear cousin, Miss Pennington, might be out on her ear?"

"Oh, indeed, 'tis a great pity," he responded, biting his lip, making Hyacinthe recall a gray rabbit she had once seen. He continued to tap his fingertips together while he seemed to decide on what he ought to say next.

"Can you tell me something of the history of this building?" Hyacinthe had found that most clerics enjoyed expounding on the history of anything, particularly their church building.

"Indeed," he said with more enthusiasm. He then stopped his tapping of fingers to clasp Hyacinthe lightly about her arm and pull her along with him while he gave a lecture on each and every contribution made by the worthies buried here. Then he proudly showed the relatively new organ installed to enhance the service. It had meant the retirement of the flutist, violinist, and harpist who had been playing at services for years.

When he paused in his recital Hyacinthe gratefully inserted, "I believe I had best return to my cousin's house."

"And I have kept you from her side, nattering on about my favorite topic. You are a very kind young lady to bear with a somewhat garrulous old man. I do recall meeting you some years ago—although you have altered a good deal. You were a bran-faced little girl with pigtails and ruffled dresses that you did not appear to like very much." He had a singularly sweet smile, albeit somewhat timid.

Hyacinthe chuckled at the memory of her freckles—of which she had but one or two remaining—and those dreadful white dresses with rows of ruffles and the blue bows that forever came untied. She bade the curate good-bye, reflecting that he might deem himself old, but she doubted if he was above forty. Hardly elderly. And about right for Jane, except he probably didn't have two pounds to bless his name with, more's the pity.

In the green once again, she caught sight of a nice-looking man, a bit younger than the curate. Brown hair peeped from beneath his tall hat. She admired the determined line of his square jaw. Could this be Sir Charles Ridgeway, whose very name made dear Cousin Jane turn a pretty shade of pink?

He was headed toward her cousin's cottage with a purposeful stride. Hyacinthe made her way across the green, skirting the edge of the pond and thinking that the many ducks and a pair of swans made a very pretty sight, if a bit messy should one look too closely at the water.

She met him at the gate to the cottage. When she drew closer to him, she observed that he had a very nice pair of hazel eyes. Curious eyes.

"I beg your pardon, miss. I had not realized Miss Pennington's company had arrived." He tipped his hat, revealing thick brown hair covering a well-shaped head.

Hyacinthe nodded in return. "I was so fortunate as to make very good time. The roads were dry," she explained.

"Ah, yes, that does help." He opened the gate and walked at

her side to the white door, which was opened in a trice by a flustered Jane.

"Oh, my. Hyacinthe, you are come home. And Sir Charles, how lovely to see you." She dithered, clearly ruffled and not quite certain what she ought to do. A pretty blue sprigged dress enhanced her delicate coloring, while the softly draped hair style created by Fosdick made her look years younger and far more comely than the day cap which she had worn.

Hyacinthe smoothly took charge in an unobtrusive way. "I am pleased to meet you, Sir Charles. As my cousin appears to have told you, I am here to help her. My dearest Jane has informed me that you may be required to move as well."

"I have found out today I will be reprieved." He turned to Jane. "I came expressly to tell you that Lord Norwood has arrived and after driving past my home believes it would be a shame to move it. In fact, it may be possible for me to buy it back again." To Hyacinthe he added, "One of my ancestors lost the manor in a card game to one of his lordship's forebears."

"Ah!" Hyacinthe exclaimed, "Then the incredible luck of the present Lord Norwood is a trait handed down?"

"His father must have ignored it, for he plunged heavily into the exchange and lost all he invested." Sir Charles's tone made quite clear what he thought of such an improvident man.

Hyacinthe was puzzled. If Lord Norwood's father had lost so much, how could his present lordship afford the expense of relocating an entire village for the whim of his view? Surely the marquess had not been *that* lucky?

Or had he? If she were more charitable, she might be inclined to believe he gambled to regain the monetary inheritance his father had lost.

Jane nervously gestured to her pleasant parlor. "Please come in. I shall have your favorite beverage in a moment," she added to Sir Charles.

Apparently Sir Charles was accustomed to come here often if Jane knew his favorite drink and kept it on hand. Hyacinthe watched him settle onto a comfortable chair, the largest in the room and located close to the hearth, although it was not a chilly day. The cottage appeared to have a poor foundation, for the floor felt damp to Hyacinthe. Small wonder a fire was kept burning to take the chill from the room.

"Sir Charles, I am very concerned about my cousin," she said softly in hope that her words would not carry into the kitchen. "She does not wish to live with our grandmother. Goodness knows, that dear dragon is a bit intimidating. Not all of us are able to stand up to her, you see." Hyacinthe smiled ruefully.

"Miss Pennington is a trifle shy, but you would think she might manage her grandmother."

"You have never met the lady, I gather," Hyacinthe replied dryly.

"What do you propose to do? I doubt if his lordship will take kindly to anyone interfering with his plans." He shifted about in the armchair as though uncomfortable with the very notion of rebellion. "He means to begin work soon."

"Yes, well," Hyacinthe declared, "I have not formed any plans as yet, precisely. But I will. That dastardly man must not be allowed to destroy this pretty village. Why, it would take years of work to create the charming gardens and pretty scene of the village green. New towns are notoriously barren and ugly," she insisted in conclusion.

"You have a point there. Perhaps if someone were to suggest a different beautification approach to Lord Norwood he might agree to it?" He turned and rose in obvious relief as Jane entered with a tray holding a glass and a bottle of fine dry sherry along with a plate of wafer-thin biscuits, and tea for the ladies.

Hyacinthe watched him as Jane poured sherry into the glass. There were no loverlike glances or hints that he was interested in Jane in a romantic way. Indeed, he appeared to look on her as he must his sister, a comfortable person with whom to chat. Hyacinthe barely suppressed a disgusted and most unladylike snort. The man did not appear even to take notice of Jane's pretty new gown or her attractive new hair arrangement.

"Perhaps we could make out a list of things that we could present to Lord Norwood," Hyacinthe suggested once he had seated himself again. "Might you be willing to discuss the matter with him? For you may as well know that I do not precisely get along very well with him. Besides, I believe it far better for men to consider these matters."

When she glanced out of the window again, she observed Mr. Wayland entering the somewhat obscured house across the way. Tudor in design, it was the oldest cottage in the village and now sat vacant. The image of a stork seeking a nesting site flitted through her mind and she barely repressed a smile.

"I believe that to be an excellent notion," Sir Charles replied, obviously pleased to be considered the one to talk with his lordship. "I agree that Norwood will respond better to another man regarding the matter. But first know that I shan't say anything until the issue of the manor house is settled. I should not like to jeopardize my purchase of it. I managed to buy some of the original land from his lordship's father when he became pressed for funds. I never had the opportunity to approach him about the purchase of my house, as he died before I could speak to him about it."

Hyacinthe decided that while Sir Charles might be a pleasant man, and one who sought to make use of an opportunity, he was not the type to set the Thames on fire. At least he hadn't set his face against her scheme. Or at least as much as he knew of her scheme.

So, with a great many suggestions from all present, a list was drawn up. When finished it contained the basic demands Hyacinthe considered important. But the list was brief—at Sir Charles's insistence. Hyacinthe thought it a very poor thing. She intended to approach the matter from another direction entirely, but decided she wouldn't upset Sir Charles by mentioning it. He appeared to be in much the same state as Jane—a bit reserved, perhaps?

They lingered in the parlor, discussing how the changes might be made. Hyacinthe thought them mad, to be so accepting of what had to be a mere whim on Lord Norwood's part.

"Where shall you live if this house is torn down? And what of your lovely roses and all the pretty flowers you grow in your garden?"

"I do not know in the least," Jane murmured. Tears gathered in her eyes, which she dabbed at with a scrap of cambric.

"And you shall not dip into your inheritance to support me when you may well have need of the money yourself," she added to Hyacinthe.

First tossing an annoyed look at Hyacinthe for distressing Jane, Sir Charles moved to place a comforting pat on Jane's shoulder, which seemed to upset her all the more.

Hyacinthe watched the scene and decided she just might enjoy the role of devil's advocate if it brought Sir Charles around to championing her dear cousin. She considered the list she had written out, then offered it to Sir Charles when Jane had once again composed herself.

"Here, Sir Charles. I wish you well in your efforts."

Hyacinthe doubted he would have any luck, but it appeared to make him and Jane happy. Hyacinthe intended to make her own list.

Across the gently rolling hills from the village and within sight of the church spire and the chimneys of Worthington where it presently stood, two gentlemen studied a list of a considerably different sort.

"Dash it all, Blase, I didn't think to come up here to do an inventory," Val complained good-naturedly. "Why do we not seek out that pretty little redhead we encountered on our way here? Perhaps she has a friend?" he concluded optimistically.

"Neither did I," Blase replied, ignoring the reference to the redhead. "But when I found certain things I believed were here to be missing, I decided that perhaps it was time to do a bit of investigation. And forget the redhead. You don't want any trouble."

Blase circled about the drawing room, making extensive notations as he went. When he compared these with the two other inventories he knew existed, he might discover precisely what had happened while he was abroad.

"Father said he hadn't been forced to sell any of the family jewels or paintings, yet when I checked the earliest inventory I noted that several of the sixteenth-century paintings are missing from the rooms where they were listed and supposed to be hanging," Blase explained. "I want to know if they were moved, stored in the attic, or . . . if they have mysteriously disappeared. I wonder if other heirlooms are gone. I hope to find out."

"Ghosts?" Val asked in mock alarm.

"More likely a thief," Blase replied grimly.

"It wouldn't be surprising considering that only a skeleton staff is here for months at a time," Val said. "At least allow me to help you. Why don't I list all the paintings? I won't be likely to miss any, as none are familiar to me."

Val picked up a sheet of paper and a sharpened pencil to begin listing the paintings in the room. Blase could transfer these items to his master list later on.

The two worked silently for hours, moving from room to room until they ended up in the attic. It was surprisingly clean, with neatly piled goods from past Montagues. A stack of paintings leaned against one of the walls. Val made for this while Blase wandered along the length of the attic poking into various piles.

By dinnertime the lack of light to see and the utter fatigue of it all forced the pair to cease work. They clattered down the stairs to the main floor.

After dinner Val and Blase drifted into the library, where they sought comfort and ease in a pair of leather armchairs and crystal glasses filled with the finest port.

"Val, I am convinced that at some time in the past a bit of skulduggery went on here at Worthington Hall. Either one of my ancestors . . . or a thief . . . absconded with some paintings, all of which would be worth a fortune today."

Val allowed a whistle to escape while he considered all the implications. "Nothing else is missing?"

Blase thought for a few moments, then left the sublime comfort of his chair to cross the room to where a magnificent oil painting of his grandfather hung. He pulled on it and one side swung silently forward on well-oiled hinges. Behind the painting a quite modern safe had been installed some years ago at Blase's insistence. For once his father had agreed. In here the family jewels ought to repose.

He gave Val a concerned look, then swiftly opened the safe. A tiny key always kept on his watch chain opened the final door. He removed several black leather boxes, placing them on the desk.

Val also left the comfort of his seat. "I say, old chap, I've heard you speak of the family gems. Wouldn't miss a chance to see them."

Blase spread out the copy of the earliest inventory, then a second from a much later year, before he opened the first of the boxes. He made a list of each item as he removed it from its place of safekeeping. Emeralds, sapphires, diamonds, and fine rubies winked and sparkled, in spite of being wrapped up and not cleaned for years.

When all had been counted and listed, Blase stared at Val. "There are a few of the gems missing. See here?" He pointed to the oldest list, his finger a trifle unsteady as he marked an emerald necklace, a bracelet of gold set with emeralds, and emerald ear-bobs. "No mention of these appears in this next inventory. I have found no record of their being sold—or given away."

"Perhaps one of your ancestors bestowed them on a lady friend and did not wish his wife to know about it?" Val remarked with a chuckle.

"I doubt such a thing . . . not that many of those gentlemen didn't have lady friends, as you so genteelly phrase it."

"What can you do?" Val queried. He returned to his chair while he watched—not too closely—as Blase restored the jewels to the safe.

Once the painting swung back into place and Blase had joined Val before the fireplace, Blase looked at his friend. "I intend to go to the muniment room and do a bit of sleuthing. My forebears were ever the ones to keep every letter and diary. Mayhap if we check the record boxes for the intervening years between the first and second inventories we might find evidence of a sort. Something to give us a lead in this mystery."

"Us?" said Val in dismay that was only partly mock.

"Most definitely us. I shall need your help. I intend to find out what happened to those jewels and paintings. There must be a clue somewhere. When did they disappear? And who took them?"

3

The next day Hyacinthe studied the countenance of her cousin with a sinking heart. It seemed clear that since Sir Charles Ridgeway appeared to have dropped his opposition to the destruction of the village Jane now wavered in her support for the plan Hyacinthe proposed.

"It looks to me that perhaps I was a trifle hasty in writing you about this, Hyacinthe," Jane said in her soft, hesitant voice the day after Sir Charles paid his call. She played nervously with the ends of her gray shawl.

"Please do not think such a thing," Hyacinthe urged. "Come, look out of this window at the charming village in which you live. It is shocking to think that all this would be torn down merely in order to provide his lordship with a change of view. I suggest that we visit a few of your neighbors, find out how they feel about this matter."

"I believe I could tell you how they think without going to such lengths." Jane said. "Follow me and we shall stroll around the village."

Not quite certain what Jane might say, yet knowing she must do as her cousin requested, Hyacinthe drew on her gloves after first tying a simple chip straw bonnet on her head. They slipped out of the front gate, Jane going first and tugging Hyacinthe along after her.

Jane looked very pretty in her enthusiasm for her mission. Delicate pink cheeks bloomed, a straw bonnet trimmed in deep pink complimented the deep pink print of her new walking dress, one of the gifts from Hyacinthe. The ruffles of her day cap peeped from under the brim of her bonnet, giving an unexpected touch of charm. She appeared a bit different from the drab young woman who had met Hyacinthe at the gate upon her arrival.

"His lordship intends to raise your rent with the new house. Can you or your neighbors afford to pay more?" Hyacinthe thrust at her cousin in the hopes that she might for once be practical about her position.

Jane bestowed a frightened look on Hyacinthe, for the amount of her competence was rather small. The very notion that her rent would be increased was a matter to consider most carefully.

At the house next to Jane's they paused while Jane whispered, "This is Granny Beanbuck's cottage. She is quite crippled, but the most cheerful soul. I buy my bread from her. Although she has difficulty walking, she bakes the most heavenly loaves. I doubt she would wish to move, for a new home might not have such a good oven, nor a boy handy to stoke her fires."

Hyacinthe mentally toted one up for her side. Granny's cottage gave evidence that someone had also planted a pleasant garden in which cabbages mingled with hollyhocks and delphinium.

The next cottaqge had only rows of vegetable behind its ragged hedge. A few sunflowers had invaded one corner of the plot. The muslin curtains hung limply at the windows, unlike Janes's crisp white window coverings. Hyacinthe gave her cousin a questioning look.

"The Hadkiss family resides here," Jane said softly. "Mr. Hadkiss, I am sorry to say, is a man not much given to work. Mrs. Hadkiss, in addition to caring for their seven children—with another about to present its hungry face to the world before long—does laundry and other tasks to keep bread on the table."

"Would they wish to move, do you think?"

"I suspect that Mrs. Hadkiss has given little thought to the matter. She appears to accept what comes her way with no question. Mr. Hadkiss would likely enjoy the move, if only to give him something else to complain about." Jane gave her cousin a stricken look. "I pray you will not think badly of me for my frank comments about my neighbors. I thought it best to be open about them."

"Not at all, for we know that people like the Hadkiss family exist, and not merely in cottages." Hyacinthe looked back at the cottage, now behind them. A tot peeked around the corner of the house, looking wistfully at the fine ladies strolling past. That family was a point for Lord Norwood's side.

"The Widow Smith lives here," Jane gestured to a trim little place, abundant flowers and vegetables intermingling in the little garden behind a low hedge.

Hyacinthe looked at the clipped hedge, comparing it to others much higher, then glanced to Jane for an explanation she felt certain would follow.

"The Widow likes to gossip and so wishes an unobstructed view. She and Mrs. Peachey—who lives across the green from here—take note of all the goings on in the village and debate them endlessly. I expect that even as we pass her house the details of our garments, the fact that I have company, will be carefully observed and discussed over a pot of tea later today."

Amused, Hyacinthe said, "We really ought to pause for a call so she might have the particulars correct."

Jane tossed her an alarmed look, then chuckled. "You are teasing. For a moment I thought you serious."

"I am. That poor woman has nothing more to enliven her life than what occurs outside her home. Pitiful thing."

After giving her cousin a considering look, Jane turned about and retraced her steps to the widow's house.

They were avidly welcomed. The widow, garbed in unrelieved black with only a lace collar to enhance her dress, patted her muslin cap decorated with delicate ruffles. "Oh," she fluttered about, "do come in."

Jane managed to place her request for the widow's daughter to help her out without offending anyone.

When they left fifteen minutes later Hyacinthe wore a somewhat stunned expression on her face. "I have never endured such a grilling. I fancy that is what an accused person must face once in jail."

"You asked for it." Jane smiled at her cousin's countenance.

Her good humor reestablished, Hyacinthe replied with a rueful moue, "But we have made her day, if not her week."

Jane's soft chuckle rewarded Hyacinthe for her efforts.

They strolled along the stone path, Hyacinthe making mental note of the likely positions taken by the Nutkin family, old Mr. Smeed, the village handyman, and the Philpotts, who were quite elderly and apt to resist change.

The little village shop proved very busy today, with ladies entering with empty baskets and exiting bearing them stuffed with parcels. The blacksmith was well occupied, but when he espied Jane, came out to say hello. He brought up the topic of the day.

"Sir Charles says he means to see his lordship about the new cottages. He's collectin' a list from a few of the ladies as to what would be most welcome."

A glance at Jane's face brought dismay to Hyacinthe's heart. She could once again see her cousin wavering. "Well, and that is only proper. What if his lordship ignores these suggestions? What then?" she challenged.

The blacksmith scratched his chin, then allowed, "That's his right, I reckon. This is his land, his village. I might see more work in a new place with people wanting all manner of things made. Perhaps there might be a few extra homes for new people." He gestured to the bench where he had been repairing a clock for the curate. "I gets mostly repairs here, with a bit of shoeing from time to time. I asked for a larger shop, for I could use more space."

"So you support a move? Just to improve his lordship's view? What if the new village site is not so pleasing, with no stream close by, nor a delightful green with a pond and stately trees? What then?" Hyacinthe queried, hoping to plant a doubt or two.

He scratched his head, then replaced the cap he'd removed when first coming to speak with them. "We'll just have to see, won't we?" With that unsatisfactory remark he returned to his workbench beneath the only window in the shop.

The two young women ambled past the graveyard and paused before the church. Hoping to offer a formidable argument, Hyacinthe pointed to the orderly graves, then said,

"These will remain here, I suppose. How can they be disturbed, even if the church is moved? How will the villagers be able to come here if there is some distance involved? Poor Widow Smith could scarcely walk very far to tend her poor husband's grave."

"He was a sailor and was buried at sea, so that is not a relevant point," Jane countered.

"It still seems sacrilegious to me," Hyacinthe mumbled, casting about for another argument. Jane looked confused and bothered, which was about the most Hyacinthe might hope for, she supposed. The curate—whom she had looked to for support—was nowhere in sight.

Not far along the street, just beyond the Peachey house, stood the shabby Tudor-style cottage that had been sitting empty for years, Jane had said. Hyacinthe noted that Mr. Wayland seemed entranced with the place, for he appeared in the doorway as they neared.

"Now, that is an odd sight," Jane murmured. "Whatever can he expect to do with that place?"

"Perhaps he decides if there is anything worth salvaging from a home of such antiquity? Shall we attempt to query him?" Hyacinthe took gentle hold of Jane's elbow to nudge her along the path. Aside from an affronted, almost scandalized glance from her cousin, nothing was said.

Jane managed the introduction with a minimum of words, evidence of her lack of regard for the man.

"Good morning, sir," Hyacinthe offered in a pleasant manner usually guaranteed to bring a smile to any gentleman's face. Mr. Wayland proved the exception. He frowned, and in a most haughty manner.

"I hope you ladies do not intend to poke about this old house. It is in deplorable condition and ought to be torn down." He tilted his head back and took a deep breath as though about to embark on a lecture on the evils of trespassing.

Just for the sake of debate, Hyacinthe slowly shook her head. "What a pity it cannot be salvaged. It has such charm. I should like to see the interior." She moved forward as though she intended to suit actions to words.

"I wouldn't do that, were I you," Mr. Wayland said in a reedy voice that well suited his anatomy. He placed a protective hand on the gate before the house. "I informed Lord Norwood that the house is dangerous and he agreed that it ought to be posted."

Hyacinthe thought the architect a trifle pompous, with his thin chest puffed out with his importance. She noted a book beneath one arm and attempted to see the title if possible.

Seeing her interest, Mr. Wayland thawed slightly. He held out the volume for her to see.

"*Vitruvius Britannicus*? I fail to see how a book detailing the best classical houses in Britain would be applicable here, sir." She was genuinely puzzled. A publication offering designs for cottages seemed more practical to her way of thinking.

That he was most annoyed with her could be seen only by his pinched nostrils and flash of resentment in his eyes that she caught just in time when she glanced up at him. "It is possible to apply the principles of good architecture to the most humble dwelling, Miss Dancy."

Jane declared, "Oh, dear, the hour has flown by. We must return immediately. Good day, sir." She tugged on Hyacinthe, who willingly joined her on a hurried walk to Jane's cottage.

"What an annoying little man," Jane murmured, the worst that she could think to say about him, it seemed.

"Well, in spite of that volume he flaunted, I suspect he is no Henry Holland," Hyacinthe added, referring to the architect who had worked on Carlton House for the Prince Regent.

"Indeed," Jane said faintly, dazzled at the very mention of the London residence. "And have you seen it?"

"Not the inside," Hyacinthe admitted, "Although I have driven past it and think it impressive." Her mind leaped to the task at hand. "So may I offer my plan for your inspection?"

Once they were safely seated in Jane's modest parlor Hyacinthe said, "I think it is abominable that Lord Norwood should oust you and the others from your dear homes. This is what I propose to do in an effort to make him see the light." And she proceeded to present her plan to defeat Lord Norwood with gasps from her cousin now and then.

* * *

Across the gentle hills two gentlemen looked over the contents of a box in the muniment room with dismay. Amid the ancient records and deeds of Lord Norwood's family, letters and diaries were scattered with little regard for dates or order.

"It is a perfect day out. Are you certain you truly wish to begin this task?" Val said in his most coaxing manner.

"Get thee behind me," Blase murmured as he delved further into the box. "Here, you plow through that stack of papers while I see what's in this pile. A task divided, and all that." He began to sort through his heap of material.

Silence reigned until Blase breathed a sigh of satisfaction. "Here it is: the inventory of Worthington Hall, done in the year 1690 in the reign of our gracious sovereigns William and Mary." He replaced the rest of the documents and letters in the box, retaining a fat diary along with the inventory.

Blase took these items and the two men strolled back in the direction of the library, chatting with ease although Blase could scarce conceal his impatience.

"What do you hope to find? The missing paintings listed?" Val asked curiously.

"Precisely."

Just then Barmore, the Montague butler, approached them with an apologetic expression on his face. "If you please, milord. Sir Charles Ridgeway to see you."

"Show him into the library, Barmore." With a resigned glance at Val, Blase quickly entered his favorite room, placing the inventory and diary on the center of his desk.

"And what might your local gentry be about, do you suppose?" Val wondered aloud in his mocking manner. "How do they view your decision to move the village? Are they about to mount a rebellion, or do they meekly fall in with your wishes to remove them from their homes?"

"Oh, I suppose it is all of a muchness—with people on both sides of the matter. These things tend to be the same, no matter what the question."

Sir Charles appeared delighted to be received when he had not written to request a meeting. "Good morning. I am pleased to see you at Worthington Hall, Lord Norwood." His bow was most correct.

"Sir Charles. Won't you be seated?" Blase signaled to Barmore, and within moments a welcoming drink was offered to the guest and to Blase and Val as well.

When they were comfortably seated and had dispensed with the usual sort of chitchat regarding weather, local crop prospects, and the like, the reason for the interview came out.

"I fear there is opposition to the removal of the cottages, sir," Sir Charles revealed after thanking Lord Norwood for leaving his home—which was actually around a knoll and couldn't be seen from the Hall—intact.

"Dash it all, don't they see that it will improve their lives? Their living conditions?" Blase clarified.

"Well . . . as a matter of fact they don't," Sir Charles admitted. "I have put together a list of suggestions from the ladies who live in one of the cottages to be destroyed and replaced. By the by, have you actually notified those who presently occupy the cottages that they will be housed in new ones? When I called upon Miss Pennington yesterday I could not help but feel that she believes she will be without a roof over her head. This, belief, I may add, is nurtured by her cousin, Miss Dancy."

"Ah, the pretty redhead," Val murmured irrepressibly.

Blase exchanged expressive looks with Val before considering the matter.

"I cannot say that *I* have, but my bailiff should have. I have scarcely seen the village in years, except from the terrace of this house. The steeple and the chimneys mar the perfection of the view, you see." Blase leaned back, calling to his mind's eye what he hoped to achieve. "I wish to develop a picturesque aspect, with extensive planting and thinning of the present layout. I may build a cascade along the stream, for Parliament has made it possible to construct a dam, so such a deed is feasible. I have found much inspiration in these books."

He gestured to the shelf behind him upon which rested copies of such books as *Elements of Modern Gardening* by John Trusler and *The English Garden* by William Mason.

Pulling a well-thumbed copy of Humphry Repton's book *Treatise on Country Residences* from this shelf, he held it up and said, "I quite like some of the things this man has to say. I should like to try out many of his propositions, and to that end have invited him to assist me in my scheme."

Sir Charles looked rather dismayed at this evidence that the plans to alter the scenery around Worthington Hall had proceeded so far.

"May I inquire just when this gentleman will arrive?"

"He answered my letter not long ago." Blase rose from his chair to search the top drawer of his desk until he found the item in question. Checking its contents, he looked up at the others. "According to this he accepts the commission and the terms I offered. He has another task to complete which is not too far removed from here. As far as I can figure, he ought to be here in another two weeks."

"And then the fur will fly," Val muttered to himself.

"What about the building of the new cottages? Have you determined a location for them? The villagers would like to have the stream go through the new village, possibly a pond in the green—for they are quite attached to the one they have at present."

"Just how much has Miss Dancy had to do with this list?" Blase inquired in a dulcet tone.

"Oh,"—Sir Charles beamed a smile at the mere mention of the young lady's name—"she was most helpful, indeed. Pointed out to me all the things that could be improved in the various cottages. The Hadkiss family really ought to have a larger place, and Granny Beanbuck must have the best of ovens."

"I suppose she'd have me installing a Rumford stove," Blase murmured to Val in an aside."

Sir Charles heard the remark and, guileless soul that he was, broadened his smile. "I believe that would be excellent. You see, Granny Beanbuck bakes the bread for the village; earns a pittance for other necessities that way."

Blase nurtured a few hostile thoughts about Miss Dancy. The chit would end up costing him a fortune at the rate she was making her suggestions.

"What else, pray tell?" he asked.

Emboldened by the patient look on his lordship's face, Sir Charles continued to enumerate the various points on the list.

"Better foundations?" Blase frowned. "This is an item to discuss with the architect, Wayland."

Sir Charles looked dubious at the mention of this worthy gentleman's name, but said nothing against him.

"What's the problem with the present foundations?" Val inquired, partly out of curiosity and partly to prod his friend into some sort of action.

"Well, the wood beams appear to be directly on the ground with little stone to support them, and the floors are not properly done at all—being of broken stone, so the damp seeps in when it rains and makes it most uncomfortable. And Miss Dancy reminded me that the ceilings are somewhat low, being scarcely seven feet in height."

"And has Miss Dancy anything else to say?" Blase inquired in a deceptively mild voice.

"Oh, yes," Sir Charles replied happily. "She says the bedrooms ought to be better lit with larger windows. and the stairs should be less dangerous—they wind around in a fearsomely steep way at present."

"It seems your Miss Dancy wants a manor house, not a cottage," Val observed with some amusement.

"Perhaps I should consult with her myself," Blase said, again with that misleading calm.

"That would be a splendid idea," Sir Charles agreed. He shifted about in his chair. Something in the atmosphere of the room appeared to make him uncomfortable.

The men talked a bit longer, with Sir Charles inquiring about the purchase of his home. Then he bade them farewell, seeming satisfied with what had been accomplished.

Once the front door had closed behind him, and Barmore's steps could be heard echoing down the hall, Val gave his good friend a curious look.

"So what do you contemplate? Do you actually intend to confront the prickly hedgehog in her lair—or wherever it is they retreat to when threatened?"

"They roll up into little balls to protect themselves, I believe. Had one as a pet when I was a lad." He considered the matter for a time, then a light of unholy glee appeared in his eyes. He rose from his chair and crossed to tug at the bell pull.

When Barmore arrived he didn't blink an eye at the peculiar request from his lordship.

"What are you up to now?" Val inquired, joining Blase by the window that looked out toward the village. "And may I go with you when you leave here?"

"I shan't tell you, and no, I had best go it alone for this," Blase replied with that same expression of wicked delight in his eyes. He gazed at the distant village with a look of boyish satisfaction.

While he waited for his request to be fulfilled, Blase contented himself with a perusal of the inventory. When what he suspected was confirmed, he gave a crow of triumph.

"I gather you found something of interest," Val said from where he still stood by the window, mulling over the possibilities offered by the events of the past hour.

"I was right. There are three paintings, all done by very fine artists of the day. These plus the jewels are listed. Although the latter are referred to in what amounts to a rather oblique way."

"Obviously, your ancestor did·not wish their existence to be widely know among his household. Curious."

Before Blase could comment on this, Barmore tapped gently on the door, then entered bearing the small canvas sack.

"Ah, bless you, Barmore. Could ever a man have a better butler than I?" Blase quickly accepted the small sack, then tossed a hasty salute at Val as he headed out of the door.

Giving little thought to what his friend might think, Blase hurried to the stables and mounted the horse that awaited him. In minutes he rode off in the direction of the village, a self-assured smile on his lips.

Since her cousin had gasped and exclaimed so often that afternoon, Hyacinthe gave little thought to another inhaled breath.

"Oh, Hyacinthe, it is he, that is, his lordship, come to seek you out. Why do you suppose he has come?"

Exhibiting patience that would astound her other cousins, Hyacinthe merely shrugged and left the copy of the *Lady's Magazine* to join her cousin at the bay window. Lord Norwood cut a dashing figure as he dismounted, tied his horse to a post on the green, then crossed the narrow road.

"Well, we shall find out soon enough what he wants. He will be here in moments."

"Mercy!" Jane whispered. She answered the door just as he tapped roundly on it.

When he entered the parlor, having to duck his head through the low doorway, Hyacinthe repressed a smile. He stared up at the ceiling with a definite frown. Apparently Sir Charles had made his call on Lord Norwood.

"I wonder if I might consult with Miss Dancy alone, Miss Pennington. I promise to be most circumspect, but I would never upset you and I fear we may exchange words."

Jane jumped to her feet, declaring she simply had to fetch a loaf of bread from her neighbor, Granny Beanbuck. She whisked around the corner, remembering just in time to grab her shawl.

"What is it that is of such a private nature, sir?" Hyacinthe said, eyeing the wiggling sack in his hands with some misgiving. "I trust you realize that we must be most careful, for Mrs. Peachey will have taken note of your arrival. Jane had the good sense to slip out of the back door. Yet—"

"It is like living in a glass bowl," he muttered, casting an annoyed look at the bay window.

Then he turned to face Hyacinthe and her heart fluttered with alarm at the wicked gleam she thought she saw in his eyes. "I repeat, what is it?"

"Since your arrival you have been doing your best—from what I have been told—to turn my villagers against me and my project. Can you not see it will be to their ultimate benefit?"

"No, actually," she replied simply.

"I offended you while at the inn. If I apologize most abjectly, you will cease this interference?"

Hyacinthe tilted her head, looking at the premier rake of London trying to assume a humble aspect. It was very difficult not to laugh. In fact, it was impossible. Her silvery laughter pealed out in the room, resulting in a look of tight-lipped outrage crossing his lordship's face.

"Miss Dancy, you live up to your reputation."

She sobered quickly at that comment. "What do you mean, sir?"

"You are as prickly as a hedgehog, 'tis said." Blase didn't add that he was the one who had coined that remark. "To that end I offer a token." He held out the wiggling sack, which Miss Dancy accepted with obvious reluctance.

She eased the contents of the sack onto her lap. "A hedgehog!"

The bewildered animal, some ten inches in length and bearing hundreds of spines as a defense, looked about it with alert brown eyes. Its nose quivered as though hunting for a familiar scent.

"*Touché*, Miss Dancy. Or ought I say, *en garde*?" His look of devilish amusement was restored, Hyacinthe noted.

"You declare war on me?" she inquired in an innocent manner. "I believe you ought to prepare for a counterattack. I am not one of your milk-and-water misses, you know. Consider yourself warned."

4

"It is a dear little thing," Hyacinthe said as she watched the hedgehog scuttle off to bury its nose in a pile of leaves and debris in one corner of the area behind the cottage. "I shall call it Harry—for rather obvious reasons."

"It is spiny, not hairy," Jane objected, eyeing the flurry of flying leaves with skepticism.

"Looked to me as though they were hairs that were stiff on the ends, but what do I know. I have heard tell that a hedgehog is a gardener's friend, eating all those nasty slugs, snails, and beetles." By now the little animal had totally disappeared beneath the leaves—for the rest of the day, most likely. From somewhere in the back of her mind, Hyacinthe recalled that hedgehogs were most active at night. In fact, they were quite busy little creatures.

"Well, I do not know what prompted his lordship to bring you such a peculiar gift. Really, to order me from my own home!" Jane declared in a miff. "I had a time of it to sneak from here to Granny Beanbuck's house without Mrs. Peachey seeing me, I can tell you."

"He issued me a challenge of sorts."

"*That* is the outside of enough," Jane said with rising indignation. Then, her forehead pleated with both worry and curiosity, she asked Hyacinthe, "What manner of challenge?"

" 'Tis odd, for I am not certain. He declared me to be as prickly as Harry the hedgehog, and said I was to be *en garde*, as though this were some sort of fencing contest."

Jane sank down on a wicker chair that Mr. Smeed had mended for her. "Contest?" she echoed faintly. "Oh, I beg of you, do not do anything you might regret."

Hyacinthe had the grace to look a bit uncomfortable at this sign of her cousin's concern. "Well . . . I did say he ought to take care of a counterattack."

"Is that a fencing term as well?" Jane asked in a faint voice.

"Yes." She could see her cousin was still puzzled, so she continued. "My brother, Peter, is a dab hand at fencing. I have learned quite a bit merely by watching him. I have vowed to have him teach me someday, for it looks to be jolly good fun."

"Oh, my," was all Jane could reply, and that in a fading voice.

"Well," Hyacinthe said, rising from where she had knelt and dusting off her hands after tossing the sack into a pile of refuse that was due to be burned, "I intend to do a bit of calling today."

"No," Jane said a bit more stoutly.

"Indeed. I have seen not one assurance from his lordship that your lot will be any better following the removal. Have you any proof that he actually intends to build new housing— other than that frippery Mr. Wayland who wanders about with book in hand?"

"Well, not exactly." Jane rose from her chair to follow Hyacinthe to the kitchen, where she proceeded to scrub her hands in a basin of water.

"What does that mean?" Hyacinthe asked.

"Sir Charles assured me that I must have it all wrong. And you know what a peagoose I am about such things. I am not like you. I cannot speak up to people. I like my peace and quiet; living in this little village is my notion of heaven on earth. The mere thought of London frightens me speechless." Jane clasped her hands together before her as if in supplication.

"I know that, silly. And because I care a great deal about you, I insist upon seeing that you continue to enjoy your quiet backwater life. Not all butterflies are gaudy and ostentatious. There are dainty little things that flutter around in rural gardens quite happily. And you are the dearest of people." Hyacinthe gave her cousin a hasty hug, then bestowed a fierce glance toward the doorway through which Lord Norwood had left not long before. "But I shan't have you hurt, nor put out of your dear little cottage."

"Sir Charles said that I shall have a lovely place to live. Really, he did," Jane told Hyacinthe.

Deciding she had best say nothing that she might regret later, Hyacinthe murmured something about changing from her morning dress and left the kitchen.

Once dressed in a suitable gown for calling, Fosdick having arranged her hair in pretty curls, one of which draped over her shoulder in a fetching manner, Hyacinthe set out on her own. Jane had declared she could not face the prospect of joining her cousin, which suited Hyacinthe to a tee.

After a casual stroll around the village green and offering a handful of crumbs to the ducks, Hyacinthe made her way toward the Peachey home. Like the Widow Smith, Mrs. Peachey preferred to keep her hedge low. Although she also embraced the widowed state, she chose to retain her married status rather than be called widow. In an unguarded moment she had explained to Jane that it made her feel younger, somehow.

Mrs. Peachey was not quite so obvious as Widow Smith. She showed Hyacinthe into her parlor, concealing her curiosity with tea preparations and a flutter of chitchat about one thing and another. Mostly she talked about the coming upheaval and what it might do to her cats.

"They are all I have," she revealed to Hyacinthe while stroking the fluffy white cat that had crawled up into her lap. Then seeming to realize her words might be construed as a bid for pity, she changed the subject.

"Lord Norwood called at Miss Pennington's cottage this morning. Odd time for a gentleman to come calling, I'd say?" her hand, threaded through the cat's thick fur, paused while her bright dark eyes watched Hyacinthe with sharp intensity.

"He brought me a gift." Hyacinthe smiled, then added, "He heard me mention that Jane had a problem with snails and slugs and had one of his men locate a hedgehog for us. I'll confess that while it is a most unusual present, Jane seemed pleased to have the animal in the garden." Hyacinthe was amazed that the heavens didn't open up to strike her for all the lies she had uttered as of late. However, she found she could not bear to spread about malicious stories regarding Lord Norwood.

"That was surprisingly thoughtful of the gentleman," Mrs. Peachey said. She resumed stroking her pet.

"I gather you are the repository of the history of this village. Have you ever considered writing it down? It ought to be done so the children of future generations would know what life was like in the little spot before it was destroyed."

"Destroyed?" Mrs. Peachey exclaimed. "I'd not thought of it like that, but you are correct. The village and its past shall be gone. So much has been lost already."

Glancing out of the window, which was bowed like Jane's, Hyacinthe observed Mr. Wayland making his way to the moldering Tudor house next door.

"My, that gentleman has a passion for old places," Mrs. Peachey commented. "Why, the other day he came to call and asked a hundred questions about the village and particularly that house. One would have thought it really did have treasure hidden in it."

"Treasure?" Hyacinthe echoed. "How fascinating. My cousin said nothing about a tale like this."

"Possibly she don't know. Mind you, there may be nothing to it, most likely 'tis all a hum, but . . . "

"Yes?" Hyacinthe said eagerly.

"Well, the old story goes that around two hundred years ago—or thereabouts—there was a redheaded woman living there who was kept by the then Lord Norwood. Mind you, I've nothing against red hair, yours is a glory, but it seems that she was declared a witch, having a rare ability with animals. His lordship-that-was-then defended her, and soon she was spending a goodly amount of time with him, if you catch my meaning."

Then Mrs. Peachey appeared to remember just who sat in her parlor and she flushed slightly. "Of course, being a single lady, you may not, for such tales really are not the sort for young ladies."

"Not at all, I find them most interesting. And yes, I believe I do know what you mean. My Aunt Bel spoke of a woman like that once. Do go on."

Reassured that it was permissible to soil the ears of a maiden lady with her tale and relishing a new audience, Mrs. Peachey continued. "The story goes that he gave her jewels and other fine things. Then hard times came, his lordship went away, and not long afterward she died."

"And so?" Hyacinthe prompted, well aware that Mrs. Peachey was trying to draw out her dramatic offering as much as she could.

"When they went in to take her off for burial not a thing could be found. She was gone, with only white curtains waving in the breeze."

"There was no body?"

"Aye. No body and no jewels or anything else that anyone could find. And believe me, they have searched the house time and again over the years with no success."

Hyacinthe took a sip of her tea, reflecting on the bizarre tale she had just heard. Did this account for Mr. Wayland's fascination with the Tudor house? Did he believe the tale and search for treasure?

"No one has lived there in ever so long. Certainly not as long as we have been here. The house just sits neglected, sinking further into decay each year. 'Tis haunted, some say," Mrs. Peachey concluded with relish.

"Haunted!" Hyacinthe whispered, captured by the image of the beautiful redheaded woman who had mysteriously disappeared so long ago. Jewels and treasure were enough to make anyone dare the risk of ghosts to search the house, but not a trace left behind? "No body ever appeared?"

"Well, some say she weren't really dead at all. That she slipped off to London to be with his lordship. That she paid her servants to tell the tale. They left soon enough, so the story goes."

"I think you ought to record every word of this story, Mrs. Peachey. And you ought to put down the history of every house in the village. I feel certain that between you and Widow Smith the entire record of this village could be collected. It would be a memorial to the village once it disappears and a great accomplishment for you!"

Mrs. Peachey was struck dumb by the words she'd just

heard. She clasped her hands to her bosom and could scarcely wait for Hyacinthe to depart so she could consult the Widow Smith on the project.

Once again strolling along the green, Hyacinthe stopped to study the Tudor house. What had truly happened to that woman so long ago? Had that particular Lord Norwood been as devilishly handsome as the present holder of the title? She simply had to find out. But, she realized, her shoulders sagging a trifle with the admission, how could she? Ladies did not call upon gentlemen. It wasn't done.

However, he had issued a challenge, one she had no intention of ignoring. What to do? A gleam entered her eyes and she hurried home.

"Do you know of any stray kittens?" she inquired of Jane after entering the cottage.

"Granny Beanbuck always has a collection of cats . . . to keep the mice and rats from her flour and breads. Why?"

"I believe I ought to repay the gift Lord Norwood bestowed upon me. He deserves a token of appreciation." A crafty expression crept into Hyacinthe's eyes.

Jane sank down upon a chair, favoring her cousin with a dismayed look. "Why is it that I suspect you of ulterior motives?"

"Because you should. Why did you never tell me the romantic tale of the Tudor house?" Hyacinthe sketched the story for her cousin.

"That lot of silly nonsense? I feel certain Mrs. Peachey made it up."

"I doubt it, for it has the ring of truth. And you needn't look at me as though I don't know what *that* is. I want to know more, and to do that I must see Worthington Hall, or at least the picture gallery. Help me, Jane."

"Mercy!" came the faint reply.

"I shall summon my coach, then call upon Granny Beanbuck," Hyacinthe decided promptly. "I do wish to compliment her on those heavenly cinnamon buns that she makes. Perhaps I ought to bring a sample along for his eminence, so he could see how important her oven is!" Hyacinthe's eyes danced with delight at her plan and she took her light cloak from the tiny stand in the hall before opening the door again.

"Hyacinthe," Jane protested weakly. She watched as her cousin skipped off along the village path in the direction of the Cock and Bull, then retired to restore herself with a cup of tea. She had been doing that quite often lately.

Within several hours all was in readiness. Tom Coachman and Warton presented themselves before Jane's cottage promptly when bade. Various curtains twitched when Jane and Hyacinthe, dressed to the nines for calling upon his lordship, left the cottage to enter the carriage, followed by the stiffly proper Fosdick.

Hyacinthe surveyed with satisfaction the sack she had made from pretty striped muslin and tied with a cherry-red riband. "My mama always taught me to give better than I receive."

"I doubt if she had anything like this in mind, dearest," Jane said.

However, she seemed to have reconciled herself to whatever scheme her cousin had in mind, for when Hyacinthe returned after obtaining a surplus cat from Granny Beanbuck, she found Jane in a receptive mood.

As though sensing something of what was in Hyacinthe's mind, Jane said as they set off in the coach, "I am fortunate to have someone who cares for me. Just think of Mr. Smeed and all the others who have no one at all." She reached over to bestow a pat on her cousin's gloved hand.

Hyacinthe turned to the window, partly to overcome her emotions and in part to survey the scenery that spread out on either side of the burgundy coach while they smartly bowled along the road that led to the Hall.

" 'Tis pretty here. Rolling hills, lovely trees, small well-cared-for farms in the distance. I cannot think what Lord Norwood means when he says his view needs improving. How can one possibly improve on this?"

"He said he wished to enhance his view," Jane said mildly.

"Enhance? And needs to destroy homes to accomplish it? Bah," Hyacinthe declared inelegantly.

The coach drew up before the house with a flourish, and Warton let down the steps for the ladies. Hyacinthe stood by the coach, examining all she saw while waiting for her cousin to gather up herself and her reticule.

"Now remember, I wish to see the portrait gallery. You must help me think of a way," Hyacinthe whispered.

Warton rapped at the door, then announced the ladies to the butler. Hyacinthe went ahead, but Jane tagged close behind, as though afraid to be two steps away from her stronger and more determined cousin. Fosdick trailed behind, set on lending countenance to her ladies.

"We are here with a small gift for Lord Norwood," Hyacinthe explained. "He was so kind as to bring us one yesterday. Oh, this is Miss Pennington, and I am Miss Dancy."

Not by a flicker of an eyelash did the butler reveal what he thought of this invasion of a gentleman's establishment by two young women and a maid.

They were ushered into a very charming sitting room and left there. Jane gave Hyacinthe a stricken look, then turned to the door as though to flee while she could. "This is insanity!" she said in a whisper.

"Nonsense. This is war," Hyacinthe whispered back.

They heard the clatter of footsteps on the stairs—at least two people. Perhaps that other man, the one with the shining dark hair and considering dark eyes, was here as well. He was far too unpredictable to consider for Jane. Sir Charles would do nicely once brought around to realize it.

"Miss Dancy? What a surprise. And Miss Pennington. To what do I owe this honor?" That he had doubts about whatever it might be lurked in his expressive eyes.

The man from the inn, Valentine, Lord Latham, sauntered in behind Lord Norwood.

"Miss Pennington, allow me to present a good friend of mine, Lord Latham."

Lord Latham bowed over Jane's hand, turning her into a flustered muddle with his polished compliments.

Hyacinthe decided she had best get to the heart of the matter immediately. The sack was becoming a trifle much for her to manage, she acknowledged when a set of claws came through the muslin.

"Since you were so kind as to bring me a gift, the very least

I could do was reciprocate," she said with a proper little curtsy.

"Why do I have the feeling that I ought to beware of the bringer of gifts?" she heard Lord Norwood murmur to his friend. He stepped forward, a hand outstretched in seeming resignation.

Smiling, Hyacinthe placed the sack into the hand, whereupon he yelped. The claws had found a target.

Obviously stifling a string of words he longed to fling at her, he opened the bag, dumping out the orange-striped kitten with little ceremony.

"A cat?"

"A tiger cat, my lord," Hyacinthe replied demurely.

The animal huffily switched a very fluffy tail, then began to investigate its surroundings.

"How novel," Val commented. "A cat from a cat."

Jane gasped at this bit of wicked language.

Hyacinthe thought it improper, cynical, but rather amusing. Naturally she did not reveal her reaction.

Lord Norwood suggested that they all be seated, and then gently queried Hyacinthe about her day while keeping a wary eye on the kitten.

She gave him full marks for perceiving that she had not made the call merely to present him with the tiger cat, which had been cleverly named Tiger by Val.

The butler appeared bearing a tray with tea and biscuits, and a bottle of ratafia should they care to indulge a bit. Hyacinthe bit back a smile when Val took note that he was expected to take tea with the ladies.

"Thank you, Barmore," Lord Norwood said, adding "please remove this animal to the kitchen." The man picked up the cat by the scruff of the neck and gingerly took it from the room accompanied by affronted yowling.

Jane fidgeted at her end of the love seat where the young women had decided to sit. Hyacinthe knew she had to act quickly or all would be lost and the daring call would have been in vain. If she could lure his lordship into a hunt, he might forget about the destruction of the village.

"You have a lovely home, Lord Norwood. While calling

upon the villagers I have heard fascinating stories of your ancestors. Indeed, I quite long to see what they looked like."
After this blatant hint, she wondered if he would deny her the
pleasure. He didn't disappoint her. He did look a trifle startled
at her request, however.

"Why, I should be pleased to show you the gallery when
you have finished your tea. I wouldn't wish to deprive you of
anything."

"Except Jane her home," Hyacinthe flashed back sweetly.

"Aha!" Val said softly. "I begin to see the light."

"You only think you do," Hyacinthe murmured back in the
same tone. She drained the cup of excellent Bohea, finished
the last of her biscuit, then rose, dusting off her fingers with a
napkin as she did. "I expect we ought not delay. I fear we are a
bit improper as it is, but I just knew you'd appreciate the kitten."

"Indeed," the somewhat stunned Lord Norwood replied. He
gave his friend a significant look, then the four walked in the
direction of the picture gallery at the rear of the house.

When they went up the stairs to the first floor, Hyacinthe
observed how polished and immaculate everything looked.
Good housekeeping was not always to be found in a bachelor
establishment, or so she'd been told. Her brother had a terrible
time finding someone who would put up with his place, but
then he had all those mummies!

"Here we are," Blase announced at the door to the gallery.
What the devil these two females were doing here, ostensibly
looking at his ancestors, he couldn't imagine. After the wicked
gift of that nasty little beast, he'd decided he had best humor
them.

They strolled along the length of the hall with Val making
suitably naughty comments along the way.

"Are you never serious, Lord Latham?" Jane asked at long
last when he had shredded the character of a particularly
bored-looking lady.

"Not if I can help it, my charming Miss Pennington. Might I
counter with a question of my own? Are you never silly?

She surprised him with her reply. "At times." Her glance at
her cousin seemed to imply a connection between the two.

At last they paused before a gentleman of the late sixteen hundreds. Blase admitted he resembled the chap, but stopped at that. From what he had read in this fellow's diary during the past four days, he had a reputation that put Blase in the nursery brigade.

"Who was this?" Hyacinthe inquired after checking the date at the bottom of the frame.

"He was also named Blase Montague. It's a name that pops up in the family from time to time." He waited for her to comment, for he was certain there was a reason somewhere in her desire to see these pictures.

"Most appropriate, I'd say." She tilted her head to give the painting a considering inspection. "Do you know that there is a fascinating story about him? Mrs. Peachey told it to me this morning. After hearing it, well, I just had to see what he looked like."

Something rang in the back of Blase's mind. "A story? One the villagers repeat?" He gave Val a meaningful look, then concentrated on the miss at his side.

"Well, and it was not so terrible, sir. Nothing scandalous, at least I doubt if it is. Unless he murdered her and hid her body someplace. I'd not thought of that before."

"Miss Dancy, *if* you will be so kind?" Blase wished he could shake the pert young woman who stood close enough so he could detect the spicy carnation scent she wore. It suited her, for she was a spicy morsel of a woman. He swung between wanting to kiss her and wishing he could shake her, for she was as naughty as could be.

With a final glance at the painting, Miss Dancy turned away to retrace her steps to the doorway. "We really ought to be going."

Blase lost his temper, something he rarely ever did. He strode up to Miss Dancy, took her firmly by the arm, then marched her along down the stairs into the library, where he pushed her onto a chair.

"I repeat, Miss Dancy. If you will be so kind? I should like to know this story you heard. I have a particular reason for wishing to hear it."

Hyacinthe glared at the man she frequently referred to as

"his eminence" because he was so intimidating. After silently debating a moment, she nodded.

"Mrs. Peachey said that when he was alive there was talk that he was involved with a redhead who lived in the Tudor house. Come to think on it, there was no mention of a family. I wonder if he established her there." When Lord Norwood gave her a dark look, Hyacinthe continued, "It was said that he bestowed 'jewels and treasures' on her. Yet, when it was known that she had died, the people who entered the house found the curtains open—no body and no treasure of any kind. Is that not a mystery?"

"Jewels? Nothing about what kind they might be?"

Hyacinthe rose from the chair where she had been so unceremoniously pushed and edged toward the door. "Nothing. But one can only wonder if they remain hidden in the house."

He strolled after her, stopping her in her tracks when he said, "And why did you wish to see his portrait?"

"Well . . . I wanted to see if he resembled you, I suppose." She knew she had upset him the moment the words left her mouth. Oh, if she could only learn to guard her tongue. Slipping away down the hall—seeming not to run but covering the marble with rapid steps—she waited for Jane by the front door. Lord Norwood had followed at her heels.

"It has been, er, interesting, sir. Thank you for the tea and the viewing," Hyacinthe said politely, then ducked out of the door before his lordship could commit murder or whatever promised by the look in his eyes.

Jane had joined them at the door. With a muddled murmur of words, she dashed after her cousin, both of them popping into the coach before the gentlemen could prevent them. Although what they might do, she didn't know. And didn't want to find out. Fosdick left the house, following her young ladies at a more seemly pace.

"What did you accomplish by that foolishness?" Jane demanded to know once they were safely away from Worthington Hall.

"His ancestor most likely did her in, for he looks to have a temper equally as bad as the present lord. Certainly they resemble one another," Hyacinthe said after examining her sleeve to see if any sign from that firm grip showed. "We can but hope my ruse works and he decides to investigate."

They discussed the matter all the way to the cottage, deciding they would prowl around the Tudor house sometime when Mr. Wayland was occupied elsewhere.

At Worthington Hall Blase walked at Val's side back to the library, a frown marring his handsome brow.

"I would wager there is something in that tale of hers," he said.

"Then you believe it?" Val asked incredulously.

"You forget, I have been reading his diary. He describes his love as having hair like flame, with a temper to match. It is my theory that he gave her the jewels and the paintings. But why did they never turn up anywhere?"

"Interesting. When do we commence a search of the Tudor house?"

Unsurprised at the conclusion his friend had reached, Blase replied, "Tomorrow morning, early. I shall assign that snooping Wayland to surveying the land I have set aside for the new cottages, and perhaps he can stake out the foundations with the help of the masons he hired. That ought to keep him out of our hair."

"But what of Miss Dancy?" Val inquired with a devilish grin.

"She is another matter entirely. We can but hope that she turns her attention to something else."

"You amuse me, Blase. If I know anything about women at all, you will have to rise early to beat her to it."

"I cannot believe she brought me a cat."

"I noticed he scratched you. Were I in your shoes, I should be a little wary of the redhead. I suspect she also has claws and would not hesitate to use them." Val smiled narrowly as though recalling something from the past.

"Perhaps a ride would be in order. I confess that this alteration I planned is assuming proportions I'd not considered when I began."

"Bit off more than you can chew?" Val taunted gently.

"Not in the least," Blase replied, stiffening slightly at the implication that he might fail in his plans. "I shall find the jewels and paintings, mark my words. And the prospect from my terrace will be developed as I envision, with the help of Humphrey Repton."

Val merely chuckled while they went up the stairs to their rooms to don riding apparel.

Across the gentle hills Hyacinthe dismissed her coachman and groom, then guided Jane inside the cottage. Fosdick took their bonnets and pellisses, disappearing without questions or remarks.

"I doubt that man has changed his intent one whit. But"— Hyacinthe spread her hands wide and excitement colored her voice—"he believes those jewels and other treasure *do* exist. Well, we shall see who finds them. Perhaps I can uncover the missing items, then use them as persuasion. And if his rakish lordship thinks he will succeed with his plans to destroy history, he can think again. I am more determined than ever that he shan't prevail!"

5

"I believe we might steal over there now. It is far too early for either Mrs. Peachey or the Widow Smith to be up and about." Hyacinthe leaned from her dormer window beneath the overhanging thatch roof to peer out into the half light of early morning. Quite a few ducks and the two swans dotted the green with their feathered presence. They were relatively quiet, with only soft quacks to be heard. Not a soul was abroad at this hour.

"This is utterly mad," Jane protested—quietly, lest she wake Fosdick. It seemed that the formidably proper abigail intimidated Jane far more than Hyacinthe, for Jane appeared quite hesitant to do anything that might shock the woman.

"Well, we do not wish the entire village to know what we are about. Come." Hyacinthe closed and latched her window, then motioned Jane to follow her from the pleasant bedroom.

They tiptoed down the stairs until they reached the tidy slate-floored entrance hall.

Hyacinthe eased the bolt on the door, then slipped outside without the slightest sound.

"What a good thing you put a spot of oil on those hinges yesterday," Jane observed in a mere whisper while they continued their almost-silent progress across the green.

A pair of ducks followed their movements, quite obviously hoping for a few crumbs, and one of the stately swans gave them a rude stare for disturbing its inspection of the morning tidbits to be found.

On the far side of the green the old house rose amid a tangle of climbing rose brambles and weeds, with an occasional clump of pinks and wallflowers gone wild peeping from the confusion of greenery. The footpath had been cleared so they were able to avoid snagging their serviceable gowns, worn expressly to tolerate the inevitable dust that haunted old places.

They found the front door well and truly locked, as were the windows to either side. Not to be deterred in what she declared to be an intriguing investigation, and recalling the daring exploits of her more adventuresome cousins, Hyacinthe persevered.

Around to the rear of the house she discovered that the entry to the scullery had been left ajar.

"Lovely!" she whispered. Not knowing how soundly Mrs. Peachey slept, the girls agreed to whisper until safely within the old house.

They slipped silently into the house, then placed the door precisely where it had stood—nearly closed.

Jane peered through the gloom. "I can scarcely make out a thing," she complained.

The floor above them squeaked and Jane reached out to cling to her cousin's arm.

Glad for the comfort of her touch, Hyacinthe said, " 'Tis nothing more than an old house. Come." She drew Jane along with her until they reached the front parlor. "We shall begin here," she decided.

Once their eyes became accustomed to the poor light, the girls looked about them with raised brows.

"It would seem that someone has begun an investigation before us," Jane observed with a noticeable tremor in her voice. "Things have been shifted about in an obvious search. There are footprints in the dust."

"How curious that Mr. Wayland did not mention that a trespasser had invaded this house when he cautioned us against coming here," Hyacinthe commented. "One cannot help but wonder if the gentleman has notions of his own."

"You mean he intends to hunt for the treasure for himself? But that would be dishonest," Jane declared roundly. The floor creaked again and she again drew closer to her cousin.

"We are hunting as well," Hyacinthe reminded her. "However, should we find something, we would assuredly hand it over to Lord Norwood, although he does not deserve it. I should be happy with the fun of finding something hidden for so long. And if it serves to persuade his lordship to forget about the ruination of the village, more to the good."

Jane shook her head. "Well, I do not see how you expect to find anything when 'tis obvious that someone else has explored this house before us."

"I suspect that Mr. Wayland has not found anything, for if he had, would he not take himself off with his loot?"

"I suppose so," Jane said doubtfully.

"Here," Hyacinthe directed, "you begin in this corner and I shall start at the opposite. There are still pictures on the walls, so search behind them for hiding places. The carpet—moth-eaten as it is—has been rolled up, so I suppose that the last hunter has already inspected the floor."

The cousins worked quietly for some time before they met at the far side of the room. Both were somewhat dusty, with cobwebs draped decoratively across the day cap Jane had donned over Hyacinthe's objections.

Hyacinthe cast a disgusted look about the room. "I doubt there is anything hidden here. Shall we go upstairs?"

"Why not the kitchen?" Jane wondered, while she followed her cousin up the worn steps. The wood had a depression in the center of each stair tread, and the girls held up their skirts to avoid gathering up the layer of dust that covered them.

"I doubt if she was well acquainted with that room were she the mistress of a wealthy man," Hyacinthe explained. "I am encouraged there's no evidence of someone else having been up here, for the dust has not been disturbed."

The floor creaked and groaned as they gingerly made their way along the upstairs hall. There were four bedrooms—all paneled, with mullioned windows—and a small storeroom. They peered into each of these, noting the absence of furniture in all but one room.

"I wonder where the ghost is said to lurk," Hyacinthe murmured while she poked and prodded everything in sight in the unfurnished rooms. She entered the room that had the remaining furniture with Jane close behind her.

"Cousin, you are anything but reassuring," Jane said as she bent to look under the bed, its tattered hangings covering elegant although dingy lines. "There is no carpet here, either," she observed while checking the inside of a beautifully decorated commode now stained with age.

"The place smells of decaying wood and mildewed fabric." Hyacinthe made her way to one of the many-paned windows, opening it just enough to allow a breath of air to wash through the room and send feathers of dust flying.

Jane sneezed, then looked apprehensively about her. "I thought I heard sounds from below," she whispered.

They paused, standing utterly still. What appeared to be footsteps reached their ears, followed by a scraping noise as though something were being dragged across the floor.

Jane turned pale and reached out to clutch Hyacinthe's arm.

"I believe there is something or someone belowstairs," Hyacinthe murmured.

"Or the ghost of that woman," Jane whispered, holding a handkerchief firmly to her nose lest she sneeze again.

"I wonder what she was like?" Hyacinthe whispered back. What sort of woman would appeal to the dashing, rakish gentleman who leaned so casually against a stone wall in that painting? While he seemed so correct in dress and manner, his eyes had held secrets. They held laughter and a knowledge of the world that Hyacinthe could only guess at.

Had he murdered her as Mrs. Peachey hinted? Or had she taken her treasures and stolen away to London? About to investigate a closet beneath the eaves at the far end of the room, Hyacinthe froze as she heard footsteps on the stairs.

"Quickly, no one must find us here!" Pulling Jane along with her, Hyacinthe scurried to the closet, then closed the door when they were safely inside. They were in what had been a paneled room, from what could be seen in the gloom. A mere slit of a window revealed little. Evidently clothing and other necessities had been kept in here, with the space used as a dressing room.

Jane tugged at her cousin's sleeve, motioning to the door, beyond which could be heard voices.

"Well, Val, this must have been her room." The steps crossed to the window that Hyacinthe had opened.

"Appears as though someone has been here recently," Val commented.

"Wayland said he had been examining the house to see if anything was worth salvaging," replied Blase.

"Well, I hardly expected it to be her ghost," Val said. He chuckled at his friend's expression. "Did you?"

"I'll confess I did not know quite what to expect. I'd not be surprised to find our little hedgehog over here poking her face into what does not concern her."

"Ah, the prickly redhead. She's a charmer, I'll wager, were you to persuade her into your arms or bed."

"She's a gently bred female, Val. Best confine those sort of observations to others, if you know what I mean." He chuckled in a somewhat suggestive manner. "Not but what I'd not relish the opportunity to do a bit of an—shall we say, investigation?—should the opportunity arise."

"Do any of the paintings we have seen so far match the description in your inventory?" Val queried while strolling about the room. He grimaced at the filthy painting above the bed. Once at the far side of the room, he tried the handle of the door to the closet, opened it to peer inside, then closed it without going into it.

"What was in there?" Blase inquired lazily while he checked under the bed to see if any of the floorboards might be of a different type or have been pried up lately.

"Dressing room. Nothing of importance there."

"Well, I expect we had better inspect it before we leave here. Who knows, she might have had a hiding place in there with her clothing and whatever furbelows a lady kept then."

"Very well," Val said, propping himself against the wall to watch while Blase continued his search. He tapped walls, pried at the broad oak planks that served as flooring, scrutinized the ceiling to see if a panel might conceal a hiding place.

"Confounded Tudor style offers far too many places for concealment. The carvings on these wooden panels could have a spring catch in any one of them."

"Or a secret door to stairs where we'll find the skeleton of the poor dear, locked in by her unscrupulous maid, foiled in her intent to flee to her lover."

"Val, remind me never to permit you access to one of those gothic novels again." Blase gave his friend a patient look, then added, "You might help, you know."

"I suspect we already have sufficient help," Val said, nodding his head toward the closet while holding one finger to his lips to silence Blase.

Blase frowned, then sighed. "Hedgehog?" he mouthed.

Val nodded.

Giving the room a final inspection, Blase shook his head in disgust. "If there is anything here, I cannot fathom where it might be."

"Think Wayland may have found it?" Val said softly.

"Stashing it away for later disposal? Anything is possible, I suppose. I believe my architect will bear close watching."

Taking exceedingly quiet steps, he edged over to the closet, turned the knob, and with a swift motion threw the door open and stalked inside.

"Good heavens," Hyacinthe complained, "you could give a person an attack of the spasms crashing in like that."

"Aha!" Blase said in a nasty tone, "I thought we had found our ghost! And how is our little hedgehog this morning?"

"Quite well, thank you. *He* is noisily settling into a cozy spot at the bottom of the garden, busily munching snails and slugs and whatever else hedgehogs eat. Harry is quite a treasure. May I ask our tom cat how he is getting along?" Lord Norwood appeared most annoyed with her comparison of him to a tom cat. She barely suppressed the grin that longed to break forth. "Mr. Wayland cautioned us so strongly against coming into this house that we simply had to find out what might be here," Hyacinthe said in a disarming way, offering Blase a conciliatory smile.

"He has been here often?"

"Every day," Jane said, while brushing away a cobweb that chanced to float before her. She smoothed out her skirts, then covered her nose again to prevent another sneeze.

Val shook his head in apparent amusement, his grin widening as he realized the disreputable sight the two young ladies made.

"What do you say we adjourn to the outside and a bit of

fresh air?" He offered Jane his arm, which she accepted with obvious reluctance. It seemed she still recalled his comment that there was nothing of importance in the dressing closet. That would rankle any lady, even one convinced that she would never wed.

"I am able to manage perfectly well on my own, thank you very much," Hyacinthe said politely to Lord Norwood when he offered her his arm. "I would like to inspect this room more than we were able. You came and we felt it best to hide, for we truly did not know who might be coming up those stairs. Why, it could have been anyone."

"Indeed. I think we shall join the others, however. I will return here later to do a bit of hunting on my own."

"You are a spoilsport, sir," Hyacinthe said with vexation. "This would be the most likely place for a woman to conceal something of value. Perhaps there is a secret compartment behind that little painting over there, the one in the shadows."

Blase strode over to examine the painting, which he proceeded to remove from the wall in order to see it better. The dim light offered by the window proved insufficient, so he left the dressing room and marched down the stairs to the rear of the house with Hyacinthe trailing directly behind him. Here he managed to wipe the dust from the picture, then studied it more fully.

"Is it one of them?" Val said softly, for Jane had made it clear to them all that Mrs. Peachey might appear in her backyard at any time.

"I believe it is. In which case the others ought to be around here somewhere. I wonder if I ought to tell Wayland to forget this house for the moment."

"Or keep him so busy elsewhere that he has no time for anything involved with this house," Val suggested.

"Excellent notion," Lord Norwood replied, a grin lighting his handsome face.

About then the sun chanced to light up the yard, reminding them of the advancing hours. Hyacinthe took Jane's hand to edge around the house. It would be best for the two of them to disappear while the gentlemen were otherwise occupied. She had a distinct feeling that Lord Norwood was not best pleased with her at the moment. Yet she had helped find his painting.

She saw the men glance up just as she and Jane began to hurry away from the house and across the green. The ducks protested, fussing in a noisy way, when the young women skirted the rim of the pond.

"We probably have awakened Mrs. Peachey—not to mention every other soul in the village—with all this racket," Jane commented when Hyacinthe tugged her past the gate and into the cottage.

"All but Granny Beanbuck, who must have been up for some time. I smell her cinnamon buns. Do you think that after we clean up we might manage to purchase a few for our breakfast?"

"Indeed," Jane warmly agreed.

They hurried up the stairs and into their respective bedrooms. In short order they were appropriately garbed for a possible meeting with two irate gentlemen. Jane's hair had been restored to shining neatness, while Hyacinthe's red tresses curled provocatively about her heart-shaped face.

Hyacinthe set about heating tea water, although she was not accustomed to such labors. One did what one must, she had long ago decided.

When Jane returned bearing a heaping plate of warm and very-fragrant buns, the aroma filled the little kitchen.

With such an incentive, Hyacinthe quickly poured the boiling water into the teapot, taking care not to spill any on herself. Rather than eat at the kitchen table, she loaded a pretty painted tray with cups and saucers, napkins, and a large plate heaped with a prodigious number of cinnamon buns inside a white linen napkin to keep them warm. There was easily enough for four.

Jane eyed the repast in the parlor with audible misgivings. "I think you are being presumptuous."

"They will be reluctant to intrude upon Granny Beanbuck," Hyacinthe declared with feminine certainty. "But I believe that the aroma of fresh-baked cinnamon buns will be nigh onto impossible for any male to resist. How thankful I am that you bought such a splendid amount."

"Yes, well, I thought that Sir Charles might stop by later this morning, and he is very fond of them." Jane blushed a painful shade of pink.

Hyacinthe had consumed the first bite of one of the delectable buns followed by a dainty sip of tea when a loud and very impatient knock could be heard on the door.

"I will handle this," she whispered to Jane. Moving from the parlor to the little entrance hall, she cautiously opened the front door just a little. Upon seeing Lord Norwood and Lord Latham waiting, she opened the door a trifle wider, looking at them with wide-eyed innocence. "Yes?"

"Why won't more girls use that word," Val muttered in a plaintive voice.

Ignoring his friend, Lord Norwood bowed slightly, then sniffed the aroma of cinnamon buns that floated from the parlor. "I believe we have something to discuss."

"Perhaps you will join us in a morning cup of tea? And fresh-baked cinnamon buns, of course." When both men surged forward, Hyacinthe stifled a grin at their boyish enthusiasm. "I feel certain that we have sufficient."

"Why do I feel that you mentally added 'even for you' after that remark?" Val said in a jesting manner.

"Well, and I did, I suppose," she confessed.

Within short order they were all seated in Jane's parlor sipping cups of strong Bohea and nibbling utterly delectable, fairy-light cinnamon buns.

Lord Norwood was exceedingly hungry after that tramp through the house, then finding someplace where he and Val might clean off some of their dirt before presenting themselves at the Pennington house. When he had consumed two cups of tea liberally laced with milk and three of the buns, he spoke.

"I believe we must have some sort of understanding. Mr. Wayland is correct about one thing. You ought not go into that deserted house. You might be hurt, or something worse."

"What do you mean, worse?" Jane inquired.

"I think he implies we might be murdered, or something equally dire," Hyacinthe explained dryly.

"But if he proceeds with his plan to tear down the village, we shan't have the opportunity to explore that once-lovely old place. It must have been very charming in its day," Jane reflected.

At this reminder of his intentions Hyacinthe grew very quiet, giving Lord Norwood considering looks over her teacup. He appeared to be unaware of her change of mood, for he blundered on.

"Precisely. I believe I shall instruct Wayland to commence laying out foundations for new cottages at once," he said, bestowing a sad look at the last bit of bun that remained on his plate.

"Even with autumn approaching? I fail to see how you can accomplish much before spring," Hyacinthe observed carefully.

"Oh, the workers are willing to proceed through most of the bad weather, except for snow," he assured her.

"Then we ought to pray for a cold winter," Hyacinthe muttered under her breath.

"Still not resigned to the move, Miss Dancy?" Lord Latham asked, his bright eyes dancing at the prospect of a good argument.

"I think it is the most stupid, insensitive, and utterly selfish thing I have ever heard of," Hyacinthe declared stoutly, glaring at his lordship in a quite defiant manner. "The very idea of destroying a person's home merely to improve a view is sheer nonsense."

She could see that Lord Norwood was barely hanging onto his composure. A dull red suffused his cheeks and he compressed his lips, no doubt to prevent him from blistering her ears with his reply to her forthright denunciation. She had to give him full marks for reasonably good manners.

"Hyacinthe!" Jane cried in a totally mortified voice.

"I cannot apologize for my excess of passion regarding this. Tell me, sir, will the rents go up on these new and splendid—and no doubt costly to build—cottages? It would be folly to construct them and not gain a respectable return for your money. That would be a poor investment."

"And what do you know about landlords and investments?" Lord Norwood said in a strained voice while failing to answer her question.

"When my dear papa was alive he taught me a great deal, perhaps knowing he had not long on earth. Since I have the practical head, whereas Peter is the dreamer of the family, Papa decided I had best know as much as possible. I understand far more about this matter than you suspect. I doubt you can toss a great sum of money away on tenant housing without a sufficient return . . . unless you have been far luckier at the racetrack than I had heard."

He frowned at her words, taking a few moments to digest them. At last he placed his teacup on the table close at hand and rose as though to depart. "I gather there is little more to say on this matter."

Hyacinthe also rose, facing him with her hands in a composed clasp before her, her little chin tilted defiantly up at him. "I daresay you have the right of it, sirrah. Unless you change your mind. I should be most grateful in that event," she said graciously, with a nod.

"I wonder what that might involve," Lord Latham murmured in his mischievous way.

"I do believe that your nurse ought to have spanked you more often, Lord Latham," Jane said repressively.

"I fear she had other things in mind, dear lady," he said, with a very distant and somewhat forbidding look on his face.

Hyacinthe thought it best to change the subject immediately before Jane could press for an explanation. While she had no notion as to what his unfortunate experience might have been, it obviously was one that still bothered him.

"Is that Sir Charles I see coming up the walk?" she said.

Jane promptly forgot the note of suppressed anger that she too had heard in Lord Latham's voice and immediately went to answer the door.

"Sir Charles," she could be heard saying in a happy voice. Jane's feelings were highly transparent to Hyacinthe. She wondered if Sir Charles might possibly be aware of them. And if he were, what did he think?

The proper gentleman entered the parlor with a look of great surprise at discovering guests in Miss Pennington's parlor at this hour of the morning. He bowed correctly, then at

Jane's urging took her chair and accepted a cup of still-hot tea with a plate bearing a large cinnamon bun.

Jane perched on the arm of Hyacinthe's chair until she rose to cross to accompany Lord Norwood and Lord Latham to the entry. "Do entertain Sir Charles, please, Jane," Hyacinthe told her. "I will tend to our departing guests."

"Pray do not leave on my account," Sir Charles protested. "In fact, I wished to ask Lord Latham about that fishing gear he mentioned to me the other day."

With a smiling look of resignation at Lord Norwood, Lord Latham again seated himself, obviously prepared to share his knowledge with Sir Charles.

Jane looked torn between chagrin that Sir Charles wished only to converse with Latham and hope that she had a possible beau in her parlor.

"I believe I will walk with you to the green, if you do not mind," Hyacinthe said to Lord Norwood as he prepared to leave. "Not having the slightest interest in fishing, I would rather feed the ducks."

"Please give Miss Pennington my thanks for the buns and tea. They were most welcome. Although"—he gave Hyacinthe a searching look—"if she is as hard-pressed for funds as you implied in your impassioned statement regarding rents, I suspect it is you who purchased the buns this morning."

"Jane's competence is very slight, barely sufficient for her to reside here. Most would deem it shocking that she lives alone, particularly when she might live with her Grandmama. But Jane is the tenderest of creatures. I fear she would wilt into nothing under our grandmama's domination. I intend that she be able to keep her home," Hyacinthe stated, giving her tormentor a frosty glare.

"Yet do I not detect an interest upon the part of Sir Charles?" Lord Norwood asked in a rather mocking tone while guiding her across the road.

Hyacinthe withdrew from him slightly. "It is not my place to speculate upon her *or* his interest, sirrah."

"You mean you have not figured out a way to bring them together?" He was on the verge of laughter, she noted ruefully.

He was a wretch—far too handsome and too certain of himself by half.

"I have not considered the matter," she answered in lofty tones, her air somewhat marred when a duck waddled over to nip at her skirts.

Blase supposed he could have reassured her that he had no intention of raising her cousin's rent. Yet he rather enjoyed these sparring matches with the delicious Hyacinthe Dancy. "I shall do what I must, dear lady," he said at last, deciding that his words could be taken several ways.

The lovely face that belonged to the most spirited and sparkling woman he had met in some time became most angry. Apparently she was not taking his words in a positive way, to say the very least.

She tossed the handful of crumbs she had carried from the cottage to the ducks that had drawn close in hope of a treat, then advanced upon him in a manner he could only think of as menacing. In fact, she reminded him of the swan that bore down upon them from the other side of the pond.

Absently he observed Sir Charles and Val exiting from the Pennington cottage, Mrs. Peachey pausing to chat with the Widow Smith, and Ambrose Clark wending his way along the path. It seemed half the village was out early this morning. Then he focused on his fiery, temperamental redhead.

"You are a beast, Blase Montague!" she hissed at him, reminding him again of the approaching swan. "An utterly wretched, selfish, inconsiderate, thoughtless beast."

With those words Hyacinthe stepped forward to give Blase a vehement push. Caught off guard by the suddenness of her movement, he had no defense. Waving his arms in the air in the hope of regaining his balance—and a futile hope to stay on dry land—he plunged into the pond.

The filthy water was chilly and, worst of all, contained duck feathers and a lot of other things he preferred not to consider. He surfaced and shook his head, then tried to climb from the pond, Fortunately the pond was shallow, so he could stand on the bottom with his head above water. However, he found himself unable to make any progress.

The rocks were covered with green slime and a goodly bit

of muck. He slipped and slid, trying to find purchase on rocks that defied him. With a determined grip on a couple of slimy rocks he made another attempt. At last he managed to exit the pond, dripping green mess and dirty water all over, feeling as though he badly needed a bath. *And* feeling most angry.

Miss Dancy, hands covering her face in presumed horror over what she had done, backed away from him—as well she might.

"Words fail me, Miss Dancy. But I daresay I shall think of some presently." He bowed, then squished his way toward where the blacksmith had his carriage and horse tied up.

If there was a soul in the village of Worthington who did not view his lordship, all wet and mucky, striding toward his carriage that momentous morning, he or she would regret it always.

Val ran to catch up with his friend, and from somewhere behind him Blase could hear the sound of laughter . . . unrestrained, bubbling, very feminine laughter of the sort that eventually hurts the ribs.

6

"I cannot believe that you did such a terrible thing," Jane scolded. "Do you think it will make Lord Norwood more kindly disposed to the plight of the villagers? Or to me?"

"He implied that he would raise your rent. I fear I just exploded. To think of all the money he has won at the racetrack . . . and then to treat you so! It is the outside of enough," Hyacinthe said indignantly. "The man has no heart, no sensitivity, no soul. He is little better than a monster!"

"I wonder why he wagers at the racetrack so constantly," Jane mused. "Surely he does not need the money? Does he?"

"Every gentleman of the *ton* is a gambling fool," Hyacinthe told her with a shrug, "with the exception of my brother." But the query set her to thinking. What if Lord Norwood truly did need the money—to run his estate, for example. What if his father had squandered the money on an ill-advised scheme, losing the lot?

It would be a good thing were Lord Norwood to take his winnings to improve the estate, the farms and homes of his tenants. But not, she reminded herself, to fritter away his blunt on such a foolish project as a picturesque view for his garden. Or turn his tenants from their homes. Who knew what nonsense Mr. Wayland would design? Likely uninhabitable places that looked pretty but were impractical to live in.

Yet to be fair, she had to admit that she had acted badly. Her Aunt Bel would have been scandalized, and well she might. A young lady simply didn't do such things. Even if it was hilarious.

Vexed with herself, she rose from her chair in the parlor to pace about the small room. Then she paused, an impish look covering her piquant face with its small pointed chin. She gazed at her cousin defiantly.

"But it *was* amusing. I tried not to laugh, really I did. To see that lofty man reduced to a green slime-covered mess was truly diverting. I have endured too many insults from him not to appreciate *his* receiving a setdown."

"I did not know he had insulted you," Jane exclaimed, her manner inviting Hyacinthe to confide but not demanding such.

Hyacinthe looked toward the window, recalling her feeling of humiliation when he had stared at her through his quizzing glass then proceeded to ignore her, as much as telling her and the world that she was far beneath his consideration. To presume to flirt with her while at that country inn was entirely too much to tolerate, an indignity for which he ought to be heartily ashamed.

" 'Tis a long story. It involves a flirtation gone awry, I suppose." She drifted from the room and out to the garden. It might be soothing to watch the hedgehog, if the little fellow would come out. So far she had only seen him at an early-morning hour, so perhaps he napped during the day?

The flowers were pretty, simple cottage-garden varieties. The lovely colors and fragrance proved an excellent substitute for the animal's antics. She wandered about the orderly garden, admiring Jane's efforts. Lord Norwood would do better to emulate Jane, with colorful flowers, restful trees, and cleverly trimmed shrubs.

What did he actually want, anyway? What, precisely, was a picturesque view? She dimly recalled reading some nonsense in the newspaper, a debate on the merits of landscaping an estate to emulate a painting, or something ludicrous like that. It seemed vastly foolish to her. Expensive, as well, if one went about demolishing an entire village to accomplish that whim.

The sound of voices from the cottage brought her about. She retraced her steps, entering the kitchen only to pause.

"So you see, Miss Pennington, it would seem to me that you have more to gain than to lose by supporting his lordship in his landscaping scheme," urged Sir Charles, his voice coming from the parlor.

"My cousin said he planned to raise my rent. I cannot afford that."

"Dear lady, is there no one to whom you can appeal? No home in which you may take refuge?" Sir Charles queried gently.

Hyacinthe pictured him leaning forward, his concern visible on his pleasant square face.

"Only Grandmama Dancy, and she terrifies me," Jane replied with a note of alarm in her voice.

Hyacinthe stayed where she was, reluctant to intrude, but deciding she had best know the direction of this conversation—just in case Jane needed her help.

Figuring that they might welcome some tea, Hyacinthe tiptoed about, placing the kettle on to boil, cutting some bread into wafer-thin slices, then adding biscuits and arranging a tray to take into the parlor.

"We shall have to see what can be done," Sir Charles said in his kindly manner. "I have often wondered that such a gently reared lady would choose to live by herself. I believe I understand now. Young women have a difficult time of it, it seems."

"Particularly if they wish to be independent. 'Tis not done, I have been told repeatedly," Jane confessed in an incensed voice. "It seems 'twere far better if we move in with some relative to become an unpaid servant."

To Hyacinthe, standing in the middle of the kitchen, these were remarkable words. She had nearly dropped the tray when that somewhat bitter voice denounced the custom that nudged spinsters to take their place where relatives might find them useful. To be sure, most unmarried ladies seemed to feel they must earn their keep. Yet all those she had met lived in fear of being sent away if they somehow displeased. It must be a dreadful existence, living in the shadows as it were.

Was she fated to end up with that as her own destiny? Would she become a patient attendant to her aunt or, horror of horrors, her grandmama? If Sir Charles failed to marry Jane, perhaps Hyacinthe would end up living here, spending her days pottering about in the garden. With her tidy income, they could manage quite nicely. It was a point to consider, she thought bleakly. Maybe they could travel.

"Oh, Hyacinthe," Jane cried from the doorway, disconcerted at finding her cousin in the kitchen, "I thought you were in the garden. Sir Charles is here and I intended to serve tea."

Hyacinthe smiled at her cousin's pink-cheeked dithering when Jane glanced at the teapot, gazed absently at the bread and bun container . . . then did nothing.

"Tea is ready." Hyacinthe carried the tray past Jane and into the parlor, placed it on a low table, then curtsied to Sir Charles in what she hoped might be considered a conciliatory manner.

He rose, bowing slightly while he studied her face. "I trust you have recovered your composure from earlier this morning?" There was the faintest hint of censure in his voice, but his eyes danced with the memory of his lordship dripping pond water while squishing along the village path.

"Indeed, sir. Mr. Clark read me a lecture on the evils of a bad temper." Hyacinthe exchanged a rueful smile with Sir Charles that spoke volumes.

"I would wager that you would do the same thing again, however," he said with a lift of his brows.

"Lord Norwood implied that he would raise the rent for my dearest Jane once she moved into his precious new cottage. If she would allow me to pay the difference it might be allowed, but she is a wretchedly stubborn and independent girl," Hyacinthe declared. "Few people know the real Jane. You ought to see her beautiful darning, sir. Why, it looks put there on purpose. I have an exquisite butterfly on my sheet to cover a hole that dared to appear. It is a wonder what she can accomplish."

"Hyacinthe!" Jane managed in a strangled voice.

"Forgive me," Hyacinthe said demurely, "I know what a modest creature you are, but once in a while it is necessary to tell the world what a splendid and talented woman you are. Is that not so, Sir Charles?"

"Hm?" he asked, his attention fastened completely on Jane.

Hyacinthe merely smiled and sipped her tea. Perhaps Jane would not find it necessary to pay the higher rent after all.

"That wretched female laughed at me! There I was, dripping wet from her having pushed me into that detestable pond, and she had the audacity to laugh!" Blase complained while tossing his ruined pantaloons in the same pile that contained a favorite coat—also ruined—hose, and a shirt that had green spots and dirty muck that he doubted the laundress could get out.

Val turned from the window to study his good friend's indignant expression. A smile lifted one corner of his mouth. "I had no idea that I would be so entertained when you invited me to visit."

"This was not my idea, and you know it," Blase fumed, stomping around to the tub. His ire subsided when Smithson assisted him into a soothing bath.

Ordering a bath in the late morning had caused some surprise in the kitchen, but the hot water quickly appeared when the staff heard that his lordship was in a towering rage.

"Ah, how good to become clean," Blase said with a sigh from behind the screen that sheltered him from a draft and close to the small fire to prevent his being chilled.

"You didn't smell particularly charming. That pond ought to have a better flow of water so it wouldn't become so stagnant . . . not to mention smell devilishly bad."

"I must remember that when arranging for the new pond," Blase said, a wry note in his voice.

"Have you thought of trying to win her over to your side?" Val asked, returning his gaze to the distant scene. "Why not invite her and her cousin, and perhaps Sir Charles as well, for tea—or something? Then you could take her out to the terrace to explain what the vista could be, how your changes will create a grand, picturesque view? I can just imagine you on the terrace, with one arm around her—to direct her gaze—pointing out your sad want of a proper prospect."

The sloshing ceased while this proposal was duly considered.

"She'd never come."

"She came with the cat, along with Miss Pennington and that sour maid," Val reminded him.

"The *tom* cat. That was an insult."

"Have you forgotten you presented her with a hedgehog? What has happened to your sense of the absurd?"

More sloshing could be heard behind the screen when Blase rose to step from the bathing tub. Before long he appeared garbed in a fresh shirt, well-made cream pantaloons, and white hose. He leaned against the door to his dressing room while footmen appeared to clear away the remains of his bath.

His hair was still damp from its washing, clinging in blond curls about his head. Blase's shirt clung to a powerful physique not gained from lolling about. His pantaloons graced well-formed legs that more than one lady had sighed over. And he looked down his aristocratic nose with the air of one well-born.

Val commented, "Pity she could not see you now. She'd forget her opposition to your scheme and chase after you. She ignored you in London, you said?" he needled.

"I ignored her," Blase snapped back, then paused. "Although I must admit, if she was interested in me, she never revealed it by the flutter of an eyelash."

"A bit of wounded masculine pride there?" Val jibed. "I don't know why you should want her attention, even if she is a delectable morsel and promises a fine time of it in . . . " His words trailed off suggestively. "There are other women. Miss Pennington would make some gentleman a fine, quiet, undemanding wife."

"Sounds dashed dull, my friend," Blase growled, pulling on first one boot, then the second.

"True," Val happily agreed. "So will you?"

"Invite them to the Hall?" Blase thought of seeing Miss Dancy again in his home, showing her the view he intended to improve. Hyacinthe? A more unlikely name he couldn't imagine. She should have offered soothing calm, like a lavender lily in a garden instead of red fire and white lightning. And then he recalled that fire and lightning were far more stimulating than a tranquil lily. Although as he recalled she was a delightfully fragrant armful, not that she had remained in his arms for more than seconds.

"All right. I shall send off the invitation. Better invite the curate as well."

"Might as well make it the entire village while you are at it. Just pray for good weather." Val stared out at the gathering clouds and wondered what the volatile Hyacinthe Dancy did now. He thought her name appropriate, for she bloomed like an exotic flower in the midst of that little village.

Hyacinthe finished her cup of tea, then excused herself, murmuring something about Fosdick coming down to keep them company.

Leaving Jane dithering behind her, Hyacinthe hurried up the spiral staircase, thinking this was another place where there could be improvement in cottage design. This staircase was murder. What might happen if they needed to go down in the dark, even with a candle, chilled her spine.

In her room, she explained Miss Pennington's need of her to the awesomely correct abigail. Once the pleased maid left to hurry down to the parlor and thus chaperone Jane, Hyacinthe got busy.

She knew that Mrs. Peachey usually visited the Widow Smith at this time of day. It was an ideal time for snooping about the Tudor house.

Had anyone questioned her enthusiasm for a house owned by her tormentor, the very man who had ignored her and now threatened to tear down Jane's home about her very ears, she would have been hard-pressed to explain. It was the legend.

Donning a serviceable gown and emulating Jane with a head covering, Hyacinthe slipped down the stairs and out the back door. Clouds gathered off to the west; it would undoubtedly rain before long. Ideal weather for snooping.

She first made her way to the pond, offering the ducks and swans a handful of crumbs as a purpose for her stroll.

Then, after a careful inspection of the village, she ambled in the direction of the church, only at the last moment turning aside into the Tudor house greenery. No one could see her now. Her dull green gown blended into the shadows cast by an old oak tree.

Her heart beat rapidly when she slipped past the scullery door and into the kitchen. Going on the same premise as before, she ignored that room as well as the next, slipping up the stairs as silently as she might.

Although there was not the least need for quiet, she felt it suited her purpose, not to mention the mood of the house. Were there spirits here? Did the ghost of that long-ago red-head—Hyacinthe had not forgotten that bit of information—linger in the shadows of these rooms?

After another perusal of the empty bedrooms, checking paneling and floorboards much as Lord Norwood had done, Hyacinthe paused on the threshold of the large bedroom.

If she had lived here, mistress of that madly handsome rake, what would she have done? If you figured that the girl had been murdered—what a dreadful word that was—it meant her treasures were most likely still hidden in the house. Unless someone over the years had found and stolen the lot.

Yet Lord Norwood had just found a painting that apparently had been part of this treasure, and found it right here, or at least in the dressing room. After one more survey, Hyacinthe crossed to enter the little room. She began to examine every panel, every irregularity in the walls.

"Oh, pooh, this window needs cleaning. I can scarce make out the design on the wall." A tattered cloth tossed to one corner served as a means to scrub the window a bit cleaner, enabling Hyacinthe to see much better.

She was just about to pry at a peculiar knob in a carved design when she heard sounds from below. Frantic lest she be found here, not knowing who the intruder might be, she hunted for a place to hide. Those steps were now on the stairs and the intruder would undoubtedly be in here before many minutes passed.

In the far side of the room she spotted a screen folded and leaning against the wall. Quickly and silently she set it up so that it would conceal her in the deep shadows and close to the wall, so unlikely to arouse interest.

Behind this screen so many years ago, the cherished mistress of that dashing gentleman had changed her elegant clothes. They must have been elegant, although Hyacinthe had no way of knowing. Yet in her experience she had noticed that those lovely women of questionable reputation seemed to dress better than the respectable but often plain, wives.

Her fears were realized moments later when the door opened wide to admit a man. She peered through the crack between two panels of the screen to inspect this person. It didn't take her long to realize who it was. She barely stopped herself from exclaiming his name aloud. Mr. Dudley Wayland!

Fortunately he ignored the screen and thus missed her presence. He went to the same panel that Hyacinthe had suspected to begin digging about with a penknife, evidence he'd been here before. In moments the catch snapped and a portion of the design opened to reveal a secret chest.

Hyacinthe scarcely suppressed a gasp of dismay. She ought to confront the man, but she was hardly of a size to do this and she had no weapon, nor could she call Norwood.

Wayland produced a soft sack from his coat pocket, velvet by the looks of it, then poured in the contents of the chest. Before leaving the little room, he replaced the chest, closed the secret panel, then glanced about the room.

Hyacinthe held her breath, praying she'd not be detected. Any man who would steal could do other nasty things as well.

She waited until she heard his steps retreat down the stairs and cross the rooms below. When he had left the house, she dared to slip from behind the screen. Dashing quietly to the window in the bedroom, she glimpsed Mr. Wayland in the tangled greenery behind the house. He tucked the velvet sack into his coat pocket, then mounted his horse. In moments he had disappeared from her view.

"Drat and double drat!" she fumed, kicking at a tattered bit of drapery. "If I had been a man, I could have stopped him, captured the treasure." Even if she contacted Lord Norwood, Mr. Wayland would have hidden the items.

Returning to the little dressing room, she touched the same place Wayland had touched on the carved panel, then inhaled with satisfaction when it sprang open to reveal the same little chest. It was empty. She removed it, then inspected the space where it had sat for so long. Back in the dim recesses she noticed a black box.

Excitement building, she daringly reached in, ignoring hazards like spiders or bugs, and pulled the box out.

It was long and slim, covered with fine leather. Taking an anxious breath, she opened it to discover a delicately wrought bracelet of gold set with emeralds. At least, she would wager they were emeralds.

A second examination by the light of the bedroom window increased her conviction. She clutched the lovely piece of jewelry to her breast, wondering what she ought to do with it. She had to give it to Lord Norwood. It belonged to him.

She took another look at the exquisite piece, admiring the rich flash of color from the deep green stones. How beautiful. With a resigned sigh, and wondering if she would ever wear anything half so fine, she closed the lid of the handsome box, then returned to the dressing room to replace the panel just as Wayland had done. The jewel chest she retained. This also belonged to his lordship and might be lost if the house was to be torn down.

A light drizzle fell on her while she ran across the village green to Jane's cottage. Skirting the pond, she recalled her father's motto: *Qui dabit recipiet.* He who shall give will receive. Perhaps in giving this to Lord Norwood she would receive a respite for her cousin?

Hurrying through the gate and up to the door, she was taken aback to find it whisked open and the man who had been occupying her thoughts standing before her. She halted.

"Come in, come in. I shan't bite you," Lord Norwood said with good humor.

"I must speak with you," she said breathlessly. "Come into the parlor, I have something to show you, that is, for you." She knew she puzzled him, but she could scarcely blurt out all that had happened in the last half hour.

When they stood in the center of the cozy parlor, Hyacinthe thrust the two items at him.

"These are yours. There would have been more, but someone else took them before I could reach them."

"What the . . . ?" He accepted the chest and the slim box. Placing the chest on a nearby table, he opened the box first. Inside he found the bracelet of emeralds in their intricate gold setting.

Jane gasped when the green jewels flashed in the dim light. Holding up the bracelet by one end, Lord Norwood studied

Hyacinthe's face. She knew she must be flushed, for she had dashed madly through the mist to reach Jane's cottage.

"Wherever did you find this?"

"Well, I located the little hiding place where she had stashed her jewels. The rest were in that chest, or casket, I suspect they may have called it. Had I just a bit more time, I might have been handing you the entire contents of that as well."

He turned to place the bracelet back in the box, then inspected the little chest. "Who took them?"

"Dudley Wayland," she said quietly. "Did you chance to see him ride off just before I returned? Had I a weapon, I would have shot him. Or something equally dreadful. I could not tell precisely how many items there were or what they were. He dropped them into a velvet sack, then made off with them while I remained helplessly behind."

At his look of inquiry, she added, "I may be silly, but I am not so foolish as to court disaster."

"There are a few who might argue with you there," he murmured.

Val stepped forward from where he had remained half hidden in the shadows. He picked up the bracelet, nodding.

"You agree with me that this matches the description I have?" Lord Norwood demanded.

"Indeed. How do we proceed from here?" Val inquired.

"He must not be allowed to leave the estate," Hyacinthe stated in no uncertain terms. Then she said, "Perhaps he believes himself safe from discovery."

"This is a nasty turn of events, for I quite like his designs and it will delay things considerably for me to find another architect, then continue *if* I can persuade him to follow the same plans. And *if* that chap will be able to work with the men that Wayland has already hired."

Something suddenly occurred to Hyacinthe and she gave his lordship a narrow look. "What are you doing here, sir? I confess that I'd not thought to see you in the village again soon."

"After our little *contretemps*, you mean?"

"Well," she confessed, "I cannot think of a more inopportune and embarrassing occurrence."

He raised his brows but did not flash that charming grin at her, and her heart sank.

"I came to invite you all up to the Hall for tea the day after tomorrow."

Hyacinthe exchanged a look with Jane, who in turn glanced to where Sir Charles quietly stood off to one side of the room.

"I believe we should be pleased to accept your gracious invitation, sir," Jane said politely. She bestowed a hesitant smile his way, then edged back to stand beside Sir Charles.

"The drizzle has let up. Could you show me the panel in question?" Lord Norwood asked, taking hold of Hyacinthe's elbow and steering her from the room even as he spoke.

"Of course," Hyacinthe said. She could not fail to observe how breathless she remained, especially since he had drawn so close to her side. Her heart did odd little flips and flops that quite puzzled her even as they left her somewhat shaken. Never had she been so intensely aware of a man as she was of Lord Norwood.

Had she actually presumed to call him Blase Montague as Jane claimed? Everyone knew his name and family, but one did not use it unless rather intimate. *That* word caused her cheeks to bloom like one of the roses in the Tudor garden. Where had her wits gone? What a crackbrained girl she was becoming!

"If you will have the goodness to go ahead, I would see the secret compartment."

Hyacinthe pulled herself together and attempted a composure that she certainly didn't feel. Once in the house she carefully made her way up the stairs. Opening the door to the dressing room, she made directly for the cleverly carved panel. By using her thumbnail she did the trick, and the hidden door popped ajar.

"Well, I'll be!" he exclaimed. He thrust his hand deep into the recesses, groping about the back of it lest anything had been missed.

"I should explain," he began, turning to look directly into her eyes.

Hyacinthe felt her knees suddenly weaken; her heart began that alarming pattering again. Those amazing blue eyes had a powerful effect on her.

"These jewels are part of a collection bestowed upon his mistress by my esteemed ancestor. That he had no right to give away something that belonged to the family did not appear to bother him. Perhaps he intended to take them back at a later date. Somehow he never did." Norwood gave her a wry smile that cut to her core. "I had heard about the missing gems, as had others in the family. None of us had done anything about it, for it was presumed to be hearsay. A fanciful story, if you like."

"What made you search?" she whispered.

"I wanted to do an inventory of the estate. When I discovered listed jewels missing, I feared a thief." He reached out to pick a cobweb out of the curls that peeped from beneath the little cap she wore.

"What will you do about Mr. Wayland? You must not let him profit from his thievery." She sounded as though she had just completed a mad dash—breathless, with a pounding heart beating a mad rhythm.

"It is a dilemma," Lord Norwood said, taking a step closer to Hyacinthe. He pulled her cap off, placing it in her hands, then ran his fingers through her tumbled curls.

She found it impossible to retreat; her feet refused to move. She stared up at him feeling trapped, assailed by a tumult of emotions she'd never known before. Why did his light touch affect her so?

She cleared her throat, knowing that if she had any sense at all she would march away from this rake. Yet she could not move.

"I must thank you for all you have done," he whispered, hovering over her, his lazy grin teasing her.

The words to the effect that it was quite all right were never spoken, for he leaned down to place a warm kiss on her lips.

She'd not been kissed like this before. Indeed, had scarcely been kissed at all. This bone-melting sensation was totally different from past experiences. When she opened her eyes, she gave him a confused look.

"You are welcome," she whispered back, bemused, then forced her feet to move and fled the room and the house as though a demon chased her. Perhaps it did.

7

Blase stood in the small dressing room feeling as though he had been struck on the head with a falling rock. He raised his right hand to touch his mouth. Was he mad? Had the pond water affected his brain? He felt like ten kinds of fool. Thrusting his hand through his hair, he considered his dilemma.

He had just kissed the little termagant who was making his life *most* complicated at the moment, whose brother was undoubtedly the finest swordsman in England, who had very protective relatives, and . . . who was eminently kissable. What a passionate delight she had proven to be. Utterly delicious.

Amazingly—all things considered—the casket holding the emerald bracelet remained in his left hand. He'd quite forgotten it in the heat of the moment.

Leaving the dressing room, he wandered down through the house and out to the tangled garden. Here he found Val leaning against one of the old oak trees, his expression of cynical amusement about what Blase expected to see. Today it rubbed him the wrong way.

"I daresay you find this all vastly diverting." Blase gave his good friend a look of exasperation.

"You have a spot of dust on your cheek. Miss Dancy did as well. Might I inquire what happened when that fiery young woman revealed the hiding place? It seemed a rather innocent occasion, although you might have been well advised to have the abigail along. She's a proper dragon," Val pointed out while strolling over to join Blase.

"You may inquire all you please. It does not follow that I shall tell you, however." Blase turned away, avoiding those sharp eyes that always saw too much. He began to walk toward the blacksmith's where they had left their horses.

Absently he noted the twitching of curtains in various cottages as they strolled along through the village. The locals were undoubtedly having a fine time with all the goings on as of late.

"Noble fellow," Val replied sagely. "Never could abide men who kissed, then told."

"I wonder if you would enjoy a splash in the pond," Blase mused, glancing toward that murky water inhabited by all the ducks and the pair of swans. "Perhaps you might think that vastly amusing as well. I wonder how you would look attempting to climb from that dreadful water while trying to find purchase on stones covered with slimy green muck."

"Enough," Val said, hastening around to the far side of Blase, maintaining a comfortable distance from the pond.

"One would think you didn't trust me," Blase complained, assuming a wounded look.

"Nor do I. If memory serves me right, you tossed me into the sea once. Ruined a perfectly good coat and vest, not to mention shrinking my favorite fawn pantaloons. Can't recall why."

"That was a relatively mild matter. Certainly not as annoying as this. However, it did serve to cool off that head of yours." Blase tossed his friend a grin that revealed his good nature had been somewhat restored.

"Well, I shall take care to avoid a repetition. Water ought to be taken in small doses, preferably heated, and with sandalwood soap."

Blase halted in his steps. "Blast," he muttered. "I had best go and reassure myself that Miss Dancy will still come to the Hall."

"Think you might have given her a disgust of you?" Val chided in innocuous banter.

Blase didn't reply to his friend's needling, but turned to stride back to Miss Pennington's cottage. Curtains twitched again, and he felt almost virtuous in providing entertainment for the village. He bowed in the direction of the Widow

Smith's cottage, to be rewarded with another flutter of muslin at her window.

"You are disconcerting them, my good fellow. They like to think they are unobserved," Val told him.

"Hah!" Blase snapped. "They are about as inconspicuous as that pond over there."

At which reminder Val strolled to the far side of Blase once again.

At Miss Pennington's cottage they were ushered inside by Jane, a pleasant smile curving her lips at the sight of the two gentlemen.

Blase decided that—given their amiable greeting—Miss Dancy must not have revealed all that had happened at the old house. When he looked at her, she fixed her gaze on her hands, but other than a slightly higher color, gave no indication of her inner feelings.

Racking his brain to think of a reason for their return, he said, "I merely wished to thank Miss Dancy once again for her help." He held the little chest up while keeping a careful watch on her.

She rose from her chair to move to her cousin's side, her hands clutching each other before her. She said nothing. Her cousin stepped forward as though to compensate for Miss Dancy's lack of response.

"Do you believe you may think of a way to relieve Mr. Wayland of the treasure while keeping him here to complete his work?" Jane asked quietly.

"Perhaps you will be forced to abandon your scheme," Miss Dancy said with a flash of those incredible green eyes.

"I feel certain I will think of something. When you see the view from the terrace, perhaps you will understand why I feel this is all necessary."

He was rewarded with a rather belligerent stare from Miss Dancy. Then she sweetly said, "Somehow I doubt it, Lord Norwood."

Feeling somewhat defeated—although he realized he ought to have expected such a reaction—Blase bowed to the ladies, then reminded them before taking his leave that they were expected at the Hall for tea.

"I should say that you have a fence or two to mend as yet, my lad," Val observed while keeping a wary eye on the pond and his best friend.

"You may say that, or anything else you please. What a tangled mess this is becoming," Blase muttered. He strode past the cottages, not paying attention to the fluttering curtains this time. At the blacksmith's he impatiently exchanged a few pleasantries with the man, then mounted his bay and rode off in the direction of the Hall, followed by Val.

From the parlor window Hyacinthe watched the men ride past the pond, then turn toward Worthington Hall.

She ought to have denounced that wicked man. Rake! He had earned his reputation in London, if this was a sample of his behavior. In the back of her mind—and heart—she almost wished that he had sincerely meant that remarkable kiss.

"Come, dear." Jane drew her to the sofa, just the right size for the small parlor. "Something has overset you," Jane probed in her gentle way.

"Nothing at all," Hyacinthe denied stoutly. She had begun to realize that if she explained what had upset her it would complicate her life. She had done her best to calm her nerves while returning to the cottage. A glimpse of Mrs. Peachey had helped enormously. It served to remind Hyacinthe that she would be as affected as that rake were she to reveal his ill behavior. Gossip would ruin all Hyacinthe's plans for her future.

"All this racketing about in musty old places may not overset your nerves, but it does not a *thing* for your hair," Fosdick declared. "Allow me to make repairs, miss."

Since Fosdick rarely insisted on such a thing, Hyacinthe suspected she must indeed look a fright. Nodding her acceptance, she preceded the abigail up the narrow stairs. It was just as well that she escape, she decided. Had she remained in the parlor, Jane might well have wormed from her the dreadful secret.

Two days later Hyacinthe, with Jane and Fosdick at her side, drove along the lanes until they reached the main avenue to Worthington Hall.

"It is an impressive place as it stands. I fail to see why he must improve his view by destroying the village," Hyacinthe murmured yet once again when their coach drew up before the entrance.

"Did you not say that Carr included the house plans in his book *Vitruvius Britannicus*?" Jane whispered as they slowly mounted the steps to the imposing front door. To either side of them tall Corinthian pillars soared in splendor. Jane gave a speculative glance at the upper windows just barely visible.

Hyacinthe nodded in agreement, then said, "I suspect that is the reason that Mr. Wayland totes that volume about with him, the odious toad. It is far too heavy a book to carry in the ordinary way."

Before they could decide who would have the pleasure of pulling the bell, the lovely carved door opened quite magically to reveal Barmore. The butler might be said to have almost beamed a welcome at them. He bowed, then led them along with him.

After settling Fosdick on a comfortable side chair in the Great Hall (Barmore tended to speak in capitals when it came to the house, it seemed), he continued on through to the next room.

"The Yellow Damask Room, my ladies," Barmore announced proudly. He ushered them along to a group of attractive chairs placed about a polished console table that held an arrangement of autumn flowers. "Their lordships will be along directly. May I say they intended to be here to greet you, but a small crisis arose."

Hyacinthe murmured something gracious in reply. Rather than settle on a chair she chose to wander about the room. She could see the elegant crystal chandelier reflected in the looking glass that hung above the marble fireplace surround.

"Could you tell me anything about the room?" Jane said. "Since you appear to have done a bit of boning up, that is."

"This is an Adam's fireplace, and I think he designed the consoles along the wall," Hyacinthe said thoughtfully, racking her brain to remember what she'd read. "The paintings are mostly Italian except for that one over there by the man called the Greek, El Greco, that is." She strolled about the room, offering details when asked. Jane remained most prudently seated on a yellow-and-white-striped chair, yet watched her cousin with great interest.

The unusual mantel clock had struck two when a stir at the door, not to mention the heightened awareness Hyacinthe felt, revealed that the gentlemen had joined them.

"I do apologize, Miss Pennington and Miss Dancy," Lord Norwood said smoothly. He strode across the carpet to reach Hyacinthe, subtly guiding her to join the others, who were dutifully seated by the console table.

"I hope it was nothing truly serious," Hyacinthe said while her eyes dared him to say it was a mere nothing that had kept him from his guests.

"Actually I was finalizing plans to have Wayland watched. His every step will be monitored."

"Oh, good," Jane exclaimed.

"I hope you know what you are about," Hyacinthe murmured in a voice only Lord Norwood could hear.

Another stir at the door brought the curate to join the group, Ambrose Clark seemed quite at ease with the party, joining Jane to converse on the problems of the church roof, particularly over his study, which leaked more badly than ever.

Before Lord Norwood could reply to Hyacinthe's provocative remark, Barmore returned, followed by two footmen and a maid. They carried trays with enough tea and splendid pastries for a party twice their size.

"Oh, I say, I fear I am a bit tardy," Sir Charles said as he breezed into the drawing room. "Had a spot of bother just before I planned to leave."

Barmore saw to his tea, thus relieving the ladies from the task of deciding who might serve as a hostess. Neither was likely to desire the position, Jane being too shy and Hyacinthe reluctant to put herself forward.

Conversation remained general, in spite of the curate's obvious desire to return to the subject of his leaky roof.

Hyacinthe set her empty cup on its saucer, then placed them on the table, glancing about the room to note the tall windowed doors which apparently led to the terrace beyond.

When she chanced to look at Lord Norwood, she met his thoughtful look briefly, then dropped her gaze to her lap.

Every time she looked at the dratted man, that kiss came to her mind, like a particularly disturbing dream.

"Would you join me for a walk on the terrace? I should wish you to see the view as it is and what I intend." His deep voice broke through her introspection.

Startled, she rose from her chair with alacrity. She did not want him to assist her or touch her in any way. Perhaps she feared her reaction?

Walking just slightly ahead of him, she stood aside so he might open the door, then swished past him. On the terrace she came to an abrupt halt, delighted with the old-fashioned geranium and ivy filled urns and fanciful stone railing. "Lovely."

Appearing to ignore her pleased reaction, Lord Norwood drew her along with him by the mere force of his presence. At last he came to a halt. Hyacinthe dutifully looked in the direction he pointed.

"See the spire and that dreadful cluster of roof lines? What I intend to create is a smooth sweep with a mass of trees planted in a diagonal line." He pulled a drawing from his coat pocket to show her.

Wishing to be fair, Hyacinthe studied the drawing, then gazed out across the verdant lawns and hills dotted with stately trees. It was utterly beautiful and she'd not wish one thing altered if it were hers.

"Well, you will do as you please, no doubt. But I think that spire rising in the distance is most charming. It adds a solid English touch to what otherwise would be a rather bland landscape." Her demure glance at him was just as bland; only those green eyes were afire with mischief.

Blase studied the saucy face turned up to gaze at him with a feeling of total frustration. He was torn between wanting to throttle her and to wrap her in his arms, smothering that adorable face with hungry kisses. He would begin with the freckles, then proceed to even more interesting places.

Moments lengthened as the silence stretched on and on. They stared at one another, measuring, sizing up the opposition as it were. He could feel a sizzling tension in the air, vibrating between them. Still she remained silent.

"Hyacinthe—" he began, speaking the name he used when thinking of her.

"La, sir, you must deem me a forward baggage, to use my given name without permission," she interrupted, a storm cloud drifting into her eyes. Hands clasped tightly before her at her waist, she glared at him with the air of one vastly insulted. He wondered if she held her hands thus to keep from slapping him and was thankful of her restraint.

Blase could think of no London miss who would have objected to any familiarity he might have used, including use of a first name. Indeed, he had found most women eager to become intimate in any way possible. Miss Dancy made her feelings regarding him painfully obvious.

"Forgive me, since we are joined in a sort of battle, I daresay I thought it easier," he said smoothly.

"Convenient," she said with a cool nod. "However, I fear it would look a trifle forward on your part, for I cannot consider calling you Blase."

She said his name in a husky whisper, the very sound of which did the strangest things to his nerves.

"Whatever you wish, Miss Dancy," he replied after clearing his throat of an obstruction.

The door along the terrace opened. Miss Pennington, Ambrose Clark, and Sir Charles, with Val at his side, emerged from the house to amble along, admiring the view, commenting on the abundant geranium blooms.

"It is a perfectly splendid view, Lord Norwood," Miss Pennington observed enthusiastically while studying the distant church spire and cluster of thatched roofs.

"You cannot detect the leaks in the church roof from here," Mr. Clark added darkly.

"Lord Norwood wishes to eliminate all the buildings from that pretty vale, replacing them with a strip of forest," Hyacinthe explained, mostly to Jane.

"Of course," Jane replied quietly. She turned quite pale, obviously recalling his intent for her cottage.

"Was this sketch drawn by Mr. Repton?" Miss Dancy inquired, holding out the paper Blase had handed her earlier.

"No, I fear it is my own poor work."

"Perhaps Mr. Repton will have other suggestions to offer? He may even *like* the church spire and the thatched roofs," she suggested in what Blase could only feel was a decidedly snide manner.

"Come, we may as well return to the house. Perhaps you would like to see a few of the rooms?" he said in an attempt to draw them all from the distressing topic of his intended alterations to the landscape.

The more Miss Dancy opposed his plans, the more determined he was to implement them. He hadn't examined his motives to see if he was prompted by pique at a woman who quite obviously detested him or by a more commendable goal.

She made appropriate comments when they again viewed the long gallery, a repository for family portraits and immense pieces of furniture that could be housed nowhere else.

"Isn't that your infamous great-great-grandmother, Blase?" Val asked with a cynical lift of his brows.

"Infamous?" Miss Dancy quickly repeated.

"Well," Blase replied with a dark glance at his friend, " 'tis said that she ran off with a friend of her husband's when she discovered the redheaded mistress ensconced in the little village cottage."

"Oh," Hyacinthe cooed, "she did not care to be supplanted. I believe she must have loved her husband very much to be so angered by his turning away from her. She appears to have been exceedingly lovely." Actually, she made a fitting wife for the gentleman with the roguish eyes.

"Rumor has it that she had a wretched temper," Lord Norwood snapped back.

Hyacinthe smiled, satisfied that she had made her little point, yet noting it seemed the Montagues did not care for women with a temper. Fine. She smiled again, then observed that Lord Norwood looked uncomfortable.

"I should like you all to call tomorrow, if possible," Sir Charles requested while they strolled back to the main entry hall. "I believe it is my turn to entertain." He appeared to address them all, yet looked at Jane when he spoke.

Hyacinthe and Jane departed shortly after agreeing that it sounded like a delightful outing.

Although Hyacinthe had her reservations about viewing the prize pigs Sir Charles touted with such great pride. She said as much to Jane later while awaiting their coach to arrive at the front door of the Hall. "I shan't wish to come overly close to their pen, for they are known to have a dreadful smell," she concluded, wrinkling her nose. "Perhaps we might remain in the house?"

Jane gave her a look bordering on indignation, then nudged her forward as Tom Coachman drew to a halt with a great flourish. Fosdick quietly followed them.

"Have you ever seen the inside of Sir Charles's home?" Hyacinthe asked as she settled back on her seat.

"No, indeed, for how could I? It would not be seemly for a single woman to call upon a gentleman," Jane reminded her with gentle reproof.

"Yet he is free to call . . . or not call . . . upon you," Hyacinthe quietly observed.

Jane's pink-cheeked silence revealed more than she knew.

The following morning glistened brightly. A shower had passed through during the night, leaving little puddles for the ducks to enjoy. The air was rain-washed fresh, and various country scents teased their noses when the two cousins drove along to the lovely old home belonging to Sir Charles.

"We might have walked, you know," Jane protested at what she termed an extravagance.

"Nonsense. I have those two men eating their heads off, not to mention the horses. We might as well use the coach and arrive like ladies rather than dusty country misses," Hyacinthe said in a spirited way.

She could see how enchanting Jane found the Tudor-style house. Upon their arrival, Jane stepped from the coach and merely stood, absorbing the gentle lines, the soft greenery that cloaked the exterior.

"Too much ivy," Hyacinthe decided. "I predict it will cause the brick to crack, and then you'll have seepage and all sorts of other problems."

Jane bristled with annoyance. "I think it is utterly charming.

And just when did you become such an expert on houses, anyway?"

With a demure flutter of eyelashes to hide her pleasure at Jane's animated defense of the house, Hyacinthe replied, "My father was ever curious about houses. He bought his copy of *Vitruvius Britannicus* when it was published in 1771. I confess to looking up the Hall when I knew that you lived close to it. And as to knowing about houses, well, that is simple common sense."

Jane's disbelieving look was quickly banished when Sir Charles himself opened the door to greet them.

"Ladies, this is indeed a pleasure. I cannot think why you have not come to call before." He beamed down at Jane, then ushered them in. Hyacinthe was quite happy to be neglected, trailing behind them with a smug little smile.

She decided that Sir Charles must be a bit neglectful of his memory, for to her knowledge they, particularly Cousin Jane, had not been *invited* heretofore. But, since Sir Charles was such an amiable man, and appearing increasingly interested in Jane, she'd not tease him about it. Her smile faded when she caught sight of the others in the room.

Lords Norwood and Latham stood by the fireplace. They bowed in the direction of the ladies, but did not move forward. Latham wore a sardonic expression as he watched Sir Charles play the attentive host to Jane.

Ambrose Clark hovered not far from the table, where an assortment of delicacies had been placed. A magnificent silver teapot sat close by a silver teakettle steaming over a flame. Mr. Clark wore a hungry look that suggested he could do justice to the entire display. Did the man never have enough to eat? Hyacinthe wondered.

Then she observed Mrs. Peachey and the Widow Smith seated by a many-paned window, looking much gratified to be included in the group.

The little party proved quite jolly, thanks to an unexpected talent for story telling on the part of Mrs. Peachey, possibly prompted by the glass of sherry she had sipped before the others arrived.

At last it came time to view the prize pigs. Much to everyone's surprise, Mrs. Peachey and the Widow Smith joined the others.

"This is like a parade," Mrs. Peachey observed with a girlish giggle.

"Did you have anything to do with the additions to the group?" Lord Norwood inquired of Hyacinthe.

Since he had spoken to her in an undertone, she replied quietly, "Not at all. Sir Charles must have taken pity on the ladies. I quite enjoy them."

"Even when they quiz you on your matrimonial prospects?" Lord Latham asked, his voice tinged with tartness.

"They mean well. And you notice that I did not respond. Indeed, I have determined to hop on the shelf, for I believe I shall journey to distant lands rather than marry. I shan't have to contend with another Season in Town, nor wonder if a man courts me for my fortune or my face."

"Likely neither," Lord Latham shot back, a grin on his handsome face. "They are more apt to seek you out for that wit you reveal when you least realize it."

"Well, it would be a comfort to think it was that," she countered amiably. Why was it, she wondered, that when Lord Latham teased and almost flirted with her, it affected her not in the least. While on the other hand, the mere presence of Lord Norwood had the power to send her nerves sizzling, her blood tingling, and her head spinning in a whirl.

"Is something wrong, Miss Dancy," Lord Norwood asked in concern. "You shake your head."

"No. Where are these prize progeny anyway? I don't detect their proximity." She sniffed the air, curious as to how far they must walk. It was disconcerting to stroll along at Lord Norwood's side. She tilted her parasol slightly so she might not see him at all.

"Allow me," the dratted man said smoothly. He removed her parasol from a suddenly limp hand, then held it over her head better to shield her from the sun. It placed him in far better view, however, and much closer.

Then a sharp turn in the path revealed a splendid pig sty, far superior to the average one. Inside, an enormous sow balefully inspected the viewers with one malevolent eye while keeping a watch on her offspring with the other.

"What a quantity of bacon and ham that would be," Ambrose Clark declared reverently.

"I daresay it would," Lord Latham agreed. The two gentlemen wandered ahead, discussing various meals of bacon and ham they had enjoyed in the past.

On the far side of the sty Sir Charles explained the pedigree of the animals to Jane. The two widows gazed, looking rather doubtful, for a few moments, then walked back in the direction of the house.

Hyacinthe glanced at Lord Norwood, wondering if he felt this most peculiar beguilement when close to her. Odd. She detested the man. Yet when he drew near, her resolve seemed to melt. No, she scolded herself, she must be strong, be firm.

"Hardly dainty, are they?" she observed in what she hoped was a serene manner.

"Indeed," he agreed.

He was laughing at her; she sensed it even though he merely smiled. Another of those little insults. Not as serious as that kiss, but it served to remind her that they were piling up. One by one those indignities increased.

Affronted by his attitude and recalling all he intended, Hyacinthe undid the ribands of her bonnet. The wind did the rest of the deed. The wickedly expensive head gear from a fine London milliner went sailing over the fence into the sty to land precariously atop a wooden box. Here it perched, ready to topple into the muck at any moment. The pig eyed the bonnet as though wondering if it was some new sort of food.

"Oh," cried Jane, "your beautiful new bonnet!"

"I fear it is lost!" Hyacinthe cried in return, clasping her hands before her in an attitude of dismay. She turned her emerald eyes upon Lord Norwood, beseeching him without a word.

He closed his eyes for a moment, then met hers, frowning with apparent resignation.

"Never fear, Miss Dancy. I shall rescue it for you."

He handed her his hat, then removed his coat and draped it over the fence. In seconds he climbed to the top of it. Unfortunately, he lost his balance on the topmost board. With a truly spectacular waving of arms and legs, he dived into the mud and mire of the sty.

His muttering might have blistered their ears but for the mud that persisted in clinging to his face.

"Good heavens!" Sir Charles cried, opening the gate to rush to his guest's assistance.

One of the piglets dashed out the gate to freedom, followed by three others before Jane had the presence of mind to close it. The piglets squealed and grunted while running around the yard. Garbled language burst forth from Lord Norwood, while Sir Charles and Jane attempted to soothe him.

In short order the two men slipped back out through the gate. A young farm lad who had lingered in the background captured the piglets, returning them to their pen.

Only Hyacinthe watched the scene as though frozen in her slippers. Had she actually intended that disaster to happen? Had she realized how utterly wretched it would be for his rakish lordship?

She had. Only sheer willpower kept a guilty grin from her face.

8

Once the piglets were returned to the sty, Lord Norwood removed from same, and the chaos somewhat reduced, his lordship turned to where Hyacinthe stood transfixed in a mixture of naughty delight and conscience-stricken remorse.

"I fear your lovely bonnet will never be the same, Miss Dancy. Pity," he observed with what she perceived to be a note of satisfaction, holding out the battered bonnet now dripping with mud. It had tumbled the same moment he made his extraordinary dive.

"It was a favorite, but one cannot predict what nature will do, can one?" she said with all due humility.

"Perhaps," he muttered, turning to Sir Charles, who was urging him to the house where a cleaning up and change of garments might be effected. The two men hurried off, Lord Norwood shaking clumps of mire as they went and Sir Charles murmuring words of sympathy and carrying the undamaged coat that had providentially been removed before the accident.

Lord Latham strolled over to join Hyacinthe, looking at her through his quizzing glass as though she were a heretofore-unknown species of butterfly.

"I particularly detest the affectation of London dandies with those odious quizzing glasses," she said quietly. "Perhaps I ought to acquire one of my own. Do you like being inspected, Lord Latham?" Hyacinthe concluded in quiet indignation, while holding up an imaginary magnifying glass and glaring at him.

"Actually, I usually use this to depress the encroachment of those green lads from the country who think they are all the crack merely because they have learned to tie a respectable cravat." He lowered the glass, then dangled it about on its little gold chain while eyeing her. "You know, I believe Blase would be well advised to bring a change of clothing with him whenever he is about you. You seem to draw disaster like a magnet. Are you magnetized, Miss Dancy?"

"Hardly," she snapped back, her eyes flashing. This man saw entirely too much to suit her.

Fortunately for all concerned Jane bustled up at that moment quite atwitter.

"Dear me, that poor man. First the village pond and now a pig sty. What next?" she mused with a thoughtful look at Hyacinthe.

Turning away from the sight of the pen with the dreadful mire that had formed from the recent rain, Hyacinthe tamped down a sense of pity for her opponent. The man was a monster, willing to oust widows and old men from their homes. She took several steps toward the house.

"How's the hedgehog?" Lord Latham asked idly.

Hyacinthe shot him a suspicious look, then said blandly, "Quite well, thank you. And how was Tom Tiger this morning? I mean the cat, of course," she added sweetly.

Lord Latham chuckled, then glanced at Hyacinthe before taking her arm, as well as Jane's, to guide them toward Sir Charles's tasteful but plain home. They sauntered along at a leisurely pace.

"The confounded animal refused to be banished to the barn," Lord Latham confided. "It has taken up residence in the house, specifically in Blase's bedroom. It seems it prefers to snuggle in the rich softness of his bed rather than the plain straw in the barn."

Darting a look at her tormentor, for she was certain there was a hidden taunt in that tale, Hyacinthe merely smiled, then turned to include Jane in the conversation. "Cats are so odd. There is no accounting for their preferences."

Jane looked rather puzzled at the exchanges between the two, which seemed to have nothing to do with Lord Norwood's spectacular dive into the pig sty. "To be sure," she murmured vaguely. When they approached the house she looked at it as though not quite certain whether they ought to enter or not.

Just as Hyacinthe was about to urge them inside, Lord Latham paused, staring off in the general direction where the new village was to be located.

"Did you know that an army of masons and carpenters have begun work on the new cottages? Several stone shells are completed and the carpenters are busy on the interiors. It will not be long before the first can be occupied. Do you know whose it will be?"

Jane spoke up. "I fancy Mr. Smeed will be first. He is hard of hearing and accustomed to being alone, so he will not mind being the first."

"Needs an ear trumpet?" Lord Latham asked. "I believe I saw one in the attics not long ago while we were hunting for . . . some things," he concluded lamely.

"The jewels, I'll wager," Hyacinthe said softly, looking at Lord Latham with a knowing gaze.

"As to that, I had better remain silent. Best for you to inquire directly of Blase." He opened the door, thus ending all speculation.

He ushered the women into the drawing room, where Hyacinthe was unaccountably glad to see the Widow Smith and Mrs. Peachey settled in for a comfortable tea before the pleasant fire. The house might be plain, but it possessed all necessary comforts.

Hyacinthe watched her cousin when Sir Charles entered the room.

"Ah, you have returned. Norwood is abovestairs. We found some clean clothes that will do him until he reaches home. It would be a shame were he to catch an inflammation of the lungs or worse." His eyes sought and held Jane's gaze as he imparted this bit of information. She nodded in wordless reply, moving toward him to converse in softly spoken words.

Hyacinthe walked over to stand by the two older ladies, who were enjoying the lavish tea set out by the capable housekeeper employed by Sir Charles.

"Poor Lord Norwood," Mrs. Peachey said after a sip of tea. "One would think the man jinxed."

"Indeed," the Widow Smith added. "Or at least when around a particular redhead." She smiled amiably at Hyacinthe. "Although this young lady does not seem the sort to inspire mischief."

"My red hair does not give me regrets in the least," Hyacinthe answered, knowing full well all the tales ascribed to people with red hair. She was certain she had heard them all. "It might be unfashionable, but I like it."

The curate, who had been quietly standing by the tea table munching on a piece of particularly delectable nut torte, now entered the conversation. "It is good to be content with what the Lord has given one," he declared piously. He quite ignored his leaking roof in that respect.

The gentle hum of conversation, not to menton the consumption of tea and biscuits, came to a pause when the object of their mutual pity entered the room. Only the crackling of the fire could be heard other than the click of boots crossing the polished wood floor.

With a bow in Hyacinthe's direction, he strolled across the room to accept a glass of restoring port from Sir Charles.

Lord Norwood went to stand by the mullioned window, the glass of ruby port in his hand. He looked remarkably fresh, his blond curls tumbling over his forehead in an engaging manner. A wry smile tugged at his lips when he observed how the others watched him.

"Well, old chap," Lord Latham said in a pleased voice, breaking the silence that engulfed the room, "Sir Charles did well by you. I vow those pantaloons could be your own, and go well with your coat."

The fawn stockinette pantaloons might have been made for the slightly shorter and stockier Sir Charles, but adapted themselves well to Lord Norwood's taller, leaner frame. The crisp white linen shirt and elegant waistcoat looked quite splendid.

But then, Hyacinthe admitted to herself, if one were to toss a hemp sack over his head, Lord Norwood would contrive to make it look dashing.

"I shall order a waistcoat much like this from my tailor in London. My mishap is not in vain, for I found something much to my liking." He raised his glass to Sir Charles in a toast. Norwood's gaze, when it settled upon Hyacinthe, made her very uneasy. He could not possibly guess that she had intentionally allowed her favorite bonnet to sail away with the wind. No woman would do such a silly thing.

"What a pity the wind took Miss Dancy's bonnet like that," Mrs. Peachey said with a nod of her own bonneted head, unconsciously echoing Hyacinthe's thoughts.

"Especially since it appeared to be securely tied," Lord Norwood murmured clearly enough so that Hyacinthe heard him. He had crossed the room, ostensibly to avail himself of the lemon biscuits that were heaped on a plate. Tart yet sweet, they were truly excellent. He took a bite, then darted her a look. "Delicious."

"No doubt," she replied with equal care.

"Things often surprise a chap. Like this biscuit." He held it up for her to see. "Expect it to be sweet, and here it has a sharp tang to it. Don't expect sweet things to bite a fellow."

"Really, sir?" Hyacinthe said innocently. "I thought nothing could surprise a London . . . beau like you."

"I consider myself duly warned."

"I understand the first of the new cottages is about finished," she said, striving for a neutral voice.

"Indeed," he said, his face turning serious. After a thoughtful glance at Lord Latham, Lord Norwood switched his attention back to Hyacinthe.

"Jane thought Mr. Smeed would be the first to move," Hyacinthe continued.

"Not all the people are resistant to improving their lives," he said with a hint of a taunt in his voice.

"I fancy the houses are made with the same damp floors, twisting stairways, and unhandy kitchens as the present?" Her smile might have been neutral, but her eyes warned him that she was prepared to do battle.

He leaned against the fireplace wall, then studied her hostile face. "Why don't you ride over soon to see for yourself? I cannot guarantee that *you* will have no ill befall you, but I trust you are a daring girl. It goes with the hair, I believe."

"*I* believe I have mentioned before that I quite like my hair color. Unfashionable it may be; it runs in my family. I would not consider a wig or dye, as some have urged," she concluded sharply.

She found the look of genuine horror that flashed across his face most rewarding. Not examining her reasons, she smiled at him. "There are some people who feel it necessary to be a fashionable blond in order to be happy. Or to marry well. Since I am not in the least interested in the latter and quite content with my red hair, my life is pleasing to me."

"That others could be as well," he answered with a pensive look, then glanced at her again. "Yet you would deny me happiness. You would stand in the way of progress," he countered, taking a sip of his port.

The room grew silent at his words. Mrs. Peachey exchanged looks with the Widow Smith. Jane drew closer to Sir Charles as though seeking support from him.

Hyacinthe chose her reply with care. "That depends on what you consider progress, I suppose. And achieving happiness at the expense of others must not be satisfying. Or so I should think," she ended meekly.

The others waited breathlessly for Lord Norwood's reply to this provocative remark. Then the plump housekeeper entered the room, whispering a message to Sir Charles.

"Mrs. Grigson tells me that a messenger has come from Worthington Hall. Mr. Repton has arrived."

The two widows put their heads together to softly discuss the latest development.

Hyacinthe turned to face her adversary. "You had best consult with him at once. I shall look forward to his reaction to your scheme. Do be sure to tell him of the antiquity of the church. Perhaps with that leaking roof he may consider it worthy to be a picturesque ruin."

"Now, Hyacinthe," Jane cautioned.

Lord Norwood inserted a comment into whatever she intended to say. "I shall ask his opinion. But, as I foot the bill for everything, he will inevitably have to bow to my wishes."

"Well, happy sawing, tearing down, planting, or whatever you intend to do next, then," Hyacinthe said.

"Ah, dear lady, your look wounds me," he replied. He placed his empty glass on the table, then took one of her hands in his. The farewell kiss he placed on it was light, his lips scarcely touching her skin. Yet she felt it acutely and trembled. And what was worse, she suspected he felt her tremble.

She flashed him a look that dared him to comment on her weakness.

He merely smiled, that lopsided smile that had melted hearts from one end of London to the other. Those intense blue eyes crinkled at the corners, and they held knowledge. He knew. Oh, he definitely knew she was not completely immune to his charm.

Hyacinthe gritted her teeth, then bared them in a parody of a smile in return. "Good-bye."

"Parting is such sweet sorrow," he murmured provocatively while slowly releasing her hand. He turned and walked across the room with jaunty steps. Hyacinthe and Jane walked behind him.

In the hall, he accepted his rumpled shirt, neatly brushed waistcoat, and cleaned pantaloons with a sigh. "Mrs. Grigson has done an admirable job, but I fear these are beyond redemption. Thank heavens my boots were easily cleaned. Hoby would never forgive me were I to confess that this pair had been ruined in a pig sty."

Hyacinthe met the challenge in his eyes with a cool look from hers. "How fortunate your tailor has your measurements. You need not interrupt your scheming here to return for fittings."

"You thought that I might?" he said with an arrested look on his face.

Vexed with her unguarded tongue, Hyacinthe said, "I merely thought it would be the thing to do. My mantuamaker always insists upon my presence for final fittings."

"How fortunate your wardrobe has not been decimated in that case." He bowed again, then left the house with Lord Latham cheerfully trailing along behind him, whistling a merry tune.

Alone with Jane in the hall, Hyacinthe also prepared to depart. Jane touched her arm and said in a low voice, "If I thought you had a thing to do with that disgraceful episode at the pig sty I would send you packing, cousin or no cousin."

"I had no control over the wind. And besides," Hyacinthe concluded triumphantly, "that was quite my favorite bonnet."

"I know you mean to help me, and I recall that list of things you might do to Lord Norwood. This was not one of them. Yet the notion that you might try such a trick with the idea it would help me lingers in my mind."

Incensed that her cousin would not immediately crow with delight at the discomfort wrought to their adversary, Hyacinthe drew her shawl over her bright hair and turned to leave. She made polite remarks to Sir Charles, who had just returned from seeing their lordships off, then walked to where Tom Coachman and her carriage awaited them.

The ride to Jane's cottage was silent for the most part. When they reached the house, Jane paused before the front door to study Hyacinthe.

"Do you plan to ride over to inspect the new cottages as he suggested?" There was no need for her to identify who "he" was. They both knew.

"I shall arrange for a horse in the morning. I believe I will find the expedition most illuminating." She turned back to inform her groom of her wishes.

Warton promised to have a suitable mount waiting for her.

The following morning after the girls had feasted on Granny Beanbuck's cinnamon buns and cups of hot tea, Hyacinthe donned her favorite riding habit of jade green with jet buttons down the front. On her head she wore a shako made of jade felt trimmed with a black plume. Her image in the looking glass appeared more confident than she felt.

"Do be careful, dearest," Jane cautioned. "There are ever so many dangerous objects around a building site."

Hyacinthe promised, then mounted the horse her groom had obtained. She waved to the curate as she jauntily set off in the direction of the new village.

It would be horrid, she knew. There would be no stately trees, just a row of plain houses, all the same with no character, no pretty gardens. She had seen one of these model villages elsewhere and detested its newness, its sameness, and its almost depressing quality of cheerfulness.

She met no one on her ride. Lord Norwood would most likely be occupied telling the celebrated Humphrey Repton just how to design his landscape. If Lord Norwood had such set ideas, he ought to have done the wretched business himself.

She rounded a bend in the road and came to a halt. Before her a sort of organized chaos met her eyes. Piles of lumber were stacked haphazardly to one side of the proposed main road through the new village. Houses were in various stages of construction. Lord Latham had not exaggerated in the least when he said that an army of masons and carpenters had descended upon the place.

Then she observed Mr. Wayland.

She dismounted with the help of a convenient block of wood, looped the reins over a branch, and set off along the road.

"Good day, sir." She approached him with curiosity. Had he hidden his cache of jewels in a safe place? She would dearly love to find them, just to taunt Lord Norwood with his own inability in that direction if for no other reason. "I see you carry out your employer's directions with enthusiasm. Such speed is truly amazing. It must keep you on the go from sunup to sundown."

He preened himself a little, and gave her a lofty look. "I do what I am paid to do."

"Have you worked with Mr. Repton before?"

"He arrived yesterday," Mr. Wayland said by way of an answer. "I look forward to adding his name to my list of collaborators," he added with a trace of pomposity.

"I should like to view the cottage that is nearly completed," Hyacinthe informed him, taking a step toward the first cottage of what appeared to be a depressing row.

He bowed, then frowningly accompanied her in her inspection tour.

She said nothing when she viewed the flagged floor, but noted that the foundation looked dry and sufficiently deep to prevent problems with damp. The kitchen had a pump, which meant the owner would not be required to venture out in bad weather to fetch water. The stairs were somewhat better than in the old village, with broader steps and less sharpness to the angle of turn, but she was not impressed with the house. Not in the least.

"I fancy all the houses will have the same design?" she inquired in a bland voice.

"Naturally," Mr. Wayland answered with pride. "It saves costs, you know. Lord Norwood does not wish to waste his money."

"He could have saved a great deal of it if he had just left well enough alone in the first place," she murmured to herself while strolling across the room to peer out of the window at the construction across the road.

Mr. Wayland gave her a sharp, curious look, but did not question what she had said.

"If you do not mind, I shall wander about, trying to envision what the village will be like—eventually—in a long time," she added softly.

Intent on completing this job as fast as he could, Dudley Wayland eagerly agreed, and bustled off to oversee the carpenters he had hired.

Hyacinthe glanced about the little parlor, then went outside. The house appeared far too close to the road to permit a charming garden such as the present Worthington cottages boasted. Why, if there would be space enough to allow a few flowers to either side of the door, that would be all. Dreary. The only variation she could note was that some of the cottages had bay windows alongside the entry door.

She trudged around to the back of the cottage, noticing the absence of windows on the sides. A thatcher had arrived, and with the help of his men commenced to work on the roof.

"Well, Miss Dancy," came a familiar voice, "what do you think?"

"Lord Norwood!" she exclaimed. "I thought you would be in conference with Mr. Repton this morning."

"And so I am. He wanted to view this site before we ride over to the area I wish to improve."

She glanced past Lord Norwood to see an older man. The gentleman did not appear well and she sent Lord Norwood a questioning look.

"He still suffers from a carriage accident he had some years back. He accepted this commission as a favor, for he knew my father. The younger man at his side is his son, John. He travels about with him now, and I suppose is in training to take his father's place eventually."

Hyacinthe felt pity for the older man. She hadn't expected this development. The poor man most likely needed this commission, unable to perform as in the past. She hastily turned away and felt her ankle twist on a scrap of lumber. With a cry of pain she ended on her posterior in a mixture of sawdust, mud, and mortar.

"Why, Miss Dancy, I believe you have met with an accident! Allow me." Lord Norwood assisted her to her feet. He brushed her off with care, then frowned in dismay when he saw how she compressed her lips in pain upon attempting to walk.

"Please, help me to my horse at the end of the road. I believe I had best return to Jane's cottage. I have injured . . ." She didn't finish her sentence, for a lady did not mention an ankle, or her leg for that matter. Hyacinthe might be a bit daring, but she was not lost to all propriety.

Suddenly she found herself scooped into his arms and carried away from the building site. He paused where Mr. Repton was studying the plans for the village with Mr. Wayland at his side.

"Miss Dancy has injured her ankle. I am taking her up to the house. Perhaps Mr. Wayland will be so good as to show you the area I most wish to improve."

She could hear the vexation in his voice and suspected he wished he had not invited her to inspect his new village. Were it not for the pain she felt, she might be pleased at this spoke thrust into his wheel.

Blase placed the young woman, who was becoming increasingly heavy, on his horse, then mounted behind her after tossing a few instructions to one of the men regarding her animal.

"You ought to have exercised more care. Anyone with a bit of sense should know there are hazards about a building site," he scolded. She was so still, so pale. Her face had turned so white that the three tiny freckles on her nose stood out in bold color. He drew her closer and urged his bay to greater speed.

"I was curious to see the new village."

Now he became truly alarmed, for her voice had grown faint, and there was none of that fiery spirit he admired.

Reining up before the front of his home, he called for Barmore while sliding down, then carefully eased Miss Dancy into his arms. She appeared even weaker, although trying valiantly to allow no sign of her pain.

"Oh, I say, sir," said the butler with anxiety. He held open the door, then barked out a succession of orders while Blase rushed down the hall with Hyacinthe in his arms, Barmore right behind him. At the end room, Blase paused. Barmore hastily opened this door, then assisted with placing the injured girl on a chaise longue near the window.

"Mrs. Earnshaw and Smithson will be here directly, my lord," he said quietly, referring to the Worthington Hall housekeeper and Blase's valet.

"I ought to have been taken to my cousin's house," Miss Dancy protested faintly.

"Miss Pennington is a lovely young lady, but not likely skilled in the treatment of injuries. Mrs. Earnshaw oversaw all my childhood afflictions, and Smithson is adept with sprains and breaks."

At this bit of information Miss Dancy looked about to truly faint. She said, "I doubt if I have a break, sir. Perhaps a sprain," she allowed, then gingerly leaned back against the pile of pillows. She glanced about her room seeming to note the feminine touches here and there.

Blase repressed a smile. "My sister stays here when she visits. It was originally my mother's room."

"I see," came the soft reply. Her lashes drifted down over pale cheeks and a look of intense pain suffused her face.

Smithson entered the room with the housekeeper right behind him. He carried a black bag that must have looked ominous to the wary Miss Dancy. She peeped at it with obvious misgivings.

Mrs. Earnshaw shooed Blase from the room and he couldn't repress a grin at Miss Dancy's patent relief at his departure.

"What's all the commotion?" Val said, strolling up with marked curiosity.

"Do you recall that I urged Miss Dancy to inspect the new village? Well, she did. And she fell—I suspect spraining her ankle in the process." Blase walked over to stare out the window.

"Pity, that," Val replied with genuine regret. "Now what happens? Your little redheaded nemesis will be unable to cause you any trouble, so you ought to have clear sailing." He joined Blase, but studied his friend instead of the view.

"I didn't wish her hurt."

"Ha!" Val laughed. "After all she has done to you? I do believe you have gone soft in the head."

"The wind took her bonnet," Blase replied to the jibe, knowing he didn't sound very convinced.

"If you believe that, I have an old racehorse to sell you," Val scoffed.

"For all her temper, she's a taking little thing," Blase said in his own defense—and possibly in hers. "She passionately defends her cousin and her home. I have to admire loyalty like that. I wonder how many cousins truly care for their family as she does." Blase transferred his gaze from the landscape to his friend.

"I hope you have ordered a new supply of coats and pantaloons in sturdy fabrics that will take a few tumbles, dousings, and shrug off mud. If she stays here you will need them." Val gave a disgusted snort, then walked through the room to the door at the far end that led to the entry hall. Here he paused and turned to face Blase.

"By the by, as we agreed, I searched Wayland's rooms after he left this morning. I found nothing, and I think I must have taken apart everything there. No jewels, no sign of that velvet sack that Miss Dancy mentioned. Are you certain that she did not take that pouch for herself? Giving you just the bracelet as a sop?"

With that explosive conclusion, he left the room.

Blase again faced the window, only this time he saw nothing. Was it possible? Could Miss Dancy in her misguided loyalty to her cousin do such a dastardly deed? He didn't wish to believe it of her. Turning away from his view that was soon to be improved, he walked back to the room where she was being tended.

Just as he was about to open the door, Mrs. Earnshaw bustled from the room, her face set in a resolute expression.

"Miss Dancy?" Blase inquired.

"You did right bringing her here so Smithson might tend her. Better than any doctor, he is. Poor mite, her ankle is badly sprained and must be paining her something fierce. I'm off to the stillroom to find her something soothing." She paused, then stared at him with a look he remembered from his childhood. "She is not to be upset, mind you."

"I must speak with her, however. It is important."

Smithson approached just then, so Mrs. Earnshaw went on her way.

"She sprained her ankle?" Blase repeated, although he knew the answer.

"And is in pain, as no doubt Mrs. Earnshaw told you. I'd advise that she remain here until the pain subsides. Perhaps her cousin could join her, lend her countenance as it were?" the valet said, knowing full well how gossip could travel.

"Ah, yes, propriety. What would we do without it." Blase murmured. Then he dismissed Smithson after a few more words of instruction.

At the door he paused to view the beautiful Hyacinthe Dancy. Could she really be capable of such treachery as Val suggested?

9

"You really ought to have taken me to my cousin's cottage," Hyacinthe Dancy insisted, albeit quietly. She still reclined on the chaise longue where Blase had placed her, the injured foot now propped on a pillow. She looked wan and fragile, those tiny freckles still standing out in bold relief. Tendrils of deep red hair clung to her forehead and cheeks.

Without thinking, Blase crossed the room to brush the strands of hair away from her face. It was a curiously intimate gesture that was lost on him, but drew a puzzled look from Miss Dancy.

"I fear that would have been a bad decision for you. Mrs. Earnshaw will take care of you far better." He supposed he sounded rather gruff, but his concern for Miss Dancy had affected him more than he had thought possible.

"I would wish that Fosdick and Jane could tend me." She gave a vexed swipe at her riding skirt. "How stupid of me to be so careless. I ought to have known there might be hazards present. 'Tis all my fault. I pray you will not blame any of the workers for my irresponsible actions." She gave him a concerned look that seemed to come from her heart.

"I shan't," Blase replied abruptly. However, he wasn't about to make it easy on his antagonist. She had countered him at every chance. She had cost him two coats with her silly schemes. Yet there was something in Hyacinthe Dancy that made him want to change her mind, make her see what he saw.

"I cannot remain here," she insisted. "You must see that. Why, the speculation, the gossip . . . It is amazing how word can wing its way about the country with such speed, particularly if the gossip is malicious." She pressed her lips together, then studied her hands now folded in her lap.

"I decided to send for the doctor," Blase said, hoping to mollify her. "He ought to lend a touch of respectability to the situation. I'll grant you this—if he says you may be moved, we will take you to Miss Pennington's. Although how you might go up those stairs is beyond me."

"Aha! You do see what I mean about those stairways! They are dangerously narrow and steep. I trust you mean to alter that in the new cottages?"

Blase was startled at the change in Miss Dancy. More animated, she leaned forward to make her point with a flash of those green eyes. Then she winced and fell back against the pillows with a sigh of frustration. When tears brimmed in her eyes, Blase sank down on the chaise at her side, taking one of her hands in his.

"If I agree to see that the stairs are indeed improved, will you agree to consider my garden plans?"

"Do your London friends know that you are become a *garden* rake?" Her color yet pale and the usual twinkle in her fine eyes dimmed, she managed a strained grin at him.

He cringed at the pun, shaking his head at her while quite forgetting to release her hand.

"The doctor is here, milord," Mrs. Earnshaw said from the doorway. She had most likely noticed his position. Fortunately she was not the sort to spread rumors. Blase dropped Miss Dancy's soft hand and left the doctor in charge.

Mrs. Earnshaw whispered that they had been fortunate to find the doctor attending an injury on the estate, so he had been close by. Then she shut the door so she might assist the doctor. After all, an ankle ought not be exposed to a gentleman who was not a husband!

Blase paced back and forth across the library while the doctor examined Miss Dancy's injury. On, she was most likely as tough as old boots with a core of pure steel. On the other hand—and here he paused to stare off across his garden—she was a delicious armful from her feathery red curls to her dainty feet, and she wore a spicy scent that reminded him of the red and white carnations in his garden. Spicy. Somehow the word, as well as the scent, suited Miss Dancy to a tee.

"I understand the doctor is here. Any verdict as yet?" Val popped his head around the corner, then strolled across the library to join Blase.

"No. I'd not thought to send for him, but Mrs. Earnshaw suggested it might be a seemly thing to do," Blase confessed.

"And what if he declares that Miss Dancy should not be moved?" Val gave Blase a sly grin.

Blase shrugged. "Then I suppose I will have to send for her abigail and Miss Pennington to lend countenance."

"It would be interesting—having your adversary under your roof." Val toyed with a paperweight on the desk while watching Blase.

"Oh, she is not all that bad," Blase felt compelled to say in defense of the young girl who had seemed so soft and womanly and now lay in the next room close to tears and in pain.

"Look at it this way . . . if she were a horse, would you bet on her?" Val said, a look of mischief dancing in his eyes.

Blase gave him a surprised look, then chuckled. "As spirited a filly as she? Why, there's no doubt she'd win any race by several lengths."

"And what about the emeralds? Have you considered that if she stays here, I could investigate the Pennington cottage— under the guise of obtaining something she particularly desires." Val's expression revealed his rather cynical notions of Miss Dancy.

"I cannot like the insinuation that she has stolen the gems," Blase protested.

"Then where are they?" Val tossed the paperweight in the air, watching the flash of color as it twirled about.

Blase gave him a bleak look. "I confess I do not know."

Before they could continue along this line the doctor opened the door, joining them with quiet steps.

"She ought not be moved for a time; that is one of the nastiest sprains I have seen. I suspect she will receive far better care while here. Although she seemed very concerned about propriety—as is only right," commented the man, who usually saw to farm injuries and not those of a gently reared young lady.

Blase exchanged glances with Val, then said, "I will send for her cousin and abigail. Miss Pennington is all that is proper."

"And," Val inserted with a twist of his mouth, "Fosdick, her abigail, is an undisputable guardian of virtue."

Giving the two peers a curious look, the doctor issued a few suggestions, then went off to have words with Miss Earnshaw.

"Do you really mean to go snooping about?" Blase queried softly lest his voice carry to the next room.

"Indeed. Who knows, I may join the Robin Redbreasts." Val hooked his thumbs inside his waistcoat, then tilted back his head to give Blase a narrow, suspicious look.

"You? A Bow Street Runner?" Blase laughed, adding, "It would take more than curiosity to turn you into a detective."

There was a sound from the next room that ended their conversation. Blase, followed closely by Val, hurried to the door. They were greeted by the sight of Miss Dancy attempting to leave the chaise longue.

"Here now, what do you think you are doing?" Blase demanded, rushing across the room to her side.

"I cannot believe I must remain here. Surely I could go?" she pleaded, then sank back against the pillows as the pain grew more intense.

Tears of frustration brimmed her eyes, eyes that reminded Blase of deep green pools. He was lost in them a moment before he came to his senses. "No, but you must be uncomfortable as you are. May I be of help until Mrs. Earnshaw returns?"

She shook her head, then apparently changed her mind. "My jacket. Help me take it off, please."

She fumbled with the little jet buttons that curved up under her bosom, succeeded with that task, then shifted slightly. Blase tugged at one cuff, easing that sleeve from her arm, then reached around to help with the other.

He discovered that in so doing he was very close to her and was momentarily dazed. She smelled deliciously spicy. She leaned against him briefly, as light as thistledown and far nicer. Then he recalled those missing emeralds. Could she truly have taken them?

The sight of her delicate cambric shirt, tucked and curving so faithfully to her figure, brought him to his senses as nothing else might. He tossed the jacket aside, then looked to where Val stood, arms folded across his chest, his eyes revealing his amusement.

"There is nothing more we can do here." A sound at the door brought Blase around. "Mrs. Earnshaw," he said with great relief. "I believe there is much you can do to make our guest more comfortable."

"Mr. Repton is desiring to speak with you, milord," she replied, bustling across the room to stand by Miss Dancy. Presumably the folds of sheer cambric draped over the house-keeper's arm constituted a nightdress. The image of Hyacinthe Dancy attired in the sheer cambric drove him from the room with more than necessary haste.

"Well," Hyacinthe observed, "you would think I was contagious."

"He is that anxious to have his plans for the garden and view implemented, miss," the housekeeper replied evenly.

She ably helped Hyacinthe from her riding costume and into the delicate, lavender-scented nightdress trimmed with white ribbons. "This was his mother's gown but she always took care of her things. You are of a size, I believe, or near enough. Now, let us put you under the covers of the bed. I believe you could use a bit of sleep after taking the powder the doctor left for you."

With that, she carefully helped Hyacinthe into the bed and tucked the covers about her with an attention that Hyacinthe found especially kind.

"Thank you for all you have done. It is an extra burden, I'm certain." Hyacinthe's eyelids drooped. She swallowed the mixture that Mrs. Earnshaw handed her to drink, then fell back against the pillows.

The housekeeper paused by the side of the bed, studying the young woman who had affected her master so strongly. She had not missed that tender look of concern, nor the gentle way he held her hand. Did he know how he felt? she wondered. Oh, these coming days were not to be missed for anything.

When Fosdick and Jane learned about the accident, they flew into action. Fosdick packed what she deemed necessary. Jane slipped over to Granny Beanbuck's cottage to obtain a few cinnamon buns, which she was certain would make Hyacinthe feel better.

It was not long before they were prepared to depart.

Jane opened the door to discover Sir Charles on her doorstep. "Oh!" she exclaimed. "You startled me. We were just about to summon the coach to take us to the Hall. Poor Hyacinthe has suffered a terrible accident."

"No!" Sir Charles cried in alarm. "May I offer my carriage, dear lady? I feel certain you must wish to drive there as soon as may be."

"What a thoughtful man you are," Jane told him. She gathered her bits and pieces, motioned Fosdick to leave the cottage, then joined Sir Charles.

When they reached Worthington Hall they found the patient asleep.

"I would like to see her—just for a moment," Jane said softly to Lord Norwood. She held in her hands a small sack from which emerged the aroma of fresh cinnamon buns.

"She sleeps," he cautioned.

Not allowing such words to deter her, Miss Pennington set forth behind the housekeeper in the direction of the bedroom.

Fosdick didn't bother to ask permission but also followed along to the bedroom where her charge slept.

Jane exclaimed softly when she saw her dearest cousin stretched out on the bed, looking so white and still. She placed the cinnamon buns on a nearby table, then edged toward the door. "There is nothing I may do for her at the moment," she admitted. She left the room, looking close to erupting into tears.

The abigail peered about the dimly lit room, then studied the strained face of the girl. The injured ankle, still elevated on a pillow, made a high mound near the foot of the bed.

"I fixed a sort of a cage to keep the covers off that poor

foot. Dear girl," Mrs. Earnshaw said, "she made not one whimper, although anyone could see she was in pain."

"She's a game one, she is," Fosdick agreed. She consulted with the housekeeper a bit longer. When the other woman left, she emptied the portmanteau of the things she believed necessary for the next few days. Fosdick was the sort of person who firmly believed in being prepared for any event, so the bag held a great deal.

In the entry, Barmore guided Miss Pennington to the drawing room, where the gentlemen awaited her. She chatted with Lord Latham and Lord Norwood while seated next to Sir Charles.

"Did the doctor say it would be very long before my cousin may return home?" Jane queried gently with a dubious look at Lord Norwood.

"As soon as the pain permits her to be moved. Between the swelling and the nasty ache from the sprain, she does not feel quite the thing at the moment," Blase said.

"Poor girl," Sir Charles murmured, looking as though he harbored a few other thoughts about Miss Dancy but was far too polite to utter them.

"Did you reach any conclusions with Repton, Norwood?" Val said, sounding quite bored with the topic of Miss Dancy's injury.

"Indeed." Blase rose to look out of the window in the direction of the soon-to-disappear village. "We will begin planting the woods to sweep up that first hill immediately. Miss Dancy will no doubt be pleased to learn that Repton believes we ought to keep the church—the tower will make a splendid ruin." At Jane's dismayed gasp, he turned to bow in her direction. "We will also build a new church in the center of the new village, of course. Mr. Clark shall have his roof that does not leak."

"Oh," Jane said with an uncertain note in her voice, "that will be splendid, I'm sure."

"How does the rest of your plan progress?" Sir Charles inquired with a thoughtful look at Miss Pennington, who wore a worried frown on her pretty face.

"Two more houses are almost ready for occupancy. I believe the Nutkins and the Philpotts are to move next," Blase concluded with satisfaction. As an afterthought, he said, "And of course their old cottages will promptly be demolished."

At Jane's second gasp of dismay, Sir Charles patted her hand in a gesture of comfort.

"And what does he say about your terraces?" Val asked slyly. "Miss Dancy seemed to admire them greatly, as I recall."

"They shall remain as they are," Blase replied, not admitting he had argued with the famous landscape designer regarding that matter. As Miss Dancy had pointed out, their beauty added to the consequence of the house. He was not so set in his ways that he could fail to see reason when presented with convincing arguments.

Just then Barmore entered the room to offer tea to Miss Pennington while Blase saw to the liquid refreshment for the men.

When she had finished her tea, Miss Pennington set off to check on her cousin, then seek out her room. It was located next to where Hyacinthe slept, and within minutes Fosdick entered to consult with her.

"Miss Hyacinthe ought to be able to come home shortly," the abigail reported with satisfaction.

"I fear there will be fireworks to rival a Guy Fawkes Day celebration when she hears that more cottages are being torn down," Jane said with a wry look at Fosdick.

"Oh, dear me," Fosdick muttered.

"At least the old church will remain . . . to become a Gothic ruin," Jane concluded, sighing. "What Hyacinthe will say to that doesn't bear thinking."

It was quite as Jane has feared. When apprised of the latest developments, Hyacinthe erupted. Fortunately Lord Norwood was off with Mr. Repton and his son, so he was spared her fire and fury.

"That heartless monster," Hyacinthe fumed from her bed.

"Dear," Jane reminded her, "he is transporting the families into their new abodes in fine style. Mrs. Nutkin is that pleased with two extra bedrooms and her husband is kept busy all day, quite exhausted come evening what with the work to be had at the new village." She exchanged a significant look with her cousin, both knowing that an exhausted man was less likely to be interested in what Mrs. Nutkin would as soon have him avoid.

Instead, Hyacinthe attacked the abandonment of the old church. "While it might need a new roof, surely it should not be allowed to molder into a ruin!"

"I cannot answer that, my dear," Jane admitted.

A gentle rap on the door brought the information that the curate desired to offer a word of comfort to the injured young lady.

Exchanging a resigned look with Jane, Hyacinthe nodded to Fosdick. The gentleman entered hesitantly, then approached the bed as though she might bite him.

"Good day, Miss Dancy. So sorry to learn of your tragic accident. But things will happen, you know. The Lord's will be done," he concluded with a look at the ceiling.

"That's very comforting to know," Hyacinthe said wryly.

"I suppose you have heard that I, that is the village, will have a new church," he said, animation lighting his face for the first time. "Not merely an ordinary roof, but slate of the finest quality. There will be no leaks in this roof, I can assure you," he concluded with great pride. "Sir Charles expressed an interest in donating a lovely baptismal font. Oh, this is a great thing for the village. Did you know that more cottages are to be built than existed previously? We shall grow. There will be progress."

"And progress is far more important than history or the security of one's loved home," Hyacinthe said softly.

He appeared disconcerted for a moment, then smiled. "To be sure," he said, apparently taking Hyacinthe's words at face value.

When Blase entered Miss Dancy's room just before dinner, he did so with caution. He had been warned that she had heard of the changes and not been pleased at all.

"It promises to be a fine day tomorrow. If your injury permits, perhaps you will be allowed to be carried to the terrace."

"So I may enjoy the view?" she shot back swiftly. "I daresay there will be fewer rooftops to mar it by then."

"I gather the curate or someone has been to call."

"He was here," she acknowledged.

"I thought you might admire the sight of the new trees being planted. There will be hundreds added to the parkland," he said with enthusiasm. "And the little stream has been dammed up to create a rather charming waterfall. When your ankle is better, I will take you to see it. Mr. Repton believes that it will be a soothing sight on a hot summer day."

"I fancy he is correct," she said, her fingers pleating the bedcover. "My injury seems to be improving. I believe it will be no time at all before I will be able to return to Jane's cottage, although I doubt if I will be up to viewing a waterfall for some time. I should like to see the village before it disappears," she concluded, her fine eyes mocking him with a flash of green.

Blase avoided meeting her eyes. He feared he might reveal something he would rather keep to himself. Val had gone to the village late in the afternoon, ostensibly to fetch something for Miss Dancy.

"Do you suppose that we might become a bit less formal? Since you reside here—even temporarily," he asked, not liking to use her surname when "Hyacinthe" was so much more charming to say.

"I scarcely believe that would be proper," she answered quickly. "I am well aware that such a change would be reported to others just too eager to gossip."

"And you have no desire to be linked with me," he finished. Odd, how it truly piqued him to know that she quite detested him. Well—perhaps that was too strong a word. Maybe disliked would be more like it. But he had always known the admiration of every lady he saw, and this cut him to the quick.

"Even if you have become the *garden* rake?" she gently chided. "Indeed, I regret to admit you are not my ideal. For it is not polite to tell your host that he fails in any aspect, is it?"

Blase decided that he had asked for that setdown and paused by the door on his way from the room. "I trust that Mrs. Earnshaw has seen to your comfort?"

A faint pink stained Miss Dancy's cheeks. "She has been quite wonderful to me. You are most fortunate in your servants, sir. And from what I have seen, you have a lovely home."

Somewhat mollified, Blase marched to the library, where he found Val hunting through the shelves.

"Looking for something to read?" Blase said in mock horror. "I am really failing in that case. Shall we plan an outing tomorrow?"

"I had enough today. Blast it all, I believed I would find the emeralds concealed in Miss Pennington's cottage."

Blase permitted himself a smile, albeit a small one. "And?"

"Not a blasted thing," Val admitted in disgust. "It is a small place and there are few spots in which to hide things." He leaned against the wall of books, giving Blase an assessing look. "Your Miss Pennington is a remarkable person, in that she doesn't collect vast quantities of absurd things. My sisters do, the silly twits."

"But no emeralds."

"No. So . . . where do we go next?"

"I wonder if Mr. Wayland has placed them in an entirely different hiding spot. See if you can nose about, learn more of his movements. Perhaps your valet, or my head groom, could chat up the locals at the nearby tavern."

"It's a thought," Val replied, rubbing his chin with a considering look. "I'll confess that I had hoped Miss Dancy had taken them."

"It would have been very convenient," Blase said, trying not to appear as pleased as he was. He didn't choose to inspect his reasons for wishing her innocent. Perhaps it was easier to view Mr. Wayland as a culprit?

Since she insisted that she was much improved, Hyacinthe was carried out to join the others in the drawing room after dinner. Blase lifted her in his arms, thinking she felt like an armful of flowers or something equally light. He took great care to prevent her foot from further injury when he placed her on a sofa.

The evening went well. When Blase rose to take Hyacinthe back to her room, she gave them all a firm look.

"I fully intend to return to Jane's cottage on the morrow. Not that I do not appreciate Lord Norwood's gracious hospitality, but I feel much more the thing. And it is better that I go." Her words were decisive.

Blase knew there was no arguing with her. Perhaps he might be able to persuade her to return to study his view later on. He still felt this imperative to convert her to his position. Yet she still looked very pale and fragile.

"Whatever you wish," he said.

"You do not really mean that, you know," she murmured provocatively in his ear while being carried back to her bed.

The next few days passed surprisingly quickly considering Hyacinthe's inability to get about. She remained in bed at first, then managed her way down the stairs to recline on the sofa in the parlor. She became adept at hopping about.

Everyone she had met in the village called to offer sympathy and inquire about life in the great house. Of course it was most subtly done, but between the Widow Smith and Mrs. Peachey there was precious little that wasn't learned about the way things were done up there.

Sir Charles called as well, but Hyacinthe soon decided that he was far more interested in how Jane fared with her invalid than in the invalid herself.

One fine day Hyacinthe could tolerate being inside the house no longer. With the help of Fosdick and a cane Sir Charles had brought for her use—bringing forth Jane's great admiration—she set out to sit on the green. Here she could watch the antics of the silly ducks and admire the beauty of the haughty swans.

While she sat relaxing in the shade of a fine old tree, one of the Nutkin children approached her. It was one of the older of the girls and she wore the saddest expression Hyacinthe could imagine.

"Sukey, dear girl, what troubles you?" Hyacinthe asked when the girl hesitantly approached her.

"Me brothers, miss." Once the barrier of actually speaking

to the pretty and sympathetic lady was broken, the girl poured forth her tale. "They tease me somethin' fierce, 'cuz I can't fly a kite for nothin'."

"That will never do," Hyacinthe declared briskly. "Allow me to help you, if I may. First, I must inspect your kite." Seeing the dubious expression on the girl's face, Hyacinthe assured her, "My brother taught me years ago, and I do not believe you ever quite forget how to do something like this."

The kite proved airworthy in her estimation. The ragged tail needed a bit of improvement, but after adding her handkerchief to the end, Hyacinthe decided it would do.

"Now you must run so, holding the kite like this before you release it." Hyacinthe demonstrated the proper way to hold the kite, then urged the girl to run across the green.

"Look, miss, 'tis flying!" Sukey cried with delight.

The success went to her head. Sukey Nutkin ran and ran until she was red in the face from her exertion and about to drop from sheer joy at besting her brothers.

Then disaster struck. The kite slipped from her tired fingers to sail up into the branches of the spreading oak.

Mrs. Peachey, who had been looking on, declared, "What a shame, Sukey was enjoying herself so much." All knew how rare an occurrence this was for the overworked Nutkin daughter.

The Widow Smith, also a spectator, suggested a gentle tug on the string, while old Mr. Smeed—who had returned here for the afternoon because he was lonely all by himself—offered the opinion that the only way to get the kite down was for some young lad to climb up to fetch it.

"Me brothers ain't about to bring it down," Sukey said, fighting the tears that threatened to fall.

Since all the other young men were over at the new village working on the new cottages, there seemed no hope. The kite was undoubtedly doomed to hang limply from the tree limb to forever decorate the tree. Hyacinthe wondered if it would mar the view for Lord Norwood.

Somehow it failed to surprise her when the object of her thoughts appeared in sight. He had a way of doing that lately. He strode to her side, a frown on his brow.

"Ought you be sitting here? 'Tis very public," he said, casting a look about at the throng of people who all seemed to be peering up into the tree for some odd reason.

"I grew bored with the parlor," she admitted. "Poor Sukey needed someone to show her how to fly a kite. And now that she's learned how, the dratted thing landed in the branches."

Every face turned to him. Blase's heart sank, for he realized what they expected. Oh, perhaps they didn't actually *expect* him to climb after the blasted kite, but he knew he would diminish in their eyes were he to walk away from Miss Dancy's appealing look. Not to mention the disappointment he knew would spring into Sukey's pale blue eyes.

"I shall climb up to fetch it for her," he said with far more enthusiasm than he felt. Remembering his previous experiences with Miss Dancy, Blase removed his coat, tossing it on her lap.

The climb was a simple affair, for the oak tree was superbly arrayed with stout limbs spaced nicely apart. He managed to reach the kite with just a little effort. Complications arose when he tried to return to the ground. The kite in one hand— for he didn't wish it to sail away—and the other hand assisting with his descent, he found the going tricky.

"Look out!" Miss Dancy cried.

Her warning proved too late. A branch broke under his weight and he felt himself slipping. He let the blasted flag go, vowing to buy another if necessary, and grabbed at passing boughs.

The ground he fell upon was cushioned by long grass, but he was well aware that his pantaloons had suffered greatly.

"Oh, sir, you've ripped your—" Sukey immediately turned as red as a beetroot and grabbed her restored kite, mumbling a "thank you" before dashing off.

She had done it again. Somehow Miss Dancy had managed to bring him to grief once more. And what was worse, she looked as though she was ready to burst into laughter at any moment.

"I am so sorry, my lord," she said in a choked voice. "What a dreadful thing to have happen." She handed him his coat to cover his exposed posterior.

The rest of the villagers drifted off to discuss the disaster, their chuckles floating back to taunt him.

"Miss Dancy," Blase said with great forbearance, "you really are a dangerous woman."

"What a lovely thing to say,'" she replied, this time breaking into peals of laughter. Blase found himself somewhat reluctantly joining her.

10

"She doesn't have the sense God gave a flea," Val chided while they rode along the track from the Hall to the new village.

"I would never go so far as to say that," Blase said sharply. "However, this last bit of teasing has gone too far."

He supposed he was overreacting to the situation. It was unreasonable to blame Hyacinthe Dancy for his fall from the oak tree, thus splitting his pantaloons and making himself a laughing stock for the villagers. That the premier rake of London should be placed in such a position was appalling, however. And she was the one who had silently urged him to fetch the blasted kite.

She had called him a *garden* rake. While he had laughed with her, it had served to remind him that Miss Dancy possessed a lamentable sense of humor.

And that cat she had saddled him with! The dratted animal had taken over his bedroom not to mention his bed, and acted as though Blase ought to cater to it. When Smithson had served the cat kippers, they had been on a china plate, if you please. No ordinary crockery for that animal.

True, the little fellow did have a winning way about him and had proven to be a good mouser. But still, a man didn't have a cat for a pet; he had a sturdy, sensible dog, for pity's sake.

"What do you intend to do about her?" Val queried.

Blase knew full well that his friend expected him to perform some devilishly nasty bit of retribution. Blase couldn't think of a thing he wished to do to Hyacinthe Dancy that was along such lines. Not after holding her in his arms. And then there was that memorable kiss. She had never mentioned it, but he found it impossible to forget. But he would. He must. It would be absurd to become more deeply involved with that red-headed tease.

"What I intend to do is forge ahead with my plans. I told Wayland to hire more stone masons to work on the church. We also need a few more carpenters to speed up completion of the houses. The sooner the new village is completed, the sooner Miss Dancy will give up and go away."

"And you wish her to be out of your life?" Val gave Blase a look that clearly told how he doubted this. Fortunately he said nothing more, so Blase didn't have to defend himself one way or the other.

"I want to find those emeralds first. I cannot believe she has taken them. Why would she give me the bracelet in that case?" he demanded.

"To put you off her trail," Val said, obviously trying to sound like a detective. "You see, if she can make you believe that by handing you the bracelet she's innocent, she can keep the rest of them. You must admit, she would look rather luscious arrayed in those emeralds on that delicate white skin with her striking eyes." Val's grin reminded Blase of Tom Tiger after it had produced a mouse for his appreciation.

"But," Blase reminded his friend, "you found nothing in her belongings."

"True," Val admitted with a frown, then brightened. "Perhaps they were in the portmanteau that the abigail brought to the Hall after Miss Dancy was injured. People often stow important possessions in peculiar places, like a portmanteau. Especially if they are away from home. And it appears she has no home, for she seems to drift from relative to relative."

"Pity you didn't find occasion to examine all her belongings while she was up at the Hall," Blase wryly concluded. The thought that the beautiful Miss Dancy was without a close family bothered him. Her brother ought to provide a proper establishment for her or take her into his own home. She needed watching over. "What about Wayland?"

"You know I have had my groom keeping a sharp eye on him whenever yours was busy. Nothing out of line has been observed. He is either innocent or dashed clever. In spite of my inclination toward the beautiful and dangerous Miss Dancy, he does bear more surveillance."

They entered the road that led through the center of the new village. It was not cobbled as yet, and the puddles of water here and there prompted caution. The entire area looked raw and unsettled. No flowers such as Miss Dancy seemed to desire graced the front of the cottages; no trees grew in the village save a few paltry beeches and willows scattered around the edges of what would be the village green. The new pond had yet to form from the stream that now flowed along the lowest part of the proposed green, but at least they were spared the abundance of ducks and the two swans.

"I must speak to Wayland about the street. There should be sufficient ground for gardens in front of the cottages."

"Yes," Val agreed. "I've noticed Miss Dancy appears quite fond of gardens. Wonder how her hedgehog is faring?"

"Last I heard it was consuming every slug and beetle in Miss Pennington's garden. I suspect Miss Dancy has been feeding it bowls of bread and milk as well, for she said something about being worried the little thing might have a difficult winter."

"Animal lover, then?" Val said with a grimace.

"Well," Blase said, "it's nice to think she cares for something. She seems to have a total indifference to men."

"Men? Or you in particular? I must say, it's dashed amusing to see that little bit of a damsel turning her nose up at you when you're the quarry of nearly every woman in London." Val grinned with decided cheer at the thought.

Blase ignored this provocative remark. Instead he stiffened, studying his architect as he spoke with a man.

"What is it?" Val murmured, reining in to see what had caught Blase's attention.

"I believe I just saw my esteemed architect accept a bribe. I'd swear the delivery chap from the quarry slipped him something." Blase narrowed his gaze.

"Wouldn't be anything new, I suppose," Val said quietly.

The two men dismounted, tied their horses to a convenient post, then slowly approached the architect from behind him.

Wayland and the man standing beside the load of stone were in deep discussion. Try as he could, Blase did not actually see Wayland pocket any money. It had been the appearance of accepting it that had struck him so forcefully. He could prove nothing.

They apparently caught the delivery man's eye, for he spoke rapidly to Wayland, then turned away to the dray.

Wayland spun around with a smile of greeting on his angular face. "Lord Norwood! I have good news for you, sir."

Momentarily diverted, Blase said cautiously, "And what is this good news?"

"We have begun tearing down the cottages in the old village and this chap will carry useable stone from there to this site, cutting down on what we need from the quarry. It will save time and money." The architect looked enormously pleased with himself. And there was not one sign of guilt in his face.

"Both would be welcome," Blase murmured. His suspicions regarding the emeralds must be coloring his entire attitude to Wayland. He had only Miss Dancy's word on the jewelry. Not that he wished to believe in her guilt.

Old Mr. Smeed had ambled from his new cottage to approach Blase. He appeared to have something on his mind.

"Good day, Mr. Smeed," Blase said courteously. He caught Val's eye, motioning with a nod of his head that Val should investigate the area for him while he kept the architect by his side.

Val nodded back ever so slightly to show he understood, then sauntered off down the road, carefully avoiding puddles. He made a show of checking each cottage as he went along.

The older man nattered on about the dust and noise from the building and the great progress that had been made, then came to the point. "Granny Beanbuck's worried that you'll not have a proper oven for her. Depends on her baking, she does. Claims she'll not move so much as a chair until she kin try it out first."

Blase exchanged a look with Wayland, then sought to allay these fears. It took much of the morning to arrange transport for the elderly Mrs. Beanbuck, then properly test the new oven. She brought the last of the morning's dough with her and set about forming her loaves with her customary skill.

Blase found he did not like her narrow-eyed scowl overmuch.

"Canny old lady, isn't she?" Val commented as the bread went into the new oven. He had silently sidled up to the group under cover of the bustle of checking the fire in the oven and cajoling the old woman to make her attempt.

"Come on, let her be while you tell me what you have found—if anything. I trust you inspected the office Wayland set up in that unfinished house across the road?" He exchanged a look with Val, who had strolled along at his side out to the center of the road.

"Indeed. Dash it all, I found not one thing that you might not expect to find in a temporary office. Of course, it was a bit difficult to hunt about, what with the carpenter popping in and out ever so often. I have become disgustingly creative with my excuses, I'll have you know." Val kicked at a small stone in his scorn of his success, or lack thereof.

"I appreciate your efforts," Blase said softly. He glanced to where his architect conferred with a stone mason. "Wayland showed no nervousness at your absence, either. Apparently the gems are not here."

"So what do we do next? Kidnap Miss Dancy so as to examine the remainder of her belongings?" Val muttered with a sly glance at his friend.

"I may try to persuade her to go on a picnic one of these days if the weather is decent." Blase glanced at a puddle, then off to the horizon where some gray clouds had formed, promising another shower before long. "Too much rain and we'll have a devil of a time finishing these cottages in time for the winter."

"Here comes Mr. Clark. I do believe the good curate is ready to do stonework himself in order to speed things up." Val chuckled at the eager expression on the gentleman's face.

Blase chuckled too. "His nimble footwork dancing around the puddles might serve him well at something, but I'm not certain it would be of any use in laying stone."

"He'd do most anything to get a roof that didn't leak."

"Good day to you, my lords." Ambrose Clark rubbed his hands together in a gesture of satisfaction while glancing back to where the church was slowly taking form.

"It seems good," Blase agreed.

"He hasn't run into Miss Dancy yet," Val said under his breath. Blase heard what he said and gave him a dark look.

"Ah, yes, the young lady does seem to have a most unfortunate propensity for accidents." Mr. Clark assumed a pious mien, then added, "One must not judge another too harshly, for you know not what lies in the heart."

"You might say that," Blase murmured. Then, with another stern look at Val that cautioned him to guard his words, he guided the curate toward where the church would one day stand in simple glory.

The curate began to inquire about certain aspects of the church plans, gesturing nervously with his long fingers. Blase decided he would beg leave of the curate to ask Miss Dancy if she and her cousin would join them on a picnic. He'd ask Sir Charles as well so he could entertain Miss Pennington. While they were away, Val—who detested anything as provincial as picnics—could sneak into the Pennington cottage to perform the rest of his investigation. Not that Blase truly expected Val would find anything incriminating, but it would silence him and remove a taint of suspicion from the lovely Miss Dancy.

Of course were Val to discover the jewelry, it would be another matter entirely.

It was sometime later before Blase was able to leave the new village. Granny Beanbuck somewhat reluctantly allowed as how the oven appeared promising. Since Blase had gone to the expense of a new Rumford stove for her, he accepted her words of probability with wry resignation.

The curate finally ran out of questions, his last act to wave a letter from the bishop offering a few words of advice for Lord Norwood. Blase accepted the letter with a slight bow, then marched away.

"I vow, I shall be more careful when I next come here," he commented to Val. "One would think *I* am the master builder instead of the one I hired."

"But you are ultimately responsible and they all know that," Val pointed out.

Which brought Blase to the matter of Miss Dancy and Miss Pennington. He was heartily sorry that he had left Miss Dancy with the idea that the rents would be raised substantially. His bailiff has suggested such a raise, but what with the effects of the war and all, there were few who could manage it. Blase figured he would have to attend a few more races in the hope of winning enough blunt to make up the difference.

The two men rode along the route to the old village, pausing when they came to where Sir Charles lived. That gentleman was out in his stable area and waved to them.

It was the opportunity Blase sought, so he motioned Val to follow.

After the usual chitchat, Blase extended his invitation. "It will be a simple thing, but I thought Miss Dancy might enjoy an outing after being confined with her injury."

"Indeed," Sir Charles fairly beamed at them. "I shall enjoy escorting Miss Pennington. You know, it is a shocking thing for her to be alone, which she will be once Miss Dancy leaves here."

"Quite," Blase said with a glance at Val. "I was unaware that Miss Dancy was planning to depart soon."

"Well, as to that I cannot say," Sir Charles replied sagely. "I confess I have been most concerned with Jane, that is, Miss Pennington." His face reddened slightly, then he added, "I've been thinking that since my situation has improved—what with my father passing on and my inheriting—I might afford a wife." He studied the faces of both men as though to know their reaction. "You did say that I might buy back the manor house my ancestor lost to yours."

"I did and you may. As to Miss Pennington, I feel certain that the lady would welcome such a proposal, for she shows a marked partiality in your direction." Blase gave Sir Charles a smile of genuine encouragement. This solution would end two problems. Sir Charles would get a wife and Miss Pennington a husband and a home without rent.

"Perhaps the day of the picnic?" Sir Charles said softly with a pleased nod.

Blase and Val left shortly after that.

Val burst into laughter once they were around the bend. "Turned matchmaker, Blase?"

"Why not?" Blase grinned at him. "Now to dispose of Miss Dancy."

When they reached the Pennington cottage a few minutes later, they found Miss Pennington about to depart to fetch the mail from the village shop where it was brought every day. She turned about to invite the gentlemen inside.

"For I must tell you that Hyacinthe has been quite blue-deviled. Why, if her ankle does not heal more quickly I fear she will sink into a green melancholy!" Jane said with some concern.

"It is slow to mend, I gather. She seemed to enjoy her time by the pond," he recalled.

"I fear she overdid. Anyway, the rain showers put an end to that. It is difficult for her to reach the garden by herself. Although she does enjoy sitting there at dusk to watch for her hedgehog."

Jane opened the door and they entered into the parlor to find Miss Dancy seated on the sofa, her foot propped up on a stool, looking for all the world like an old lady with gout. Her greeting revealed mixed emotions—joy at a change of company and dismay that the callers should be Lord Norwood and Lord Latham.

"Good day, sirs. From the touch of sawdust I gather you have been over to the new village. And how do things progress?" she asked politely.

Blase detected a flash of fire in those green eyes that warned him to tread cautiously.

"Well, I do believe," he replied blandly.

"And when do you tear down the lovely old Tudor cottage across the green? I am surprised that Mr. Repton did not consider that in the vein of a rustic refinement for your distant prospect. It reminds one of an old painting." Her face wore a pensive expression, one almost of sadness.

"As a matter of fact we did discuss it,'" Blase admitted. He was totally unprepared for the sparkle of hope that lit her beautiful eyes. Indeed, her entire face came alive and she leaned toward him with eagerness.

"And what did you decide," she asked, quite as though his reply was the most important decision to be made.

Blase found himself in a quandary. Mr. Repton had definitely felt that the house offered a touch of the picturesque, but Blase had thought to tear the cottage down. Instead, he now found himself gazing into Miss Dancy's remarkable eyes and saying what he'd not intended to say.

"It shall be allowed to stand. At least until it may become dangerous."

"How utterly delightful!" she exclaimed as though Blase had done something wonderful. "Did you hear that, Jane? That lovely old place shall remain as a memory of the village that once was. I am so glad," she said with genuine warmth.

Blase smiled, then wondered if she perhaps recalled that kiss they had shared in the closet of the Tudor cottage. Could she possibly have a sentimental attachment for that reason? He did not flatter himself it might be so, merely reflecting that the cottage was an appealing sight. He decided to proceed with his picnic plan.

"We hoped to invite you both to a picnic on the next fine day," he said with a half-smile. "Miss Dancy could do with some fresh air and Sir Charles declared he would enjoy escorting Miss Pennington. I can promise some fine views," he coaxed with a cautious eye on Miss Dancy.

Jane Pennington blushed, while Hyacinthe Dancy resumed her pensive look. It was Jane who answered.

"We should be pleased to accept, my lord. I will bring some of Granny Beanbuck's famous cinnamon buns as a treat. Fosdick intended to go shopping one day soon. That would be ideal."

The gentlemen professed themselves delighted and left shortly after.

"Do you think?" Jane cried. "Could he actually? Oh, I suppose it is nothing more than Lord Norwood inviting him along and his being polite," she concluded, her face losing its animation.

"It is difficult to know what gentlemen think. When I see

Lord Norwood I cannot help but recall the little song about the sad maiden. You know, the maiden who begs the man not to deceive her, and how can he use a poor maiden so? The last verse is particularly apt." She sang it in her high, clear soprano, a rather shrewd gleam in her eyes:

> "Soon you will meet with another pretty maiden,
> Some pretty maiden, you'll court her for a while;
> Thus ever ranging, turning and changing,
> Always seeking for a girl that is new."

"Well, while I think that a nice little song, I do not believe it applies to Sir Charles. He has not been in the way of chasing young maidens. Only lately has he come into some money, and he attends to his estate rather than socializing."

"It quite relates to Lord Norwood, however," Hyacinthe said. "I wonder how long before . . ." Then at the sight of Jane's frightened face, she stopped. "Well, we can only believe we do the ladies of England a favor by keeping him occupied so that he cannot inflict his charm elsewhere."

"Perhaps the mail has arrived," Jane said hurriedly, moving toward the door. "It is usually here by now."

"Would you be so kind as to buy us some peppermints when you go?" Hyacinthe begged, hoping to cheer her cousin with a treat. "And take my reticule in case there is a letter for me. I vow the postage seems to increase every month. Fancy, I must pay at least twenty shillings for a letter from my aunt!"

"Of course I shall," Jane said, taking the reticule from the sofa and leaving at once.

Hyacinthe had not meant to upset her cousin and regretted her thoughtless words. However, she could not help but worry. Unless Sir Charles came to the rescue there was nothing left but to persuade Jane to permit Hyacinthe to assist her. For some time she contemplated ways in which she might accomplish this.

Hyacinthe heard the front door shut and turned to greet her cousin. Sitting quietly on the parlor sofa had taken its toll and she welcomed a diversion.

"The mail has come and there is a letter for you. It's two

sheets, so must have a great amount of news. It was franked by Lord Crompton. Do you know a Lord Crompton, my dear?" Jane said, sounding much impressed. She handed the letter to Hyacinthe, who promptly broke the seal and unfolded it.

She read the letter with a growing sense of dismay. While lovely news, it was not the sort she had hoped to receive.

"What is it, Hyacinthe? You look as though someone has died." Jane sank down upon the sofa, her face full of concern.

Hyacinthe refolded the letter, trying to think just how she would tell Jane the bad news.

"The letter is from Aunt Bel," she began.

"With whom you stayed before you came here," Jane prompted.

"Indeed. She is to marry the Earl of Crompton shortly."

"But that is wonderful. I am so happy for her. Why the long face?" Jane gave Hyacinthe a puzzled look.

"Because," Hyacinthe said with deep regret, "I had hoped we might go to stay with her until we could find another place for you to reside, some little cottage you would like. Cousin Chloe will go to live with Grandmama Dancy while Aunt Bel and her new husband go off on an extended wedding trip. We can scarcely invite ourselves to stay in a house where everyone is gone. Indeed, Aunt Bel will have had her things removed to her new home and Montmorcy Hall will sit empty until Cousin John returns from wherever he is traveling."

"That means you have nowhere to go, does it not?" Jane gently queried, her eyes soft with sympathy.

"Well . . ." Hyacinthe desperately sought an answer to their dilemma. "We might try staying with my brother. Only . . . as you know, Peter is fascinated with those horrid Egyptian mummies and that dreadful collection of peculiar objects our father brought back from Egypt. I truly do not think I can bear to live with a nasty old mummy."

Jane gave Hyacinthe a horrified yet fascinated look. "Do you mean he actually has them in the house? How frightful!"

"Then you agree with me on that? We must find another place to live. Surely there are other cottages to rent. I shall help you."

"I like it here," Jane said stubbornly. "It is quiet, charming, and I have friends." She no doubt thought of Sir Charles, as her face looked wistful and her eyes grew dreamy.

"If we were to put our money together, might we not afford something rather nice? With a lovely bit of garden for you. And my hedgehog," Hyacinthe added as an afterthought.

"I know of no such situation," Jane said, shaking her head thoughtfully. "I spoke with Lord Norwood's bailiff the other day. I did not wish to trouble you with what I learned, but it is not good. He told me the rents are to be higher, much higher, on the new cottages. It is more than I can manage. And I know of no other place to which I would care to go. Now that Cousin Chloe has moved in with Grandmama Dancy, that rather eliminates her as well. Not that I particularly wished to live with her," she added.

"Then what are we to do if you will not permit me to pay more of the rent, stubborn girl?" Hyacinthe said quietly. She clasped her hands in her lap, suddenly speculating on a life amid the decay of the Tudor house. "It is all his fault, you know. What a pity he wasn't stuck in that pig sty," she said grimly. "He'd have succumbed to something dire by now and we could remain here." She shared a look with Jane and sat wishing Blase Montague to the ends of the earth.

"I do so want to retain my independence. Oh, Hyacinthe, I am truly afraid," Jane said in a whisper.

"I am as well," Hyacinthe agreed, then handed her clean handkerchief to a quietly weeping Jane. Another line from the little song returned to her. "Oh, my innocent heart you've betrayed."

11

The following days brought significant activity and change to the old village of Worthington. Granny Beanbuck's cottage began to tumble as the workmen tore it down stone by stone. What wood could not be used again was trundled away for fuel. Windows and doors were carefully removed for future use elsewhere. Nothing would be wasted.

Jane stood in the garden, watching as the chimney toppled to the ground, a cloud of dust rising in its place.

"How I shall miss the aroma of cinnamon buns in the mornings," she murmured to Hyacinthe, who stood at her side also watching the destruction of the cottage.

"I fail to see why his elegant lordship could not have been satisfied with his view as it was," Hyacinthe complained to Jane and the hedgehog, who had been startled from its sleep by all the racket and now poked a drowsy head from under a leaf.

"What did I hear you call him yesterday?" Jane said, beginning to stroll to the house.

"The garden rake," Hyacinthe snapped. "All of London society will be vastly amused to see how rustic he has become. The premier rake of the Town, reduced to tree plantings and fertilizer. I vow they will think he has gone to seed!" She chuckled when Jane groaned at her joke.

"But you do not go to town, so how will they know?" Jane said, holding the door open for her cousin to enter the cottage.

In the house all was neat and smelled faintly of lavender and carnations, a distinct contrast to the uproar and musty dust next door. Hyacinthe gave a look about her, then turned to Jane.

"We could forget about those nasty mummies and fling ourselves upon my brother in the city. Perhaps he will store them elsewhere if I beg him prettily. Otherwise, we will have to find another cottage at a rent you can afford . . . unless you will swallow that silly pride of yours and allow me to help you. Can you not see that *if* you will let me pay most of the rent, you could have one of those dratted new cottages? I am certain Sir Charles would wish you to be close by," Hyacinthe concluded, hoping this might be a persuasive finish to her argument.

Jane gave her cousin a distressed look, "I cannot diminish your inheritance in such a manner. You may have need of it." Then she confided, "I fear that Sir Charles is not as interested in me as you seem to think. He has never sought my company for any purpose other than casual conversation. I doubt the man knows how to flirt."

"Think what a blessing that will be, then," Hyacinthe crowed. "How many women would love to have a husband who did not persist in flirting with another?"

"Who said anything about a husband!" Jane cried, looking most alarmed.

"Well, any woman of sense being single and in need of a home must necessarily look about her to see if there is an unattached and eligible gentleman in the neighborhood. And Sir Charles is all of those, you must admit."

"True," Jane agreed. She paced about the room, wringing her hands as she went. "But I could never be forward or try to trap him, as I know some women do to catch a husband. That is why I failed in my Season . . . I could not flirt with that in mind."

"I know what you mean," Hyacinthe replied quietly. "I fled London for several reasons, one of which was that I could not see myself wed to any of those beaux who clustered about me."

"And the one who attracted you?" Jane said with a gleam in her gray eyes.

Hyacinthe turned away from her cousin to study something out of the window. Rather than answer this probing question, she looked at the Tudor house. Mr. Wayland could be seen wending his way—empty-handed—in the direction of the new village.

"Did you not say that Mrs. Peachey wished to consult with you about a particular design for a cap? Why do you not bring it over to her now?" Hyacinthe said softly.

"Of course," Jane said, her bewilderment at this complete change of topic quite clear in her voice.

"And I will do a bit of looking about the village, since my ankle is so improved," Hyacinthe said in the mildest of tones.

Jane gave her a sharp look, but said nothing regarding her cousin's overly innocent expression.

They left together. Hyacinthe tucked her cousin's arm in hers and chattered about the ducks and whether or not they would peaceably make the move to the new village. Jane concluded that it would take a bit of coaxing to bring them all, including the swans, to a new home.

Just when they drew even with the Tudor cottage, Hyacinthe paused. "Think about my offer—*do*. Unless you can bring Sir Charles up to scratch, you must decide upon some path for your future."

"I promise, although I meant what I said about your inheritance. But what a horrid expression, 'up to scratch.' You make him sound like a chicken." Jane made a face that quite expressed her feelings.

"Well?" Hyacinthe chuckled at Jane's grimace, then sobered. "I intend to do a bit of hunting about. Should Mrs. Peachey wonder, tell her I am investigating the old garden. She will never question that, I believe."

"Since when have you become enamored of old gardens—just in case she should ask?"

"Ever since I saw Mr. Wayland leave this house not long ago. He carried nothing in his hands, which I think rather curious. And just what was he doing here when Lord Norwood said that this house is not to be torn down?"

"Oh, do be careful," Jane whispered. She searched the area about them with a casual turn of her head, then set off toward Mrs. Peachey's cottage with a light step.

Hyacinthe clutched her shawl about her more tightly, then entered the tangled web of a garden with hesitant footsteps.

Someone had made an effort to clear away the worst of the weeds. The grass, such as it was after many years of neglect, had been scythed.

She wore a small, neat bonnet tied securely under her chin. Fortunately her gown was of plain stuff, not likely to suffer from dust and cobwebs. Although she devoutly hoped the spiders had not been busy since she was last here.

The rear door again stood slightly ajar. Hyacinthe slipped inside with practiced ease, then began her inspection of the interior.

Nothing in the kitchen area appeared to have been disturbed. The dust covered all surfaces in an even layer and no trace of footprints could be seen other than on the path that had been made by herself and Lord Norwood and Lord Latham when they searched. She must not forget that Mr. Wayland had also roamed the premises. Which were the prints he had left today? she wondered.

In the paneled parlor, she saw nothing untoward. Sadly shredded draperies hung at the windows but it mattered little as the panes of glass were so dingy that it was difficult to see anything anyway.

Hyacinthe grew thoughtful while slowly plodding up the stairs. If Wayland had left no trace of his visit on the lower floor, whatever he had been doing here must be found upstairs. She hurried on to the first of the rooms.

Considerably later and covered with a film of dust and cobwebs—the spiders seemed to have been busier than ever before—she entered the largest bedroom. The tattered bed hangings swayed in a draft of air.

Checking about her, she noted that one window was cracked open a trifle. She walked over to investigate the area, but found nothing. Then she turned to face the dressing room as she called it. She had not returned to it since that day of the momentous kiss.

Taking a deep breath, she walked across the room, then opened the door. Nothing appeared to have changed. She began a more minute inspection, going over panels, studying the floor. She thought Mr. Wayland had been in here, but it was difficult to tell. The little hiding place didn't have anything in it that had not been here before.

That did not mean that he could not have concealed his loot elsewhere, however. Hyacinthe felt a strong urge to find those jewels. She wondered if Lord Norwood suspected her of keeping them, giving him only the one piece. Naturally she would never do such a thing, but he didn't know that. He might have seen her around London, but that hardly constituted a knowledge of her character. She did not give him high marks for his powers of observation.

Except, she noted, he must pay attention to race horses to have won such enormous sums in betting on the races.

She listened a moment to the creaking of the house. A gentle wind tore at the trees that hovered over it, causing branches to brush against the roof and walls. No other sounds reached her ears. Had she perhaps hoped that someone would come? Certainly not Lord Norwood, she scolded herself.

Feeling frustrated at her inability to discover where Mr. Wayland had concealed his stolen goods, she walked to the window, wiping a small place on the pane with her sleeve. From here she glimpsed the village store. What on earth was going on over there? Then she realized that the shop owner must be in the process of removing to the new village. The new shop was barely ready to accept the goods transferred, yet away they went. Even as she watched, another load of goods was carried from the shop to be placed on the dray, which was ready to depart. The lad in charge of the transfer set off toward the new village, plodding along the track with care.

Jane would feel more isolated than ever. One of these weeks Mrs. Peachey and Widow Smith would go, and then Jane and Hyacinthe would be the last people left. At least Lord Norwood had promised to leave Jane's cottage until last. Although that wasn't of great help.

Drat it all, why could she not have persuaded Lord Norwood to abandon his stupid scheme? Giving up on her hunt— only for the day, mind you—she marched down the stairs and across the green until she was again inside Jane's modest home.

Fosdick was clearly horrified at her appearance. She tut-tutted and fussed over her charge like a mother hen. Hyacinthe submitted to a change of clothes after a rather thorough washing. Mostly her hands and face were in need of repair; the gown merely needed scrubbing in soapy water.

Once restored and garbed in a charming moss-green mull trimmed with clusters of ivory ribands and pale pink satin roses, she hurried from the house, Fosdick trailing her. At the Cock and Bull she found her coachman and groom. They chatted quietly while working on the coach leathers.

"How soon can we be ready to depart? I wish to go on an errand." She gave Tom Coachman an expectant look.

The men allowed as they could have the coach ready in a trice, which Hyacinthe interpreted as about thirty minutes at best.

Strolling away, she watched more of the contents of the shop being hauled to a dray.

"She ought to have offered a few things at a special price so she would not have had so much to move," Hyacinthe observed to her maid.

"Well," Fosdick said sagely, "as to that, she will need the same items at the new shop."

As soon as the coach was ready, Hyacinthe climbed inside with Fosdick following, and they set off along the road that led to the Hall.

"I do not approve of this gamboling about, young lady," the proper abigail said with a sniff.

"You do not have to approve, dear Fosdick. Just manage to attend me." Hyacinthe folded her hands meekly in her lap while she considered precisely what she would say to his lordship when she confronted him. It was far too late to stop the destruction of the village. What could she best hope to accomplish with this visit?

She firmly rejected the notion that she might wish to see the dratted man. While he was as handsome as could be, he was totally ineligible. What woman wanted a husband who preferred fertilizer and planting to her! That he might not always be absorbed with altering this view didn't occur to her.

Barmore hurried down the front steps to greet her, escorting her into the house with flattering promptness. Fosdick quietly trailed behind, once inside seeking a chair in the vast entry hall.

"I failed to send word that I wish to see Lord Norwood. Dare I hope that he is in this afternoon?" Hyacinthe asked with a demure smile.

"As a matter of fact, I believe he just finished his nuncheon. Allow me to inform him of your arrival, Miss Dancy." He paused, then added, "May I also hope that your injury is entirely healed?"

"Indeed, Barmore," Hyacinthe said, flashing the famous Dancy smile at the butler, "I feel quite the thing, I assure you. How kind of you to ask."

Looking gratified at this fulsome reply, the butler disappeared from the drawing room, leaving Hyacinthe to amuse herself until Lord Norwood should deign to appear.

She did not have long to wait. That peculiar sensation that had assailed her heart before startled her again when she turned from the window to see him enter the room.

"Miss Dancy," he said while crossing to join her. "To what do I owe this pleasure?"

"I fear my wits have gone begging, sir," she admitted, suddenly thinking she was a silly peagoose to come here. "It is far too late to halt the destruction of the village, much as I wish I could. Jane is terribly upset and that distresses me. I cannot persuade her to allow me to help her with the rent. Perhaps you would allow me to pay part of her rent? She has such impossible pride."

"Yet you admire her, for I can hear it in your voice." He thought for a minute, then offered his arm. "Come with me. I would have you look at my view again, for it is constantly changing."

Hyacinthe reluctantly permitted him to take her arm and usher her out to the terrace. The geraniums still bloomed in spite of the chill that now hung over the countryside at night. Their spice scented the air when she broke off a leaf to crush in her hand.

"Well, sir?" she said, not encouraging him in the least.

"The trees must grow some, but surely you can use a bit of

imagination to see how it will be in the future," he said with enthusiasm, pointing off toward the village.

Young saplings marched up the hillsides; a great deal of earth had been moved since she was last here, creating a different contour. And she was forced to admit that it truly looked lovely. What vision to be able to see that the change would be so charming.

"I believe I can envision some of what it will be," she allowed. "I shall miss the old village."

"The church steeple and the roof of that Tudor cottage you admire so greatly still stand," he reminded her.

"And lovely they are, too." Recalling what she had seen that morning, she turned to face Lord Norwood. "Have you discovered anything more regarding the missing jewels? The reason I ask is that I saw Mr. Wayland coming from the Tudor house shortly after Granny Beanbuck's old cottage was razed. He walked rapidly toward the new village, not stopping to check on the dismantling. He carried nothing in his hands, and since the house is not to be torn down, why was he there? I thought it most curious."

"I'll wager you went over to investigate."

Hyacinthe dropped her lashes in confusion at the gleam she observed creep into his eyes. Did he recall what had happened when they had been at the old cottage? Surely a rake such as he would likely forget a bit of dalliance. It was only a brief kiss, after all. But, her heart reminded her, it had affected her most strongly.

"I did," she managed to reply. "I found no evidence he had hidden something there. However, it would be logical if you think about it. He may believe we have thoroughly investigated the place, so feels safe to return his loot there."

"Interesting theory. I had best bring Val along and do some more investigation." He turned back to his new gardens. "But come with me for the moment. I wish to show you my new planting of roses. Come next June, they will perfume the air with their fragrance. I also discovered a new variety that blooms in July, so to extend their season."

"Perhaps one day we shall have roses that bloom until frost," she said, willingly going across the terrace and down the steps into an area neatly planted with a clever layout of rose bushes. There were a great many plants. The ground around them was covered with a mixture of straw and manure, judging from the smell. She wrinkled her nose in distaste, but said nothing. After all, this sort of smell one encountered every day while on the road or in town.

"And over here," he continued, while tugging her along with him, "I intend to have an Elizabethan knot garden. Val and I found some old plans in the muniment room with a list of plants and their arrangements. I think you might admire it very much."

Puzzled why he might care what she thought of his new gardens, Hyacinthe admitted that this particular one appealed to her. She said as much. "Perhaps it is the charm of the old cottage, but I like the idea of an old-fashioned garden. What a pity you could not restore the garden around the Tudor cottage. Did your ancestor also include plans for that, or did his plans extend only to the occupant?" Her smile was mischievous, but she was still relieved when he grinned back at her.

"Do you recall she is recorded as a pretty redhead?" His grin widened when he saw her discomfiture.

"Perhaps I ought to restore the place, then," she said. "I could take up residence with your permission and pity."

"I cannot see that you would need my pity, Miss Dancy," he teased. "I might be able to offer something else, however."

She turned away from him, feeling that the conversation had taken a perilous turn.

"The weather has improved and Val insists that tomorrow will be better. No rain, he declares. Could we plan our picnic?" He guided her along various paths which now held an occasional yellow chrysanthemum or purple China aster. A few other fall-blooming flowers were clustered in a bed near the steps.

She paused at the bottom of the steps to look about her. "That would be lovely, although I will confess that I doubt you could find views that might rival these gardens. *You* may have the distant perspective. *I* prefer the detail and scent around me."

"We shall see," he promised, then returned her to the entry hall where Fosdick awaited.

The abigail wore a disapproving frown and gave Lord Norwood a frosty glare.

On the way back to Jane's cottage, Hyacinthe considered her call to Lord Norwood. It had availed her nothing, but it had planted an idea in her head.

"Fosdick, do you think that the Tudor cottage is beyond hope?"

"Not in the least, miss. My mother lives in a house of an age with it and goes along right well." The maid gave her mistress a shrewd look, then added, "I fancy were it to receive a good cleaning it would improve considerably."

"Have you been there?"

"No, but I saw the gown you wore—nothing but dust and cobwebs on it. There must be several girls in the village who would like a bit of pocket money what with moving to a new house and all."

"Are you actually encouraging me to clean a house that does not belong to me?" Hyacinthe gave Fosdick a disbelieving look.

"Aye. What better way to draw rats from a hole?" the maid replied with an innocent air.

"Hm, I shall think about it," Hyacinthe murmured in return. She resolved to seek out all the willing hands she could find. The Widow Smith's girl would be the first to approach.

Across the gentle hills Val chided his host. "You mean you had the chit here and you did not let me know? I wondered why you disappeared so hastily after our meal, not to return for ages."

"You are ever the gallant with ladies. I was only protecting Miss Dancy from your charms." Blase gave his friend a teasing glance, then strolled along the hall in the direction of the muniment room.

"What? Are we to bury ourselves on such a perfect day?" Val cried in dismay.

"I wish to look over that box once again to see if perchance there could be a paper or two I missed the first time. I would like to know more of the history behind that Tudor cottage. By the by, Miss Dancy informed me that Wayland had been snooping around there this morning. She didn't see the chap arrive, but he left there conspicuously empty-handed."

"You think he may have returned to the scene of the crime, so to speak, to replace the jewels in what he considers a safe hiding place?" Val said, excitement coloring his voice, supplanting his usual air of ennui.

"It could be. Miss Dancy said something about cleaning up the garden, and I believe I'll see that it is done. Shame to have the place go to ruin."

"When it will remain empty? Why bother?"

Blase felt like a fool to reveal that he did so because Miss Dancy wished it done. Rather, he gruffly replied, "Sound management practice. I believe it would be possible to find someone who prefers the country to the village."

Val didn't refute his remark, but he gave his friend a very curious look. Blase ignored it.

They spent an hour or so in the muniment room, then took the papers Blase unearthed to the library. Here he relaxed in his favorite chair while studying them.

"Do they help?" Val inquired. He had established himself in a comfortable chair by the window where he could see the distant hills and still view the cozy fire burning in the grate.

"I found the floor plans of the cottage. It seems my esteemed ancestor had a clever passage built so he might slip down the hidden stairway in the event that someone was coming up the main steps."

"You mean in case his wife sent someone looking for him? I say, that seems unlikely."

"Why else would he put in such a thing?" Blase studied the plans, which included a scheme for a garden. The writing was faded and difficult to read. "Come over here to see if you can decipher this print. Time has not improved it."

They huddled over the old set of plans until between them they felt they had figured out the original.

Blase gave his friend a satisfied look. "I believe I should like to duplicate the original garden. It would be a curiosity."

"By all means. I think it would add to your picturesque view." Val said this with no change of expression to indicate he was other than his usual cynical self.

Equipped with dustcloth and broom in hand, Hyacinthe daringly marched over to the Tudor cottage. Behind her several of the village women straggled along similarly equipped. All were dressed for the purpose of attacking the dusty house.

Hyacinthe acted the general and deployed her troops most efficiently. In short order, the tattered draperies went out to the rubbish heap and the windows began to sparkle, pane by pane. Following the generous application of lemon-scented beeswax on the paneled walls and other surfaces, the spice of sweet-smelling rushes and herbs strewn across the freshly scoured floors, and fresh air sailing through the rooms, the house soon took on the appearance of a habitable cottage.

Hours later Hyacinthe looked about her with great pleasure. Jane had joined her at midpoint and added her efforts.

"I am a dab hand with polishing, if I do say so," she said with modest pride.

"Everyone has been marvelous," Hyacinthe said. She sought out her reticule and promptly paid each woman a generous amount for her work. Not only had they come when asked, they must have left their own work undone. Hyacinthe doubly appreciated that.

Once alone, she and Jane sank down on the bottom steps of the staircase, looking about with satisfaction.

"Did you realize it would be so lovely? Just look at that floor. The parquet pattern must be as beautiful as the day it was put down."

Hyacinthe glanced at Jane, then took a deep breath before imparting her information. "I mentioned the house to Lord Norwood and said it was a pity that it go to ruin. I also said we might move in here, since he does not plan to tear it down. It is larger than your cottage and certainly more attractive, what with the patterned windows and all the other little touches given it. It must have been built with love," she said softly.

"You do recall the story about it, that his lordship's ancestor housed his doxy here."

"Are there any ghosts?" Hyacinthe inquired idly.

"None I know about, but one never knows," Jane answered gloomily. "I shouldn't feel comfortable thinking that first redhead was lingering about here."

"We had best clean up, then have our supper. I, for one, am famished," Hyacinthe declared as she rose and walked to the rear door. There she paused, looking about the spotless kitchen with a tired smile. "What a shame that girl of long ago couldn't see this place now."

"It wants only furniture, I believe," Jane agreed. Then she gasped and blushed. "I forgot to tell you in all the general commotion. Sir Charles met me after I left Mrs. Peachey. He invited me for a little drive to the new village, then insisted he take us up to the picnic tomorrow. He believes the weather will be fine, but suggested I bring an umbrella anyway. Oh, Hyacinthe, he was so *caring*." Jane gave her cousin a pleased smile, then slipped past her and hurried toward her cottage.

Hyacinthe looked about her again, thinking of the fine wood, utterly worm-free, used for the bed upstairs. Well, she thought with a philosophical shrug of her shoulders, she could always move over here. If Jane married Sir Charles, she would be able to spare a few things. And Hyacinthe could purchase the rest in Woodstock. All she had to do was convince her garden rake that it would be a good idea.

Firmly closing the door behind her, she also considered the other reason she'd had the house cleaned. No sign of the jewels had turned up. Yet she felt they had to be here. Her instincts told her they were. Her instincts were never wrong. In which case, she reflected as she entered Jane's cottage, she had best prepare for a wedding between Sir Charles and Jane and hope that Lord Norwood would not object to a tenant in the Tudor cottage. He hadn't said no.

It was some hours later when she awoke for no reason at all. She remained perfectly still, listening. Nothing.

She slid from beneath her covers, grabbed her soft velvet robe, donning it while crossing to the window.

Across the way she could see small rays of light coming from the Tudor cottage! They wavered, most likely because of branches that were in the way. But there was no doubt in her mind; someone was in that house. *Her* house to be. The one she had cleaned up so she might move there.

She stuffed her feet into her morocco slippers and skimmed down the stairs as quietly as she could.

Without considering the impropriety of her actions, she slid back the bolt on the front door, than began to cross the green. A glance at the upstairs windows revealed the lights up there. Was it Wayland? She picked up a stout limb, just the right size for knocking a man over the head, and continued on her way.

12

"What do you make of all this?" Val said while looking about the spotless bedroom. A light aroma of beeswax and lavender scented the air. No dust motes or tattered draperies remained. The carved oak bed frame—what remained of the mattress had been consigned to the rubbish heap—glowed with the patina of age and diligent rubbing.

"A band of pixies has descended upon this place since we were last here," Blase replied with amusement. He scratched his head in bewilderment. "I wonder why? I vow the fussiest housekeeper could not find fault with the house. Who could possibly wish to turn this old place into a habitable cottage? What happened to the tales of ghosts or whatever prevented others from renting it over the years?"

"Do you suppose whoever cleaned this house also searched for the jewels?" Val strode to the dressing closet to fling open the door and peer inside. "Why did we think it necessary to come here at night?" he complained. He motioned for Blase to bring both lanterns into the room.

Blase followed, standing bemused when he surveyed the efforts of his particular pixie. Not only did the room shine with polish, the windows sparkle, and the floor gleam sufficiently for it to serve as a looking glass, but the folding screen had been joined by a pretty little pine chair and a small table—both equally well-polished.

Blase set one of the lanterns on the table, then began examining the paneled walls. "I have the feeling that whoever did this intends to move in here," he said over his shoulder. "Perhaps after the others have moved to the new village he will settle in here to set up housekeeping with no one the wiser."

He quite forgot he had tacitly given Hyacinthe Dancy permission to live here.

"You would see the fires in his chimney, however," Val reminded him.

"Perhaps. It could be that he is counting on my going off to a Christmas party elsewhere, then haring off to London following that." Blase turned to face his friend, a speculative look on his face. "You also think Wayland has something to do with this?"

"He would appear the logical one," Val agreed.

"Well, we will have to upset his plans. Let's comb every inch of this room, for we both sense the gems must be here. How fortunate I have the original plans and my pixie removed the dust. Now to find the concealed catch that leads to the secret stairs."

He showed the plan to Val again, and they set to work. The house was chilly, the work frustrating, but both men were most determined to succeed.

Hyacinthe stared at the cottage, watching the light move from room to room. With only starlight and a half moon to guide her, she had stumbled all the way across the green. The stout limb had helped her keep from falling. She hoped it would serve her as well when she hit the prowler over the head with it.

Taking a firm hold of the tree limb and her courage, she advanced upon the house, sneaking around to the rear and the door that opened to her touch. Although after today she would be able to enter through the front, for she had found the key and oiled the lock and hinges.

She glided across the kitchen floor, thankful she need not worry about bumping into furniture. With the floor plan well imprinted on her memory, she went mostly by touch and recollection. Once she found the stairs, she began a cautious assent, one step at a time.

Blase paused in his examination of the spot he felt most likely to have the secret catch. Raising his head, he listened, then shushed Val.

"I think I hear something."

"A pixie?" Val teased.

Blase tossed him an annoyed look, then tiptoed from the dressing closet out to the bedroom. With only the light that escaped from the closet, this room was dimly lit. He could see well enough, certainly sufficiently to see the intruder. Looking around, he could discover nothing to hand to use as a weapon. He crept up to the door, standing to one side, waiting.

Hyacinthe rounded the top of the stairs, hoping that the intruder had not heard that squeaky step. Why hadn't she oiled *that* dratted thing? With painstaking care she edged her way along the hall until she reached the main bedroom. Here she paused, listening. She heard nothing, but she could perceive a faint light coming from the small dressing closet. Her nerves tightened and her heart pounded faster. In moments she would face this man.

Raising her trusty stout limb over her head, she nudged the door open wider with one foot, then slowly entered the room. From the corner of her eye she sensed a figure to her side.

Spinning about, she crashed the limb down upon the hapless intruder's head with all her might—which admittedly wasn't great. The man staggered, then fell back against the wall, sliding down to rest on the floor with a satisfactory thump.

Then Hyacinthe realized who it was!

She sank to the floor in horror at what she had done. While it might be forward to be so bold, her concern outweighed any propriety. She drew his head upon her lap and bent over him. Stretching out a hesitant hand, she gently probed Lord Norwood's head, seeking a wound. "Oh, I am dreadfully sorry, my lord," she said softly, wondering if he would be all right.

"Blase! What the . . . ?" Val dashed around the corner with a lantern in hand, then abruptly halted before succumbing to laughter.

Blase gazed up at his nemesis with a resigned look, then winced as her hand touched the injury to his head. The only tolerable part of this all was being cuddled in her lap.

"I believe your pixie has returned to the scene," Val said, trying to control his chuckles.

"Miss Dancy, may I ask what brings you here in the middle of the night?" Blase said with what he thought was praiseworthy restraint. He nudged the tree limb away with his foot, waiting for her reply and reluctant to move.

"I saw lights. Since this house is unoccupied, I grew worried. It would never do for some vagrant to set fire to a perfectly habitable cottage when I had just finished having it cleaned." She drew herself up, a righteous tilt to her chin and an indignant fire gleaming in her eyes. Had she not presented an amusing picture in her lace-edged nightcap and green velvet robe, she would have passed for a dragon.

Blase unwillingly rose to his feet, opened one of the windows to toss out the branch, then turned to face her again. "Why did you clean the house? Not that it doesn't look splendid, but it *is* unoccupied, as you just pointed out."

She clasped her hands together and stared down at the floor. "I thought it a shame that this house should be neglected. Jane suggested that the local women would welcome a bit of money—what with moving into new houses and all—so I hired as many as I could to help. And besides . . . you said I might live here." She gave him an accusing glare.

"I see." Blase glanced at Val, then winced, for his head hurt like the very devil when he moved.

"So you had a sort of protective interest in the house?" he said mildly. "And when you saw a light over here you felt it necessary to investigate—even if it was the middle of the night?"

"Indeed," she replied eagerly. "The very thing. How clever of you to guess." Then she appeared to recall her improper dress and began to back toward the open door.

"You are to leave us now? Just when we are about to open the secret panel?" He had no idea what possessed him to reveal their intent. Why would he want this exasperating and dangerous female around?

She stopped her retreat. "Secret panel? There is a concealed passage in this house? How exciting!" She took several steps toward him. "May I see? Then I promise I shall vanish from sight."

"I told you she was a pixie," Val muttered.

Blase gave him a look that quite silenced him. Motioning them to follow, Blase returned to the other room, dutifully trailed by Val and Miss Dancy.

She quickly espied the plans and eagerly scanned the layout before joining him where he had been puzzling over the secret entry.

Running a delicate hand over the wood, she paused at a knot—or what appeared to be a knot. "How odd," she murmured. With a twist of her hand, she pressed her thumb against the knot and the panel slowly creaked open.

A rush of stale, dust-laden air greeted them. Cobwebs draped the walls and ceiling of the staircase, festooning it with ghostly shadows when the lantern was brought to play on it.

"I say," Val murmured.

"Quite," Blase replied.

"Well," Miss Dancy said in a bracing voice, "do you intend to stand there all night? I would like to know where this goes." With that observation she took one of the lanterns and began to march—most carefully, mind you—down the steps.

Blase grabbed the other lantern and with Val directly behind him hurriedly followed the intrepid Miss Dancy.

The steps made a sharp turn, then continued until they reached the bottom and a door. Miss Dancy depressed a dull brass lever and the door swung open, squeaking its protest at being disturbed after all these years.

Miss Dancy stepped forward and looked around her. Blase followed. Val paused on the threshold, assessing what they all saw.

"The rubbish heap!" Miss Dancy exclaimed.

"I see where the old mattress went," Blase observed.

"And the mice that had made it their home. This house needs a cat," she snapped.

"I'll be happy to volunteer Tom," he offered in what he considered a magnanimous gesture.

"That will not be necessary," she whispered back as though suddenly mindful that voices could carry in this little village in the silence of the night. "Granny Beanbuck has a spare cat she will be pleased to offer. A sister to Tom if I make no mistake."

Blase stepped forward, although he didn't know quite what

he could say to her. He was furious, intrigued, ached like the devil, and wondered what she was *really* up to. To top it off, he felt a nearly uncontrollable urge to gather the delicious Miss Dancy into his arms and kiss her until she was as senseless as she had intended him to be after that knock on the head.

"Good night," she said softly. "I am truly sorry about your head. Is the picnic still to be?"

"What? Of course," he muttered, trying to gather his wits about him.

Feeling oddly dejected, Hyacinthe hurried off into the darkness, stumbling here and there. She had not taken a lantern and now wished she had. But someone might have seen her and that would never do, gossip being what it was.

She hurriedly slipped back into Jane's cottage, drew the bolt into place, then walked up the stairs as quietly as a mouse.

From her window she glimpsed the light from the lanterns as it flickered about the yard. Then it disappeared into the house and she guessed that the two men had returned to the upper floor. In minutes the light glimmered from the bedroom and she knew she'd been right.

She waited, watching. After a bit the light disappeared. Figuring that they must have gone back to the Hall, Hyacinthe made her way to her bed, curling up under the covers with a great deal on her mind.

She drifted off to sleep while trying to figure out how to persuade Lord Norwood that she would be the ideal tenant for the Tudor house even after bashing him in the head with a stout limb.

In the morning Blase met his guest at the breakfast table with a yawn and a wince.

"Head still hurt?" Val inquired, placing his coffee cup down on its saucer with a clink.

Blase gingerly rubbed the offending part of his head. "You might say that. For such a slip of a girl, Miss Dancy is most capable."

"I wonder if that is part of the curriculum at Miss Twickenden's School for Young Ladies of the Gentry, or wherever Miss Dancy went," Val mused. "It could be that we have touched upon a secret training—that of preparing girls to defend themselves against all comers."

"I rather believe it's instinctive—at least with her." Blase filled a plate with food, then joined his friend at the table.

"She is a walking disaster, isn't she?" Val commented while selecting another slice of cold, dry toast. "I do not know why your cook cannot bake rolls like Granny Beanbuck's. Would Cook's feelings be irreparably damaged if we sent off for some? They were very good," he concluded wistfully.

"Send for some if you like. Doubtless the groom would be more than willing to fetch them—especially if he could sample one or two."

"I shall remember that for the morrow," Val said. "So . . . weather permitting, you are to picnic today while I search her cottage. Are you prepared? With Miss Dancy along you had best wear something old and ready for the rubbish heap. And certainly ascertain that you have a supply of liniment and bandages about the house before we leave."

"I do not know why I tolerate that young woman," Blase grumbled between bites of egg.

"Usually one does that sort of thing when one is more than fond of said young woman," Val said obliquely.

Blase gave Val a sharp look but offered nothing in rebuttal. Indeed, words failed him. How *did* he view the delicious Miss Dancy? What a fetching little thing she had been last night in that lace-trimmed muslin cap and soft velvet robe. Those lovely eyes had flashed green fire at him, and she had snuggled him against her in a delightful manner.

"I wonder what she's up to," he murmured.

"Wants something, you may be certain," Val said dryly. "They all do. There isn't a female alive who does not wish for more than she has."

"Ah," Blase countered, well acquainted with Val's jaundiced view of the female portion of the population, "but what does she wish?"

"I'll wager she will let you know soon enough." Val finished his coffee, then pushed his chair away from the table.

"You don't suppose . . ." Blase said slowly. "No, it could never be that. It would be highly improper."

"What? Do tell," Val urged. He propped himself against the wall by the window, tilting his head while awaiting Blase's reply.

"With Miss Pennington smelling April and May around Sir Charles, do you suppose Miss Dancy actually intends to live there? I could not credit what she said last night. She had mentioned something about not liking to live with her brother or her grandmother. She previously lived with her aunt. I read that *she* recently married and is off traveling with her new husband, the Earl of Crompton. It would seem that Miss Dancy has no home to call her own." He exchanged looks with Val.

"And she would rather live in a haunted old Tudor cottage than rent one of your new houses," Val concluded with a nod.

Blase also rose from the table, crossing to the window to join his friend. "I shall take great interest in her request. For I believe you are correct—she has something up her sleeve besides her arm."

Hyacinthe splashed some of her precious carnation scent on her bosom and neck, then dabbed a bit on her wrists. It would never do for a lady to reek of scent, but she did adore the perfume.

"Are you nearly ready, love?" Jane asked from the doorway. She looked charming in a soft golden-yellow wool gown trimmed with gray rosettes. Her brown hair peeped from beneath her chip bonnet decorated with tiny yellow roses and knots of gray riband.

Accepting her coquelicot Poland mantle from Fosdick, Hyacinthe wrapped it over a matching gown, a particular favorite of hers. Fastening the mantle at her shoulder with an antique brooch, she turned to face her cousin. "Well? Will I do?" She touched the brim of her most cherished bonnet, one trimmed with bunches of red cherries.

"Fetching," Jane declared with admiration. "That shade of poppy red is most becoming on you, in spite of your red hair. Hurry, Sir Charles is to come at any moment."

"And you do not wish to keep him waiting?" Hyacinthe

chuckled, then followed Jane downstairs after thanking Fosdick for her excellent efforts and wishing her a lovely day in town.

Sir Charles drew up before the cottage promptly, his smile of greeting flattering Jane.

Hyacinthe took a good look at the pair and decided she would not have to worry about Jane. Rather, she had best find a place for herself.

It was not time for her to depart as yet, however. Jane would need bolstering until the wedding, for wedding there would be even if those two were not aware of it yet.

The picnic was to be held not far from the home farm of Lord Norwood's estate, in a pleasant glade through which flowed the same stream that made up the village pond.

When they arrived at the scene Hyacinthe found herself hard put not to smile at her cousin and Sir Charles. They had said little but exchanged discreet smiles and looks all the way.

With a sigh, Hyacinthe turned to greet Lord Norwood, then looked about for his friend.

"Val detests things like picnics. He decided to remain at the Hall. I suspect he may go riding later. Something to do with Granny Beanbuck's cinnamon buns, I believe."

"Jane brought some with us, for she had noticed he seemed very fond of them. What a pity."

"I doubt they will remain uneaten." Leading her along the stream, he softly inquired, "You slept well last night after all the excitement?"

"Once I saw the light had gone, I popped into bed and slept like a top until morning. And you? Your poor head. It must ache something fierce this morning. May I repeat how sorry I am?"

"Oddly enough, I believe you."

That exchange appeared to permit both of them to relax. Hyacinthe enjoyed his company for once. He seemed to take pleasure in hers as well.

The repast that the cook at the Hall had prepared was likely enough to feed a small army, but Hyacinthe and Lord Norwood attempted to do justice to it.

Jane and Sir Charles appeared lost to most everything. At

last he murmured some nonsense about showing her the late-blooming flowers he had observed along the stream, and the two strolled off in that direction.

"Smelling April and May," Lord Norwood said quietly.

"Do you think he will offer for her?" Hyacinthe dared to ask.

"Shouldn't surprise me in the least. The man needs a wife to help him on his estate. Fortunate he inherited instead of his elder brother. That character was a fool of the worst sort. He was killed while traveling, which enabled a good man to receive what he ought."

"With those acres restored and the manor house once again in his possession he will have a proper farm?" Hyacinthe inquired, figuring someone ought to ask on behalf of Jane.

"Indeed." Lord Norwood looked amused. "Sir Charles came over this past week to settle the matter. The house has returned to his family, where it should have been these many years."

"Gaming can bring terrible losses. Yet you do well at the racetrack, or so I have heard. Has no one ever wondered at your amazing luck?" she had the temerity to ask.

"If they have, it has not reached my ears. I may be a rake, Miss Dancy, but I have the reputation for being an honest rake." He gave her a look that made her wish to disappear.

Hyacinthe could feel her cheeks turn pink. Embarrassed, she sought for something to say in reply and couldn't think of a thing except to apologize. "I did not mean to cast aspersions, sir."

"I expect you did not. People are naturally curious. And I confess I have an uncanny bit of luck at the racetrack. I avoid cards, however, for my luck does not extend to them."

"How interesting," she said politely, knowing she ought not inquire further. "Do you suppose we might also take a stroll? That chicken was delicious, but I think I ate more than my share."

"Ah, yes. With Miss Pennington and Sir Charles scarcely touching their food, someone had to eat," he said approvingly. He rose to his feet, then extended a hand to assist her.

The scenery proved exceedingly lovely. Golds and yellows splashed the trees with autumn color. An occasional patch of russet peeped through the remaining greens and browns on the hillsides. The stream flowed quietly over pebbles and past the rushes, in no particular hurry to reach its goal. Hyacinthe felt the same.

She was glad they had chosen to walk in the opposite direction from the others. She'd not wish to interrupt something promising.

"You look well in that color, most surprisingly," he suddenly offered.

"I know, it is curious given my red hair. I believe I explained before how I feel regarding the color. What is that up ahead? A garden in the country?"

"Wildflowers, I expect. They seem to do remarkably well along here."

"But they look like a garden! Oh, do say I may have a little bouquet. Not all of them, for I'd leave seed, but a few, please?" She clasped her hands together, thinking the array of autumn flowers quite lovely. They were on the other side of a fence, but it did not look to be a formidable obstacle.

"When asked so prettily, how could I possibly refuse?" he said as gallantly as anyone might wish.

"Mind the fence," she felt obliged to caution.

"Hang the fence, it's the bull on the far side of the pasture that I'd best steer clear of," he replied with a laugh.

She could see no sign of the animal and said so. "Perhaps your man has moved it to another pasture for the day?"

"We can but hope so. Val would say I am tempting fate," Lord Norwood muttered as he vaulted over the fence to advance upon the mass of wildflowers.

He bent to gather an armful of wild angelica, woodbine, wild asters, white campion, harebells, and clustered bellflowers with a bit of greenery for contrast.

Hyacinthe was absorbed in finding a piece of moss so she might keep the flowers damp until she reached the cottage. When she looked up after locating a particularly nice clump, she froze in horror.

"Blase," she whispered, so forgetting herself as to use his first name, "that bull you mentioned before? The one you wished to avoid? I fear he is advancing on you. *Now*. What can I do?"

Lord Norwood slowly straightened, then turned to see a nasty-looking bull approaching him from over the hill. It seemed evident that the fellow did not like having his territory invaded. Not in the least.

"I've heard tell that the chaps in the Spanish bullrings wave red capes at them," he murmured.

Hyacinthe had already dropped the moss. Now she swiftly undid the brooch at her shoulder, dropped it into her reticule, and slid the Poland mantle down until it hung limply to the ground.

"He is coming nearer," she cautioned, edging closer to the fence. She placed a foot on the first rung of the fence, thankful that it was neither a stone barrier nor a hedge. "Can you take my mantle?"

He turned again to cross to her side. It proved a mistake. The bull charged at him, covering the ground at a frightening speed. Poor Lord Norwood didn't have a chance, really. He was picked up and tossed aside like a limp rag. He fell to the ground with a ghastly thump. With a sideways glance she could see his body . . . exceedingly still.

She swung herself over the fence, forgetting any care for propriety or her clothing. Taking the bright coquelicot mantle in the hope that the color would deflect the bull from its target, she waved it about, slashing the air with red.

"Can you edge away from that nasty animal?" she cried. No reply was forthcoming.

The bull paused in his attack on the intruder, then inspected the bright cloth being waved at it with curious eyes. Hyacinthe daringly advanced, attempting to come between Lord Norwood and the animal. She continued to wave the mantle about, her fears for her dear Blase's safety foremost in her mind. It didn't occur to her that she was placing her own life in great danger.

Behind her she could hear what sounded like someone slowly making his way through the long grasses and flowers. A few soft groans reached her ears, making her more determined than ever to keep the bull at bay until Blase could reach the other side of the fence.

"Hyacinthe!" Jane cried in dismay.

"Be quiet, woman," Blase said, sounding clearly in pain. "Unless you wish to see your cousin trampled to death."

There was a pause, then Hyacinthe heard him say, "Keep waving the mantle, but begin backing up. There is nothing in your way," he instructed in a gruff, pained voice.

She could hear how difficult it was for him to speak. Following his directions, she sidled across the pasture until she reached the fence. Before she could think of how she was to negotiate that, what with the bull still advancing on her and not being able to turn her back on it, she was snatched from behind. Over the fence she sailed, landing on her feet with a thump.

At first she thought Sir Charles had pulled her to safety. When she saw him standing by Jane, she turned to look at Blase, and was utterly horrified by what she saw. He leaned against the fence, his blue coat sadly torn, grass stains on his fine gray pantaloons, and his face covered with stains and dirt. When he moved toward her, he limped slightly.

Without consideration as to how her words or actions might appear to the others, she said, "Thank God, you are all right. I would never forgive myself if anything serious had happened to you." She gently brushed off his face with her mantle. "You poor man. Was ever a person so beleaguered as you?" she murmured. "Another coat, and those poor pantaloons are quite ruined, I fear. First your head, and now your leg. You will wish me to Jericho."

"Hyacinthe!" Jane blurted out, "you did not do this on purpose, did you?"

Hyacinthe stopped what she was doing. She could see the doubt creep into Blase's eyes. "Of course not," she stoutly denied. But the doubt had been planted. Blast Jane, anyway. Why did she have to say something so utterly dreadful?

How could Hyacinthe convince Blase that she couldn't hurt him, not intentionally, not anymore? Not since she had realized that she loved the dratted man. Her garden rake.

"It was an accident," Lord Norwood said evenly.

"He went in there to pick me some wildflowers. The bull was nowhere in sight at the time," Hyacinthe cried. She darted looks at Jane and Lord Norwood. "I truly did not wish him harm. Truly!" Tears of frustration and reaction stung her eyes and she turned aside to fumble in her reticule for a handkerchief.

A somewhat crumpled and partially soiled scrap of linen was thrust into her hands by the man at her side.

She mopped her eyes, then gave Jane a defiant stare. "I may have harbored a few unkind thoughts about Lord Norwood in the past. But, dear cousin of mine, I'd do nothing to willfully hurt him. Not *ever*." She turned away to take Lord Norwood's arm with the intention of assisting him to where the carriage had last been seen.

"Val will never let me hear the end of this, you know," Lord Norwood said with a wince when he stumbled on a rock.

"I shall try to explain. You must have a doctor examine you carefully," she insisted, guiding him away from a rut.

They reached his carriage and with a stricken face she watched his painful climb into it. He leaned forward slightly to stare at her a moment.

"Tell me, Miss Dancy, what is it that you would wish above all . . . in regard to the Tudor cottage, that is?"

"Why," she said, looking at him with wide eyes. "I should like to live there. You said I might," she reminded him.

"I was afraid of that," he muttered. "I'm not certain I'd survive it, my dear."

Hyacinthe stood very still in the center of the road when his carriage drove off toward the Hall. He detested her. He must. She wondered how she could endure without him.

13

The reaction of his staff at the Hall was about what he might have expected, given the sad state of his appearance.

Val merely took one look at his torn coat, grass-stained pantaloons, and battered person . . . and laughed. "At least you did not wear your best remaining coat," he said after his amusement had abated.

"You might at least express a bit of sympathy, old chap," Blase complained to his friend while they walked up the stairs to the master bedroom after Blase had ordered hot water to be brought up.

"I told you she was a dangerous woman," Val countered. "You are dotted with scrapes and bruises from head down as far as I can see." They walked down the hall until reaching Blase's room, then entered. Val strolled to the windows, where he found a seat with a view of the hills.

Smithson must have anticipated a calamitous end to the outing, for he had a tub awaiting the hot water, towels set out, and clean clothes spread on the bed. In short order the water arrived, even before Blase had stripped off his shirt and the ruined pantaloons.

Blase gingerly eased himself from the remaining pieces of clothing, then sank into the tub of hot water behind the screen and in front of a glowing fire. "You don't know the whole of it," he replied in response to the charge against Hyacinthe. "Do you know that when that bull tossed me toward the sky Miss Dancy whipped off her mantle, clambered over the fence, and deflected the perverse animal from a second stab at my carcass? Just before he charged I had muttered something about the bullfighters in Spain using red capes. She may never have seen such a display, but she certainly saved my hide by waving her mantle about beneath his nose. I was able to crawl to the fence, slither under it, and reach safety. She was remarkably brave."

"Champion," Val murmured, quite subdued by this revelation. "She endangered her life to protect you? Amazing. Sounds like a regular Boadicea."

"And she did not ask for anything while on the picnic, either." Blase sighed with pleasure while he soaked in the hot water, then began to soap his face and arms to remove the mud that smeared them.

However, he refrained from mentioning the doubts that Jane Pennington had raised with her accusation. Could Hyacinthe Dancy hate him so much that she might wish him dead? Preposterous. Why would she have dashed to his rescue if that were the case? Still, she might think he would be sufficiently discouraged to abandon his plans.

That was a piece of nonsense if ever he heard any. Even were he so inclined, things had progressed too far to be altered at this late date. No, he did not want to accept the idea that she harbored malicious intent toward him. Regardless, he would do well to be on his guard when near her.

The memory of her close to him, his arms about her when he pulled her to safety, returned. Combined with that promising kiss in the cottage and her gentle, remorseful caress (true, that was after hitting him over the head), it created a tantalizing recollection—one that was hard to dismiss. He wanted Miss Dancy, but dare he pursue her? It could be a hazardous course! She certainly did not encourage a fellow, what with her concerted efforts to half kill him.

"You have not asked what I found," Val said quietly some minutes later.

"Well, *did* you find something of interest?"

"Nothing," Val admitted. "I approached from the rear, and since there are a number of workmen tearing down another cottage in the area, I doubt if I was noticed. They don't bother to lock the back door, foolish women. Wonder there was a thing in the house."

"But?" Blase urged, relieved to hear Miss Dancy proven innocent.

"The remarkably neat Miss Dancy has an impressive lot of jewels, a nice collection of gowns and whatnot, and everything else you expect to find in a woman's room, but no emeralds of any kind, antique or otherwise, stashed in the bottom on her portmanteau and other luggage. Odd, that. You would think that some man would have given her stones to match her eyes ages ago." Val tilted his chair back to rest against the window surround while he apparently considered Miss Dancy's eyes and lack of emeralds.

"She isn't that old, my good fellow, not too long out of the schoolroom," Blase said, oddly pleased that Miss Dancy did not possess signs of gifts from gentlemen—not that any proper miss could or would accept such things. But Miss Dancy was not the ordinary run-of-the-mill woman. She appeared to have her own set of rules to live by.

"So what do we do next?" Val said with a sigh. "Oh, I just remembered, your curate chanced by just as I was leaving the old village, full of messages for you. Had I known of your injury, I'd not have suggested he present them to you in person."

"I will be a little sore, nothing more than that. No broken bones, thanks to Miss Dancy." He allowed Smithson to spread soothing ointment on his scrapes after reluctantly leaving his bath, then pulled on his clothes hurriedly.

"Correct me if I'm wrong, but wasn't she the reason you landed in this pickle in the first place? She has been behind every disaster that has occurred so far."

Blase refused to discuss it further. Picking a bunch of wildflowers seemed innocent to him, but Val could read catastrophe into anything a woman did. The two men went down to the drawing room where the good curate awaited them, having decided to promptly do as suggested.

"Oh, I say, Lord Norwood, you look to have had a bit of an accident," Ambrose Clark declared in dismay.

"Nothing, nothing," Blase muttered with a look directed at Val daring him to say otherwise. "What is it you wish to discuss?"

"Well, it is this, my lord: I do believe we ought to bring as much as possible from the old church—associations, you know. The cross, the font, pulpit, the screen as well, all ought to fit in the new building. I should think the bells might be re-hung as well. Certainly the new organ should be moved," he finished, looking at Blase with hope in his eyes.

With a glance at Val, Blase sought to reassure the curate that the organ would be transported as soon as possible along with the other items, and that he would also try to see that the good man received an elevation, since the vicar assigned to this church hadn't been seen in these parts in an age.

Across the hills from the favorable meeting between lord and curate, Hyacinthe stormed about the little parlor in hurt frustration.

"I cannot think how you could say such a thing," she accused her cousin for the third time. "Surely you know me better than that, to even *think* for a moment that I might wish him dead—for he could have been killed had that bull not been lured away from him."

Dismayed by the outburst, Jane tried to soothe her cousin as best she might. "I confess I was a trifle upset, as it appeared Sir Charles was about to propose to me, and your cries stopped that. Perhaps I am merely dreaming, to believe he has an interest in me," she concluded with a sad face. She accepted her cousin's regrets, then left the room to prepare a tray of tea and biscuits.

Hyacinthe sank down upon the chair close to the window, staring out with unseeing eyes. Now that she considered what she had done, she felt all trembly. Nerves, she decided. After all, she didn't challenge a bull every day.

There was, however, another matter to consider—her discovery. She had most unfortunately fallen in love with the very man she opposed. Why, she detested him. He would force all these villagers from their old homes, then raise the rents on the new ones—just to improve his view. That was reprehensible. Dreadful.

She wished it might be otherwise. But, she reminded herself, he had ignored her all the while in London, flirting with every other woman in sight. He was exceedingly good at charming the ladies. He certainly charmed her without half trying.

"Miss," Fosdick said from the doorway, "I believe someone has been in the house while we were gone."

Hyacinthe snapped from her considerations to stare at her abigail. "You cannot be serious."

"Your belongings have been shifted about; nothing is in quite the same place as it was," the maid asserted.

From the doorway Jane gasped at this revelation. "Nothing like this ever happened before all this tearing down began," she said. "It must be one of the strangers."

"Have you seen evidence that anyone forced entry?" Hyacinthe asked, ever practical.

"Why would they need to? The back door was left unlocked," Fosdick said with a disapproving look at Jane.

"I never did need to lock up before," Jane said in her own defense.

"Was anything taken?" Hyacinthe asked while she hurried across the room out to the bottom of the stairs.

"Not a thing, which is most curious, if you get my meaning," the maid replied in a voice laden with import.

Hyacinthe paused, slowly turning about to face Fosdick. "That is *most* curious, indeed. Why bother to enter a house, go through belongings, then take nothing? Not even my jewelry?" she added in disbelief.

"Nothing," the abigail confirmed.

"Why?" Hyacinthe sank down on the bottom step, contemplating the matter.

"Well, if you were to ask me," Fosdick continued, "a person might search for a particular item, and if he did not find it, leave without taking anything else."

With a gasp, Hyacinthe jumped to her feet, then dashed up the stairs, taking care not to bump her head on the low part at the top. Her room seemed as always, neat and orderly. Fosdick had followed and now watched.

"Everything has been shifted about," her maid said, pointing out a few.

"Mr. Wayland would have an excuse to be in this area. He comes over here quite often to see how the men do. Maybe

Lord Norwood found the jewels, has taken them away, and Mr. Wayland believes *I* have them."

"Excuse me," Fosdick inserted, "but Lord Latham did not join you on the picnic today. Remember, I was nowhere near here; Tom Coachman took me in for a bit of shopping."

"Surely you do not think Lord Norwood would send him to spy on me?" Hyacinthe cried, hurt at the very notion that the man she loved would further distress her. "That would be utterly horrid!"

The abigail failed to respond. Hyacinthe returned to the parlor to relate what she had seen and discussed.

Jane ventured a strained smile and suggested they consider the problem over a cup of tea.

Later, while strolling about the village—ostensibly to relax her nerves and enjoy a bit of air—Hyacinthe mulled over the mystery. Someone had entered her room—for nothing else in the house had been disturbed—but had taken not a thing. It bothered her to think that either Mr. Wayland or Lord Latham would go through her possessions. Obviously someone believed she had the antique jewels.

But that puzzle aside, she must face her real dilemma. Lord Norwood. She had seen the look of doubt in his eyes when Jane accused her of deliberately luring him to the field. While she had admittedly pushed him into the pond, and assuredly permitted her hat to sail into the pig sty, she hadn't intended him to fall when he rescued the kite. And she certainly had never intended his life to be imperiled while venturing to gather a few wildflowers.

Yet would he believe that? Would he suspect her of wanting him dead? No! her heart cried. Not the man she had come to care for—even if it was against her will. But there were good reasons for him not to have complete faith in her.

She knelt down to examine a duck that nestled along the bank of the pond. "You do not think I could be so heartless, do you?"

The duck rose, shook itself, then waded into the pond and swam off.

"So much for evidence of innocence."

"Miss Dancy, are you all right?"

Hyacinthe jumped to her feet, startled by the high, thin voice of the angular architect. "Mr. Wayland, you quite surprised me. Have you been in the village long?"

"No, I had to supervise some work on the church," he replied in an important manner.

"I see." Which meant that Lord Norwood's friend had come around to snoop in her things if Wayland could prove he was elsewhere. The knowledge pained her, for it doubtless meant that Lord Norwood had planned the picnic with that very thing in mind. It hadn't turned out the way he planned. Nothing had been found in her room, and he had ended up somewhat battered and bruised.

Mr. Wayland glanced at the Tudor house, then sidled up to her. "Have you observed people around that house?" He gestured in that direction with a nod of his head.

"Why, I hired the village women to clean and polish it. I intend to move into that house, for it is most charming and I do not mind being in the country. I daresay I can persuade a distant cousin of mine to join me here to maintain propriety if Jane requires an extra person." She dare not hint that Jane would wed Sir Charles, for the poor man had not mustered up his courage to propose.

Dudley Wayland paled at her words. Hyacinthe considered it an odd reaction to her innocuous proposition.

"Why, surely you would not wish to live so far from others," he said, his manner most agitated.

"I like a serene life," she said, quite forgetting that her life had been anything *but* that since coming here.

He muttered a few more sentiments along the same lines, then marched off in the direction of the new village with a few backward glances that seemed rather ominous.

"He most definitely does not wish me to move into the Tudor cottage. I believe I shall consult with Lord Norwood's bailiff regarding the rental of it. Surely he cannot resist the notion of an income from property that would just decay otherwise." With a somewhat calculating look in her eyes, she retraced her steps to Jane's cottage. "I can tell him that Lord Norwood agreed."

Once in her room, she again paused to look out of her window across the hills in the direction of the Hall. With all that had happened he must surely detest her. Never mind that she had detested him for ages. All had changed. The shoe was on the other foot, so to speak.

"Fosdick, I intend to rent the Tudor cottage. There is something quite havey-cavey going on over there. What better way to find out than to be on the premises?" She pulled on a gray pelisse over her coquelicot gown. Best to be inconspicuous in what she did.

The maid assisted her efforts, then stood by the door before Hyacinthe made her way down the stairs. "You are no doubt walking into danger, renting that place. However, I won't leave you, rest assured of that."

Hyacinthe gave her a grateful smile, then hurried from the house in search of the bailiff.

She found him not far away in the old village. He was looking over the remains of several cottages that had been torn down.

Hyacinthe might love Blase Montague, but she thought him mad to attempt so silly and expensive a scheme. Nevertheless she wished to make atonement for all she had done to the poor man, even if she had undoubtedly ruined any chance she might have had in charming him. And she must rent the Tudor cottage to do so. She felt it in her bones.

"Sir? I have something to discuss with you." Since the man rarely chatted with the guests in the village, he was clearly startled at her request.

Sometime later, and much pleased with her success, Hyacinthe returned to Jane's cottage waving a written agreement in the air when she entered the parlor.

"We may move into the cottage across the way anytime we please," she declared to an astounded Jane. Behind her, Fosdick nodded as though she had quite expected this.

"I shall hire some of the workers to carry your belongings over there if you will agree to the scheme, and Tom Coachman and my groom will help as well. We shall be settled in a trice! In fact, perhaps I ought to buy your furniture, for I feel certain that Sir Charles will come up to scratch one of these days."

Jane looked unconvinced, but a hit of pink crept into her cheeks as she considered her cousin's words. "I suspect you pay more than your share," she scolded gently. "We will settle that matter later."

"I shall begin to pack," Fosdick declared, then disappeared up the stairs.

"I wonder if Sir Charles will think me comfortably settled if we transfer my things over there," Jane said with a worried frown sometime later. "Do remember that his concern was for my homeless state."

Hyacinthe shook her head. "I truly doubt that is the case now. I believe he is quite smitten. You might mention that I intend to invite a distant cousin of mine to move in here with us. Then he will have no qualms about asking you to marry him. Nor will he fear that I shall come along with you." Hyacinthe knew full well that often a single lady would be invited to live with relatives. It placed a strain on all, particularly in the early days of a marriage. She did not intend to create more problems.

With the abundance of workers available in the village, it did not take long for her coachman, groom, and several strapping men to remove the belongings from Jane's cottage over to the Tudor place.

Mrs. Peachey and the Widow Smith bustled across the green to find out what was happening.

"I declare, such goings on!" Mrs. Peachey exclaimed while keeping a careful eye on the furniture passing beneath her nose. Since none of the ladies had ever inspected the bedroom pieces, it proved illuminating. Jane had acquired several lovely articles of furniture, mostly from the attics of her relatives. All were lovingly polished and in excellent repair.

The kitchen table was the last to be carted over and Hyacinthe stood in the road watching as it disappeared around to the rear of the house. She turned as she heard hoofbeats approaching. Certain the bailiff was returning to take a month's rent from her, she was dismayed to see Lord Norwood, with Lord Latham right behind him, bearing down on her. And here she stood with a dust cap on her head and most likely a smudge on her nose.

"Miss Dancy, what is afoot?" He glanced about with curiosity, obviously noting the men who straggled away from the Tudor cottage back to where they had been working.

"Then you do not know?" she said in confusion. Why else would he come here—unless it was to tell her to get off his property forever.

"You are all right? In my desire to reach the Hall, I neglected to see if you had been harmed when I hauled you over that fence. Your gown?" He glanced at the simple green sprig muslin she now wore.

"A few minor tears, nothing serious," she said, unless, she thought, you considered the damage to her heart.

Jane and Fosdick left the old cottage where Hyacinthe had first come. Jane paused to look it over, as though saying farewell to an old friend. Then she turned and made her way to where Lord Norwood now stood beside his horse.

"Here is the key to that cottage, not that it is important any longer, for I expect it will be torn down ere long." She handed the large key to him, then excused herself. Fosdick took a sharp look at the trio remaining, then followed Jane.

"I do not understand this in the least. What has happened? Why are they going over there?" He gestured to the Tudor cottage, revealed in all its old charm with the weeds and grass trimmed, the windows shining. He watched, quite perplexed, as Jane and Fosdick entered through the front door now restored to polished beauty.

"I am renting it," she declared with pleasure. "I intended to give the rent to your bailiff, but you may as well take it instead." She handed the packet to a very bemused Lord Norwood, then watched when he checked the contents.

He looked up at her, clearly puzzled. "For how long a period does this cover?"

"One month, sir," she replied. She would have to write to her solicitor to see that more funds were sent. Perhaps she might arrange to have a bank in Oxford open an account in her name. She would enjoy an occasional trip to that town for a bit of shopping.

The two men exchanged looks, then Lord Norwood turned to her again. "Tell me, what were you told regarding the amount of rent for the new cottages?"

Hyacinthe sensed something in his voice. He was angry. At her? She couldn't help that. She told him the sum that the bailiff had revealed. That look of anger hardened into cold outrage.

He remounted, then gathered the reins, preparing to leave. "I shall return later to deal with this removal you have affected. But know this—the amount of rent for the new cottages is no different from the old, in spite of my teasing you on the matter. I see that I shall have to have words with my bailiff."

She watched, quite frozen, as the two men galloped off along the road to the new village. His words went around and around in her mind. The amount of rent as given her by the bailiff was wrong! He had lied. The rent had not been greatly increased. Hyacinthe had not only acted in the wrong, but dreadfully misjudged Lord Norwood.

It was as though a cold hand clutched her heart. If she thought him indifferent to her before, he would positively scorn her now. But it was a mistake! An honest mistake. Yet perhaps she should have taxed Lord Norwood over the sum directly, and it would have been revealed. Now she would never know. She taunted herself with the knowledge that she was undoubtedly her own worst enemy.

With a resigned sigh she began her way to the Tudor cottage, although she was reluctant to face Jane with the truth of the matter. So many things were the result of that lie. How could she possibly correct everything to what it ought to be?

The dust had settled when Sir Charles approached from the other direction. What now? she wondered while pausing before the gate.

"What has occurred? I heard that Miss Pennington has moved." He was clearly alarmed, almost amusingly so.

"She has," Hyacinthe agreed.

"But she cannot. That is, she said nothing to me about removing from here. Where did she go? Why did she not inform me? I must speak with her. Tell me where I may find her."

Taking pity on the poor man, Hyacinthe walked forward to where he sat on his horse. "Follow me. We do not have a stable, but I trust you may tie your steed to a tree." She gestured toward the cottage. "I have rented the Tudor house. Jane and Fosdick are there arranging our things."

"She is still in the village, then?" His relief was almost diverting.

"Yes, she is. For the moment. You know, Jane is a very pretty woman. One of these days some fortunate man could well sweep her off her feet and carry her away."

Now he looked even more alarmed. "I must see her."

With that he jumped from his horse, looped the reins on a branch, then surged ahead, hurrying up the path to the cottage where a serene Fosdick ushered him inside with the grace of a born housekeeper.

Hyacinthe observed his greeting to Jane with narrowed eyes. The man was a slowtop and would need more nudging, most likely. But Jane clearly loved him as he was, and she should have him. All it would require would be a bit of intrigue.

When he was safely away from the house, Hyacinthe confronted her cousin in the hallway. Jane carried a stack of clean huckaback towels, most likely unaware of what was in her hands from the expression on her face.

"He desires to take me for a drive on the morrow. He is concerned about the ghosts in this house. I told him not to worry." She gave Hyacinthe a distracted look. "You do not believe we will be pestered by ghosts, do you?"

"Not live ones," Hyacinthe muttered. Seeing her cousin's confusion, Hyacinthe assured her, "The ghosts are likely figments of overactive imaginations and little boys bent on mischief. Put your mind to what you will wear on this momentous occasion."

With that happy thought planted in her mind, Jane sailed up to the linen closet, tidied the things already in place, then went off to her new room, larger and sunnier than the one in the old cottage.

Hyacinthe stared after her. She ought to have informed Jane of the awful lie the bailiff had told. Maybe things would quickly work out so Jane could marry Sir Charles and Hyacinthe wouldn't need to reveal all. Knowing Jane, this might be the better course to take. Hyacinthe's heart yielding to the persuasion of this argument, she followed her cousin up the stairs.

The floorboards squeaked as she entered the larger of the bedrooms. Since, in spite of Jane's objections, she paid the bills now she'd chosen this one—and Jane would soon be gone. Besides, she had a sentimental regard for it. But she wondered how sound the building might be. Her groom and coachman had gone over the house, pronouncing it free from bugs and serious decay. Still . . . there was the secret passage that went down from her dressing room.

Crossing to the closet, she went in, pressed the little wooden knot, then watched the secret panel swing open as it had before. Chilly air rushed up to greet her. Rather than go down to the lower level, she studied the upper portion. Could the jewels be here?

"Hyacinthe? Where are you?"

Upon hearing her cousin, Hyacinthe hurriedly closed up the paneled entrance, then pretended she had been hunting through her gowns hanging in the wardrobe brought from Jane's former house.

"In here, dear. I thought I would have the Widow Smith and Mrs. Peachey over for tea tomorrow while you are off gallivanting with Sir Charles. They are bursting with questions," Hyacinthe invented. She figured it was close enough to the truth and she could quickly send a note to the ladies, who would leap at the chance to snoop. "What does one wear when being interrogated?"

"Oh, Hyacinthe, you are so silly." Jane leaned against the paneled wall not far from where the knot seemed conspicuously present. "That pretty green India mull you think so plain will be lovely. They do not expect city elegance."

"You think not?" Hyacinthe shook her head. "I expect they will like me to dazzle them. After all, I owe something to my image."

Jane laughed, then joined her cousin as she went to leave the little room. Before closing the door, Hyacinthe glanced back to where she knew the passage to be. Later on she intended to inspect it inch by inch. Now that she had a perfect right to be here, there was no need to rush. Tomorrow, while Jane was on her drive and before the ladies came to tea, she could search. For she fully intended to find those jewels before Mr. Wayland found some excuse to return.

Then a terrible thought struck her. Perhaps he could enter from below!

As soon as possible, Hyacinthe excused herself from her cousin, making her way to the rubbish heap with the explanation that she needed to oversee the disposal of the trash. That was a patent untruth, but it was necessary to make certain that no one could get inside.

The door proved easily found when one knew where to search. It didn't take long for Hyacinthe to decide that it could be opened with little effort. She hunted around until she located a hammer and nails, then made certain that for the moment there was no way Dudley Wayland could sneak up those secret stairs. And she intended to find the jewels before he found a way, for she was convinced Dudley Wayland had hidden them somewhere in the passage.

14

The evening meal, the very first in their new abode, turned out well, prepared by the Widow Smith's girl, Fanny. Hyacinthe was a preoccupied diner, however, for her thoughts kept wandering alternately to the lie she must keep hidden and her need to explore the secret passage.

She had a truly deep conviction that the old family jewels were concealed in the walls of the passage. But where? She ought to have good light, and there was nothing but candles to be had in this house. What she needed was an Argand lamp with a shade. The efficient tubular wick of this oil lamp burned more brightly—without smoking—and increased illumination tenfold.

Quite unaware that Jane and Fosdick were deep in a discussion of what gown should be worn on the momentous outing with Sir Charles, Hyacinthe broke in. "Does either of you have any idea where I might buy an Argand lamp? I enjoy needlework of an evening and candles are a poor substitute."

Both women stared at her with perplexed looks on their faces for a few moments.

Jane said, "I believe you may purchase one in Woodstock, or if not there, you could go as far as Kidlington."

"I should think you might even order one, if you are in a hurry and cannot find the time to go," Fosdick added.

"That is true," Jane said. "But it ought not take long to run in to Woodstock." She gave Hyacinthe a curious look. "I had not realized that you were so fond of needlework."

"That is because she has been so busy with other things," Fosdick inserted helpfully. "Why, she is one of the finest needlewomen I have ever seen in all my years of service."

Hyacinthe stared at her abigail. Had being persuaded to join them for dinner while in Worthington gone to her head? Though she certainly enjoyed a bit of needlework from time to time, Hyacinthe could hardly aspire to such heights.

"Thank you, Fosdick," she murmured, then resumed mulling over her problem. She would send a message to the coachman first thing in the morning, then dash to Woodstock for the lamp. When Jane went off for her ride and before the ladies came to tea Hyacinthe could begin her exploration.

She supposed she might confide in Jane, but there were two reasons to remain silent—Jane might blurt out the truth at an inauspicious moment, or she might insist upon helping. Hyacinthe knew a fierce desire to be the one who found the missing items. She didn't delve into her underlying motives.

With the problem of a proper lamp solved, she sat back in satisfaction. The other problem—that of the horrid lie told by the bailiff—would wait. It would have to wait. Nothing must keep Jane from that outing with Sir Charles. Hyacinthe prayed the weather would not change. Clouds hovered toward the horizon. They must just go the other way, for rain would ruin everything.

"Pudding, miss?" Fanny inquired.

"What? Oh, yes, I adore pudding—of any kind," Hyacinthe blurted. She really must pay better attention.

The remainder of the evening went normally. Fosdick resumed her more retiring nature and Jane bubbled with delight on the prospects of her future until it was time to retire.

In the morning, Hyacinthe did as planned. Since Jane slept late she was not obliged to prevaricate about her errand, and anyway, Jane knew she wanted a lamp; just not *why* she wanted a new lamp

With a bit of searching in Woodstock, the exact shop she hoped to locate was found and two Argand lamps purchased. Hyacinthe decided that if one was good, two were better.

"Miss Dancy! What a surprise to find you in town."

Hyacinthe swallowed with care, then turned to face the man she feared to see. "Lord Norwood. Fancy meeting you here of all places." She motioned the shop assistant to where her carriage waited, whispering that he should just place the lamps inside.

"Out shopping bright and early, I see." He glanced at the shop, then back at her. "Lamps? You desire to entertain?"

"Oh, no," she said truthfully. "I enjoy a bit of needlework of an evening, and candlelight is dreadfully hard on the eyes." She must buy a bit of canvas and yarn or else look utterly silly, what with telling this tale so often.

She glanced about her, noting that nothing frightful seemed about to happen. Lord Norwood looked perfectly safe. "Well, I had best hurry home. Jane is to drive out with Sir Charles today, and I must not miss this occasion."

"I gather he is finally coming up to scratch."

Hyacinthe grinned. "Jane said that made him sound like a chicken."

He laughed at that and Hyacinthe hoped that perhaps all was not lost between them.

"I gather you are settling in well enough? I find it hard to understand why Miss Pennington preferred that place to a new cottage." He leaned on his cane while watching Hyacinthe with an intent regard.

"Actually it was the misunderstanding that caused it," she confessed, quite flustered and fiddling with the cords of her reticule with nervous fingers. "You did not help, sir, with your teasing," she reminded him.

"I promise I shan't hold it against you," he said. There was no twinkle in those blue eyes and his smile had faded when he met her gaze. In fact, all seemed to dim about them, for she noticed nothing but him.

"Look out, sir!" cried the shop assistant who had lingered before the door.

Before either of them could move, a boy being chased by four others came barreling into Lord Norwood, knocking him off his feet.

Hyacinthe heard the tearing of fabric with a sinking heart. All the poor man had to do was talk with her and he ended in disaster.

The shop assistant rushed to help the gentleman, offering to chase the boys.

"Never mind, I trust they are far from here by now, all much chastened, no doubt," Lord Norwood said wryly. He turned to Hyacinthe, remaining carefully erect. "I must bid you farewell. It seems I must find a tailor immediately."

Knowing she must look guilty when it wasn't her fault in the least, Hyacinthe agreed, then whisked herself into the carriage and bid her coachman to hurry on his way. She peeped from the window to see Lord Norwood entering a shop a few doors from where the altercation occurred.

Bouncing along the rutted road back to the old village, she considered what had been said and had happened. She truly did not know if he would ever forgive her for all the appalling things that had taken place since they met. She could only hope to atone for a few of them by finding those wretched jewels.

Jane was in alt when she viewed the fine lamps. Nothing would do but that they had to be lit and admired.

"I believe I shall take up sewing something other than mending of an evening with this fine light," she declared.

"I noticed that Sir Charles has a pair of them in his drawing room. Be sure you buy sufficient canvas to work a new set of chair seats," Hyacinthe said.

Jane blinked at this forward thinking, then went off to inspect her gown for the tenth time that morning.

Taking both of the lamps, now extinguished, Hyacinthe brought them up to her room. Fosdick took one look and shrugged.

"I gather you have something up your sleeve. I misdoubt you intend to commence all that needlework you spoke of in the middle of the day."

"If you like, you may take yourself off to visit Mrs. Grigson over at Sir Charles's house." Hyacinthe would find it easier to work with the house empty. Fanny was off at her mother's for the day, helping pack for her removal.

"Hmphf," Fosdick said, following this utterance with a sniff of disdain. She left the room and shortly was heard going down the stairs. Bless the good woman, she'd never say a word about Hyacinthe's odd starts.

Once alone, Hyacinthe hurried to the closet after donning a

mob cap and an enveloping apron, then lit one lamp. Quickly pressing the little knot of wood, she entered the passageway, her lamp now lighting up the area far better than a branch of candles ever could.

She began with the left side of the passage, starting at the top, working her way down, pressing every inch. She knew that whatever was concealed here would be in between the walls, for there was little space allotted to the secret passage. But what could be the solution to the riddle of the hidden treasure? Lord Norwood had hinted that more than jewels were missing.

If she could find whatever else had been hidden here years ago, she could at least feel absolved of all the wrongs she had committed, to say nothing of the dreadful things that seemed to happen whenever she drew near the man.

Minutes passed before she heard Jane calling her. Having found nothing of interest, Hyacinthe quickly put out the lamp, then placed it on the little table she had brought into the closet. She pulled off her cap and apron, tossing them aside before scurrying around the corner.

In the hallway, Jane stood with an uncertain look on her face. "Oh, there you are. Fosdick is nowhere to be seen and you appeared to have vanished as well."' She fidgeted with a lace reticule that Hyacinthe had given her. Then she slowly twirled about. "Will I pass inspection?"

Hyacinthe felt guilty for neglecting the all-important drive. "You look better than a dish of comfits. I vow that if Sir Charles is not swept from his feet by the sight of you, the man needs spectacles."

With a soft little giggle, Jane made her way to the front door where she greeted Sir Charles. By the looks of him, he was struck all of a heap. Jane glanced back at her cousin and winked.

With the drive off to such a promising start—not even a sign of rain in the sky—Hyacinthe went to the kitchen to boil water for tea after washing her hands of dust. A tray had been nicely arranged in anticipation of the visit from the village gossips. When a faint rap was heard at the front door, Hyacinthe was ready.

Actually, things went quite well, far better than Hyacinthe had hoped they would. The two ladies revealed that they had embarked on the village history just as Hyacinthe had suggested. They went on to offer details unearthed through a search of attics, the records kept in the church, and the tombstones in the graveyard.

"I had no notion this would prove so fascinating, Miss Dancy," Mrs. Peachey confided. "Why, Eloise and I have scarce had a moment to look out of our windows the past week."

"Have you learned anything more of the woman who lived here?" Hyacinthe inquired of the authors.

"The dashing redhead? Precious little. There are references to ghosts and such from time to time. But it strikes me as odd that although the house was kept more or less in repair, no one has lived here for any length of time," the Widow Smith said with a sage nod. "And whoever lived at the Hall saw to the repairs through the years. What secret do you suppose is hidden in these walls?

She was uncomfortably close to the truth. Hyacinthe forced a laugh. "You have a wonderfully fanciful mind, Mrs. Smith. I doubt if anything sordid is concealed, for I have slept extremely well, and I doubt if I would were something nasty hidden here."

Hyacinthe could almost see the thoughts that ran through the widow's head. Disappointment vied with pleasure that Mrs. Smith was actually having tea with Miss Dancy and in the wicked Tudor house. After all, a kept woman had once resided here!

When the call came to a conclusion, Hyacinthe graciously walked the two ladies to the door, saying, "I wish you well in your efforts. I expect that once you have it completed, Lord Norwood will wish to publish it for the shire records."

This consideration so astounded the two women that they merely gasped, then fled down the front path deep in discussion.

Hyacinthe watched them for a few moments before going out into the garden, or what remained of the garden. It occurred to her that she ought to find the hedgehog and bring him here. Poor little thing would be frightened half to death when they tore down that cottage.

With that thought in mind she crossed the green, entering through the gate to skirt the cottage—now looking quite forlorn—around to the rear of the house.

"Whatever you doin' here, Miss Dancy?" Sukey, the Hadkiss girl of the kite episode, asked.

"I intend to find my hedgehog. Would you like to help me?" Hyacinthe decided that it should be safe enough. Lord Norwood was miles away from here as far as she knew.

In short order the two were prowling through the garden, poking under piles of moldering leaves, prying up fallen branches, hunting into any likely spot where a hedgehog might hide. Hyacinthe thought she had found him when it happened.

"Whatever are you doing, Miss Dancy?" said an unfortunately familiar voice.

Conscious of her now-rumpled mull gown hiked up well above her ankles and being crouched on the ground in an improper position, Hyacinthe looked up at him. "Good afternoon, Lord Norwood. It wanted only you, I expect."

"I daresay I'm better off not knowing what that means," he muttered. "But you failed to answer my query."

"If you must know," she said somewhat ungraciously, "we are hunting for Harry, my hedgehog. The one you gave me," she added for further illumination. "Perhaps you recall Sukey?" she concluded as an afterthought.

"How could I forget? I trust you have kept your kite from further harm, Sukey?"

The little girl blushed then retreated at such notice.

"I suppose I had best help you," Lord Norwood continued. "I was reckoned to be a dab hand at gathering up hedgehogs when I was a boy. The little things seemed to like me." At Hyacinthe's amused expression, he added, "And please do not say that it is very apt, for you would be repeating something that has become trite over the years."

"Well, you can be a trifle prickly at times," she said with a grin. "I am not the only one," she concluded virtuously.

He removed his coat—placing it carefully to one side—pushed up his sleeves, and plunged into the garden. He was not there very long before he emerged triumphant, hedgehog in hand. "Harry, I believe!" he declared with pride in a job well done.

"And so it is," Hyacinthe agreed after a close look at the little fellow. Then she took a look at his lordship and swallowed with effort.

His broad chest covered in fine cambric had become damp from the moldering leaves and now clung to him, revealing a fine, manly chest. He was more muscular than her brother. He was also much closer to her than she deemed prudent. She wanted nothing more than to be enfolded in those strong arms and held close to him.

But, she realized with horror, he was daubed with mud all over that beautiful cambric shirt. With a sigh she rose, the spell broken.

"I fear your shirt must be consigned to the wash, sir. Gardens are notorious for producing soil, and Harry adores grubbing in the dirt."

Indeed, it also appeared the little fellow had no fear of the man who held him so cautiously. Lord Norwood rose, and with Hyacinthe trailing behind him, crossed the green to the Tudor house where he carefully deposited Harry in the garden. The animal quickly disappeared beneath a pile of autumn leaves and debris.

Hyacinthe handed him the coat she had thought to bring along, then watched while he brushed off his soiled shirt before donning the well-tailored coat of a fine gray cloth.

"Have you tended to the secret passage?" he asked, looking ready to depart.

She gave a guilty start, then realized he must refer to the sealing off of the entrance. "Indeed." She turned from the rear of the house, hoping to draw Lord Norwood to the front gate and safety. "I nailed it shut so anyone who wished to sneak up those stairs would find it impossible."

The perverse man would not follow her. Rather, he strode around past the ashes of the rubbish heap, now carefully raked down by Warton. "Where is it?"

Resigned, Hyacinthe walked along the house until she spotted the slit that indicated the hidden door. "I nailed it shut along here." She pointed out where each nail had been driven. To do so necessitated her coming very close to his lordship. He refused to budge and she rejected the idea of admitting she was so strongly affected by him.

So she daringly turned to face him, awaiting his verdict of her efforts. After all, he did own the house, and she supposed she ought to have sought permission to pound nails in the place.

"Hyacinthe . . ." He stared down into her eyes with an indescribable expression on his face. She would have said he looked hungry, except this was not the time of day for a meal.

Nervous, she rubbed her hands together. Licking suddenly dry lips, she answered, "Yes?"

His fingers brushed her cheek, dusting off a leaf she supposed. But his very touch seemed a caress that sent tremors through her. She ought to move. They ought not be here. For although she had red hair and lived a somewhat unconventional life, inside she was a very proper woman.

She might even flirt just a bit, but always with discretion. This was not prudent. She sensed that a strange sort of danger threatened her.

He stepped closer to her. Scarcely an inch was between them. "Hyacinthe," he whispered.

Suddenly she was crushed against him, his lips finding hers in a kiss that was infinitely sweet. Flee she ought, yet she clutched his coat with trembling fingers.

"Norwood," called a voice from around the other side of the house.

Hyacinthe found herself swiftly abandoned as Lord Norwood strolled around to hail his friend.

"Over here, Val. Miss Dancy has been showing me the results of her efforts at nailing shut the passage door."

Hyacinthe stood where he had left her. Another brief kiss, yet more intense than the first. The sweetness and tenderness she'd experienced made her long for more, unfortunately. While she had no one to warn her of the risks involved, she sensed that she flirted with far more than in the past. Was this what that redhead of long ago had known? Was this intense longing to be close to the man she loved what had compelled the woman to flout society's laws to be with him?

Hyacinthe knew that she could not follow that path. Either she was not as strong, or merely more sensible.

"Well, Miss Dancy," came Latham's mocking voice, "you have many talents."

She wondered what he meant by that.

"So she has," Lord Norwood agreed quietly.

Somehow she managed the next few minutes with far more aplomb than she would have believed possible. She smiled and gestured, thought she acted naturally, when all she could think of was the feel of his mouth on hers and the warmth of his hands on her arms. She shivered.

"You are cold," Lord Norwood exclaimed. "What thoughtless nodcocks we are to keep you standing here." With that masterful manner he could conjure up, he swept her along to the rear door, then inside to the kitchen.

Lord Latham followed. He glanced about the spotless room, then noted the cinnamon buns on a tray, covered lightly with a cloth. A teakettle steamed gently on the hob before a banked fire.

"I believe we could all enjoy a cup of tea with one of those buns," he observed, apparently oblivious to the tension between his friend and Hyacinthe.

She forced herself to set a tray for them with pretty cups and saucers, plates heaped with fragrant buns, and crisp linen napkins. What a sight she must make, her gown stained and crumpled, hair likely in a mad tangle. Well, when had anything ever been normal when she was around Lord Norwood?

"My mother likes to collect old china," Val said after they had settled in the sparsely furnished parlor and he had enjoyed a bit of bun. "Do you like old things, Miss Dancy?"

"Yes, I believe you might say that I do. My mother left me her Wedgwood and I hope to have it in my own home someday." She gave Lord Latham a curious look. His face wore a hostile expression when he thought she wasn't watching him. Why? Did he so deeply resent the things she had done—accidently or on purpose—to his friend? She set down her cup and drew her shawl more tightly about her shoulders. While assuredly never pampered in her life, she had not known antagonism such as this before.

She heard Fanny moving about in the kitchen, a sign that the packing had been concluded for the Widow Smith.

"More families are leaving here. The Widow Smith goes soon and the Hadkiss family tomorrow, according to Sukey. Before long we will be alone." She hoped her smile assured that she did not mind the loss.

"I almost forgot to tell you—I dismissed my bailiff," Lord Norwood said. "The man intended to raise those rents, keep the difference for himself. As it was, Tombler definitely had been skimming. I surmised that as soon as I saw your rent packet. It was not the amount I had told him to charge. You may skip the next month's payment," he added casually.

"My goodness!" she exclaimed. "What a wicked man."

"I intend to set things to right with the villagers. Contrary to what you seem to think, I am not a monstrous landowner."

No witty reply popped into her head. The only thought that persisted was that she had definitely ruined her chances with the man she now loved. Oh, he might dally with her, trifle with her a bit, but there was nothing serious. Hyacinthe might be an innocent, but she knew full well that such a flirtation rarely ended in something more permanent.

At last she said, "I am pleased to discover you are not what I thought you were." And with that observation she stopped.

A subdued Hyacinthe bade farewell to the gentleman. Jane was still gone. That could not but offer hope for her. Hyacinthe was grateful that Lord Latham did not quiz her about her intentions for the future, a future without Jane or anyone else.

Since she doubted Fanny—busy with preparations for supper—would come hunting for her, Hyacinthe ran lightly up the stairs to her room and into the closet. What might have been didn't bear dwelling upon.

Instead she lit the lamp again and returned to her inspection of the secret passage.

There was a peculiar indentation about ten inches up from the third step down. Hyacinthe, thankful her already-crumpled gown could become no worse, knelt to examine it more carefully. She pressed the wall inch by inch, a hope growing within her that she might have found something.

Suddenly a panel of wood swung open. Elated, Hyacinthe grabbed the lamp to peer more closely. A painting! What would a painting be doing here? Replacing the lamp, she removed the landscape from where it had been concealed for likely many years. A bucolic Dutch scene met her scrutiny. She blew off a film of dust, then marveled at the detail, the colors. Surely this must be one of the "treasures" Lord Norwood had hinted at.

Eager to uncover more, she set to work with renewed zeal. Aware that the indentation meant something, she searched for another. In twenty minutes of intense examination she located another such spot.

She excitedly pressed along the same pattern as before. As before, a panel opened to reveal a second painting. She withdrew this larger oil with an awed gasp, for while she might not know the artist she recognized the quality of the work. It was truly magnificent.

After she carefully placed this painting with the first, she set to work with determined intensity. A third indentation was found about a foot below the other. Another panel opened to reveal still another painting.

She studied this one slowly, for it was of a redheaded woman. Clearly a work of great merit, it had an intimate warmth about it as though the artist painted this on a commission. Could this be a painting of the woman who had lived here so long ago? Green eyes seemed to tease her. There was no way to tell. No clue existed.

Hyacinthe sat back on the top step. Jane had still not returned. There was yet time to continue her exploration. With lamp in hand Hyacinthe inched her way along, almost nose to wall.

At last she thought she saw a difference in the wood. Heart pounding, she pressed a knot similar to the one that opened the panel to the passage. At first it appeared she had been wrong. Then slowly, ever so slowly, a small piece of the paneling opened.

"Hyacinthe?" The voice came from below.

Drat. Jane was home. Hyacinthe could not stop now, and indeed if she was right, didn't need to stop. She wrapped trembling fingers around the parcel that had been hidden and withdrew the square box.

"Hyacinthe, whatever are you doing?" It was a measure of Jane's excitement that she did not realize the significance of what Hyacinthe had found. "Come, I have important news," Jane declared with excitement ringing in her voice.

Hyacinthe had already guessed the news, but would never destroy her cousin's joyous moment. With the dusty box concealed in the folds of her skirt, she hurried up the few steps to the top, turned off the oil lamp, then faced Jane with what she hoped was deserved interest.

"Sir Charles has made me the most happy of women! We are to be married as soon as the banns have been read. And if the work continues apace, we shall be married in the new church." Jane fairly danced in her joy.

With great fondness, Hyacinthe kissed her cousin on the cheek. "I can but wish you happy, dearest Jane."

"You will write that distant cousin you mentioned," Jane said, considerate of Hyacinthe even at this time.

"Of course," Hyacinthe promised. That didn't say *what* she might write.

Once the glow had dimmed a trifle, Jane looked around the closet, then frowned. "Whatever is going on here? I do not recall those stairs before. Where did those dusty paintings come from?" Then she studied Hyacinthe and said, "Why are you wearing a most gloating expression? I doubt it is for me, for you must have guessed the outcome of this drive."

Slowly Hyacinthe withdrew the box from the folds of her skirt. Holding it up before her, she opened the lid. Both girls gasped at the contents.

"This is it!" Hyacinthe chortled with glee. "The missing jewels!"

"Oh, my," Jane whispered as she retreated. "You had best send for his lordship. I'd not wish to be responsible for them. Not at all."

"I shall, Oh, I shall with great pleasure, you may be assured." Hyacinthe stared down at the glittering gems, the necklace that must have graced a lovely neck so long ago. The gold gleamed softly in the dim light; the emeralds winked and sparkled in spite of the years.

This would surely atone for all that had happened these past weeks. Perhaps . . . just perhaps. . . .

15

"I take it you can easily explain that dirt-smudged shirt you wear," Val said on the ride back to Worthington Hall.

"Of course," Blase replied with his jaunty grin, one that tilted up at a corner of his mouth and was called rakish by any number of ladies. "I put my expertise at hedgehog snabbling to work—to catch Harry."

Val closed his eyes and shook his head in disbelief. "Every time you go near that redhead it ends in disaster. I fail to see why you must bother with her. Or is it impossible to leave her alone?" Val gave his good friend a speculative look.

"A fatal attraction? Hmmm, I doubt it. Think on this, each time the disaster lessens—witness that I only soiled my shirt this time, and that was my own fault." He thought for a moment, then continued, "And you can scarce blame Hyacinthe for that lad who careened into me while we were in Woodstock."

"What were you doing there, by the by?"

"Checking up on a few things. I need a new bailiff what with dismissing Tombler. I heard of a well-qualified man and wish to interview him. Sent off an express from Woodstock."

"So what do we do in the meanwhile?"

"There is a race on at Newmarket this weekend. Prinney's supposed to enter one of his nags. I believe I should like to see that race," Blase said in a musing tone.

"I can see where you might feel in need of funds, what with all this building. You aren't short, are you?"

"The new church is costing more than I expected. Blast it, everything has gone up in price." They rode over the final hill that offered a splendid view of his ancestral home in all its autumn splendor. Blase paused to survey his domain for a moment, content he was pursuing the right course.

"With your incredible luck you ought to acquire enough blunt while there," Val said encouragingly, seeming anxious for a diversion.

"Trouble is, they all know me," Blase muttered. "Odds will change if I bet on a particular horse—the one that Frank Buckle is to ride. I believe I shall ask Sir Charles to join us, place my bets for me. Better odds that way, you know," he said with a perceptive look at Val.

Val sighed with pleasure. "I don't mind telling you it was becoming dashed dull around here, what with you conferring with Repton and his son and clashing with Miss Dancy every other day. I'll wager Smithson will welcome the respite from the afternoon baths." He grinned at the irritated look from Blase but ceased his teasing.

They clattered into the stable yard and handed over their horses' reins to the head groom before strolling out to the terrace in front of the house.

"It is beginning to take shape as I had hoped," Blase said to Val.

They stood gazing at the nicely altered view for a few minutes, then both strode into the house.

In the library Blase penned a brief missive to Sir Charles requesting the pleasure of his company for a short trip to Newmarket. He sent it off immediately, requesting his groom to wait for a reply.

Val ran up the stairs to alert Smithson and his own valet that they best pack for more than several days, just to be on guard against accidents. The new coats Blase had ordered from London had yet to arrive. Both valets were all too aware of his frequent misfortunes and would be eager to fend off catastrophe.

Across the gentle hills splashed with autumn colors of gold and russet, Hyacinthe sat in the front parlor at a little desk she had seen in Woodstock and ordered delivered immediately. Designed for ladies, it had a hinged front that folded down flat to make a writing board. It had bookshelves above to hold the little novels that Hyacinthe enjoyed. Her hot-pressed and lightly scented paper could be tucked inside the single drawer. It was from here she took a sheet to write her momentous summons to Blase Montague, Lord Norwood.

"How best to persuade him to come without revealing all," she wondered aloud to Jane after nibbling on the end of her pen for some minutes.

"Why not simply inform him that you have found the missing heirlooms?" Jane said with irrefutable logic, glancing up from her now ever-present sewing.

"No." Hyacinthe rejected that idea immediately. "I wish to see his face when I tell him what has been here all these years. I believe he will be very pleased." She wondered if that painting of the redhead would provoke some interesting debate.

She thought on for some moments, then shook her head. "I can think of nothing else but to request the pleasure of his company as I have some information for him."

"That is certainly obscure enough," Jane said with a frown. "What makes you believe that he will pay any attention to such a request?"

"He must," Hyacinthe declared, but without a great deal of conviction.

Before she could summon Warton to deliver the message, she decided she had best have tea. Perhaps she might think of something better while sipping Bohea and nibbling one of Granny Beanbuck's buns.

Fanny had just brought in the tea tray when a rap was heard at the front door. Shortly, Fanny ushered Sir Charles into the parlor. He wore a distressed look on his face that brought Jane to her feet in dismay.

"What is it?" she cried, crossing to his side in a flurry of muslin.

"Now, now," he soothed. "It's nothing terribly serious. It is just that Lord Norwood has urgently requested I join him and Lord Latham on a jaunt to Newmarket for the weekend. I feel I must go along, given the wording of the missive." He gave Jane a fond look. "I had especially wished to attend church this coming Sunday when our banns are first read."

Jane offered a forgiving smile. "I quite understand. You

know, there are some who think it bad luck to be present at this time."

"Well," Hyacinthe inserted, her positive feelings for Lord Norwood suffering at this revelation, "I think it wretched. If the dratted man wants company he can surely find it there."

Sir Charles directed a serious look at her. "You do not understand in the least, my dear girl. I think it important that I spend this time with his lordship. I am dependent upon his good will for a number of things."

"It is an excellent idea, Sir Charles," Jane added with a scowl at Hyacinthe.

Retreating from what was, after all, none of her business Hyacinthe considered the matter from her point of view. This meant that she must shelter and protect those valuable jewels and priceless paintings for the weekend. What if Mr. Wayland took a notion to prowl about in search of them? She dare not leave the house for anything!

She owned a gun. Her brother had purchased a fine pistol from Manton and trained her in the use of it. She could hit a wafer dead center. Whether or not she might have the courage to aim that same gun at a villain she didn't know. But, she thought optimistically, she might frighten him with it. He wouldn't know she had never shot at a person before.

With a murmured excuse, for she could leave the lovers alone now that they were engaged to be married soon, she hurried up to her room to prowl through her trunks.

"I might be of help were I to know what you look for, without your tearing things to bits and pieces," Fosdick said dryly from the doorway.

"My gun," Hyacinthe informed her.

"I see. You intend to shoot his lordship over them jewels?" the maid said, walking over to a small chest beneath the window and near the secret panel.

"Fosdick!" Hyacinthe said, looking askance at this bit of plain speaking. "You are pledged to secrecy. And besides, I may think his rakish lordship a sad scrambler, what with his dashing off to Newmarket for the weekend, but I would never go so far as to shoot him for it. No, I must protect the jewels and paintings until he claims them. What if Dudley Wayland comes sneaking around here?"

The abigail rubbed her chin at this idea, then knelt to open the little chest. " 'Tis in here," she said quietly. "You will have to oil it up some, perhaps test it out back at some sort of target. You have not fired it in some time," she reminded Hyacinthe.

"With his lordship gone away, there is no need to fear I shall accidently hit him," Hyacinthe joked softly.

"Pray you need hit no one," the maid said, a sober look on her face.

After finding the bullets and all else she needed, Hyacinthe went downstairs. Jane was out in front of the house at the gate, saying a tearful but brave good-bye to her betrothed. Hyacinthe swiftly walked to the rear of the house, then out to the garden.

Warton was there, raking up some debris and in general making himself useful.

Hyacinthe rapidly explained what she wished to do. Knowing her expertise, the groom hurriedly set up a sort of target for her, then watched—after seeing to it that she didn't forget one bit of preparation.

Her aim had not suffered in the least, in spite of the elapse of time since her last attempt. Of course the noise brought Jane scurrying to the rear of the house, peering from behind a shrub at the sight of her cousin taking aim at the makeshift target.

"Heavens, Hyacinthe! What a racket you make," she said when her cousin paused to reload.

"It is my duty to protect what is not mine," Hyacinthe reminded her.

"Oh, dear, I had not thought it would come to this." Jane continued to watch, then urged her cousin back to the parlor so they might discuss the matter at greater length. "We need to plan," she concluded.

Deciding that her ability had not diminished, Hyacinthe cleaned her gun properly, then joined her cousin in the parlor, with the gun now safely in its case.

Jane eyed the gun case with misgivings and said, "You are certain you must have that thing handy?"

"Mr. Wayland may be desperate; we do not know."

"Well, I hope no one paid any attention to all the noise over here," Jane said before sipping her replenished tea.

"How could they, what with the demolishing of the cottage along the road? A gun shot is not much different from a tumble of stones," Hyacinthe reassured her with confidence.

They plunged into a plan for the defense of the house. Hyacinthe decided to reinforce the fortification of the door to the secret stairs. Jane prudently decided that the less she knew of the matter the safer she would be.

When Warton had returned to the Cock and Bull—which had already partially removed to a new location—Hyacinthe began.

She pounded more nails along the edge of the door, then dragged—with Jane's reluctant assistance—a barrel over to nudge in front of it. Once that was completed, she stood back, most pleased with her efforts.

"I misdoubt if he can sneak in past that barricade," she declared. Brushing off her hands, she found a rock to tote inside. From within the passage, she placed it so that were Wayland to manage entrance somehow or other, he would trip on the rock. If nothing else, it would serve as a warning, enabling her to meet him at the top of the stairs with gun in hand.,

All this work was tiring, but oddly satisfying.

The days passed in quiet activity. With Sir Charles and Lord Norwood away, not to mention the cynical Lord Latham, there was no social life at all.

Jane worked at a steady pace assembling a proper wardrobe. She embroidered and added lace to petticoats, sewed a sheer shift of finest cotton and trimmed it with delicate lace from a supply Hyacinthe offered.

Hyacinthe also sewed for her cousin, wishing they had time to send to London for a proper wedding dress. Jane elected to be married in a palest blue Gros de Naples trimmed with yards of Bruges lace. It was a dress Hyacinthe had brought her cousin from London and never been worn as yet. Jane thought it excessively beautiful.

When she tried on the gown, Hyacinthe had to agree, but she would have wished for better.

"You are blooming, Jane. I have never seen you in better looks. Sir Charles is a most fortunate man."

"I shan't have the sort of wedding clothes you might find in the City, but I shall do well enough," Jane replied with a hint of complacency. "And I do intend to take your advice on the chair seats."

Having completely forgotten what she had uttered about the needlework, Hyacinthe gave Jane a blank look.

"I will purchase canvas and yarns on my first opportunity. When last I looked, those chair seats appeared prodigiously dreary."

Murmuring something suitable, Hyacinthe set aside her sewing, thankful for the light from the Argand lamps this evening, and went to the windows. There had been no attempt to enter the house by any means last night. She'd taken the precaution of requesting Warton to sleep belowstairs after Fanny went home. There was comfort in knowing a man, even one as old as Warton, was in the house.

She had silently acknowledged that Wayland might attempt to enter from the front door. A surreptitious inspection of both front and rear doors did not offer a great deal of comfort. He could force entry at either—or even enter through a window. The knowledge did not console her.

The next morning Hyacinthe saw Mr. Wayland on the green. At first it looked as though he was inspecting the demolition of one of the remaining cottages. Then she observed him staring in her direction. Or did he peruse the Tudor house instead?

"Good day to you, sir," she said after crossing to meet him with what she hoped to be an agreeable manner.

Flattered to be noticed, he smiled. This sent his angular face into peculiar contortions, rather amusing ones. "You are not displeased with your temporary abode?"

"Temporary? Why do you say that? We find it most congenial." She watched his changing expression with interest. Wherever had he acquired the notion that she would be moving shortly?

"Well," he blustered, "with Miss Pennington shortly to wed Sir Charles, I assumed you would move on. Perhaps join a cousin or an aunt." He smiled again, but this time Hyacinthe felt not the least amused.

"For the present I intend to remain here. I may invite a cousin to join me. I do not care for London in the winter, much preferring the charm of the countryside."

He paled. "You plan to go with your cousin on her honeymoon?" he ventured, hope clear in his voice.

While she knew it was fairly common for a bride to have a companion along, she had no intention of leaving here, and said so. "I have not been asked, and besides . . . I think they will do well enough without me."

"But Miss Pennington is a very gently bred woman; she might find need of your company," he put forth in a persuasive manner.

"Nonsense," Hyacinthe snapped back, quite out of patience with the man. "She will have Sir Charles. Besides, I intend to do a bit of decorating, with Lord Norwood's permission, of course." Dare she hint more? "I should like to enlarge the window in the closet, for the light is dreadfully poor in there."

He frowned and in a hatefully superior voice said, "As an architect, I would not recommend that. You are likely to encounter all sorts of problems in an old place."

"Rubbish," she countered, sensing she might be hitting close to the bone. "In spite of a certain neglect the place is sound enough. I will also order a bit of painting and certainly some more furniture." With that observation she left him, returning to the garden that she and Warton were laying out along one side of the house. She well recalled the plan she had seen among the papers Lord Norwood brought.

The effect of this was one of permanence, of settling in for a long stay, precisely what she intended.

Once in bed that night it was not long before she heard noises, her room being toward the rear of the house. She slipped from between the sheets and tiptoed to the window, taking her gun from its case on the way.

Down below her room and to one side, right before the secret-door location, a shadow moved. Hyacinthe returned to her room to load her gun, don her green velvet robe, then cross to the closet. In the improbable event that Mr. Wayland did enter

he passage, she would be prepared to defend the priceless her-
tage that belonged to Lord Norwood.

She had not closely examined her reasons for such fierce
determination. Except . . . she had always been intensely loyal
to her family and friends, and she supposed she might classify
him as a friend. She had no other designation for him, goodness knew.

She placed an ear against the paneling, but could hear noth-
ng. Perhaps he had been thwarted? Hearing nothing more, she
returned to the window to search the grounds below. A
shadow moved across the future garden, stumbling from time
to time. She deduced that Mr. Wayland had given up, for she
recognized his lanky, angular form immediately. But for how
long? He must have counted upon her moving away from
here, hoping to leave the jewels in the passage until the house
again stood empty and he could retrieve them at will. She
wondered if he even knew about the paintings. She doubted it.
They had been very dusty and looked not to have been
touched in ages.

Once again in her bed, she wondered just why Lord Norwood had to leave *this* particular weekend.

On Sunday she remained home from church, explaining to
an annoyed Jane that this was precisely the moment when Mr.
Wayland might break into the house, figuring that everyone
would be at worship services. Jane accepted that justification,
but with obvious reluctance. Jane never missed divine services
unless she was seriously ill.

It was therefore quite understandable when Jane chided Hyacinthe on her mistake.

"Mr. Wayland came to church this morning. Albeit he entered rather late," she added conscientiously.

"Well," Hyacinthe replied, heroically refraining from permitting a smug note to enter her voice, "he came snooping
around here shortly after you left. I was right to send Fosdick
along with you. He saw two figures leave and thought it us.
He was ever so shocked when I came around the corner of the
house. I never saw anyone disappear so quickly."

"Oh," Jane said, much subdued. She didn't argue with Hyacinthe again regarding leaving the house, other than to re-

mark that she hoped Lord Norwood appreciated the sacrifices Hyacinthe was making on his behalf.

As to that Hyacinthe could not speculate in the least.

The three men who cantered along the road to Worthington Hall were in the best of spirits.

"I say," Sir Charles declared with enthusiasm, "I have the greatest respect for your knowledge of horses. I can see where you earn your reputation. Well done, old chap."

"It helped a good deal to have you serve as a front for me. Wouldn't have had a chance at half the blunt had you not assisted," Blase said amiably.

"We were rather clever, if I do say so," Sir Charles replied with a grin. "Had them all fooled. Good idea to separate before we entered town and only meet by chance at the races. Shrewd bit to slip me your wagers on paper when we shook hands. No one suspected a thing. I wagered a little myself, trusting you not to let me down. Appreciate the extra sum, what with wedding costs and all."

"Miss Pennington does not come with a large dowry?" Val said without his usual wry manner.

"No, but it does not matter. I'd have her were she penniless." At that he lapsed into contemplative silence.

Val exchanged a look with Blase, then quietly said, "You will be well set now, I presume."

"Aye," Blase replied with satisfaction clear in his voice. "I can finish the church and village, complete the gardens about the house, and turn my attention to finding the jewels and paintings with no concern."

"And Miss Dancy?" Val probed.

Darting a cautioning nod at Sir Charles, Blase shook his head to indicate he'd discuss that matter later.

"Well, at least you did not have one accident to ruin your clothing," Val concluded as they rode up before the Hall.

Sir Charles took his leave shortly after. Suspecting the gentleman wished to see his Jane, Blase thanked him again for his part in the plan to increase the sum for the rebuilding of the village.

"I have a vested interest in the village, you must know," Sir Charles said as a disclaimer. "We all prosper in proportion."

Val and Blase entered the house to be met by a grave Barmore, a crisp white missive in his hand.

"What is it?" Blase asked. "You look unusually serious."

"As to that I do not know. Miss Dancy sent this message up by her groom, who said it was most urgent. It came several days ago."

"Blast!" Blase said softly. He broke the seal, unfolded the paper to read the message, then looked at Val in puzzlement. "She requests the pleasure of my company."

"That sounds innocent enough," Val replied, slapping his gloves against his thigh with impatience. "I shall leave you to decide just how urgently she desires your company while I go to my room to clean up. I feel in urgent need of a bath myself."

"I'll do the same," Blase said, somewhat abstractedly. He turned to Barmore, who looked as though bursting to say something. "Do you know anything else about this mysterious request?"

"Miss Dancy was not in church last Sunday. One of the workers told one of our grooms that he had heard something that sounded like gunshots at the Tudor cottage on Saturday."

"Zounds!" Blase exclaimed. He dashed up the stairs and into his room.

"Sir?" Smithson said, when he observed his master's haste in removing his garments.

"I'll merely wash up, for I've no time to wait for a bath. I must get to the village immediately."

In less time than he could have believed, Blase washed, changed garments, and hurried out of the house. He vaulted on a fresh horse that stood awaiting him—thanks to orders sent down by Smithson—and rode off toward the old village without a thought to Val.

He went straight to Hyacinthe Dancy.

"My lord, what a surprise," she said demurely when Fanny ushered him into the front parlor.

"You sent for me," he replied bluntly, standing before her while waiting for her explanation.

Rising gracefully from the chair where she had been sewing, she motioned him to follow her upstairs, holding one finger to her lips to urge silence.

Blase watched the slim figure before him ascending the steps with a gentle sway of her hips. Very womanly, was Miss Dancy.

They entered the closet, Blase first noting the feminine aspect of the bedroom; cheerful fabrics and bedhangings, a warm rug on the floor. Yet it appeared sparsely furnished compared to most homes he had been in, particularly ladies' bedrooms.

She crossed the closet to open the secret passage, then removed each painting from where she had again concealed it. "I believed it safest to keep them here," she said over her shoulder. After he had exclaimed over the treasures revealed—with no comment on the redheaded lady of one painting—Miss Dancy again returned to the passage and retrieved the gems. Her satisfaction in handing this box to Blase was marked. Not that he could blame her, once he opened the box.

"They are all here," he said softly, draping the necklace over his arm to admire it. "Did you encounter any problems? Someone reported he thought he heard gunshots here. I see you are not injured, so may I assume another poor soul got shot?"

"I only tested my aim, sir," she replied with a twinkle in her fine green eyes. "But I would have shot Mr. Wayland had he been able to move the barrel, then force entry to the secret passage."

"By Jove," Blase said in admiration.

"Fortunately I was at home when he came snooping around. However, I was prepared for anything."

"How may I ever thank you, Miss Dancy . . . Hyacinthe? . . . for I feel that we are far too good friends to be so formal." He cast her a speculative look.

"I should feel better were Mr. Wayland captured and sent away from here. Surely someone else could finish the project he has begun?" She did not comment on his use of her given name.

Blase rubbed his chin with his free hand. "I imagine that

could be done. I fancy Repton could recommend someone. But how best to capture Wayland?"

"Well," Hyacinthe Dancy said in a musing tone, "Sir Charles and Jane are due to wed soon. Perhaps you might give a betrothal ball for them up at the Hall? Mr. Wayland would assume us all to be there. But *I* could remain here. If he comes, Warton and I could handle him."

Brave words, indeed. But Blase observed that her confident words were not reflected in the way she said them. He thought for a few moments, then offered his own plan.

"We could leave Warton on guard, as it were. The jewels and paintings will be safely up at the house, but we will tell no one. Once the ball is in progress we can slip off here—first making certain that there is good music, not to mention ample food and drink, for the celebrants. With Sir Charles and Jane as the center of attention, I believe we might manage that. What do you say?"

She gave him a cautious nod. "I believe it might very well work." This was followed by a shy grin. "I am pleased I was able to find your missing things for you."

"Dashed amazing bit of detective work. Val will be crushed, for he fancies himself a bit of a sleuth."

Hyacinthe offered a sack for the box of jewelry, then showed Lord Norwood how to cushion the paintings with a length of velvet so they'd not be damaged in route to the Hall. It made an unwieldly parcel, but she doubted if anyone would comment. For one thing, few strangers strayed onto Montague land and his own people would not think to question his behavior.

When she met Jane belowstairs, she countered any quizzing with the announcement of the coming party. "He is sending invitations to everyone in this area—all who know you both. It is to be right away, for he feels it important to show his approval of your match."

"Oh, my," Jane breathed in excitement. "A ball! It has been ages since I last attended one. To dance with Sir Charles . . ." She drifted upstairs to plan on a suitable gown, eyes full of dreams.

Hyacinthe hied off to the tavern where she found Warton in the stables with Tom Coachman.

Quickly explaining what was to come, she secured the support of both men. They knew so much she didn't need to explain the necessity for secrecy.

Alone on the green, Hyacinthe looked about her. So many houses were gone, with scarcely a hint of a wall remaining. How sad, she reflected. Future generations would not know this place, save for the records being compiled by the Widow Smith and Mrs. Peachey. And all to satisfy a whim of the landlord.

But she had to admit in all fairness that he had told her he would not raise the rents. She did not wish to interfere in his business in this regard. His new bailiff would obey his wishes in this respect and inform the villagers.

Hyacinthe also reminded herself that she had misjudged him badly.

He had behaved with perfect fairness according to his own standards. And, what's more, he had refrained from a retaliation for her deeds. He would certainly have been justified to order her far away, off his land forever.

Instead he had been most forgiving. But he was hardly loverlike. He had been so terribly correct when he thanked her for restoring his heirlooms.

What had she expected? A warm kiss and embrace? her heart wondered. She would have welcomed both. Instead she was rewarded with a plan to catch a thief.

Still, she wouldn't give up yet. She had a few ideas.

16

"It is a lovely house when all lit up for a party," Hyacinthe admitted while the coach made its way to the front entrance of Worthington Hall. "Not that it is unacceptable otherwise, mind you. But the candlelight shining forth is especially nice."

"Well," Jane said after a sigh of great satisfaction, "I think it prodigiously kind of Lord Norwood to have this ball for Sir Charles and me." She gave Hyacinthe and Fosdick an anxious look. "Will I do?"

Assessing her cousin's glowing looks above the plum taffeta gown trimmed with falls of delicate Point de Venise lace, Hyacinthe replied, "You resemble nothing more than a delectable comfit, the sort one has at Christmas."

"You are in best looks," Fosdick confirmed in her proper way.

"Well, were it not for your excessive kindness in giving me this splendid gown, I should look a dowd. I can never thank you enough for all you have done, dear Cousin."

"I am pleased to see you settled and off my hands, if you must know," Hyacinthe said with a gay laugh.

"We must have a serious chat about your future one of these days. You insist upon avoiding the matter, but I shan't allow that forever." Jane studied Hyacinthe with a penetrating look, one that probably saw more than Hyacinthe wished to be seen. She was relieved when the coach stopped and Warton opened the door for the women.

Jane went on ahead to greet Barmore and discuss last-moment arrangements with him. Fosdick retired to the end of the hall, pleased to greet someone she knew.

Hyacinthe paused by the coach. "All is in readiness? You are to return to Tudor cottage. I doubt if you need hide, but just remain inconspicuous, perhaps?"

"His lordship told us just what to do, miss." Warton touched his hat in a respectful gesture, then stood stiffly at attention while Hyacinthe walked up the steps to the open door. She wondered what his lordship's instructions had been.

Lord Norwood walked up to greet her just inside the large and glittering entrance hall. The gray walls took on a warm tone from the myriad of candles; tall arrangements of autumn flowers and leaves graced the corners, adding to the appeal. Pleasant fires burned brightly on either side of the room. But Hyacinthe noted little of her surroundings in her concern.

"I trust you are prepared," she said in an undertone.

"Once the ball is well in progress I shall drop our little bomb in Wayland's ear. When he leaves, Val and I will be right behind him."

"You are far off the mark if you think I intend to be left behind in all this," she whispered vehemently. "I will be one of that party as well."

He gave her one of those amused, superior looks that men tend to bestow upon a woman when they believe men know better. Hyacinthe fumed, but silently, for she would do nothing to spoil Jane's happy moment. However, she intended to join those two men. She could shoot a gun as well as either of them, and they could use an extra person were Wayland to become violent.

When she entered the long gallery she could see that nearly everyone from the village was already present. The Widow Smith wore a rustling black taffeta gown of simple elegance that amazed Hyacinthe. Her graying curls showed from beneath a fashionable turban.

Mrs. Peachey wore a plain gray sarcenet cut in modest style and adorned with a pretty cameo pin to match her earrings and looked years younger.

If there was a faint aroma of camphor in the air, it was shortly banished by the scent from the flowers. It seemed that his lordship had emptied his conservatory of every decent bloom to be found.

Hyacinthe was quite touched by this gesture. He was giving this little ball, which consisted of the villagers and local gentry from nearby manor houses, mostly to catch a thief. But he was doing it with a grace and style that surprised and impressed her.

He had hired—Jane said all the way from Oxford—a musical group that now played softly in the background. Servants hovered along the edges of the growing throng.

She turned to face her host and admitted, "I could not have done better. This is something Jane will remember with fondness forever."

"But will you, I wonder?" he murmured, then walked away to greet new arrivals.

Blase thought she looked ravishing in the pale green taffeta gown. The neckline bordered on the scandalous, but even so it served as a foil for her exquisite skin and magnificent hair of rich deep red. He smiled. She couldn't quite hide those few freckles on her nose, in spite of what he suspected was a discreet application of rice powder.

Somehow those tiny specks of brown only served to make her more appealing if she but knew it. He greeted the guests, then turned them over to Val, who in turn guided them to where he felt they would be comfortable.

"She give you a bit of trouble?" Val muttered when he returned.

Not bothering to inquire who "she" was, Blase looked after Hyacinthe and shrugged. "She insists she is coming along with us. Why, I can't imagine. How does she think she will get there? I can't quite see that delectable gown perched on a horse, in spite of her determination."

"I would not make the mistake of underestimating her, my good friend," Val advised.

Mr. Wayland came from the rear of the house where he now stayed alone, Mr. Repton and his son having been called elsewhere. He wore a coat in a violent shade of puce over biscuit pantaloons. When Blase saw Wayland's patterned waistcoat in bright orange, he shuddered with horror.

"Good grief!" Val murmured. "It wanted only that."

"Look at it this way, we shall be doing the world a kindness by eliminating him, at least from English shores. For it will be transportation for him, I feel certain."

"I see your local Justice of the Peace is present with his good wife." Val studied Squire Knowler, then went on, "Looks to be a rather shrewd fellow. You intend to bring him in on this?"

"He has already been apprised of what has happened. I showed him the original papers, then the restored jewels and paintings. How fortunate that the next Sessions comes in Michaelmas, not too far away. Although I doubt if Wayland will like his stay in the jail until then."

"He'll like his trip to Botany Bay even less," Val said with evident satisfaction.

"The squire agreed that Wayland cannot be permitted to go free to practice this sort of thing again. Next time he might not have a Miss Dancy about to thwart his designs."

"Ah, yes. Miss Dancy. How do you intend to keep her here?" Val gave Blase a mocking smile, then added in an ironic tone, "I cannot see her standing idly by while you have all the fun. Be careful, she'll probably end up shooting you!"

Blase listened to his friend laugh and not for the first time wondered precisely why Val remained so bitter—or perhaps jaundiced would be a better word—toward women. Saying nothing, for he knew he'd receive no reply to any query, Blase merely shook his head, then wandered into the throng of happy guests.

It was not long before Blase chose to toast the betrothed couple, offering them his felicitations and hopes for a good future. The Justice of the Peace extended his good wishes as well, noting that Sir Charles was acquiring a wife who was well liked by all and who promised to be a fine helpmeet. Then the musical group struck up a joyous waltz and Sir Charles led his chosen lady into the dance to the gentle applause of the assembled.

Blase positioned himself close to where Wayland stood. The man was eyeing Mrs. Peachey's unexpectedly simple elegance.

"Amazing how a woman can bloom given the chance, what?" Blase commented to the angular architect.

They watched as Ambrose Clark led a blushing Mrs. Peachey into the dance. Then Wayland said, "Your curate is behaving unseemly, I think."

"Ah, perhaps he is merely celebrating his acquiring the title of vicar with greater things to come, once he has settled into his living."

"Vicar? The old one die?" Wayland said with a sneer.

"No. He failed to do the job he was supposed to do. I do not tolerate fools about me, once I uncover them. Crooks or cheats either," he added softly. "Witness my ex-bailiff, Tombler."

Wayland did not reply, but Blase observed that the chap's collar seemed to have become excessively tight all of a sudden. A sheen of moisture glistened on his forehead.

"By the by, did you know that I have decided to tear down the Tudor cottage after all? Miss Dancy has other plans for her future." That was no lie if Blase had his way. He would inform her later that she must alter her way of life considerably.

"Really?" Wayland said with distinct alarm. "How soon?"

"Quite soon. Miss Pennington will marry in two weeks and until then the two ladies are sure to be busy day and night preparing for the wedding. Once the wedding is over, the place comes down." Blase noted Wayland's worried frown with satisfaction. He believed what Blase said was true.

"But," the architect sputtered, "I thought you said Mr. Repton agreed it was a most picturesque house and added to your view."

Blase gave a negligent wave of his hand. "I changed my mind. The church spire is enough."

"I think Miss Dancy will be unhappy to leave there," Wayland said, obviously attempting to insert a bit of controversy.

"Miss Dancy," Blase said sharply, "has nothing to say in the matter."

"Excuse me," Mr. Wayland said, clearly agitated, "it has become somewhat warm in here. I believe I shall catch a bit of air on the terrace."

He turned to leave the room. Blase gave a nod to Val, then caught the squire's eye before sidling through the crowd to the main doorway. It was time for action and he felt primed as though for battle.

With the strains of music drifting down the stairs, he silently followed Wayland. Fortunately the chap was in such a tearing hurry he never looked behind him. He most likely believed his host content to entertain his guests.

Blase waited in the shadows of some drapery while Wayland slipped from the house to the terrace, then followed before the door could shut. Val and Squire Knowler were close behind him. Blase paused after letting the other two out of the door, thinking he heard something.

A rustle of taffeta clearly reached his ears. Miss Dancy sailed down the stairs, her soft kerseymere cloak billowing about her.

"I suspected you might try a trick like this," she fumed quietly when she confronted him. "If you think you will go without me, think again."

"And what could you do if I chose to leave you behind, my sweet?" Blase reached out to suggestively trail a finger down one petal-soft cheek in a most daring manner.

"I shall scream the house down, and most likely alert Wayland to trouble!"

Blase gazed into those fiery green eyes, eyes which promised trouble if not a great deal more. Could he resist their appeal? Knowing he would likely regret this, he nodded.

"Good," she said with a snap. "Let us be gone before Wayland stumbles into the trap set for him and we miss the entire event."

Blase couldn't fail to admire the way she whisked herself around the corner and dashed across the terrace, not making a sound in her soft slippers.

When they came up to his waiting horse, she merely turned to face him, an expectant look on her face. "Well?"

Resigned to his fate by now, Blase lifted her to the horse, then leaped up behind her, holding her as close to him as could possibly be allowed.

"Sir?" she questioned, turning her head to look up at him. She was just tantalizing inches away.

"All things will be explained in due time," he said, knowing he must sound obscure, but she couldn't be allowed to have everything her way.

The horses' hooves had been wrapped in sacking, as though they were highwaymen set on a robbery. They followed Wayland just close enough to see the fellow, yet distant enough so he should not hear them.

Hyacinthe nestled snugly against the man seated behind her. His arms came around her—to hold the reins, nothing more—but he had such a manly form and such comforting arms. She balanced as best she could, given the jouncing ride.

The oddest sensation that his lips touched her hair assailed her. But that was preposterous. The man detested her; she was certain of that. Although there had been recent moments when she had hoped. But no more.

Blase. What an appropriate name for a man who had started an unquenchable fire within her. It was a fire she must douse, however. She refused to pine for him once this was done and he went on his way. And considering the state of her fragile heart, that had best be soon.

They tore through the night, Hyacinthe relishing her closeness to Blase. Faint shadows cast by the half-moon crossed their path. She leaned into his strength.

They halted and she found herself abruptly hauled to the ground. Once certain Wayland had reached the Tudor house and tied his reins to a limb, Blase, Hyacinthe, and the others silently stalked toward the house on foot, leaving their horses tied near the green.

Tom Coachman hurried forth to take charge of them.

Unwilling to break the silence to deliver Blase a deserved scold for the rough treatment, Hyacinthe contented herself with giving him a dirty look.

"Follow me . . . and try to stay out of trouble, please?" The pleading note in his voice indicated he did not hold great hope of this.

"I never get into trouble of my own making," she whispered back at him. She thought she heard a derisive snort, but it was very faint.

Deciding they intended to trap Wayland at the base of the secret entry, Hyacinthe left them and ran to the front door, slipping inside without a sound. Even in here she could hear

Wayland frantically at work prying the door open. One by one the nails popped out.

Hyacinthe crept up the stairs and into her room. In her drawer she found her loaded gun, then prepared to wait at the top of the secret passage in her closet. She propped open the panel, but Wayland couldn't know that someone waited there for him. If he had naught but a candle, he wouldn't see beyond the immediate area he searched. He was in for a surprise.

At last the final nail was pried out and the secret access slowly opened. Wayland paused, as though to see if he had been detected. Since Fosdick had made herself conspicuous in the entry of the Hall, Wayland must feel certain the cottage now stood empty.

Hyacinthe heard his footsteps coming up toward her and she raised her gun, hoping he'd not hear her cock it.

The light of his lone candle wavered and flickered in the draft. He shielded the flame with his other hand, thus having no defense should someone rush him.

All was silent save for his steps. Then he reached the spot where the jewels had been hidden and stopped.

Hyacinthe backed away a trifle lest the shimmering green of her skirt be seen. Her gun remained aimed at her target.

He tore at the paneling, having no regard for the fine old wood. When he had removed the last panel he grabbed the box within, little knowing that it contained mere trumpery.

"Stop where you are, Wayland," Blase ordered from the bottom of the secret stairs.

Wayland immediately turned to flee to the top. Here he came face-to-face with Hyacinthe and shrieked in fright, seeing no more than a hooded cloak in the shadows.

In the ensuing minutes nothing was clear except that they could have used some light. Dudley Wayland dropped his candle, which was immediately stomped on by Hyacinthe to prevent a fire.

Then she fired her gun in the direction of his footsteps, hoping to hit the villain even with poor light, and was pleased to hear a man cry out.

But . . . the voice did not sound like Wayland's in the least.

"I've got him," Blase shouted with satisfaction from the far side of the room.

Hyacinthe quickly located her lamp, lit it with trembling fingers—for she suspected she might be in for a scold—then turned about.

"Oh, no!" she cried in dismay. She beheld a sobering sight.

Blase did indeed hold Wayland and was in the process of binding him up with the aid of Squire Knowler. Lord Latham slumped against the far wall, his hand clamped around his arm. Blood seeped between his fingers.

Hyacinthe felt ill.

"I did not know I displeased you so greatly, Miss Dancy," Lord Latham managed to say between gritted teeth.

"*I* did not know that you trailed behind Wayland, sir. I am most sorry," Hyacinthe said, hoping she sounded as regretful as she truly was. She found a stack of linen cloths and made a pad to place over the wound. Warton, who had entered from the hall, assisted her. He located a tin of basilicum powder, then went for a basin of warm water from the kitchen. He returned shortly.

While Blase informed Dudley Wayland of what he knew about Wayland's theft of the jewels, Hyacinthe worked over a now-seated Lord Latham. She removed his coat with difficulty, then—after a moment's deliberation—tore off the sleeve of his shirt. It appeared to her in the lamplight that the wound was but a graze. Nevertheless, it ought not have happened and she felt remorse that she should be the one to hurt him.

Within a brief time she had cleaned the wound, sprinkled on a bit of basilicum powder, placed the pad over it, and tightly bound his arm. When done, she gathered up the torn sleeve and his coat, then waited.

"I fancy Blase is safe enough now," Lord Latham said in his more familiar wry manner. "It is his friends who must take care."

"I did not hurt you on purpose, you know," Hyacinthe said, quite on the verge of tears.

"I shall turn this fellow over to my deputy," Squire Knowler announced. "I doubt if he will like his imprisonment, but he ought to have thought of that before he ventured forth on a life of crime," the squire added, prodding Wayland in the back with a not-too-kind finger.

"And we, with a few adjustments for Val, will return to the ball," Blase replied. "I had hoped that none would be the wiser regarding our absence. Pity you had to get yourself shot, Val."

"I suspect it is time for me to leave your house, Blase. If Miss Dancy is turning her dangerous attentions in my direction, I dare not remain." The old familiar mockery could be heard along with another, almost pensive note.

"Nonsense," Hyacinthe declared briskly. "I shall take great care to stay out of your way, sir. And as to the future, who knows what may happen? I may throw myself on my dear brother's mercy."

"Poor fellow," Lord Latham muttered ungraciously. He winced when Hyacinthe placed his coat over his shoulders, then they all straggled down the stairs.

Tom Coachman insisted that Miss Hyacinthe ought to ride in the coach to keep an eye on poor Lord Latham.

And so she did. She kept a nervous watch on his skeptical lordship, maintaining a dignified silence all the way. He said nothing, staring out of the window into the dark of the night as though he saw something of interest.

It said much for the food, drink—especially the fine drink— and the company that the conspirators had not been missed.

Hyacinthe handed her cloak to Barmore, smoothed her curls from her face, then braved the stairs to the gallery. Warton assisted Lord Latham, with Lord Norwood on his other side.

"Not much of an injury," Lord Latham insisted, although somewhat weakly.

"Good thing you won't be missed from the celebrations, then. For you, my friend, are to retire with a splitting headache. Or do you have another ailment in mind?" Blase said in a jovial manner only a trifle forced.

"Make me sound like a dashed wetgoose," Val complained.

"I shall say an old wound is troubling you if anyone asks," Blase said. "Something from our Oxford days."

"Fine," Val muttered, "just fine."

Blase ran lightly down the steps to where his guests still

mingled. Excellent music drifted toward him as he entered the room. Knowing he did not show any damage—save a faint aroma of horse, which would scarcely be detected, here what with the perfumes, sweat, and scents of food and flowers—he felt safe.

And then he saw Hyacinthe.

She stood quietly chatting with the new Vicar Clark, listening for the most part. Those pert freckles stood out in bold relief. She appeared fashionably pale.

Wending his way through the appreciative throng of increasingly happy guests, Blase found a path to her side.

Ambrose Clark exchanged glances with his lordship, then found he urgently required a glass of negus.

"Are you all right?" Blase clasped her elbow, guiding her along to a sofa close to the door.

"Yes, indeed. I drank some of your excellent champagne when I came in here, then found the good vicar. You were not gone very long." She blinked several times.

"No one has commented on our absence?"

She grinned at him, a small parody of her normal dazzling smile. "I have received two hints that I was away with you too long to be quite proper. I fear you have another shocking tale added to your list." She waggled a finger at him in a mock scold.

"Blast," Blase murmured, distressed that she would be harried in such a way. "You realize that you simply cannot remain in the cottage, gossip being what it is."

"You mean that the locals may link me—a redhead—to the lady your great-great-grandfather housed there? And what is more link you to him?" She smiled wanly. "I do not believe I should like to become your mistress, sir, even if you are a handsome brute. I suppose you could make me an offer. Perhaps I may find it irresistible." She giggled.

"How much champagne did you consume, anyway?"

"One, two, perhaps three glasses. I was very thirsty," she explained carefully.

"Hyacinthe, I hope you do not make a practice of driving a man mad." Blase wished he could whisk her out of here to a more private location.

"Never," she proclaimed somberly. "How is Val?"

Surprised at her use of his name, Blase replied, "He will do well enough. You saw to his care so he ought to mend, at least his arm. Do you fancy him as well, Hyacinthe?" he said boldly.

She merely blinked, then said, "Not at all. He needs someone who can gently nurse him from his misery. I want a man who can offer me a challenge, but of a different sort." With that she ceased to speak, turning aside to look where Jane danced with Sir Charles. "She is as happy today as she may ever be, unless you count her wedding day. It was kind of you to give her this. You are a very good man, I believe."

With that pronouncement she slid gracefully from the sofa to the floor. Or would have had Blase not caught her in his arms and carried her from the gallery.

He found Fosdick lurking in the hall.

"I think it best we see that Miss Dancy return home," he stated, defying the maid to comment.

"Aye, she has sustained more shocks this eve than a gently bred lady ought. But then, her father always said she's as tough as old boots." With that, the maid disappeared down the stairs. Blase could hear her giving Barmore instructions.

If ever a man had been more frustrated than Blase at that moment, he couldn't imagine who he might be. He stood alone with a deliciously beautiful woman in his arms . . . and she had to be unconscious. Or asleep. He didn't know which was worse.

Fosdick returned with the cloak Hyacinthe had worn on the dash across the hills to the old village. "The coach will be in front of the house shortly, my lord. Come."

It was not long before Blase deposited Hyacinthe in her coach, then watched Tom drive it off toward the old village. Well, he thought, so much for carefully laid plans that called for soft music, moonlight, and well-rehearsed words.

The following morning Hyacinthe woke feeling tired and out of sorts. She was not permitted the luxury of suffering in silence.

"Are you awake? Poor dear. Lord Norwood sent you a vast

array of flowers. Warton explained everything." Bearing a tray, Jane tiptoed into the room.

Hyacinthe eyed the contents of the tray and consented to a cup of tea and some dry toast. "I am well enough. *You* had a lovely evening, I believe."

Jane went into raptures over her splendid evening, the likes of which had never been known to anyone before. When she had praised everything from the music to the food, the lovely guests and all else, she became silent a moment.

"I think we need to talk. I will be leaving this house before long. You have avoided explaining what you intend to do with yourself. Did you actually write to anyone?"

"I suspect you know that I did not," Hyacinthe admitted, pushing herself up in bed.

"Well?"

"I believe I shall visit my brother in London after all," Hyacinthe said at long last.

"In spite of the mummies?" Jane asked with a smile.

"Bother the mummies. I need a change. Who knows when his whimsical lordship may decide to tear this place down?"

She faintly recalled saying some shocking things to Lord Norwood last evening. Words about his great-great-grandfather and his mistress. She groaned at the very idea.

"Did you see that the painting of the beautiful red-haired lady was hanging prominently in the gallery? A few people think you resemble her."

"Merely the red hair," Hyacinthe grumbled. She pushed aside her covers and left her bed. "I intend to dress and go for a stroll on the green. Will you join me?"

"Too much to do. But you go; the fresh air will do you much good," Jane observed sagely.

Hyacinthe rapidly did as intended, then slowly made her way along the pond with a bleak heart. She had come here with such noble purposes. Yet, in spite of all her mistakes, Jane had found a gentleman who truly cared for her and she would have a happy future with him.

This left Hyacinthe alone, on the shelf, no one to turn to other than a brother who really didn't wish her presence in London and a grandmother who was likely up to her ears with cousin Lady Chloe. It also left Hyacinthe yearning for a gentleman she could not have.

"Do you intend to fall into a green melancholy?" said a curious male voice from behind her. "If so, you had best douse yourself with tinted powder, for I have it on good authority that you look far too delicious."

Hyacinthe whirled about, teetering on the edge of the pond, waved her arms to regain her balance and lost. She knew she'd end up in the pond and shut her eyes against that slimy green water.

Instead she found herself captured in strong arms and drawn close to a manly chest that smelled faintly of costmary and spice. "Blase," she whispered. When he refused to put her on her feet, she tilted her head. Below her was the pond. He wouldn't, would he?

"We have some unfinished business, my love."

She blinked at the endearment. "I owe you an apology, at least I think I do. Something about your great-great-grandfather and the redhead?"

He drew her even closer. Hyacinthe grew worried at the gleam in his eyes. Did he mean to tease her, then?

"He had the right idea, only she came along too late for him. I do not intend to make the same mistake. Will you marry me, my love? Say you will, or I will drop you in the pond. Only fitting, considering our past."

Hyacinthe threw her arms tightly about his neck and plastered herself against him quite firmly. "Before you acquire any notions, I agree to wed you whenever you wish."

"I already have the notions, my dearest," he murmured, then kissed her with all the fire he possessed.

Behind them a couple watched in fond contentedness. Her red hair had faded, as had her Tudor-style gown. The gentleman, garbed in doublet and hose, gave his lady a pinch on her posterior and grinned. "They'll do fine now, I believe." The redhead winked saucily in response. And then they vanished from sight with naught but their laughter remaining.

P9-EIG-173

INDIA:
BUSINESS
CHECKLISTS

An Essential Guide
to Doing Business

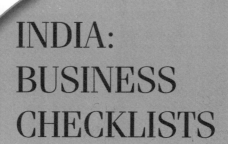

INDIA: BUSINESS CHECKLISTS

An Essential Guide to Doing Business

Rupa K. Bose

John Wiley & Sons (Asia) Pte. Ltd.

SCHAUMBURG TOWNSHIP
DISTRICT LIBRARY
130 SOUTH ROSELLE ROAD
SCHAUMBURG, ILLINOIS 60193

382

BOSE, R

Copyright © 2009 John Wiley & Sons (Asia) Pte. Ltd.
Published in 2009 by John Wiley & Sons (Asia) Pte. Ltd.
2 Clementi Loop, #02-01, Singapore 129809

All rights reserved.   **3 1257 01823 7668**

No part of this publication may be reproduced, stored in a retrieval system or transmitted in any form or by any means, electronic, mechanical, photocopying, recording, scanning or otherwise, except as expressly permitted by law, without either the prior written permission of the Publisher, or authorization through payment of the appropriate photocopy fee to the Copyright Clearance Center. Requests for permission should be addressed to the Publisher, John Wiley & Sons (Asia) Pte. Ltd., 2 Clementi Loop, #02-01, Singapore 129809, tel: 65-64632400, fax: 65-64646912, e-mail: enquiry@wiley.com.

This publication is designed to provide accurate and authoritative information in regard to the subject matter covered. It is sold with the understanding that the publisher is not engaged in rendering professional services. If professional advice or other expert assistance is required, the services of a competent professional person should be sought.

Other Wiley Editorial Offices

John Wiley & Sons, Inc., 111 River Street, Hoboken, NJ 07030, USA
John Wiley & Sons, Ltd., The Atrium, Southern Gate, Chichester, West Sussex PO19 8SQ, UK
John Wiley & Sons (Canada), Ltd., 5353 Dundas Street West, Suite 400, Toronto, Ontario M9B 6H8, Canada
John Wiley & Sons Australia Ltd., 42 McDougall Street, Milton, Queensland 4064, Australia
Wiley-VCH, Boschstrasse 12, D-69469 Weinheim, Germany

Library of Congress Cataloging-in-Publication Data

ISBN: 978-0-470-82421-4

Typeset in 10/13 point, Quorum Book by C&M Digitals (P) Ltd.
Printed in Singapore by Markono Print Media Pte. Ltd.
10 9 8 7 6 5 4 3 2 1

Contents

To my father, Ashim C. Bose, in memoriam.

Acknowledgments

This book was inspired by a short report that my late father, A.C. Bose, and I wrote some 20 years ago, called *India: Business Checklists*. The country had barely taken the first steps toward liberalization, and remained extremely restricted. Nevertheless, for companies willing to take the time (lots of it) and trouble (also lots of it), substantial payoffs existed. Our report was aimed at multinational companies interested in those payoffs. India has liberalized a great deal since then, and it's been interesting looking back at the advice we offered.

This book, which is triple the size of that original report and based on new research, has the same basic mission: to provide a realistic, pragmatic view of doing business in India. It's intended as an intensely practical guide for companies and individuals.

The finished product is the result of interviews or correspondence with many individuals both inside India and outside it. Some of them gave me information, or introduced me to others who would. Some facilitated my visits and my discussions. Others helped me by reviewing sections of the book, and making suggestions. Although I cannot acknowledge all of them (and some would not wish to be acknowledged), I thank them all. I'd like to mention some names:

Adit Jain, Air Commodore Banerji (retd.), Alok Agarwal, Ambi Venkateswaran, Bettina Bernhardt, Deepak Jolly, Gautam Bose, Geetha Iyer, George Russell, Girish Ahuja, John Kivel, Kavish Arora, Mark Langhammer, Mohini Banerji, Mukul Shukla, N. Madhavan, N. Shankar, Nigel Marsh, P.C. Abraham, Paul Moreton, Pavan Behl, R. Balakrishnan, Rajeev Gowda, Rajiv

Bali, Rajiv Luthra, Ramesh Padmanabhan, Sanjoy Chowdhury, Shyam Ananthnarayan, Sujata Madhok, Tim Jones, Vikram Talwar, and Vishwavir Ahuja.

I have tried to make this book as accurate and comprehensive as possible, but India's business environment is changing rapidly. For that reason, I would recommend double-checking any crucial facts.

India: Boom Town!

India these days feels like a boom town. Economic growth is transforming the urban areas of the country. Consumers are feeling wealthy, and buying a much greater range of goods and services than before, at hundreds of shops and in glittering malls. The entrepreneurial energy is electric. Opportunities appear everywhere. At the same time, many of the problems of a boom town have appeared: strained infrastructure, chaotic growth, pollution, shortages of skilled workers, and, possibly, increased corruption.

India has always been a tantalizing opportunity for international companies.

India's population passed one billion in the 2001 census, and was estimated to be about 1.1 billion in 2007. It is growing at an estimated 1.4 percent annually. With half the population under 21, it is also a youthful market. The introduction of satellite TV in the past decade has changed tastes, and has created unsatisfied demand for a range of new goods and services. A consumer boom is under way; the fundamental demand for goods and services is huge.

India's unprecedented growth rates in recent years astounded those who had grown accustomed to the "Hindu rate of growth" of 3–4 percent or even the early liberalization rates of 5–6 percent. Now, growth rates of 8–9 percent seem normal. The per-capita income is low, but in recent years, rapid growth in GDP has lifted a large number of people into the middle class, and disposable incomes have risen sharply. India is now ranked as the twelfth-largest economy in the world (and third largest by purchasing power parity).

The magic of these large numbers ensures that despite education being far from universal, even a relatively small percentage of people with good education—most in schools teaching in English—results in a very large base of well-educated jobseekers, consumers, and entrepreneurs. India has become known for all kinds of operations, from simple call centers to heart surgery.

Add to that is a legal system that is recognizably based on the British one, and the use of English as the language of business and government, and the country seems to be a remarkably accessible business opportunity.

And so it is—with caveats.

It's an extremely challenging place to do business, primarily on account of governmental regulation. Despite substantial improvements over the past 15 years, India remains regulated.

"It has a federal system," said Narayanan Madhavan, a former Reuters correspondent, "so you must check regulations at the central level, state level, and local level. Apparent business-friendly regulations can turn out to be implemented in contrary ways."

"There's been a lot of deregulation at the center," a business executive noted. "But now, you have to deal with the states." (India has a federal system, with 28 states and seven "union territories"—effectively mini-states. The central government is based in New Delhi.)

Getting a project under way may still mean dealing with the government on many levels: the center for overall approval; the state in which the project is to be situated; and local authorities—the municipal authorities in cities, and the *panchayats* (local councils) in rural areas.

In 2008, the World Bank ranked India as 120th out of 178 countries in the difficulty of doing business. At that, its rank had improved from 2007, where it ranked 132nd. Most of the improvement came in only two areas: getting credit and trading across borders. India ranked above the median in employing workers, getting credit, protecting investors, and trading across borders. It ranked a dismal 177th in enforcing contracts.

Despite all the regulations, India is also a "soft state." Regulations are frequently flouted, and enforcement is patchy, especially at an individual or small-company level. Large companies, which are more visible, are more likely to face enforcement—but as in many countries, they may also be better prepared to deal with it.

The other critical problem (and opportunity) is an infrastructure under strain. Already stretched 15 years ago when India started its rapid expansion, it has not kept pace with the country's economic growth. Ingenious workarounds, although expensive, have allowed companies and the country to continue growing.

This book of checklists is meant to prepare an expatriate businessperson for the realities of doing business in India.

India: huge, confusing, difficult, accessible, easy

N. Madhavan, the former Reuters correspondent and an experienced business journalist, had this to say: "There's an old saying—Everything you say about India, the opposite is also true. Hurried impressions can be misleading.

"India has a vibrant democracy," he noted, "which means the pace of change is slower, but there is more stability. Comparisons with China are pointless, mainly because India is a democracy. Regulations and red tape are a part of life. It's a long-term market; few opportunities exist for quick profits. There's a high level of entrepreneurial energy in India, and it quickly saturates any opportunity.

"Regulations can change in response to situations. Obstacles can be created by influential Indian groups. They have social and political influence, and it's better not to take them head-on. The groups are transforming into powerful well-connected global players.

"Certain industries remain intensively regulated: insurance, retail, telecom, entertainment, defense, and food.

"India is currently in a confused situation regarding environmental issues. While the government is increasingly aware of the environment, it is not the top item of anyone's agenda. Solar power, despite initial promise, has gained little traction owing to high costs—including servicing costs, poor reliability, and lack of grid access.

"The flipside of the demographic win—the huge and growing market—is population pressure on all resources.

"The immediate bottleneck is infrastructure: the current five-year-plan focuses on power, roads, and telecommunications. No one expects the problem to be solved soon, but substantial investments will be made, and the infrastructure improved."

MAP OF INDIA

New Delhi
(NCR)

Kolkata
(Calcutta)

Mumbai
(Bombay)

Hyderabad

Bangalore

Chennai
(Madras)

PART 1
The Context

This set of checklists is about the historic, economic, and political context. Companies that understand this background will have a better appreciation of the direction in which policy and the economy are moving.

1.1 Basic Facts

India is a huge country, with considerable differences from region to region. With a population approaching 1.2 billion, and a ground area of 1.3 million square miles, it is better understood as a continent than as a single country.

- **The climate:** India's climate varies by region, but in general, there is a hot summer, tempered by the arrival of the southwest monsoon—the country's main rainy season—followed by a gradual fall in temperatures through a cool winter. The winter tends to be the peak travel time; the heat of summer is uncomfortable, and the rains frequently play havoc with the overstretched infrastructure. However, different cities are differently affected. The monsoon, which is critical for agriculture and freshwater supplies, is watched very carefully each year, and its progress charted in the news. A good or bad monsoon can affect the GDP growth in that year.

- **Time zones:** India, fortunately, has only one time zone, and no daylight saving time. It is five and a half hours ahead of GMT.

- **Government:** India is a parliamentary democracy, and elections are held every five years (unless the government is dissolved before that). The President—elected by the parliament and the state legislatures—is the head of state, with powers that are largely ceremonial except in case of a crisis. The prime minister, selected by the party that wins the elections, is the head of government. Voting is not compulsory, but there is nevertheless a fairly high rate of participation.

- **The census:** India conducts a census every 10 years (the next one is due in 2011); and for such a vast country, with such a huge rural hinterland, it achieves a remarkably accurate count. Most population projections are based on census data.

- **Demographics:** India's population at the most recent census was 1.01 billion, growing at 1.3–1.4 percent annually; it was estimated to have exceeded 1.14 billion by end-2007. Perhaps 370 million of these are children under 15 years old. The sex ratio is skewed in favor of males; there are an estimated 107 men for every 100 women. (For under-15s, it is about 110 boys for every 100 girls.) The generalized cultural preference for sons has been strengthened by the availability of modern technology for prenatal gender determination, and the means to afford it.

- **Languages:** India has more than 200 mutually unintelligible languages. Most—but not all—belong to the Indo-European group of languages. Unlike in China, there is no common script. As a result, English and Hindi have gained importance as link languages, particularly in large cities.

- **States:** India is divided into 28 states and seven union territories, largely along linguistic lines. (Language is used as the primary determination of ethnicity in India.)

- **Religion:** About 80 percent of Indians are Hindus, 13 percent are Muslim, 2 percent each are Christians and Sikhs, and the remainder a mixture of Buddhists, Jains, and other religious groups. For the most part, the religious groups coexist reasonably harmoniously, but there have been vicious and violent attacks on occasion, in the form of riots and murder.

- **Cities and villages:** India remains a primarily rural country, despite the rapid growth of cities and towns. More than 70 percent of Indians live in the villages, and only 30 percent in urban areas. The 2001 census listed

34 cities with populations exceeding one million. Seven cities—Mumbai, Kolkata, Delhi, Chennai, Hyderabad, Bangalore, and Ahmedabad—had populations greater than five million.

- **The stockmarket:** India has an extremely active domestic stockmarket, and more than 5,000 listed companies. Foreign companies are allowed to buy stocks, but with restrictions. India has several stock exchanges, but the Bombay Stock Exchange (BSE) and the National Stock Exchange (NSE) are the most significant. Each has more than 4,500 listed companies, and market capitalization exceeding US$1 trillion.

- **Inflation rate:** India's inflation rate has averaged 4–6 percent annually in the past five years, down from a historical rate of about 8 percent.

- **Airports:** India has about 80 actual airports, and hundreds of basic functional landing strips. Of the 80 airports, 24 account for most of the traffic. Some 16 offer international services, but most international flights mainly connect to Delhi, Mumbai, Chennai, Kolkata, Bangalore, and Hyderabad. The country plans to have 500 airports by 2020. Major airports are being modernized.

- **Ports:** The country has a long seaboard to the east and west, with 11 major ports and more than 130 minor ports. However, most of the freight goes through Mumbai and Mormagao (the alternate spelling is Marmagao) in Goa on the west coast, and Chennai and Visakhapatnam on the east coast.

  India's ports still have limited capacity. Delays in handling are normal. Coordination can be a problem: ports sometimes get backed up because the containers cannot be moved out onto the railway lines. "We need dedicated freight corridors," said a consultant. "We expect Indian ports to go from handling 580 million tons to 1.3 billion tons by 2013, but we haven't invested enough to achieve that."

  They are in the process of modernization; money has been sanctioned, and prefeasibility studies started.

- **Clearing and forwarding:** Clearing and forwarding agents reach all large cities and even most small towns.

- **Internet:** India has 183 ISPs, of which 41 are all-India. The Indian government occasionally blocks access (or encourages ISPs to block access) to sites that are considered subversive or pornographic, or to be promoting gambling, racism, violence, and terrorism. Issues of computer security are handled by the government organization CERT-IN, which also handles such problems as phishing and cyber-attacks. (CERT-IN parallels other CERT organizations around the world, such as USCERT.)

- **Driving:** International driving licenses are valid. Vehicle are supposed to keep to the left of the road. Traffic is chaotic, and observance of traffic rules poor.

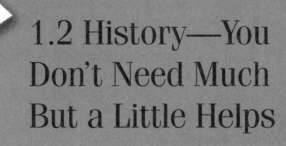

1.2 History—You Don't Need Much But a Little Helps

Some books suggest that a business visitor needs to understand India's history to be effective. Perhaps—but all that's really needed are the main points below.

- **India became an independent democracy in 1947:** In 1947, India became independent from the British rule, winning independence by diplomacy, not war. It became a secular parliamentary democracy on the British model, with a president as head of state and prime minister as head of government. Unlike many nations that became independent about the same time, India has been able to preserve its democracy, and most Indians are intensely proud of this, while also taking it for granted.

- **The Partition of India was a crucial event:** As the British withdrew, India was divided into two states: India and Pakistan—at that time, West Pakistan and East Pakistan, now Bangladesh. (Burma had been separated earlier.) This is known as the Partition. The plan was to create a Muslim state in Muslim-majority areas.

  The process of Partition was botched. There were mass migrations of Hindus to India and Muslims to Pakistan (although millions of Muslims decided not to leave). This exchange of populations was accompanied by riots and bloodshed on both sides of the new border, and left deep scars, particularly in north India.

- **India has fought three wars with Pakistan—and one with China :** The state of Kashmir has been a cause of dispute since 1947. Both India and Pakistan consider it part of their territory. The de facto line of control actually divides the state into two parts, controlled by the two countries. The whole issue is further complicated by some Kashmiri interests that want independence from both countries. The two countries have fought three wars, including the one that ended in Bangladesh becoming independent.

- **British rule had a lasting impact:** More than 50 years after independence, the effects of the British rule on the political system, the legal system, education, the use of English, and other areas continue to be felt.

   British colonization—and earlier influence—in India lasted for about 200 years. Before 1947, India—which at the time constituted the present Pakistan and Bangladesh, as well as Myanmar (then Burma)—was a British colony. The British came to India to trade, but eventually established themselves as a political power. The East India Company became a de facto government, operating through the existing princes. By 1850, it governed nearly all of India, which became a British colony, governed by the Crown. Some princely states continued to exist, but they owed fealty to the Crown.

- **India chose a semi-socialist economic path:** After independence, India chose a "mixed economy," based on the most progressive thinking of British intellectuals in the 1940s. It blended capitalism, state capitalism, and socialism, with an emphasis on controls. In the 1990s, it became apparent that this path, which might have furthered social justice and established the Indian industry, was doing little to encourage rapid growth.

- **In the 1990s, India liberalized its economy:** Some 45 years after independence, India shifted toward a more capitalist, market-driven economic system.

Its economic growth rate has climbed from about 3 percent per year to about 8–9 percent per year. Many of the controls in place since 1947 have been removed or reduced to a large extent.

- **India was once a Hindu country with mainly Muslim rulers:** Before the British era, India was ruled primarily by a Muslim monarchy for centuries. Starting about the eighth century, invading Muslim monarchs established city states in India, and gradually came to rule much of a majority Hindu nation—although some Hindu kingdoms existed right up to the British era. India was essentially a Hindu land. Hinduism evolved from local religions and Iranian influences, and refers not just to religious beliefs but a whole way of life.

  The greatest of these Muslim monarchs were the Mughal emperors, starting with Babur in 1526. The resulting Indo-Saracenic culture spurred a flowering of art and architecture. This dynasty governed Northern India for close on 250 years, and its power sometimes extended far into the south. Urdu and Persian were the languages of law, the courts, and scholarship. By the end of the period, it had weakened considerably, and the British moved into a fragmented India.

- **For most of its history, India was a region of multiple kingdoms:** Before the Mughals, India was not a single nation, but a continent, an amalgam of many kingdoms, and whenever the central power weakened, it tended to revert to this form.

  These kingdoms sometimes paid homage to a central authority, whose reach depended on military, economic and political factors.

1.2.1 Historic Names and References

Ashoka: An emperor of the Maurya dynasty who reigned from about 273–232 BC, Ashoka was considered one of the greatest kings of India. He conquered and unified most of India, and became a Buddhist out of respect for its humane ideals in reaction to a particularly brutal war. He spread a doctrine of tolerance, equality and humanitarianism.

Akbar (1542–1605): Considered the greatest Mughal emperor, Akbar worked to reconcile Hindu and Muslim interests, and unlike some other emperors, respected Hindu rights of worship, and repealed a differential tax on Hindus. He married a Hindu princess to establish ties with the Rajputs, the royal families of Rajasthan.

Shivaji (1627–1680): Revered in Maharashtra as an idealized Maratha leader, a leader and king in western India, he is best known for carving out an independent Maratha kingdom and defending it against powerful surrounding kings, including the Mughal emperor, Aurangzeb.

Mahatma Gandhi (1869–1948): Mohandas Karamchand Gandhi, revered as the "Father of the Nation," was a lawyer who turned to social activism and became the leader who captured the hearts and minds of most Indians. He fought against the British rule with a policy of non-violence, but was assassinated by a Hindu extremist shortly after Independence.

Subhash Chandra Bose (1897–1945?): A respected freedom fighter who opposed Gandhi's philosophy, Bose believed that direct action would be necessary for success. He joined the "enemy of his enemy" during World War II, and sought alliance with the Axis powers, particularly Japan. He is believed to have been killed in a plane crash.

Jawaharlal Nehru (1889–1964): Nehru was India's first prime minister, and a leader of India's Congress Party. He fought for freedom, but remained on cordial terms with the British through the process. An idealist and a believer in Fabian socialism, his long term in office allowed him to stabilize India's democracy in ways that did not occur in many of the countries that became independent in the same era.

Muhammad Ali Jinnah (1876–1948): Jinnah was Nehru's counterpart in the Muslim League, and crucial to the founding of the nation of Pakistan. He became its first governor-general, but died of tuberculosis and cancer barely a year later. His daughter, Dina, married a Parsi industrialist, and remained in India.

Louis Mountbatten (1900–1979): Mountbatten was the last viceroy and first governor-general of India, and was closely involved in Britain's withdrawal. In business terms, he was a key member of the transition team. He was assassinated by the Irish Republican Army in 1979.

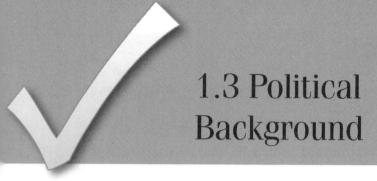

1.3 Political Background

- **India is a multiparty democracy:** In recent times, coalitions have been necessary to enable any party to form the government. Since the country works on the federal system, elections are held separately in the states and at the center. Some parties are national parties; others have a base only in a particular state.

  Regional parties can be critically important in helping building coalitions in what is often a fragmented vote. This can impact policy, since even small parties may play a crucial "swing vote" role.

  In the past few years, the increasing strength of regional parties is changing Indian politics. No single party is likely to win an election outright, so the dominant party must compromise in order to build a stable coalition. Many observers feel this will slow the pace of market reforms, and more populist policies are a likely outcome. The general direction of reform, though, seems stable, having weathered several changes of government.

- **The national parties:** The single largest party is the *Indian National Congress*. It leads the governing coalition at present, and has, in some form, governed India for most of the years since independence in 1947.

  The *Bharatiya Janata Party* is the largest opposition party. It was in power between 1998 and 2004, and leads the opposition at present.

The other national parties are:

◆ the *Communist Party of India* (CPI)
◆ the *Communist Party of India (Marxist)* (CPI(M)), which is strong in the states of Kerala, West Bengal and Tripura
◆ the *Bahujan Samaj Party* (BSP), which seeks to represent people at the bottom of India's caste system, and is particularly strong in Uttar Pradesh
◆ the *Nationalist Congress Party* (NCP)
◆ *Dravida Munnettra Kazhagam* (DMK), a regional party based mainly in Tamil Nadu but also in Pondicherry.

All five are currently aligned with the Congress Party coalition, though only the NCP is actually part of it.

• **Political history:** The Congress Party, a key player in the freedom movement during the British era, held power for 30 years from independence in 1947. It was led by Prime Minister Jawaharlal Nehru until his death in 1964, then by several other leaders until Indira Gandhi took over in 1966.

In 1975, Indira Gandhi, then leader of the Congress Party, imposed the "Emergency," a period of suspension of civil rights during which some observers feared that India's democracy was dead. She lifted the Emergency in 1977, and called an election.

The opposition parties united against the Congress; the Janata Party ("People's Party") headed a coalition in 1977 in a surprise win. It was India's first non-Congress government in 30 years. Morarji Desai became prime minister at the age of 81. (He was to live to 99.)

The Janata-led coalition fell apart in two years, forcing the President to call a general election.

Early elections in 1980 returned the Congress to power.

Its leader, Prime Minister Indira Gandhi, was assassinated in 1984, but her son, Rajiv, headed the party to an electoral win.

The Congress Party lost the 1989 election. The second-largest party, the Janata Dal, ("People's Group") formed a coalition government.

Internal disagreements led to another early election in 1991. While campaigning, Rajiv Gandhi was assassinated.

The Congress Party won in 1991 election, but lost the next in 1996.

The Janata Dal formed an unstable government initially headed by V.P. Singh, and then by Chandra Shekhar.

Early elections in 1998 again returned an unstable coalition, this time led by the BJP.

This forced yet another election in 1999, and again the BJP coalition came to power. This time, it was able to complete its five-year term under Prime Minister Atal Bihari Vajpayee.

Election in 2004 returned the Indian National Congress, led by Sonia Gandhi, to power.

She declined to become prime minister, and instead nominated the respected economist Manmohan Singh to the post.

Elections are due to be held in 2009.

- **Timeline**

1947	Independence; Congress Party comes to power and remains there for 30 years.
1975–1977	"Emergency"—a two-year period of suspension of civil rights.
1977	Congress unseated for first time in 30 years by a Janata Party-led coalition.
1980	Coalition falls apart; early election won by the Congress party.
1984	Indira Gandhi assassinated; son Rajiv takes leadership of the party, which wins the election.
1989	Congress party loses the election; Janata Dal forms an unstable coalition government.

1991	Another early election; the Congress wins again.
1996	Congress loses the election to a BJP coalition.
1998	Early election returns another BJP coalition.
1999	Even earlier election returns yet another BJP coalition, which this time is stable.
2004	Congress Party, led by Sonia Gandhi, wins the election; she declines to be prime minister and nominates Manmohan Singh, a respected economist and former finance minister.
2009	Next election due.

1.3.1 The Nehru–Gandhi Clan

Few families have been as involved in Indian politics over several generations as the Nehru–Gandhi clan. They all have been members of the Indian National Congress Party, except Maneka Gandhi and her son Varun, who are members of the opposed BJP.

Jawaharlal Nehru (1889–1964): freedom fighter, and then India's first prime minister from 1947 to 1964. He died in office.

Indira Gandhi, his daughter (1917–1984): prime minister from 1966 to 1977, and again from 1980 to 1984. She was assassinated in 1984.

Rajiv Gandhi, son of Indira Gandhi (1944–1991): prime minister of India, 1984–89. He was credited with starting to dismantle some of the controls on the economy. Assassinated in 1991.

Sonia Gandhi, Italian-born wife of Rajiv Gandhi (born 1946): president of the Indian National Congress Party, she declined the role of prime minister after the party won the national elections. She is credited with reuniting the party and holding it together.

Rahul Gandhi, son of Rajiv Gandhi (born 1970): a member of Parliament, and active in the Indian National Congress Party.

Maneka Gandhi, daughter-in-law of Indira Gandhi (born 1956): married to Indira Gandhi's younger son Sanjay, who was killed in a flying accident in 1980. She is a member of the BJP, and particularly well-known for her compassionate work for animal rights. She has been a minister four times.

Varun Gandhi, son of Maneka Gandhi (born 1980): a member of the BJP, and is expected to seek election to the *Lok Sabha* in 2009.

1.3.2 Other Major Political Figures

Morarji Desai (1896–1995): first non-Congress prime minister of India, from 1977 to 1979.

Atal Bihari Vajpayee (born 1924): former prime minister of India, 1998–2004. Senior politician of the BJP.

L.K. Advani (born 1927): senior politician of the BJP, and leader of the Opposition from 2004. He may be the party's nominee for prime minister should they win the election in 2009.

Mayawati Kumari (born 1956): leader of the BSP, and chief minister of Uttar Pradesh.

P. Chidambaram (born 1945): currently minister of finance, and widely regarded as one of the key figures in the liberalization of the economy from 1991. Member of the Congress Party.

1.4 India's Economy

Note: India's fiscal year starts April 1, so financial years referred to as, for instance, 2001–2002 refer to the year starting April 1, 2001, and ending March 31, 2002. Single-year references are to the year starting April 1 of that year.

- **It's become a lot less agricultural:** The rapid growth of recent years has shifted the structure of the Indian economy toward one that is more industrial and commercial, and less agricultural. In 10 years, the share of agriculture has fallen nine percentage points, and that of trade has grown four points; manufacture is up two points, and finance and business services are up two points as well.

  Until 2003–2004, India's single largest sector was agriculture and mining. Now manufacturing (including construction and utilities such as power) contributes 27 percent to the GDP. Trade, transportation and communications come next with 25 percent, then agriculture with 21 percent. Finance, insurance, real estate, and business services contribute 14 percent, and the government, 13 percent. (All figures are based on the Indian government's *2008 Economic Survey,* using estimates for 2006–2007).

  Only 10 years earlier, agriculture had contributed 30 percent; manufacturing, 25 percent; trade, 21 percent; finance and services, 12 percent; and the government, 13 percent.

- **The GDP growth rate has risen:** India has always achieved growth in its GDP. Only four times since 1950 has the growth rate fallen into the negative, mostly after a very poor monsoon season in the years when agriculture was the single largest contributor to the GDP. Since 1992, the lowest rate of growth in any year was about the average for the previous 30 years.

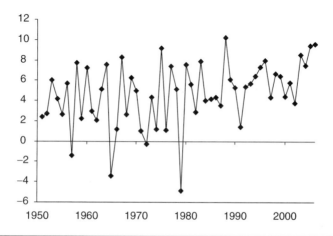

Figure 1.1   Indian GDP 1950–present

- **India's inflation rate is moderate:** India's rate of inflation has historically been below 10 percent (though with some spikes), and stands at 5–8 percent in 2008. (Effective inflation may be higher, depending on the goods and services considered. Food prices spiked in 2008.)

  Unlike countries in Africa and Latin America, India tends to have moderate inflation environment. Since 1999, inflation (measured as the Wholesale Price Index (WPI) and the Consumer Price Index for Urban Non-Manual Employees (CPI–UNME)) has been in the range of 4–6 percent per year, but rising oil prices increased prices in 2007 and 2008, forcing both years into the 5–8 percent range.

The actual number varies considerably, depending in part on how it's measured: the government provides a WPI, as well as several consumer price indices, and these can be calculated on an average or period-end basis.

The WPI is the one usually talked about: it is available weekly, and comprises a large basket of goods. However, for most business purposes, the CPI–UNME may be more representative. India's inflation environment is likely to remain moderate, although it is vulnerable to imported inflation, particularly from oil prices.

Inflation in India tends to be seasonal, higher in the first half of the fiscal year (March-September), and lower in the second. This is probably tied to the agricultural cycle, and may not persist over time as agriculture's share of the economy falls. Instead, globalization and the relaxing of price controls may synchronize India more closely with the rest of the world, at least for tradable commodities.

- **The balance of payments is improving:** Invisible exports and capital inflows have improved the balance of payments.

  India's balance of payments, traditionally under pressure, benefited greatly from the liberalization. As of February 2008, India had sufficient reserves to cover 13 months' imports. (At its lowest, in 1991, they had fallen to two weeks' worth.)

  While the balance of trade has always been negative—India imports more than it exports—it made up for it in other ways. The exports of invisibles, particularly IT and related services, grew sevenfold in the four years between 2001–2002 and 2005–2006. Remittances from non-resident Indians (NRIs) have also been significant. The other major factor has been the rise in portfolio investment, particularly from 2003; in dollar terms, its value in 2005–2006 was six times that in 2001–2002. The latter is a concern for government authorities, since it is volatile, and the effects of money pouring into the economy in the short term are inflationary.

  The Reserve Bank of India (RBI) has been performing a stellar balancing act to manage these issues. The *Economic Survey* refers to the "trilogy of objectives"—a stable rupee; low inflation; support for growth and maintaining a flow of credit. Though many voices have supported further liberalization of capital markets, others fear it could cause short-term desta-bilization that would benefit speculators more than businesses. The RBI's pragmatic attitude to monetary policy seems to be succeeding.

- **The value of the Indian rupee has stopped declining:** The rupee's value is a "managed float" against a basket of currencies including the U.S. dollar, the Japanese yen, and the euro, among others. Generally, the rupee has depreciated slowly against the other currencies, reaching a low point of Rs49:US$1 in May 2002.

- **Foreign investment has risen sharply:** According to the government's "Factsheet on Foreign Direct Investment," nearly US$75 billion of foreign investment flowed into India between 1991 and February 2008. Of that, some US$20 billion came in the last 11 months—from April 1, 2007 onward.

- **The *Economic Survey* provides excellent information:** For those interested in further reading, the Indian government's annual *Economic Survey* is published each February, in conjunction with the budget. It is a detailed document, and is available in its entirety online. It is also available from the Oxford University Press for a fee.

1.5 Why Everyone Talks of Liberalization

One of the attractions of the Indian market is that it is not yet saturated, since it has only in recent years become quite open to foreign companies. Any visitor to India will hear talk of "liberalization." To understand where they are coming from, the historical context is important. It also explains many of the restrictions that remain.

- **India's economy was carefully planned in infancy:** Immediately after independence, India's government chose to take it in the direction of a planned "mixed economy." Government-owned companies were to occupy the "commanding heights" of the economy. The private sector would be allowed, even encouraged, but with strict controls to prevent monopolies and exploitation. Most companies would need industrial licenses to operate, and to prevent monopoly and wasted capital, those would specify a maximum quantity they were allowed to produce. High tariff barriers would protect India's markets, and behind those barriers its infant industries would grow to economic strength. India's economic direction was expressed in a series of five-year plans.

  At the time, it seemed a rational and humane set of decisions. India was extremely poor. The growing population was beginning to put pressure on food supply. India was short of capital; the private sector had even fewer resources. A planned economy to manage these scarce resources seemed an obvious choice. In a 2004 interview, Prime Minister Manmohan Singh (a respected economist himself) pointed out that given those constraints, India would have been unlikely to develop an industrial base without central planning. There were other successes: the Green Revolution allowed India to feed itself without food aid. The industrial base did develop, but as the economy grew, albeit slowly, the system became a constraint on progress, rather than an enabler of it.

- **This evolved into the License Raj:** The unintended consequence of this was an uncontrolled breeding of controls, restrictions, permits, and license requirements. Any kind of economic activity beyond the most rudimentary cottage industry required permission. This is the era sometimes referred to as "*License Raj*," or "*Permit Raj*."

  The second unintended consequence was that it stifled competition. The most useful capability was understanding how to navigate governmental approvals; management and entrepreneurship were secondary. In that shortage economy, everything that could be produced, sold. Marketing was frequently a mixture of distribution and rationing.

  In the 1970s, the ruling Congress Party tried to use government controls to deal with economic issues. Banks and oil refineries were nationalized, and the Foreign Exchange Regulation Act forced foreign companies to reduce their equity to minority positions unless they exported much of their product, or imported technology.

  The economy grew about 3–4 percent per year. The population grew about 2 percent per year. By the mid-1980s, it was apparent that the economic paradigm was no longer stable, let alone successful.

- **Telecommunications presaged a change in the early 1980s:** In the early 1980s, the economy changed direction. The initial focus was on technology and telecommunications. At first, the change was neither drastic nor very apparent, but it was a break with 35 years of history. India's leadership started thinking in terms of growth. India had not done badly:

of the countries that had become independent around the same time, many were no longer democracies, and the majority had done worse in economic terms. There were economic crises in Latin American and Africa, while India's growth rate climbed to about 5–6 percent annually.

It was not enough. In 1991, foreign exchange reserves fell to two weeks' worth of imports. The deficit was about 8.5 percent of GDP. This was when India made a commitment to a major change in direction, an economic liberalization that was unprecedented. Import controls were sharply reduced. Almost all controls were relaxed at least somewhat. The economic successes of this strategy were encouraging.

- **Everyone's for liberalization now:** The reforms gathered momentum as the leaders found that reducing controls and opening the economy led neither to economic disaster nor to disasters at the polls. Instead, almost all the political parties eventually came round to accepting liberalization as the way forward.

   The process is not complete, and it is unclear when or whether it ever will be. In this, India is pragmatic rather than ideological. Restrictions remain, but compared to where the country started in 1991, the entire economic philosophy of the government has been overhauled.

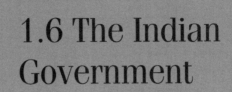

1.6 The Indian Government

- **India's government is a parliamentary democracy:** The President is the Head of the Nation, and the Prime Minister is the Head of State. India's government has two houses of Parliament; the lower house is called the *Lok Sabha*, and the upper house, the *Rajya Sabha*.

- **It is a federal system:** The central government and the states have their own spheres, though the central government has more powers than, for instance, the US federal government. The states each have their own government, for which elections are also held. Each state has a governor.

- **General elections are held every five years:** Despite voting not being compulsory, a substantial portion of the electorate casts a vote—about 600 million people. (Every citizen over 18 is eligible to vote.) Indian elections are widely recognized as being free and fair. The *Global Integrity* report for 2007 rated India's elections as high for election integrity and for citizen participation (although it rates poorly on political financing).

  The country is divided into 543 constituencies, each of which returns one member to the *Lok Sabha* in a first-past-the-post election. The party that wins the greatest number of seats forms the government—often in a coalition with other parties if it has only a plurality and not a majority—and nominates the prime minister.

- **The President is indirectly elected:** The President of India is elected by the members of parliament and of the legislative assemblies. Usually, this amounts to a selection by the ruling party. Presidents of India are usually chosen to demonstrate inclusiveness. Their role is ceremonial unless there is a political crisis, in which case they may decide whether the government should be dissolved and elections called.

- **The ministries make and implement policy:** The ministries are typically headed by a minister, who is supported by the bureaucratic structure of the ministry. It is the responsibility of these ministries to make governmental policy, within the framework of the legislation passed by parliament.

   Bureaucrats are selected through a competitive examination, and usually devote their entire careers to government service. The number and description of the ministries can change as needed, but some that usually remain are the ministries of home affairs, external affairs, commerce and industry, finance, and defense. The most senior bureaucrat in each ministry is the secretary. Other ranks (in descending order) are additional secretary, joint secretary, director, deputy secretary, and undersecretary.

1.6.1 The Ministries

Central Government (Ministries)

Ministry of Agriculture

Ministry of Chemicals and Fertilizers

Ministry of Civil Aviation

Ministry of Coal

Ministry of Commerce and Industry

Ministry of Communications and Information Technology

Ministry of Consumer Affairs, Food, and Public Distribution

Ministry of Corporate Affairs

Ministry of Culture

Ministry of Defense

Ministry of Development of North Eastern Region

Ministry of Earth Sciences

Ministry of Environment and Forests

Ministry of External Affairs

Ministry of Finance

Ministry of Food Processing Industries

Ministry of Health and Family Welfare

Ministry of Heavy Industries and Public Enterprises

Ministry of Home Affairs

Ministry of Housing and Urban Poverty Alleviation

Ministry of Human Resource Development

Ministry of Information and Broadcasting

Ministry of Labor and Employment

Ministry of Law and Justice

Ministry of Micro, Small, and Medium Enterprises

Ministry of Mines

Ministry of Minority Affairs

Ministry of New and Renewable Energy

Ministry of Overseas Indian Affairs

Ministry of Panchayati Raj

Ministry of Parliamentary Affairs

Ministry of Personnel, Public Grievances, and Pensions

Ministry of Petroleum and Natural Gas

Ministry of Power

Ministry of Railways

Ministry of Rural Development

Ministry of Science and Technology

Ministry of Shipping, Road Transport, and Highways

Ministry of Social Justice and Empowerment

Ministry of Statistics and Program Implementation

Ministry of Steel

Ministry of Textiles

Ministry of Tourism

Ministry of Tribal Affairs

Ministry of Urban Development

Ministry of Water Resources

Ministry of Women and Child Development

Ministry of Youth Affairs and Sports

Department of Atomic Energy and Department of Space (Independent Departments)

PART 2
Preparing for India

This set of checklists addresses the kind of concerns that are likely to come up early in an India effort: planning a trip, travel issues, cultural pointers that enable a traveler to India to manage a trip more effectively, and a heads-up on the mindset a successful business visitor is going to need.

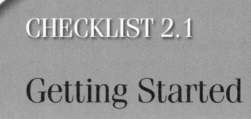

CHECKLIST 2.1

Getting Started

☐ **It is important to visit India:** India is not a country you can understand at a distance. Even though exploratory visits can be expensive, they can head off a great deal of confusion and misapprehension. Anyone who plans anything there should definitely visit India, preferably several times.

☐ **Try to make contacts before a visit to India:** While some of the contacts will develop while on the ground, it is worthwhile to set up meetings beforehand, since you will want to talk to as many people as you can on these visits.

Appointments should be lined up in advance, as far as possible, and enough flexibility provided for a changing schedule. This is particularly true of appointments with government figures. Confirm the appointment a day or two in advance of the meeting.

☐ **Some embassies can be very helpful:** If your embassy or high commission has a significant presence in India, it is often a good place to start. The US and UK have particularly well-connected and knowledgeable people.

If you plan to visit the embassy or high commission, check their timings on their websites, or call first. Some embassies have fairly restricted or unusual timings, and many observe holidays from their own country as well as some Indian holidays.

Become familiar with lakhs and crores: It is a good idea to become familiar with the Indian counting system, using the terms lakhs and crores.

India uses the terms lakhs (sometimes written lacs) and crores much more than it uses millions and billions. A lakh is a hundred thousand, and a crore is 10 million. These terms are commonly used in financial matters, newspaper reports, government publications, and importantly, in negotiations.

While most often used for rupees, it can refer to anything countable, including people and unit sales of any product. Since these can be confusing at first, it's best to know them before going in rather than discovering them on the ground. One manager said, "If you aren't familiar with them, people sometimes take advantage of that when negotiating."

Americans: in written dates, the day comes before the month: In America, dates are written with the month first; in India, people generally write dates with the day before the month. It's written the English way: DD/MM/YY (or even DD.MM.YY). This can lead to confusion regarding dates for meetings, contracts and correspondence. It is preferable to spell the month out, if possible.

Learning the Indian (Hindu) calendar has little practical benefit: A separate Indian calendar exists, and visitors will occasionally encounter it. It is culturally relevant, and has official status, but it is little used in a business setting.

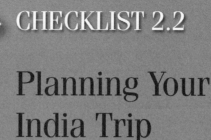

CHECKLIST 2.2

Planning Your India Trip

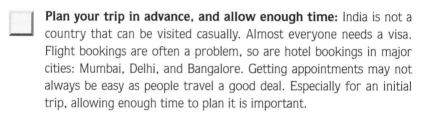

Plan your trip in advance, and allow enough time: India is not a country that can be visited casually. Almost everyone needs a visa. Flight bookings are often a problem, so are hotel bookings in major cities: Mumbai, Delhi, and Bangalore. Getting appointments may not always be easy as people travel a good deal. Especially for an initial trip, allowing enough time to plan it is important.

Obtain a visa; almost everyone needs one: Almost all foreigners (including US citizens, whether of Indian origin or not) need visas to travel to India, whether as a tourist or on business. The Indian consulates have outsourced the visa process to various outside agencies; in the US, the agency is Travisa; in Singapore, there are two agencies: Mustafa Air Travel Pte. Ltd. and Serangoon Air Travel Pte. Ltd.

It usually takes two to five working days to get a visa. They are typically valid for 180 days, starting with the day of issue. Business visas can be extended; tourist visas not. However, getting a visa extension is tedious.

Apply for a visa where you are legally a resident: Generally, you can get a visa only in your own country (that is, the country of which you are a national), or, if you are resident in another country, you can get a visa in that country.

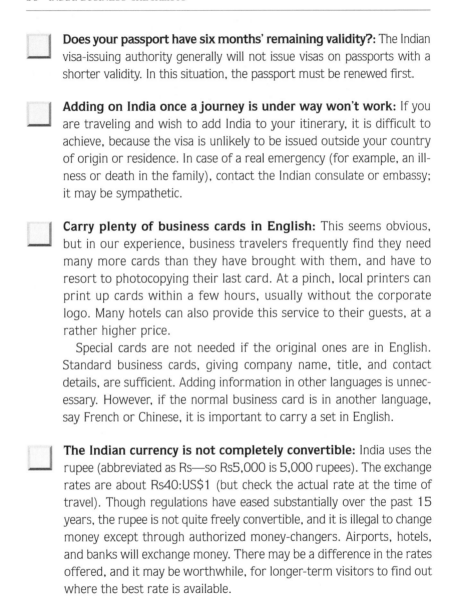

Does your passport have six months' remaining validity?: The Indian visa-issuing authority generally will not issue visas on passports with a shorter validity. In this situation, the passport must be renewed first.

Adding on India once a journey is under way won't work: If you are traveling and wish to add India to your itinerary, it is difficult to achieve, because the visa is unlikely to be issued outside your country of origin or residence. In case of a real emergency (for example, an illness or death in the family), contact the Indian consulate or embassy; it may be sympathetic.

Carry plenty of business cards in English: This seems obvious, but in our experience, business travelers frequently find they need many more cards than they have brought with them, and have to resort to photocopying their last card. At a pinch, local printers can print up cards within a few hours, usually without the corporate logo. Many hotels can also provide this service to their guests, at a rather higher price.

Special cards are not needed if the original ones are in English. Standard business cards, giving company name, title, and contact details, are sufficient. Adding information in other languages is unnecessary. However, if the normal business card is in another language, say French or Chinese, it is important to carry a set in English.

The Indian currency is not completely convertible: India uses the rupee (abbreviated as Rs—so Rs5,000 is 5,000 rupees). The exchange rates are about Rs40:US$1 (but check the actual rate at the time of travel). Though regulations have eased substantially over the past 15 years, the rupee is not quite freely convertible, and it is illegal to change money except through authorized money-changers. Airports, hotels, and banks will exchange money. There may be a difference in the rates offered, and it may be worthwhile, for longer-term visitors to find out where the best rate is available.

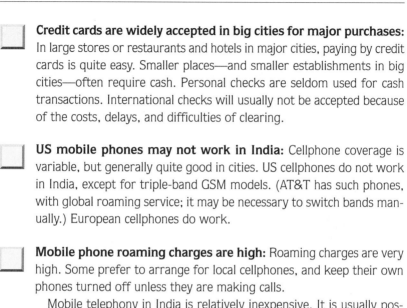

Credit cards are widely accepted in big cities for major purchases: In large stores or restaurants and hotels in major cities, paying by credit cards is quite easy. Smaller places—and smaller establishments in big cities—often require cash. Personal checks are seldom used for cash transactions. International checks will usually not be accepted because of the costs, delays, and difficulties of clearing.

US mobile phones may not work in India: Cellphone coverage is variable, but generally quite good in cities. US cellphones do not work in India, except for triple-band GSM models. (AT&T has such phones, with global roaming service; it may be necessary to switch bands manually.) European cellphones do work.

Mobile phone roaming charges are high: Roaming charges are very high. Some prefer to arrange for local cellphones, and keep their own phones turned off unless they are making calls.

Mobile telephony in India is relatively inexpensive. It is usually possible to make some arrangements; "pay-as-you-go" phones are available, as are rentals. Sometimes, the local Indian office or partner can make a loan of an Indian cellphone. Cybercafes also provide an inexpensive option for international calls in an emergency.

Internet access is available, but security can be an issue: Most good hotels will provide Internet access, but the line may not be as fast as travelers get back home. Most business centers also have computers, and India has numerous cybercafes, but security is a major issue.

Users should be aware that security is a risk with publicly used computers, travelers have reported acquiring viruses from business center computers. The computers may also harbor keystroke loggers (which record every keystroke a user makes, including login names and passwords) and other malicious programs. In Mumbai, the police plans to require all cybercafes to install keystroke loggers that would be downloaded to the police.

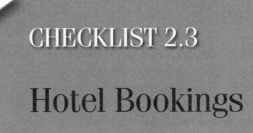

It is a good idea to book hotel rooms early: India's hotels are of good quality. The facilities are acceptable, but the service is usually well above average. In addition to recognizable foreign names, the Oberoi and Taj groups have excellent reputations. However, they tend to be expensive, particularly in the busy season, and are often sold out a month or more in advance. Advance bookings are strongly recommended.

Differential charges for foreigners are being phased out: In late 2007, most upscale hotels switched to a single rate for Indians and foreigners (earlier, almost all of them charged foreigners a premium). Some travelers report that Internet booking rates are better than the rates they are quoted by phone or through their travel agents. A local contact may be able to get you better rates on a hotel room than is available overseas. The corollary to this is that you may be required to pay in rupees, whereas earlier, most hotels required payment in hard currencies.

Confirm the hotel room prices you have accepted: Travelers have mentioned problems with room rates at some hotels—being told one rate and charged another on arrival. All room rates should be confirmed by fax or email at the time of booking. Also, get clarification on taxes; hotels have sometimes charged taxes on a higher room rate than the one actually paid by the guest. Hotels have also been known to charge taxes on a "complimentary" breakfast. The government imposes a special luxury tax on good hotels and other services that are considered luxuries in India.

Arrange to be met at the airport if possible: It is preferable to be met at the airport. The better hotels can arrange a driver with a sign. Taxis are available, but it is not always easy to find a driver who speaks English, and they are sometimes unsafe. In some cities, criminals who prey on foreigners work with taxi drivers at airports. If it is not possible to be met, try to take a prepaid taxi if they are available. If you do this, book the car before exiting the building. It may be difficult to go back in, and it may be difficult to resist being importuned by waiting taxi drivers.

Consider staying in a serviced apartment: In the major cities, good serviced apartments may offer a less expensive and more settled option than a hotel room for long stays. They are usually some distance from the city center, but the commute may be worthwhile to save costs and for comfort.

Some companies maintain resthouses in cities to house staff from out of town. This is typically an apartment with a cook/manager running it, and may be under the management of the local office. While they do not provide the luxury of a hotel, they are often less expensive and more convenient, especially for extended stays.

Some visitors do the opposite. Infrastructure issues (power, water, cooking gas, and Internet connections) can be problematic for a visitor planning to stay for weeks rather than years, in which case, a long-term arrangement with a hotel may provide a better option.

CHECKLIST 2.4

Plan for All Seasons

☐ **India has a busy season and a slow season:** Travel to India is seasonal. Winter is the busy season; the weather is usually comfortable, even chilly, and there is (in most places) little or no rain. All prices tend to be higher, and travel bookings more difficult to get.

☐ **Allow for climatic differences if visiting many cities:** The major cities in India are all quite distant from one another, and have noticeably different climates. It is useful to check the temperatures in all the cities on the itinerary, not just the one where you will spend the most time.

☐ **Delhi in winter feels colder than the temperature indicates:** In winter, only Delhi is uncomfortably cold among the major cities. Temperatures fall to 4°C, or occasionally even less. A lack of central heating in homes and many offices, and unheated automobiles and taxis can make this more problematic than lower temperatures in Western countries. Carry warmer clothes than would be suitable in equivalent weather at home.

☐ **Allow for winter fog disruptions in air travel from Delhi:** Winter morning fog in New Delhi can complicate scheduling. It sometimes will delay air traffic by making arrivals and departures impossible until mid-morning, and occasionally has a cascading effect throughout the country, causing delays and cancellations. It is impossible to plan for this completely, especially because it is fairly unpredictable, but some visitors deal with it by building slack into their schedules so that a day's delay is not disastrous.

Prepare for extreme summer heat in Delhi and Chennai: Visitors should be aware that summer heat can be extreme in Delhi National Capital Region (NCR) and Chennai. Mumbai and Bangalore tend to have more moderate summers. Light clothing, sunscreen, and sunglasses are all advisable. (Shorts are seldom worn in any but the most informal settings, even by men. Light slacks are suitable wear, as are light—though modest—skirts for women.)

Expect logistical difficulties during the monsoon: Most of India's rain falls in tropical downpours for about three months in summer, and during this time, flooding of low-lying land, traffic snarls, and occasional disruptions of transport occur. Mumbai is especially vulnerable. Much of the city is low-lying reclaimed land, and when a heavy rain coincides with high tides, substantial flooding can occur, and brings commercial activity to a standstill for a day or two.

Plan around holidays: Business visitors may need to be aware of holidays in planning their visits. The Indian official calendar has many holidays, and some additional local ones are also observed. If you are on a short visit, it is preferable to check with the organizations you plan to see; it can be frustrating to discover that two days out of a four-day trip become useless for business. October, in particular, is the peak of the festive season in most of India.

The central government has a list of 14 compulsory holidays. In addition, there are 35 other holidays listed that may be observed by individual employees or offices. Complicating the situation, some of the holidays are on a lunar calendar, and may be observed on different dates each year.

State governments are allowed to declare any 15 holidays, as long as they include the three national holidays: Republic Day (January 26); Independence Day (August 15); and Mahatma Gandhi's birthday (October 2). It is worthwhile getting a list of major holidays in each of the states you plan to visit. These should be available on the Internet, but ensure that the list is updated.

Finally, although most follow the government holidays, some individual organizations may have additional holidays of their own. Again, it is worthwhile to check with the companies in advance to ensure that they will be open.

Plan around parliamentary sessions in Delhi: For those business-people needing to meet senior government officials, it may be worthwhile to check whether the parliament will be in session. If it so, officials may be called away at short notice, forcing them to reschedule appointments. (Actually, senior government officials may actually be called away by the ministers at any time, but this tends to be more frequent when the parliament is in session.)

2.4.1 Holidays Gazetted by the Central Government

Muharram	January 8
Republic Day	January 26
Milad-un-Nabi (Birthday of Prophet Mohammed)	March 10
Holi	March 11
Ram Navami	April 3
Mahavir Jayanti	April 7
Good Friday	April 10
Buddha Purnima	May 9
Janamashtami	August 14
Independence Day	August 15
Id ul Fitr	September 21
Dussehra (Vijaya Dashami)	September 28
Mahatma Gandhi's Birthday	October 2
Deewali (Deepawali)	October 17
Guru Nanak Birthday	November 2
Id-ul-Juha (Bakr Id)	November 28
Christmas day	December 25
Muharram (falls twice in Calendar 2009)	December 28

List of Restricted (Optional) Holidays

New Year's Day	January 1
Guru Gobind Singh's Birthday	January 5
Makara Sankranti (North India)	January 13
Makara Sankranti (Bengal)	January 14
Pongal	January 14
Basanta Panchami/ Shree Panchami	January 31
Guru Ravidas's Birthday	February 9
Sivaji Jayanti	February 19
Swami Dayanand Saraswati Jayanti	February 19
Maha Shivaratri	February 23
Holika Dahan	March 10
Chaitra Sukhladi/Gudi Padwa/ Ugadi/Cheti Chand	April 7
Easter (Sunday)	April 12
Vaisakhi	April 13
Vishu	April 13
Mesadi	April 14
Vaisakhi (Bengal)/ Bahag Bihu (Assam)	April 15

Rabindranath Tagore's Birthday	May 9
Rath Yatra	June 24
Hazrat Ali's Birthday	July 7
Raksha Bandhan	August 5
Parsi New Year	August 19
Ganesh Chaturthi	August 23
Onam	September 2
Jamat-Ul-Vida	September 18
Dussehra (Maha Saptami)	September 25
Dussehra (Maha Ashtami)	September 26
Dussehra (Maha Navami)	September 27
Maharishi Valmiki's Birthday	October 4
Deepavali (South)	October 17
Naraka Chaturdasi	October 17
Govardhan Puja	October 18
Bhai Duj	October 19
Guru Teg Bahadur's Martyrdom day	November 24
Christmas Eve	December 24

CHECKLIST 2.5

Getting Around
In India

☐ **For domestic travel, fly if possible:** Generally, it is preferable to fly, rather than drive, where possible in India.

Several domestic airlines now operate in India, including the government-owned Air India, and a few air-taxis flying limited routes. This has eased domestic air travel considerably. However, they vary in coverage, punctuality, and reputation. Jet Airways is considered the leader. The typical flight time from one major city to another is about two hours, and a flight is the best way to make the journey.

Although it is often possible to drive, the road conditions make this uncertain and rather risky. In some cases, train travel is a feasible—if not a very comfortable—alternative.

☐ **Be prepared for some uncomfortable airports:** India's main international airports are Delhi and Mumbai (formerly Bombay). There are also international flights into Kolkata (Calcutta), Chennai (Madras), and Bangalore. As of early 2008, most of these airports were small and old-fashioned by international standards. However, Bangalore has a brand new airport some distance from the city, so does Hyderabad. The distance has become an issue with travelers, because the transport costs are high. Bangalore's airport startup was delayed until May

2008 by a court case regarding contracted user fees to be imposed on air travelers, and by training schedules for air traffic controllers.

Major renovations are under way in Delhi; and the situation is expected to improve by 2010, by which time, there should also be a new airport in Mumbai.

As of 2008, most Indian airports are uncomfortable and rather bleak for flying out of. There is nothing to do in most of them; two or three shops and a snack bar constitute the amenities. Computers go down from time to time, causing delays and inconvenience at check-in. Arriving at an Indian airport is not so bad; because they are small, it is often possible to get through fairly quickly, especially for business-class travelers.

There is a lack of sophistication among the traveling public, noted one expatriate, which can lead to inconsiderate behavior—late arrival on the plane; use of cellphones past the time allowed; and inordinate demands on the cabin crew.

Try to hire cars with drivers who speak some English: Self-drive cars are difficult to get, and in any case, it is probably better for outsiders not to attempt driving in India's chaotic traffic. (However, Hertz car rentals are available in many major cities to drivers with Indian or international driving permits.) Long-term visitors may wish to obtain international driving permits in any case as other foreign licenses are not valid in India.

Cars with drivers can be hired for around the same price as an ordinary car rental would be overseas. In early 2008, this was about US$25–50 per day. For most purposes, it is better and safer to hire a car and driver than to take taxis, or to attempt to use a self-drive car. This is particularly true for businesswomen.

Any good hotel—or an Indian contact—should be able to arrange for an air-conditioned car with a driver who speaks at least some English, and knows his way around the city.

It is usual to give the driver time off to eat meals—usually when you expect to be at a particular location for at least one hour. It is good form to give part of the tip at that time, in case he does not have enough money with him to buy food.

Be realistic about travel time when scheduling appointments: As in many large cities around the world, travel time in India's larger cities is quite variable. This can limit the number of appointments possible in a day.

The production—and affordability—of cars has outpaced the road infrastructure, and a journey that takes an hour without traffic can take more than twice that during rush hours, or if an accident or other problems cause blockages. Particularly in Delhi, VIPs may block traffic a clear passage for their motorcades to create.

Public transport—where it exists—may be a feasible option: Public transport is limited, and may be extremely crowded. Bus travel has little to recommend it, but the trains may be a feasible option.

Delhi has a new metro line, which is undergoing major expansion. Completion is planned for 2010. Meanwhile, two lines operate. Although the section from Rajiv Chowk to Chandni Chowk tends to be packed during business hours, it still is an effective way to commute.

Mumbai's ancient suburban train lines are still the fastest way to travel between the north and the south, but travel needs to be carefully planned around rush hours, and is not comfortable. Metro railways are also being built elsewhere in the country—in Bangalore and Chennai, but were not yet put into operation in 2008.

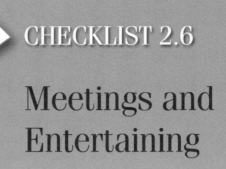

CHECKLIST 2.6

Meetings and Entertaining

☐ **Punctuality tends to be variable:** Some Indian businesspeople are extremely punctual; others less so. Bureaucrats may be delayed by factors beyond their control, such as demands from the ministers or from their seniors. While things are better than a decade or two ago, when Indian Standard Time was known as Indian Stretchable Time, visitors should allow a certain amount of flexibility. It is advisable not to schedule appointments too closely; allow an hour between appointments, plus travel time, if any.

☐ **It is unusual to schedule breakfast meetings:** Most offices start between 9 a.m. and 10 a.m. and close between 5 p.m. and 6.30 p.m. Some offices are open for half a day on Saturdays; others do not work at all. Afternoons are often preferable for appointments. In general, although most Indians are early risers, the work day does not start until 9 a.m. at the earliest, and breakfast meetings are rare. Most business meals take place at lunch or dinner. (The financial service industry may be an exception in which breakfast meetings are common.)

☐ **Foreign travelers will encounter dual pricing and puzzling taxes:** Foreigners often have to pay for services (hotel bills, for instance) in dollars, and pay perhaps 10–50 percent more than an Indian customer paying in rupees. (Changes started to take place in 2008: check with the hotels.) Credit card companies also make money from the currency conversions.

Admission to tourist sites is much higher for foreigners than for locals; the famous Taj Mahal in Agra is Rs20 for Indians, and Rs500 (about US$12.50) for foreigners. However, most places charge Indians Rs5–10, and foreigners pay about US$2–5. Some Indians living overseas have been charged the foreign rate, even though they were Indian. Domestic airlines have recently stopped discriminatory pricing, as have major hotels.

Generally, foreign visitors should plan to pay restaurant bills and taxi fares in rupees, although they may be asked to pay in dollars. Paying in foreign currency is not legal, except when the recipient is an authorized money changer. Paying with foreign credit cards, where they are accepted, is allowed.

The usual tip is 10 percent: Foreigners are expected to be better tippers than Indians. The usual tip at restaurants is 10 percent. Normally, taxi drivers and doormen are not tipped, although staff who actually provide assistance—for example, the bell boy who carries your luggage—would be. In hotels much frequented by foreigners, expectations tend to be a bit higher. It is usual to tip the driver of a hired car at the end of the day.

Hotel bars charge a lot for imported alcoholic drinks: By Western standards, alcoholic drinks are generally expensive in India once levies and taxes are added; it is even more so for imported ones. Meeting someone for drinks can be more expensive than dining out. A tab for three drinks can be US$70–80 or more. A less expensive option is to buy a bottle of liquor from a local "wine shop," and invite your guest to your room.

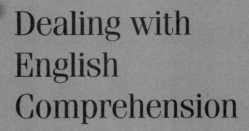

Dealing with English Comprehension

☐ **English works fine:** For most business purposes, English speakers will not need to learn another language, or to hire translators; English is the language of business, the government, and the legal system. The Supreme Court conducts its business in English. Only a few local matters are transacted exclusively in an Indian language, and those can be handled case by case.

☐ **Be aware that spoken English may be strongly accented:** A foreign visitor to India is likely to find communication hampered by two things. First of all, although English is widely spoken, it is generally a second language. A visitor may encounter a huge variety of accents, depending on the speaker's mother tongue. Even Indians from different regions sometimes have problems understanding one another's accents. English competence and grammatical correctness will also vary, depending on the speaker's background and education.

Secondly, Indians often speak fast, and interrupt or speak over one another—a behavior not considered rude in most situations.

Experienced visitors recommend that the best way to deal with this is to speak slowly, and ask for something to be repeated slowly if you do not understand it. After a while, as one's ears become attuned to the various accent, intonations, and pronunciation styles, it becomes easier to follow.

Learning an Indian language may yield few business benefits: Enthusiastic internationalists, particularly those with a talent for languages, sometimes consider learning the local tongue. In India, it is difficult. First, there are many of them: 21 official languages. The main language, Hindi, is spoken by perhaps half of all Indians, and that in a number of somewhat mutually incomprehensible dialects.

Of the major cities, only Delhi NCR is actually in Hindi-speaking territory; Mumbai (Bombay) has Marathi as its language, Bangalore has Kannada, and Chennai (Madras) has Tamil. Complicating this demographic is that large cities attract residents from all over India, so the Indians a foreigner would deal with might all speak different languages at home. This is one reason English is so widely used in places of business: it is India's common language.

Indian languages can be difficult to pronounce: Indian languages can be daunting owing to a different range of consonants. For someone who has not grown up with these sounds, they can be difficult to discern, let alone reproduce.

For those who decide to try anyway, it is not necessarily easy. Most Indian languages are less complicated to learn than English, but for English speakers, the sounds may be difficult. Hindi, along with most Sanskritic languages, has consonants that are not distinguished in English. The south Indian languages have different sets of consonantal sounds that even Hindi speakers find difficult.

Written English may be easier to understand: The varied accents of spoken English don't carry over into written communication. Most English-speaking Indians write reasonably clearly. Even if the writing is not perfectly grammatical, it is generally easy to comprehend. This sometimes makes email a useful means of communication in cases where the accent is an issue.

India uses a lot of acronyms: India's print media—and even Indians in conversation—use a large number of acronyms that can be mystifying for those unused to them. (See "Acronyms You May Encounter" for a useful list.)

There are differences in body language: Shaking the head, for instance, is not negation; it usually means acknowledgment or agreement. This can be difficult for people from cultures where it is seen as disagreement or disapproval.

Similar issues may arise around eye contact. If people look away while you are talking to them, it is usually a sign of respect, or at least politeness. Most Indians will not look anyone in the eye for any great length of time.

Etiquette and Expectations

☐ **Most rules have exceptions:** India is best understood as a continent. The number of different languages, religions, cultures, and subcultures ensures that no generalization is entirely accurate. However, it is easier to point out ways in which India may surprise foreigners, particularly those from the West.

☐ **Foreigners may be asked questions that seem intrusive:** It's a warm and nosy culture. People are generally friendly toward foreigners, at least on a superficial level. Visitors may be asked personal questions about brothers and sisters, parents, spouses, offspring, schooling, and background. This is considered to be a matter of taking an interest in a person, and the matters closest to them—which are their families. These are the questions that help Indians understand one another.

☐ **Indians tend to dress quite modestly in business contexts:** This applies to both men and women. The norms vary from organization to organization. Suits may be worn, or the norm may be shirt, tie, and pants. In some places, suits are worn in winter, and safari suits or "bush shirts" in summer. For women, pant-suits are generally appropriate in any setting. Bare legs are recognized as acceptable for foreign women, but skirts should nonetheless be fairly long.

Some regions are more conservative than others, and smaller towns and cities more conservative than a metropolis. "Conservative" for women is defined as clothes that are not very form fitting, and cover the body and legs, (and not by color). However, *saree* blouses are very form fitting, and bare the midriff. Men seldom wear shorts, even for casual wear.

When foreigners wear Indian clothing, it is considered casual: For those who want to experiment with Indian clothes, the tunic and pants combination of the *kurta-pajama* (also known as Punjabi suits) are suitable for social events and easier to manage than *sarees* (for women) or *dhotis* (for men). *Dhotis* are seldom worn by urban Indians except ceremonially, although in south India, the *lungi* (a long wrap that substitutes trousers) is casual wear.

Flirting should be approached with extreme caution: There is little flirting in the workplace. Although there are men and women, especially in urban settings, who may respond, there is a danger of misunderstanding. This could seriously affect a person's credibility as a serious executive—particularly for women.

Women are generally treated with respect: Men should treat women with traditional respect (and vice versa). Usually, men should not touch women, or even shake hands, unless of course a woman extends her hand, in which case, it is proper to shake it. Otherwise, a nod and a greeting are just as appropriate. A businesswoman may shake hands; to establish her intent to do business as an equal.

The custom of the peck on the cheek, or the social hug, is limited to a small subset of urban Indians. Although India is a patriarchal culture, it is also a country that has had several women leaders; women in senior and powerful positions face no special problems.

Use first names only if invited to do so: Indians do not usually use first names casually; in a work setting, it is appropriate to use surnames with honorifics, especially if there is a difference in status or age (that is, both those above and below the speaker would be addressed as Ms. X, or Mr. X, or Dr. Y).

Food and Hospitality

☐ **Accepting invitations to share a meal is usually appropriate:** Indians often freely invite people home for meals, even if they do not know them well. It is fine to accept, unless there are organizational issues: crossing hierarchical boundaries, or appearing to show favoritism. In these cases, sensitivity is essential. If you plan to take a gift, do not take anything alcoholic unless you are certain it would be welcome. Many Indians do not drink at home. A box of chocolates is generally suitable.

☐ **After accepting an invitation, it is polite to eat what is offered:** Guests should eat at least a small portion of the food served. It will have been especially made. If spicy food is an issue, politely inform your hosts in advance that much as you would like to, your stomach cannot take fiery spices. The host should be discreetly made aware of any dietary restrictions. This is best done in private, so as not to give the appearance of distrusting the host's ability to make guests feel welcome.

☐ **Avoid double dipping or anything that could "contaminate" food:** When eating with Indians, it is extremely important to be aware of the taboo on anything that contaminates food. Most Indians observe a strict etiquette with regard to *jhoota* food or utensils. Once a dish or utensil has been used by one person for eating, it is *jhoota*, and no one else can use it until it has been washed. It is considered extremely bad form to share saliva—so a utensil that has been used for eating, even accidentally, cannot go back into the serving dish. If eating with your fingers—as is customary in India—the hand that has been in the mouth cannot be used to take food, even finger food, from the serving dish.

Ask for cutlery if you prefer it: In most situations, it is fine to use cutlery to eat even if others are eating with their hands. It is usually perfectly acceptable to use a knife and fork—or even a spoon and fork. Many Westernized Indian families routinely use cutlery as a matter of convenience.

If eating with fingers, the left hand should never be used for eating: The left hand is considered contaminated, and is not used for picking up food. The actual etiquette for eating with the fingers varies from region to region in terms of how much of the finger may be in contact with the food.

Be aware that Indian customs include many food taboos: It is important to be aware of, and respect, personalized food taboos. Most Indian men drink, as do some of the more Westernized women—although in many cases, they do not drink at home. In general, most Hindus (80 percent of India's population) avoid eating beef; many are vegetarians. For that reason, they may also avoid gelatin, unless it is the Indian vegetable gelatin. Some women observe weekly or monthly fasts, and may not be willing to accept invitations on those days. Some vegetarians do not eat eggs either, but milk is universally acceptable. Muslims avoid pork, as do many Hindus.

Punctuality tends to be more relaxed in a social setting: It is not unusual for guests attending a lunch or dinner to come an hour or more late. If in doubt, check with your host when you should really plan to arrive. Festivities associated with weddings, in particular, seldom occur at the time expected or printed on an invitation.

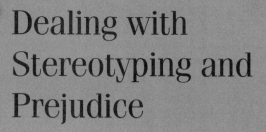

CHECKLIST 2.10

Dealing with Stereotyping and Prejudice

☐ **Some may find a surprising degree of stereotyping in India:** Americans and people from cultures where sensitivity to racism is learned early may be surprised by considerable open stereotyping. Racism is not as clearly defined as unacceptable in India as, for instance, in the West. Even within India, "ethnic" jokes about people from elsewhere in India are common, as are stereotypes along ethnic lines. Often, the stereotypes are accepted, to some degree, even by those being so typecast. Although these generalizations are often broadly accepted, they have very limited effect on work situations.

☐ **In general, there is a cultural bias toward the fair-skinned:** This has no impact in the workplace, but is quite evident in matrimonial advertisements. Foreigners who are Caucasian have reported, overall, a warmer reception socially than people who are not, although this is seldom significant enough to be more than a minor annoyance.

☐ **Foreigners may find social stratification in India unusually strict:** It is a very stratified society (although it is actually more mobile than many Indians perceive). As incomes grow, the middle class is more confident than before, and less deferential. For the most part, Indians are very conscious of the hierarchies of which they are a part, and of their place in the world. It is important to be sensitive to status symbols, and not act in ways that would seem to denigrate someone's position.

Caste gets a lot of airtime, but has little workplace impact: Caste is much talked about, but for most business purposes, irrelevant. (It is quite important in weddings and politics.) Unless you are operating in rural India, caste considerations do not usually enter the workplace.

Class can be very important: Class, on the other hand, is something that is very important in the workplace. It is intimately linked with the hierarchical structure described. As a rule of thumb, people of upper classes would be insulted by being asked to do a menial task. They may volunteer to do it, which is different.

Most middle-class families have domestic servants: Household servants are still commonplace in India. It is unusual to interact in any way with the servants at a host's house, except for a nod. In some cases, a host may introduce a servant, but this is unusual. It is appropriate for house guests to tip the staff, but they should consult the host on the proper amounts.

Unlike the domestic staff in places like Singapore and Hong Kong, household servants in India tend to be relatively unsophisticated. They are generally not integrated into the family, although there may be ties of loyalty between long-time servants and the families they work for. In those cases, the people of the household may help the servants (or their children) in several ways, particularly in getting an education or a job. This can be a significant factor in upward mobility for servants of affluent households.

CHECKLIST 2.11

Health and Safety

- [ ] **India is reasonably safe and healthy to visit:** Indian cities are physically safer than most large American cities, although probably less so than Singapore or Tokyo. Indian health care is generally good for people who can afford the better clinics and hospitals. However, we do recommend precautions.

- [ ] **Do not drink tap water ever:** The water in large cities is chlorinated, but may still carry contaminants and bacteria. It is best to avoid drinking tap water, and use bottled, boiled, or UV-treated water. This is not a matter of acclimatizing to local conditions—residents don't drink it either. Most Indian homes use "Aquaguard" or boiled water.

- [ ] **Salads, raw fruit and vegetables may not be safe:** When eating out, hot cooked foods are the safest. Raw produce is easily contaminated while being grown, transported, sold, or prepared. If you are buying raw fruit or vegetables, wash them, preferably in bottled water, before eating.

- [ ] **When eating out, Western food is usually available as an option:** Some stomachs are sensitive to Indian spices—in particular, chili peppers. It is possible to order Western-style meals at restaurants, or ask the waiter before ordering. Indian food, particularly in restaurants, is often quite salty and spicy.

Foreigners out late at night should be cautious: On the whole, Indian cities are approximately as safe as European ones, and probably a lot safer than US cities, at least as far as severe bodily injury goes.

Nevertheless, a foreigner alone late at night may be perceived as vulnerable. It is best to be cautious, and check with your hotels or your hosts. India tends to be crowded and buzz with life all the time, so only a few places are really isolated at night.

Women traveling alone should be particularly careful, especially in Delhi, where a foreign woman alone may be perceived as an easy prey.

Driving in India can be dangerous: Traffic is not orderly—some observers consider it the worst in Asia—and the accident rate is fairly high. It is also necessary to be careful when walking in traffic and crossing the roads. Assume that drivers will not necessarily obey the rules on the roads, but they will try to avoid hitting you. Pedestrians, especially, should try to be visible to drivers.

Be careful with your belongings to reduce risk: Petty theft is very common in India; it is advisable to secure valuables, and take care not to display them in public. Foreign passports are still an attractive target. Leaving your passports and other important documents in hotel safes is probably the best option. Foreigners are rarely asked for proof of identity once they have checked into the hotels.

Avoid trouble spots when strikes and demonstrations occur: Almost all major cities in India have occasional strikes, demonstrations, and similar social disruptions. They may be accompanied by stone throwing and other vandalism. They are seldom violent, and even when they are, they do not target foreigners. Observe reasonable safety precautions: avoid the fray, stay indoors if the disruption is in the area, follow the suggestions of the hotel staff or local associates.

Swimming in the ocean may be dangerous: India has very few, if any, safe beaches, and almost no lifeguards. Currents off even popular beaches can be powerful and treacherous. Most Indians do not know how to swim, and someone in trouble in the water is unlikely to be rescued.

Malaria tablets are a judgment call: Some travelers prefer to start a course of malaria tablets before departure. Many others avoid them, and some take them only if traveling during or shortly after the rainy season. Malaria does occur in India, as do other mosquito-borne diseases, but the side-effects of these medications can be uncomfortable.

It may be convenient to pack any necessary medications: A wide range of drugs is available in India, at prices that seem derisory to Americans (though not to travelers from universal-coverage countries such as the UK). However, it may not be easy to figure out the Indian equivalents, as the drug and brand names may be different.

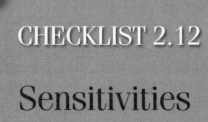

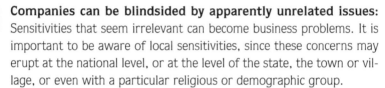

Companies can be blindsided by apparently unrelated issues: Sensitivities that seem irrelevant can become business problems. It is important to be aware of local sensitivities, since these concerns may erupt at the national level, or at the level of the state, the town or village, or even with a particular religious or demographic group.

Problems can be triggered by disgruntled former employees or former suppliers; by local power figures, political and otherwise, by activists who oppose an action or activity of the company, or by nationalist ideologues.

A local public relations company can help head off problems.

Be proactive: When a problem occurs, proactive engagement with it is more likely to succeed than keeping quiet and hoping the issue will go away.

Generally, the market's memory may prove longer than in many Western countries, both for good and bad. Companies may find that consumers are aware of brands that have not been marketed in decades. Conversely, that controversies may remain alive for years.

When soft-drink companies were accused of selling products containing a high level of pesticides, many observers felt that the companies' reactions were not effective enough: they kept silent and hoped the problem would die down, but the silence was interpreted as guilt. A more immediate response and greater publicity effort to address the issue regarding it might have prevented it from recurring.

☐ **Any printed material with maps of India may be a problem:** The Indian government is extremely sensitive about maps of India and how they depict the country's boundaries, particularly those with Pakistan. This can be a contentious issue, because India and Pakistan have an ongoing dispute over the state of Kashmir. (The border with China is similarly disputed in some areas.) Many international sources do not indicate the boundaries as the India government requires. If any kind of printed materials—books, magazines, brochures—is imported, the Customs authorities have the right to stamp the map with big disclaimers, or even destroy the product. In early 2008, an organization that attempted to bring in 300 corporate brochures to hand out to clients had the shipment held up, and Customs informed it that the consignment would be burned.

☐ **Social factors can play out in unexpected ways:** Companies may find that social or environmental factors affect them in unexpected ways. Ultrasound scanner suppliers, for instance, found themselves being blamed for the falling sex ratio of childbirths in India. Baskin-Robbins in Gujarat was accused of competing with locally produced ice-cream.

India has a strong cultural preference for sons, and the arrival of ultrasound scanners has encouraged a cottage industry in the selective abortion of female fetuses, so the sex ratio of new births for girls has been dropping. Although it is illegal to tell prospective parents the gender of fetuses, this rule is difficult to enforce. Suppliers such as General Electric are being blamed for aggressively marketing its machines and making them widely available, thus enabling prenatal gender selection.

Fears that Baskin-Robbins was competing with locally made ice-creams heightened tensions in Gujarat, and in 1998, a retail outlet was burned down by nationalist demonstrators.

☐ **Anything involving limited resources can be a problem:** The most contentious issue is often land, and conflicts—not limited to foreign companies—have arisen in cases where state governments have provided companies with formerly agricultural land. Other resources can also be contentious: water is one.

Many industries use water in their processes, either as an input or as a coolant. They may compete with local villages and farms.

This can be problematic, both logistically and in terms of relations with the community, partly because the companies need the more valuable land that has access to water, and they have to compete with other uses for that water.

Some Coca-Cola plants, for instance, are situated in water-short areas, leading to allegations that the company is depleting the water available to local agriculture. (See "Coca-Cola in India.")

Foreign companies may be held to higher standards: A manager who has worked for both Indian and multinational companies once said, "In the Indian companies, I was very comfortable because we were part of the community. In a foreign company, you have to be much more careful. There are some things you cannot do at all..."

In 1995, a health inspection discovered a couple of flies in the kitchen of a KFC outlet, and temporarily closed it down. (Flies are widespread in India, and most restaurants and food shops are troubled by them.) It became an excuse for nationalist sentiment to build anti-multinational publicity, but it had no long-term impact.

In August 2006, a group of environmentalists released a report saying that Pepsi and Coke in India were tested for pesticides, and the contents exceeded the limits the government planned to impose. This was not the first time: In August 2003, a similar allegation impacted sales. (See 2.12.1, "Coca-Cola in India.") This resulted in action against the two products by six states in India, which partially banned their sale. A Pepsi spokesman pointed out that no other products had been tested, and that pesticides are ubiquitous in India, being found in groundwater, human milk, and most potable products. These residues are nearly impossible to remove. A spokesman for the testing organization suggested that soft drinks should be held to a higher standard than milk, since they lack nutrition, and consumption is purely optional.

Any denigration of a revered character or person carries risk: This is true, whether the person is contemporary, historical, or mythical. There have been reactions to depictions of *Bharat Mata* (Mother India) by artist, M.F. Hussain; to a disrespectful portrayal of the seventeenth-century warrior-king, Shivaji, (who is strongly identified with the state of Maharashtra) in the social networking site Orkut, and to a scholarly book on Shivaji. In addition to demonstrations and violence, legal cases may be brought under a clause that prohibits anyone from doing something that would inflame the sentiments of a particular group or cause enmity between groups.

Section 153 of the *Indian Penal Code*, in the interests of trying to prevent the provocation of unrest and trouble between groups, prohibits anyone from saying, writing, representing, or doing things that would promote enmity or ill-will among people of different religions, or racial, linguistic, or regional groups, castes, or communities, particularly if they disturb "public tranquility."

In the Hussain case, an art gallery showing his work was attacked. Several lawsuits are still being heard. There have been attempts to attack his Indian properties.

In the Orkut case, rioters attacked cybercafes in Mumbai. Later, the police tracked down and arrested the people suspected of uploading the work (after first imprisoning the wrong man for nearly two months). They used information from the Internet service provider and the phone company to locate the IP address of individuals in another state. The erroneously arrested man, who was allegedly beaten while imprisoned, is suing the ISP company.

In the case of the book on Shivaji, publisher Oxford University Press decided to withdraw the book from India (although it remains available elsewhere). A violent attack on an Indian research institution mentioned in the foreword resulted in the disappearance of a number of rare books and manuscripts. A scholar acknowledged in the book was also personally attacked; the government subsequently provided police protection. A court case under Section 153 was brought against the author; the court ruled against the complainants, on the grounds that there was no ill intent.

Companies can be inadvertently affected by religious issues: Any religious issue, particularly one pertaining to Islam or Hinduism, can be extremely sensitive.

Taslima Nasreen, a writer of Bangladeshi origin whose novels have been interpreted as being critical of Islam, at first moved to India after several of her books were banned in Bangladesh. Islamic groups in India reacted negatively to her writings, and she was forced into hiding. Eventually, she left the country.

M.F. Hussain, arguably India's best-known artist, made a series of nude drawings depicting Hindu deities and other revered figures. This triggered attacks on his apartment and property, as well as a court case alleging that he deliberately sought to offend Hindu sentiment. He now lives in London and Dubai.

Terrorism is an ongoing concern: Given the background of various rifts in India's social fabric, and several explosive incidents, the government is always concerned about terrorism.

Companies and individuals should be aware of these concerns, and recognize that some erosion of privacy is likely. Communications companies have been required to share information with the government authorities, including the police.

2.12.1 Coca-Cola in India

Coca-Cola has had a long presence in India, and was widely available until 1977, when the government's decision to enforce the then provisions of the *Foreign Exchange Regulation Act* would have forced it to dilute its foreign ownership to 40 percent. Many companies complied; Coke was not one of them. It closed down its Indian operations. In 1993, when the India market became deregulated, it returned to being more competitive. Not only had several domestic cola brands been established, its key competitor Pepsi had also entered the Indian market a few years earlier.

Coke acquired one of its key competitors (the Thums Up brand), as well as four other local brands from the Indian company Parle, which also entered into a partnership with Coke.

After a few false starts, it is now estimated to have more than 50 percent of the cola market in India. It owns 24 bottling plants, and another 25 are run by franchisees. According to a published interview with Coca-Cola, the Indian operation became profitable in 2007, after investments totaling about a billion dollars.

The company has faced several road-bumps:

◆ In 2003, the Center for Science and the Environment (CSE) alleged that Coke (along with Pepsi) contained a high level of pesticide residues in the drinks. These allegations resurfaced in a follow-up study in 2006, when the CSE claimed little had changed.

The situation was further complicated by reports that some farmers were spraying Thums Up instead of pesticides on their crops. It was implied that this worked because the pesticide content was so high. One scientist guessed that it might have worked because the sugar coating attracted ants, which consumed the other pests. Another determined that it was ineffective as a pesticide.

◆ At Plachimada in Kerala, local farmers used Coke's plant sludge as a fertilizer. A report later aired on British television alleged that the sludge had high levels of cadmium and lead, metals that can have toxic effects. Coca-Cola refuted this allegation.

◆ An ongoing issue is water. Coca-Cola production requires water, and the plants were in areas where they were assured of access through tube wells or bore wells. However, tube wells can affects the overall water table.

The Plachimada plant was closed when the *panchayat* (local village authority) refused to renew its operating license. On appeal to the Kerala High Court, the company won its case. However, the panchayat gave a conditional license that the company does not find practicable for continuous operation, and the plant remains closed.

In 2006, students at the University of Michigan prompted that organization to review Coke and water use in India. In response, Coke commissioned The Energy and Resources Institute (TERI), an independent organization based in New Delhi, to assess and report on the situation, including a review of six bottling plants.

The report confirmed that Coke met all government requirements, but also noted that the concerns of local villagers. They made recommendations about greater community involvement in areas around the plants. TERI further suggested that one plant in particular, Kaladera (in the arid state of Rajasthan), was likely to remain problematic in its water use, particularly due to insufficient rainfall in the preceding years.

Coke has responded by putting in rainwater harvesting and aquifer replenishment systems that it says will put back up to 15 times the amount of water it withdraws. It has indicated a commitment to achieving a net zero balance in groundwater usage across all its plants by 2009, both through water conservation and large-scale initiatives in the surrounding communities. In Kaladera, for instance, it has worked with the community to construct groundwater recharge shafts, and restore ancient step wells. The university confirmed that it was satisfied with Coke's response.

It will also work toward achieving TERI's recommendations on community involvement. In Kaladera, aside from water conservation efforts, it has introduced scholarship programs for local students, including one specially targeted at girls.

CHECKLIST 2.13

Warnings from the Twice Shy

Interviews with expatriates, visitors, and managers in India yielded the following warnings.

Know your limitations despite the common language: In particular, do not assume that because you speak English, and all legal and commercial matters are in English, that you can do it yourself. "It's easy to be misled," said an expatriate. "There are complexities here that take years to understand. You need local intelligence and help."

Foreigners may find it difficult to manage operational issues: Someone coming into the country without direct experience is likely to find the operating environment very complex. This is an area best delegated to someone with local experience.

"They should focus on the business, and ensure they have someone local looking after the operations," advised one Indian manager at a foreign company. "The problems here are different."

Yes doesn't always mean yes: It may just mean that the person doesn't want to say rudely no. "They don't like to say no," said an Australian manager, "even when they should. I guess it's like that everywhere in Asia."

Don't be misled by efficient professional Indians: Sophisticated urban Indians, particularly those with some international exposure, may give the wrong impression about how the country functions (or, sometimes, doesn't function). "People meet the smart engineers and managers who make presentations overseas, and they get the idea that that's how the whole country is," a local manager said. "Then they come here and are disappointed. They are not ready for India as it is."

Don't be fooled by appearances when assessing candidates: Apparent sophistication is not necessarily the same thing as business acumen. It is easy for foreign executives to be misled by a polished exterior. "Golf-course decisions, I call them," a manager said.

India is information-rich: India is an information-rich society, and, unlike many other Asian countries, not closed or secretive. That English is the language of business and government helps. People are generally helpful.

"Do your research," recommended one expert. "There is a lot of information out there to be gleaned and bought."

Plan for disruptions: *Bandhs*—general strikes, power outages, and other disruptions—are not uncommon; businesses have to learn to work around them. Although they contribute to inefficiency, they can generally be managed.

Be aware that political connections matter: Foreign companies need to be careful how much they will develop these, because being close to one government may be a negative with its successor. However, agents, distributors, and even your consultants may have political connections.

Be ready to accept differences: "You must keep an open mind," recommended a senior entrepreneur. "Work the way Indians work. Europeans and Asians seem more comfortable with this than Americans."

Be ready for both Indias: At present, said a British expatriate, he encounters two Indias: the old India of government-owned companies, with long negotiations and bureaucratic procedures; the new one of the new airlines and shipyards—with external experience, quick decisions, and easy access to decision makers. People have to be prepared to deal with both.

Plan for exit costs: Not all ventures are successful, and leaving India can be harder—perhaps more expensive—than going in. "Most companies don't think about this," said an American expatriate, "and they end up surprised."

Expect complexity: "Everything was more complex than in any other market we operate in, much more than in the rest of Asia or in China," said the manager of a US consumer product company. "Whether it's distribution or retailing, legal issues, establishing property ownership, moving products between states, different taxes in each state, everything is complicated. You have to get involved, and you need reliable local partners."

Keep in mind the six "Ps" for success: A manager of a British company operating in India suggested the following Ps:

- ◆ Personal effort. It is 24/7. It never stops. People expect complete is personal commitment.
- ◆ Presence. You cannot win over the India market with brief visits. You have to give up weekends, and holidays, and build relationships. You need to get on the ground.
- ◆ Professional behavior. If you fail, you don't leave. You dust off and try again.
- ◆ Patience. India requires a huge amount of patience, from traffic to business.
- ◆ Persistence. Keep going or you won't get anywhere.
- ◆ Partners. You need an Indian partner to interpret nuances and give wise counsel.

PART 3

Entry to India

The checklists in this section cover the kind of ground companies may want to think through as they decide to do business with India: What, exactly, should they seek to achieve? Is it the market or the potential workforce that is the draw? How should they set up shop in India? What are the options? These checklists should get a company started on building its entry strategy.

Planning for India

☐ **Decide objectives for being in India before going in:** India offers two major draws to foreign companies. The first is as a low-cost provider of services and, perhaps, goods. The second is as a rapidly growing and unsaturated market. It is critically important for a company to understand whether it is coming for the first reason or the second—or both. The approaches relevant to the two factors can be quite different.

Some companies jump in without actually knowing why they want to be in India, recognizing it as an important geography, but unsure how to optimize their presence there. While this approach is quite practical in some countries, India is too complex. They are likely to run into difficulties from a lack of clarity in their objectives.

If it is too early for a clear decision on why your company wants to be in India, consider an option some companies with adequate resources have used: they have established liaison or representative offices as listening posts and ways to learn about India, while raising the company's market profile.

☐ **Establish a realistic time frame for results:** Most things in India take longer than expected to happen, and companies should factor in a time frame of about one or two years. In recent times, it has become easier to set up a liaison office, but businesspeople should still expect it to take months, not weeks, to get an Indian operation under way. A manager who has been through it three times between 1990 and 2007 notes that the time required fell from about two-and-a-half years to about eight months. Setting up an outsourcing operation, or an offshore one, will take at least an annual cycle to work out the glitches. It may take longer than that to see profits or cost savings come to fraction.

☐ **Establish a local liaison person:** Having a competent and well-known person on the ground makes everything easier, and reduces the likelihood of mistakes. This person could be an employee, an agent, or a specific individual in a partner company.

☐ **Locate good Indian advisors:** Conditions in India are quite different from elsewhere, and it is extremely important to have locally relevant advice. Some of the areas where companies should ensure they have local advisors: legal, tax, government dealings, travel, and later, executive search, marketing, and advertising.

All the major international service providers—except law firms—have a presence in India, but good local alternatives also exist. Most of the well-known US accounting firms have Indian operations, as do executive search firms such as Heidrick & Struggles, Korn/Ferry, and Egon Zehnder.

As of May 2008, foreign law firms were not allowed to practice in India, though the government is reportedly considering giving them access; serious discussion of the subject started in September 2007. Foreign legal firms do have informal relationships with Indian law firms.

Said R. Balakrishnan, now of the Centrum group: "I think getting a good law firm or a good global audit firm is the key starting point. For example, if the client is routed through, say, PWC US or Deloitte US, he is more likely to touch the right bases in India. One key thing is that the accounting or law firm can help in identifying the local talent. I also understand that some large headhunting firms are getting into this business of liaison."

The quality of the advisors is extremely important, noted one business executive from a small company. "I think we went in with the wrong people," he said. "It seemed that everything that could go wrong did go wrong. Documents weren't clear. Requirements weren't clear. Some things were supposed to be done online, but they couldn't actually be done online. There were comprehension gaps and other inefficiencies. It's easy for the large companies, I suppose. They can go to the international companies that all have a presence in India. But mid-size companies don't know where to go. They have to rely on recommendations from other expatriates."

Expect communications issues and time zone differences: As an organization, it is important to recognize the communications issues and time-zone differences inherent in managing ventures in India.

Some companies reduce the problem by managing their Indian operation from an Asian regional office in Singapore, Malaysia, or Hong Kong; but companies without such an international presence do not have the option. Mid-size and smaller companies, in particular, should bear in mind the resources and open-minded attitude that the head-office contact for the Indian operation will need. Decentralizing greater authority to the people on the ground reduces the need for head-office involvement, but it is impossible to eliminate.

Allow for infrastructure issues: For instance, if telecommuting is important—and it is for many companies in an international setting—ensure that key executives have industrial-strength power backup. Modern apartment and office complexes provide diesel generators, but in the delay before they kick in, teleconference access can be lost. An additional battery-inverter system may be useful. Also allow for increased internet traffic, and therefore bandwidth congestion, around the end of the day. Broadband access (through DSL) is, needless to say, critical.

Consider exit costs at the time of entry: "Lots of companies, particularly small ones, don't think about exit costs if things go wrong," said an executive in the healthcare industry. "They can be pretty high. You have to pay off employees and break your lease. It can run to US$10–12 million for a 2,000-person operation."

Prepare a startup budget consonant with the plans: Estimated costs at startup vary, depending on the company's requirements. A bare presence can be established for about US$150,000 in the first year; a small country office with a local manager, perhaps, US$500,000 million; and an expatriate manager with an office in a prime location, perhaps, twice or three times that.

Entrants cannot rely on single-window clearance: It is a buzzword without a real impact, said several executives in India. Although the process of getting required approvals is much simpler than before, many permissions will probably be needed, and several ministries may be involved.

Patience is critical to success in India: Most things—not just getting approvals—are more complicated than expected.

"Nothing was easier than I expected," said a multinational manager of his company's entry into India. "There's more complexity than in any other market in Asia."

An entrepreneur who had set up a business in India found the first step of getting his company registered delayed by a clerk at the Registrar of Companies, who kept rejecting the proposed names, declaring they were too general, or too specific, or did not reflect the planned activities of the company.

Pragmatism is essential: On the whole, companies cannot expect to change things, so it is important to find ways to deal with the roadblocks. India is full of workarounds.

Persistence and a long view are useful: India is not a good market for quick profits, but may be very lucrative for companies that think long term. Foreign visitors to India often find aspects of it frustrating, so persistence is a prerequisite for success.

A liberalized India offers many entry options: As India liberalizes, it has become easier for foreign companies to enter the market, and many entry strategies are available.

For decades, India has been an interesting but rather inaccessible market for international companies. In the past decade or so, the easing of the regulations has opened up new opportunities. Many companies interested in India are seeking market access. Foreigners approaching a potential business in India will find several options available, and these can be used individually or in combination.

One option is to export directly to clients in India: Some companies export to India and rely on the clients to order the goods and clear them when they are shipped. This requires the least commitment of corporate resources and management, and is usually part of a purely opportunistic strategy: the company makes sales when it finds an opportunity, but does not attempt to develop the market.

For some companies—particularly those making very expensive products, typically machinery, a small market in India, there does not justify the point of going beyond opportunistic sales. If they expect to sell only a few units annually, or maybe even less than that, it may not be worth the trouble to even appoint a distributor.

3.2.1 Case Study—Audi

Audi is an example of a company that started with exports to India, before developing a presence and starting CKD production there. (CKD stands for Completely Knocked Down.)

Audi started selling cars in India in 2004. It set up three dealers, in Delhi, Mumbai, and Bangalore, and introduced several models, initially all imported into India, beginning with the Audi A8, Audi A6, Audi A4, and Audi TT.

Three years later, Audi started Audi India as a division of the Mumbai-based Volkswagen Group Sales India Pvt. Ltd. This entity was responsible for sales and marketing in India. In November 2007, the company announced it would assemble about 300–400 units of the A6 model locally in 2008, at sister company Skoda's plant in Aurangabad, Maharashtra. The Audi A4 would be added by the end of 2008.

By March 2008, Audi announced it would invest €30 million by 2015 in Indian manufacture. Audi told the press that it intended to assemble the Audi A4 and Audi A6 for the Indian market in India, with components imported from Germany. Until it achieved that objective for the Audi A4, it would price the Audi A4 cars as though they were Indian made. (Imports of cars attract substantial customs duties.)

With the start of the CKD production of the Audi A6, the company estimated that it saved about Rs140,000–210,000 in costs at the consumer level.

Audi's dealer network had grown from the initial three to seven by April 2008: it added dealers in Gurgaon, Pune, Hyderabad, and Chandigarh. All the dealers have opened new Audi showrooms with Audi "corporate design and corporate identity." The new exclusive showrooms—the first of 10 showrooms across India Audi expects to have in place by the end of 2008—allow Audi to display its model range

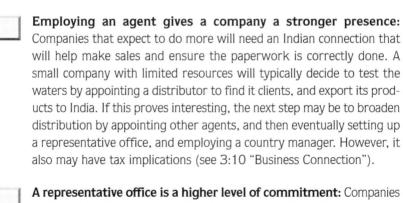

effectively. The flagship Gurgaon showroom is more than 13,000 square feet in size, the Hyderabad one about 5,500 square feet.

The model range from 2007 onward includes the Audi A8, Audi A6, Audi A4, the sports car Audi TT, and the SUV Audi Q7.

The luxury car market in India is tiny at present; only about one percent of all cars sold fall into this classification: an estimated 4,000 cars annually. But Audi estimates that the luxury segment is growing at perhaps 50 percent per year.

Audi competes with the better-known and well-established market leader Mercedes for a share of this market, and also with BMW. Both those companies also make cars in India: Mercedes builds 2,000 to 2,500 cars annually, and BMW increased the production capacity of its plant in Chennai from 1,700 to 3,000 cars. Mercedes, which has been in India for more than 50 years, has a dealer network covering 26 cities, while BMW has nine dealers and plans to expand to 12.

Employing an agent gives a company a stronger presence: Companies that expect to do more will need an Indian connection that will help make sales and ensure the paperwork is correctly done. A small company with limited resources will typically decide to test the waters by appointing a distributor to find it clients, and export its products to India. If this proves interesting, the next step may be to broaden distribution by appointing other agents, and then eventually setting up a representative office, and employing a country manager. However, it also may have tax implications (see 3:10 "Business Connection").

A representative office is a higher level of commitment: Companies ready to take the plunge usually set up representative offices.

Many companies establish a local presence through liaison or representative offices as their first move into India. These offices can coordinate with local agents and distributors, and gather market intelligence. In some cases, they hire local managers for their knowledge and access. In other cases—and particularly if the home country is not English-speaking—they may prefer to have an expatriate present, especially in the initial stages.

According to one country manager for a US company, it is preferable for a company that is at all serious about establishing itself in India to set up an office first. The choice of distributors is crucial, and for a company that has never done business in India before, the question is "How do you know you are appointing the right agents?"

It is better, he argues, to make the first step a search for a really good local country manager, and let that person establish a distribution network. It may be easier to find and assess a country manager than a bunch of distributors, and foreign companies—especially those with limited resources, who may not even be in a position to evaluate their agents' performance.

An Indian subsidiary or joint venture is the next step: A company ready to commit to India can set up an Indian company, either as a joint venture or as a wholly owned subsidiary.

Liaison or representative offices cannot legally do any business, so many companies move to the next stage: a presence in India through joint ventures or subsidiaries. These companies are allowed to sell and manufacture, and are treated as Indian companies. They are permitted to own property (except agricultural land), not merely lease it.

Licensing technology offers returns with less involvement: Licensing arrangements may be a way to enter India with low-involvement, or sweeten the returns on a more extensive arrangement.

Foreign companies can license technology to Indian firms as a way of doing business without a major investment. It is useful for those that are not ready for a deeper involvement in the Indian market, or in those areas where foreign companies are still restricted.

Until recently, involving a minority-held affiliate was also a strategy. With the liberalization of regulations regarding foreign ownership, this has become less important. It is nevertheless an interesting option for some companies as a way to provide regular returns from the Indian operations.

In April 2008, Arcadia Biosciences announced it would license technology regarding nitrogen use and salt tolerance for a number of crops to the Indian seed company, Maharashtra Hybrid Seed Company Ltd.

In 2007, Georgia-Pacific Chemicals of Atlanta, Georgia, signed a seven-year technology licensing and manufacturing agreement with India's Thermax Ltd. It covered chemicals used in the paper industry. The company also has a joint venture in Vadodara, India, for thermosetting resins: Georgia-Pacific Kemrock International Pvt. Ltd. was formed in 2006.

3.2.2 Case Study—Crocs India

Crocs, the innovative Colorado-based shoe company, brought its products to India in 2006.

Crocs was founded in 2002 by three entrepreneurs who designed a new type of boat shoe made of a flexible lightweight resin. The product was a hit; sales soared from US$1 million in 2003 to US$108 million in 2005, and US$847 million in 2007. Between 2004 and 2005, the company acquired its supplier, a Canadian manufacturer called Foam Creations, and changed its name from Western Brands to Crocs Inc. A professional management team—consisting of past alumni of the electronics company Flextronics—was brought in. It went public in 2006, listing on the US stock exchange NASDAQ. Its profits have risen tenfold between 2005 and 2007, to US$168 million. Although its primary market was initially North America, the company decided on an international strategy quite soon after it started, and Crocs are now sold in more than 80 countries; international sales now exceed domestic sales. It manufactures shoes at eight factories in international locations including Mexico, Brazil, Bosnia, Italy, Vietnam, and China.

Crocs entered India when three independent entrepreneurs based in Singapore acquired the distribution rights in 2006, and set up distribution arrangements in India through local agencies. It has three distributors for its lifestyle brands, which constitute 95 percent of its Indian business. (It has separate arrangements for its medical shoes, used for such conditions as diabetes.)

However, within a short time, its management decided it wanted direct access to the Indian market, and bought out the distributors and brought them into the company. The next step, in February 2007, was to set up a subsidiary, Crocs India Pvt. Ltd.

The Indian government permits single-brand retailers to operate in India, but caps foreign equity at 51 percent. Crocs got Foreign Investment Promotion Board approval for a joint venture with one of its distributors.

Marketing challenges: From the start, it was apparent that Crocs would need to tailor its global marketing strategies to India. "Globally, we do three things," said Mark Langhammer of Crocs Asia. "First, we focus on public relations—articles in the press and so on—so that consumers get used to seeing our new breed of footwear. Second, we participate in events that allow the consumers to interact with our shoe products, so they can see the benefits for themselves. Finally, we have very broad and visible distribution, so the shoes are accessible and visible."

There were several challenges to this approach in India.

◆ The underdeveloped retail sector. Despite the new malls that have come up in recent years, retail in India is still dominated by small family-run stores. Langhammer estimates that organized retail accounts for about 10 percent of the footwear market. This limits the amount of shelf space they can devote to new, relatively expensive brands, so it limits distribution opportunities. In India, the typical Crocs display in a multibrand or multiproduct outlet is perhaps 200 pairs, whereas in a place like Dubai, they would display maybe 800 to 1,000 pairs.

◆ Few events. India has relatively few of the business-to-business (B2B) and business-to-customer (B2C) events that Crocs typically participates in elsewhere: B2B and B2C trade shows; school events; county fairs; and so on.

◆ Noisy media situation. Though India has well-developed print, broadcast and cable media: it is a very competitive and noisy field. It is difficult to rise above the clutter and media "noise."

These factors prompted Crocs to modify its marketing plans in India. To build its brand, it is establishing flagship stores in the major metropolitan cities that constitute three-quarters of its market: Delhi NCR, Mumbai, and Bangalore, as well the main secondary markets of Chennai and Kolkata. These will allow it to display a much broader range of products than it can do in multiproduct stores, and help it to build its brand image. The stores are located in "high street" areas (and malls that enjoy high traffic) such as Connaught Place, Saket, and Gurgaon in the NCR; Colaba and Linking Road in Mumbai; Brigade Road in Bangalore.

It had opened five stores by end-July 2008—in Delhi, Mumbai, Pune, and Gurgaon—and planned another eight by the end of 2008, and 15 more in 2009.

The stores help the company to build its brand, both through visibility and through a status effect: a brand that has its own store in a good location would be perceived as having arrived. It also allows Crocs to show a much broader product range, with perhaps 2,000 pairs on display, and present the opportunity to interact with consumers.

"Crocs is an experiential product," said Langhammer. "The stores allow consumers the opportunity to touch, feel, and try on this different and innovative type of footwear. Once they try on a pair of Crocs, they really begin to understand our brand and uniqueness."

In addition, Crocs distributes its shoes through major retailers, and its products are in more than 300 multibrand outlets across the country, including specialty footwear stores (such as Metro, Regal, Inc. 5, and Reliance Footwear), major department stores (such as Lifestyle, Central, Pantaloons, and Westside), and sporting goods stores (such as Planet Sports).

Crocs is also launching an advertising campaign through cinema, television, and radio in India to position the product more effectively.

Some of the characteristics of the Indian consumer may also require a different strategy.

◆ Buying behavior. Women, just like elsewhere, do most of the buying for the whole family, as well as for themselves. However, in India, unlike in many other countries, women tend to spend money on the others in the family, and look for inexpensive products themselves.

Some of the Crocs retailers have recommended differential pricing for men's and women's shoes—a strategy that Crocs has yet to adopt. Despite all this, women are Crocs' number one customer.

◆ Conservatism. The Indian consumer is quite conservative. Crocs is perceived as a brand suitable for children and the beach; the company is expanding this brand image to be much more of a lifestyle product, a brand position that has been effectively established in most other countries.

◆ Price sensitivity. Although the target consumers are sophisticated and aware of international products, they are price-sensitive in actual purchasing. They do not spend a great deal of money on shoes, and often prefer cheaply made indigenous footwear. In India, Crocs are priced at about 12–15 percent more (after tax) than in the US, (but this is significantly less than in Europe and other markets) due primarily to import duties and local taxes.

◆ Spectators rather than participants. Indian consumers tend to watch rather than participate in physical activities. This reduces the impact of efforts to get consumers to interact with the shoe. It also implies a smaller market for products that are marketed to an active or sporting lifestyle.

◆ Presently, Crocs has not introduced a special product for India as India tastes are found to be very similar to those in other major markets. Crocs currently offers 40 of its 100 styles, and will be introducing over 50 new styles in 2009. But the five classic styles still account for 50 percent of our sales, and black remains the top-selling color— reflecting the conservative nature of the country.

He adds: "While we are focusing on introducing our international styles to the India marketplace, we are exploring the development of specific styles for India, and are working with local designers."

Langhammer acknowledges that Crocs' strategy requires a significant investment. Although company policy is not to disclose investment numbers or sales, he estimates that a store would cost perhaps US$250,000 to set up. The scarcity of sophisticated retail space and the intense competition are driving up costs. Rents alone can be as much as Rs1,000 (or more) per square foot per month in the kind of upmarket locations the company seeks. Typical terms require a six-to-ten-month deposit, and one month's rent in advance. "It ties up a lot of cash."

Other approaches may require less investment. Franchising is an option. Crocs, as a new and relatively unknown brand in India, did not initially get as much interest as older established brands. The company also wants more control than franchising would provide in the early stages of brand building, but it does not rule out franchising later on as a way to grow the market faster.

Some of its competitors are choosing to license their products: Levi's, for instance, licenses an Indian manufacturer of Levi's shoes; and Florsheim, perceived to be a premium brand, also uses the franchisee model. This approach requires significantly less investment, but also much less involvement and control.

Another option is to work entirely through the wholesale system. This may be suitable for companies with well-known brands that do not want a great deal of involvement in India.

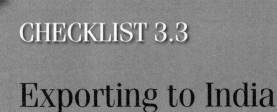

Exporting to India

India is importing an ever-increasing amount of products: As the country has lowered trade barriers, imports have risen not only in volume but also in variety. In 2005–2006 (April–March), India imported merchandise valued at approximated US$149 billion. (Its exports were about US$103 billion.) Imports and exports are growing at about 18–22 percent per annum (Source: Department of Commerce, Government of India.)

India now permits a broader range of imports than before. Tariffs have been substantially lowered. Almost all imports are directly to the end-user; distributors are permitted to stock and sell only a limited range of products, for example, spare parts.

Check whether India permits import of the product: A shortlist of prohibited imports (animal fat, rennet, wild animals, and unprocessed ivory) and a longer one of restricted products still exists.

Some imports are "canalized," that is, they must be routed through government-owned companies. (These are mainly petroleum and its products, vegetable oils and grain.)

Imports of materials and equipment to be used in exports are usually duty free. Import duties are still levied on many consumer goods, particularly luxury goods or those that compete directly with important Indian industries. In some cases—for example, new automobiles—the rates can be very high.

In addition to import restrictions, other requirements—such as emissions standards for automobiles—may make exports difficult without substantially modifying the product.

Ascertain the actual duties that would be payable: Duties on imports are aligned with indirect taxes paid on local manufacture. Though these are all trending downward, they can still be quite high in some products. Imported goods may attract countervailing duty; anti-dumping duty; and additional customs duty.

Harley-Davidson, the motorcycle company, can now export to India after changes in required emission standards brought their bikes (which comply with European Union standards) into compliance. But it estimates that duties and taxes could result in its motorcycles being twice as expensive in India as in the US. In February 2008, it was reported that with a customs duty of 60 percent and about 30 percent in other taxes, the market was still far from promising.

An optimal strategy may simply be to make opportunistic sales: Some companies do nothing; they sell to India on an occasional and opportunistic basis, on the basis of unsolicited orders. Especially for small companies selling products that have long lifecycles, this may be a practical approach to an otherwise high-involvement market. Companies can capitalize on the approach by using good websites, by advertising in industry journals, and by word of mouth.

Consider opportunistic exports to India if your product is unlikely to find a substantial market there, or if your company resources are limited.

Other companies may prefer a more permanent arrangement: If so, you may wish to appoint a distributor or agent, or even several of them. It may be worthwhile to establish a presence through a liaison office.

When exporting to India, ensure that the packaging is sturdy: Aside from the rigors of the sea journey or cargo flight, the goods will be subject to cargo handling that may be rougher than in developed countries. Standard packaging would easily be damaged.

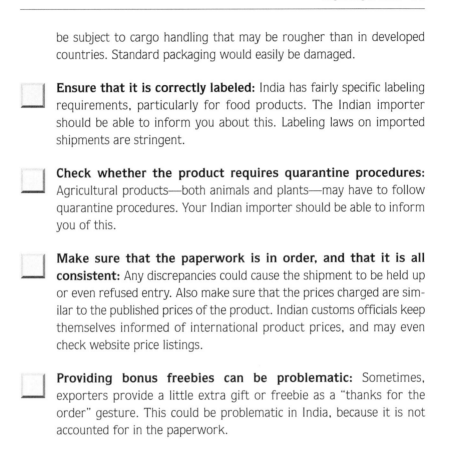

Ensure that it is correctly labeled: India has fairly specific labeling requirements, particularly for food products. The Indian importer should be able to inform you about this. Labeling laws on imported shipments are stringent.

Check whether the product requires quarantine procedures: Agricultural products—both animals and plants—may have to follow quarantine procedures. Your Indian importer should be able to inform you of this.

Make sure that the paperwork is in order, and that it is all consistent: Any discrepancies could cause the shipment to be held up or even refused entry. Also make sure that the prices charged are similar to the published prices of the product. Indian customs officials keep themselves informed of international product prices, and may even check website price listings.

Providing bonus freebies can be problematic: Sometimes, exporters provide a little extra gift or freebie as a "thanks for the order" gesture. This could be problematic in India, because it is not accounted for in the paperwork.

CHECKLIST 3.4

Selecting an Agent

☐ **Companies should consider the selection process carefully:** A company that plans to export to India, rather than manufacture there, depends on its agent, or agents and distributors for access to the market. The selection of the associate or associates is probably the single most important decision for its success.

☐ **Is a dedicated sole selling agent best for the company?:** A decision the company must make is whether to have a multiproduct or dedicated distributor. Some companies prefer dedicated distributors that only deal in their product lines. Others note that their business alone is unlikely to sustain the kind of infrastructure they want to access.

It may be a tradeoff between an agent that is focused on your business but too small to be effective, or one that is substantial but does not pay enough attention to individual clients. A company must decide whether to sign a large distribution company, which will have a strong infrastructure, but may have several products and principals clamoring for its resources, or a smaller distributor, which will focus on its product, but may not have the critical mass to provide a strong infrastructure.

☐ **Check the credibility and reputation of candidates:** This is difficult for a visitor to discern; the only way to find out is to ask around. References from existing clients may be useful, but must be checked.

Places to start the investigation would be:

- ◆ your country's embassy or high commission if it has a substantial commercial presence
- ◆ industry associations such as CII, FICCI, and NASSCOM
- ◆ other businesspeople in the country.

Check that the agent has the necessary infrastructure: A company must verify that the agent has sufficient infrastructure to meet the requirements of its clients. It is a good idea actually to inspect the infrastructure claimed, or at least the crucial parts of it. Most agents would be happy to take you around.

Check that the agent has a comprehension of local laws and taxes: The distributors should understand the legal aspects of the business, and not inadvertently embroil the principals in violations of the law. In particular, they should be aware of all the state and local regulations and levies.

Companies cannot assume that the relationship will be permanent: Although business relationships in India are often stable over long periods—in part, because family-controlled businesses may have more predictable policies and objectives—they are not immune to rethink on both sides.

For instance, in 2003, Kraft Foods severed a distribution arrangement with the Indian company Dabur for its orange powder drink, Tang. Launched in 2001, Tang faced severe competition from local products and gained little traction. The company relaunched Tang in India in 2006, and is now planning to introduce many of its cookie (biscuit) brands.

Seek local legal assistance in drawing up a contract: Rather than using standard inhouse contracts, it is worthwhile to seek local legal assistance in drawing up contracts, paying particular attention to equitable exit clauses.

Although India is moving toward a more impersonal setting, relationships are still very important. A graceful parting that does not cause bad blood is in every way more desirable than one that leaves the two parties at odds. Disgruntled former associates can easily spoil a company's reputation, and the effects can continue long after the event.

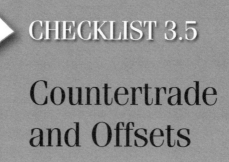

☐ **The government prefers offsets for all large deals:** Any company selling to the Indian government should be aware of the preference for countertrade or offsets. For large deals, it is a requirement, whether stated—as for defense purchases—or not. Savvy companies can use this to strengthen their competitive position in bidding.

☐ **Offsets and countertrade mean slightly different things:** Companies should bear in mind the difference between offsets and countertrade in the India context. Offsets usually refer to investments in related industries; countertrade usually implies counterpurchases, that is, the sourcing of exports from India.

☐ **Offsets will likely be demanded for major government sales:** Companies should expect that major sales to the government may require offsets or countertrade. In some cases, the requirement is built into governmental guidelines. Guidelines for defense purchases specify that 30 percent of any deal amounting to more than US$3 billion must be offset by investment in, or purchases from India's defense industry.

☐ **It may be possible to convert an offset into a counterpurchase:** Though this is not necessarily routine, it may be possible to convert an offset requirement into a counterpurchase. This provides more flexibility, since it frees the company from the obligation to invest in or purchase from the industry. It can source other goods and services, depending on the agreement reached, to meet the terms of the deal.

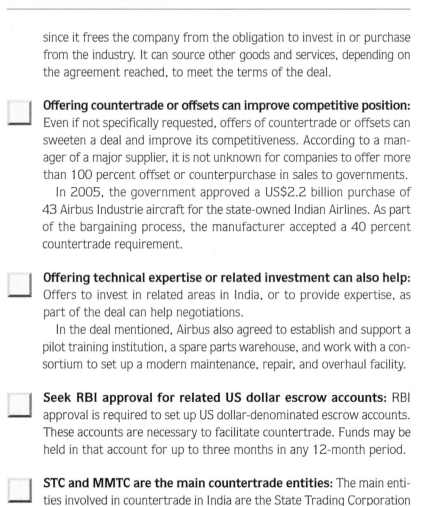

Offering countertrade or offsets can improve competitive position: Even if not specifically requested, offers of countertrade or offsets can sweeten a deal and improve its competitiveness. According to a manager of a major supplier, it is not unknown for companies to offer more than 100 percent offset or counterpurchase in sales to governments.

In 2005, the government approved a US$2.2 billion purchase of 43 Airbus Industrie aircraft for the state-owned Indian Airlines. As part of the bargaining process, the manufacturer accepted a 40 percent countertrade requirement.

Offering technical expertise or related investment can also help: Offers to invest in related areas in India, or to provide expertise, as part of the deal can help negotiations.

In the deal mentioned, Airbus also agreed to establish and support a pilot training institution, a spare parts warehouse, and work with a consortium to set up a modern maintenance, repair, and overhaul facility.

Seek RBI approval for related US dollar escrow accounts: RBI approval is required to set up US dollar-denominated escrow accounts. These accounts are necessary to facilitate countertrade. Funds may be held in that account for up to three months in any 12-month period.

STC and MMTC are the main countertrade entities: The main entities involved in countertrade in India are the State Trading Corporation (STC), and to a lesser extent, the Minerals and Metals Trading Corporation (MMTC).

For example, in October 2007, STC signed a memorandum of agreement with the Philippine International Trading Corp (PITC). STC would coordinate the sale of bulk pharmaceuticals, medical equipment, and commodities such as rice, sugar, wheat, corn, flour, and cement; it would import fatty acids and coconut oil, ores and fertilizers, processed food, cosmetics and personal care products, and a range of other products and substances.

They may be involved even if the deal is concluded separately: For instance, the government appointed STC as the coordinator in the countertrade and offset component of the aircraft purchase deals. In 2007, the government-owned Bharat Heavy Electricals Ltd. signed a memorandum of understanding with MMTC that its power-plant equipment would be promoted as exportables against countertrade agreements.

Planning in advance may strengthen your position: If selling to the Indian government or state-owned entities is an important element in your strategy, planning in advance may allow your company to forge a stronger position in meeting offset requirements.

Positioning itself as a player in the countertrade market, Lockheed Martin, the US-based defense supplier, has announced it was in discussions with about 20 Indian companies to qualify suppliers. It also indicated that it would consider exceeding the offset requirement as it has done in some other countries.

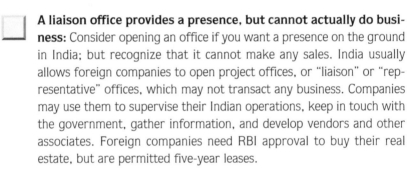

CHECKLIST 3.6

A Presence in India

☐ **A liaison office provides a presence, but cannot actually do business:** Consider opening an office if you want a presence on the ground in India; but recognize that it cannot make any sales. India usually allows foreign companies to open project offices, or "liaison" or "representative" offices, which may not transact any business. Companies may use them to supervise their Indian operations, keep in touch with the government, gather information, and develop vendors and other associates. Foreign companies need RBI approval to buy their real estate, but are permitted five-year leases.

☐ **A subsidiary or affiliate is a better business vehicle:** If the company wants to do business directly, an Indian company may be a better vehicle, and is now relatively easy to achieve.

After decades of discouraging foreign investment in India, the government has liberalized its stance, and now actually encourages it. Previously, foreigners had little hope of getting a majority share in an Indian venture, unless it exported most of its production. Now, it is permitted in most cases, and the procedure has been streamlined. This is called the "automatic route," and companies, whose Indian investments qualify need neither ministerial nor Reserve Bank approval.

They will still need to notify the Reserve Bank on receiving money from overseas, and on issuing shares to foreigners or foreign entities.

Not all foreign investment is automatically permitted: Check whether your company's business is restricted; exceptions to the automatic route remain. Foreign investment is not permitted in areas to do with gambling, lotteries, atomic energy, retail trade (with some exceptions), and agriculture (again with some exceptions, mainly in agribusiness).

Any company whose products are subject to industrial licensing (see below) requires approval from the Foreign Investment Promotion Board (FIPB). If a company needs FIPB clearance, it adds perhaps one-to-three months to the time required to complete the formalities.

The FIPB is a board within the Department of Economic Affairs in the Finance Ministry. Its role is to deal with foreign direct investment into India. Its members include the secretary for industry, finance secretary, commerce secretary, and secretary for economic relations in the Ministry for External Affairs (the "Foreign Ministry").

Some companies still need industrial licenses to operate: Companies may need to check whether industrial licensing still applies their industry.

India formerly had a comprehensive system of production controls, known as industrial licensing; its intent was to prevent monopoly, but it also had the effect of creating scarcity by penalizing increased production. This system was greatly relaxed as India liberalized. Foreign investments in any industry that requires industrial licensing (see the following) also requires prior approval from the FIPB.

Industrial licenses currently apply mainly to the following:

◆ Industries with social impacts—alcoholic beverages; tobacco products including cigarettes; electronic, defense, and aerospace; explosives; and hazardous chemicals—need licenses.

◆ Some products are reserved for the small-scale sector (that is, companies with an investment in plant and machinery or equipment of less than Rs50 million, or Rs20 million for companies providing services). Larger companies may be permitted to make these products if they export half of their production in India; they will require prior permission by way of an industrial license.

3.6.1 Branch Office: Activities Permitted to the Indian Branch of a Foreign Entity

◆ Exports and imports

◆ Providing professional or consultancy services

◆ Research

◆ Planning and arranging joint ventures with Indian companies

◆ Representing the parent company and group companies

◆ Acting as an agent for purchase or sales

◆ Providing IT services and developing software

◆ Providing technical support for the company's products

◆ Representing a foreign airline, shipping company, bank, or insurance company

Non-resident entities require RBI approval if they wish to set up a branch office. (Banks and insurance companies get this approval automatically as part of the larger approval process they undergo.) Unlike liaison or project offices, branches are allowed to generate revenues, and need not be paid for from overseas funds. A branch cannot manufacture goods in India, but it is allowed to subcontract manufacture to an Indian company.

As of February 2008, some 35 products were reserved for small-scale companies. Most of these were in the general area of food (such as pickles, bread, pressed vegetable oils, and processed spices); wooden furniture, exercise books, some plastic products made of PVC or polyethylene, polypropylene; some chemical products; some simply made mass-consumption products including matches, fireworks, laundry soap, padlocks, aluminum or stainless steel cookware, and glass bangles; steel products including furniture and rolling shutters; and small electrical motors and electrical wiring accessories. The products on this list are changed from time to time, so checking the current situation is recommended.

◆ Generally, companies that wish to locate their production facilities within 25 kilometers (15.5 miles) of any of the 23 major cities will need licenses. Exceptions are made for certain industries, mainly in electronics, software, and printing. Companies that set up in areas already designated industrial zones before 1991 also do not need licenses.

Some companies need specific environmental clearances: Companies investing in a range of polluting industries may need clearances to show that they are dealing effectively with pollution, although even here, the requirement may not apply if the investment is fairly small (less than Rs1 billion). Certain geographic areas are considered ecologically sensitive, and companies may be prohibited from establishing industries there, or may have more stringent guidelines to follow.

A branch operation may suit in some specific cases: Some companies—especially banks and airlines—prefer to set up branches. Branches are allowed to do business. For banks, the critical factor is the capital requirement and the reputation, and operating as a branch offers a better option since the entity is legally part of its parent. However, if it wants to engage in nonbanking operations, it may need to have a subsidiary instead.

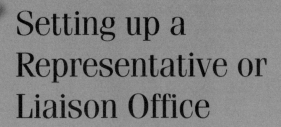

CHECKLIST 3.7

Setting up a Representative or Liaison Office

☐ **An office is not a substitute for an agent or a subsidiary:** When setting up a representative office, companies must recognize that it can only be an adjunct to a business, since it cannot actually engage in any transactions. Many firms use it to boost their marketing efforts and develop a long-term India strategy, while the actual business flows through agents or joint ventures. (The terms "liaison office" and "representative office" are used interchangeably.)

☐ **Some companies prefer to rely wholly on agents:** This is less expensive, and can be satisfactory, particularly if the company has an agent that works solely for them. The agent then functions as the company's representative in India. It is not quite as arm's length as exporting to India with no agents at all, but still represents a fairly shallow involvement. It provides substantially less control and less scope for market development than having an office.

☐ **Allow for reasonable costs in setting up such an office:** A very rough estimate is about US$1–1.5 million (2007 dollars) annually for an office staffed by an expatriate and two local officers with support staff. Relying entirely on local personnel will save perhaps half the cost.

(However, some businesses find that having an expatriate manager, more than justifies the extra expense, especially when the operation is new.)

Said one Indian country manager who set up a liaison office in Gurgaon recently, "You can start up with about US$150,000 in the first year. All you need is a local country head, who would cost you about US$50,000-60,000, and space in a business center to set up shop with. That would be about US$12,000 per year. Travel costs would be roughly equivalent to the salary, so that would be another US$50,000–60,000. Legal fees would be in the range of US$4,000–5,000. Then, there are miscellaneous service costs. When you subsequently move into your own rented space and add support staff, it can still be done for under US$500,000."

Another source estimated the total costs to come up to about US$0.8–1 million, for an expatriate country head, support staff, a couple of assistants, and a location in the center of New Delhi, with rent estimated at about US$120,000 per year; secretary and three staffers at about US$50,000 per year; domestic and overseas travel at about US$80,000–100,000; cost to company of an expatriate country head at about US$400,000; and miscellaneous costs and fees, of about US$150,000–200,000 annually.

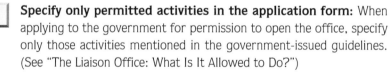

Specify only permitted activities in the application form: When applying to the government for permission to open the office, specify only those activities mentioned in the government-issued guidelines. (See "The Liaison Office: What Is It Allowed to Do?")

Even minor deviations could stall or block your applications. A liaison office is not meant to be turned into a business-producing entity. If a company sets up a liaison office, and decides to do business other than through an agent, it will need to incorporate an Indian company.

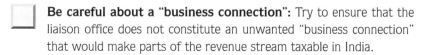

Be careful about a "business connection": Try to ensure that the liaison office does not constitute an unwanted "business connection" that would make parts of the revenue stream taxable in India.

This is a gray area at present, and companies expect greater clarity in the next year or two, especially after the resolution of the Vodafone case. Said one expatriate, "A company can start with a liaison office, but if it doesn't move to the next step, it may look suspicious and attract tax authorities' attention." Companies can use this route, but should be prepared to have their cases heard if needed.

3.7.1 The Liaison Office: What Is It Allowed to Do?

◆ It can represent the parent company/group companies.

◆ It may promote exports and imports.

◆ It can plan and arrange joint ventures with Indian companies.

◆ It can act as a communication channel between the home office and Indian companies.

Any nonresident who wishes to open a liaison office or project office in India needs approval from the RBI. This is based on the *Foreign Exchange Management (Establishment in India of branch or office or other place of business) Regulations 2000*, amended twice in 2003 and again in 2005.

The office is not allowed any commercial or industrial activity; it must be entirely paid for by money sent in from overseas (or, for a project office, payments from a multilateral aid or project agency). It must report its annual accounts to the RBI.

CHECKLIST 3.8

An Indian Company

☐ **Do you want a subsidiary or a joint venture?:** While many companies set up wholly owned subsidiaries, some prefer to have joint ventures with Indian partners.

Despite the Indian government liberalizing its stance on foreign direct investment—so that foreign firms are more easily allowed majority ownership (or even 100 percent ownership), many foreign firms prefer to take stakes of less than 50 percent, with the understanding that the Indian partners will be primarily responsible for the operations. Companies from countries where English is not the main language may find this route particularly convenient.

☐ **Joint ventures can help with the complex business environment:** Given the complexity of India's operating environment, consider the advantages of a joint venture.

◆ It brings the local knowledge of an Indian partner to bear on regulatory issues.

◆ It makes use of the Indian firm's expertise on marketing in India.

◆ It allows the business to operate according to local norms.

◆ It is likely to be more cost-effective than bringing in foreign managers.

In December 2007, Volvo A.B. announced a deal with Eicher Motors Ltd., with a plan to pay US$350 million for a 45.6 percent share in Eicher's truck and bus business. (Formerly associated with the German Eicher Tractors, the company has been owned by Indian shareholders since 1965.)

Mahle GmbH is planning a 50:50 joint venture with India Pistons. The Indian company's existing factory at Maraimalai Nagar near Chennai will be spun off into the joint venture, and double its present capacity to more than six million pistons annually. The company plans to make pistons for automotive engines that meet Euro IV and higher standards, and oil-cooled pistons for diesel engines.

In February 2008, Tata announced a joint venture with Boeing to make aerospace components for the defense industry.

Roca, a Spanish company making ceramic bathroom fittings, has entered into a 50:50 joint venture with Parryware in Chennai.

Sanyo has a 50 percent joint venture in India with BPL in the field of consumer electrical products. The company is planning to sell separately branded Sanyo and BPL products to different market segments.

The question of control can sometimes become contentious: In some cases, the foreign company leaves the operation of the Indian joint venture to its local partner. This can be useful in cases where the foreign company has little international expertise and limited resources. In such a situation, it is important to ensure that both sides have clear and mutually acceptable expectations. Some kind of written memorandum is a good idea, not so much as a legal document but as a way of clarifying objectives.

Since liberalization, the foreign company generally has management control of the joint venture. This allows it to function more or less as a wholly owned subsidiary, while still providing access to the Indian partner as an advisor.

Equal control is the most difficult option: In some cases, the foreign company and the Indian partner have equal holdings and equal control. This is, by far, the most tricky operation. Even if there is a complete meeting of minds at the early stages of the venture, interests inevitably diverge. This can be further complicated by the people involved—especially in the foreign company—as they tend to change with normal promotions and reassignments. An arrangement that depends on relationships and individual trust may falter at that stage.

Things can fall apart: Not everyone considers joint ventures a good idea. One manager we interviewed thought them risky. "Corporate partnerships are inherently unstable," he commented.

A powerful, well-connected Indian partner can help get things done, but can also be tricky: after the Indian government passed protective legislation requiring foreign companies to get no-objection certificates from their Indian partners before starting competing operations in India, some companies felt that it blocked them from getting out of unsuitable arrangements, since the Indian partners could block their return.

A February 2007 article on Rediff.com noted that many of the joint ventures set up earlier fall apart once Indian deregulation permitted greater foreign ownership, and the markets grew large enough to be interesting. The objectives of the two partners frequently diverged, particularly in the matter of long-term investment balanced against short-term profits. Often, the foreign company, having developed India expertise through the joint venture, had no reason to share future opportunities with a local partner.

One observer noted that in the 1990s, a number of alliances were formed. The Indian partners expected them to last forever, and the foreign partners wanted to be the main drivers of those ventures. For the most part, neither expectation was realized.

Joint venture agreements should specify appropriate exit clauses: International companies in joint ventures should be aware that if the situation changes, it is important to be able to abrogate the arrangement without damage control becoming necessary. They should ensure that they have a mutually acceptable buyout clause or some other procedure for a graceful exit.

Commented R. Balakrishnan in Mumbai: "Most joint ventures in India have perished or floundered due to domestic entrepreneurial greed.

Ultimately, a foreign company must use domestic involvement to start up, and then, plan for the divorce well in advance."

A wholly owned subsidiary is a feasible and popular option: With the government becoming favorably inclined toward foreign investment, wholly owned subsidiaries are permitted in most industries. In most cases, they are incorporated as "private limited companies."

A senior manager with local knowledge is critical: Even more so than with most setups, it is essential to have senior managers with local knowledge in the top tier of wholly owned subsidiaries. Their skills in negotiation and their familiarity with the environment can make the difference between succeeding and failing.

Recognize that it requires relatively high involvement: Having an Indian subsidiary will probably involve a greater commitment of managerial time and effort than a joint venture, whether at the initial startup, when the company will need to do all the work of setting up the company and hiring staff, right down to the management and implementation of corporate goals and norms. It will probably be more closely integrated into the global operations. The level of involvement required may make this less attractive to companies with limited resources, or for which India is not central to their global strategy.

Carefully balance centralization and local autonomy: Especially in a wholly owned subsidiary, the balance between centralization and local autonomy is exceedingly important.

While having the Indian company follow parent company norms may be the most comfortable way to do business, it can devalue the subsidiary's expertise in responding to local conditions. Highly centralized companies may also face more challenges in attracting and retaining good people, who would want more control of the operation.

Consider ownership through an offshore subsidiary: Although the tax benefit of this is less clear now than it appeared to be (see "Checklist 4.18: Taxes"), it may still be easier to structure ownership of a subsidiary through an offshore entity. This may be worth discussing with the tax advisors.

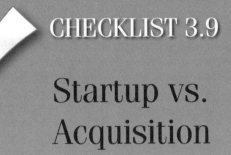

CHECKLIST 3.9

Startup vs. Acquisition

☐ **Acquisition of local companies is one way to create an Indian presence:** After making a decision to invest in India, a company will also need to determine whether the best strategy is to start an operation from scratch, or to acquire all or part of an existing Indian company. Both approaches have their proponents.

SiRF Technology Holdings Inc, a US-based global positioning systems (GPS) company, set up its Indian subsidiary in 2004 in NOIDA. Launching it with an initial investment of US$1 million, SiRF expected to invest an additional US$3 million the following year. The company also planned a development center in NOIDA.

Lionbridge Technologies, a UK-based acquired Mentorix, a 700-person company in Mumbai, at a reported cost of US$21 million.

☐ **Acquisition can be immensely helpful in getting access to a scarce resource:** Foreign companies have acquired Indian companies that can offer licenses of some sort; a particular market position or production facility; or even a good technical team. Some instances of companies that have decided on acquisition:

◆ In 2007, US IT company EMC acquired Valyd Software, a privately-held company in Hyderabad. Valyd has some specialized data security software. EMC's first acquisition in India was of a company called SANWare in 2003, picked up through the purchase of its bankrupt parent company, Sanrise, for US$2.5 million.

◆ Walt Disney acquired the children's TV channel, Hungama, (by acquiring United Home Entertainment, the producing company) for about US$31 million in 2006.

◆ News reports in 2007 said that EDS Corp acquired Bangalore-based RelQ Software Pvt. Ltd. for about US$40 million. RelQ is a software testing company. EDS had earlier acquired a position in the well-known outsourcing company, Mphasis BFL.

Acquisitions can kick-start a market entry: When Lionbridge Inc. of the UK announced its 2003 purchase of Mentorix, a 700-employee company in Mumbai, it noted that it was getting a mature, well-established operation.

Tecumseh, the US compressor company, established manufacture in India through its 1997 purchase of Siel Compressors Ltd. in Hyderabad, and Whirlpool India Limited's compressor division in Ballabgarh, near Delhi. They were folded into the wholly owned subsidiary, Tecumseh Products India Ltd.

Vodafone, the UK telecommunications company, bought out the interest of Hutchison in the Indian mobile phone operator, Hutchison Essar. This gives it a majority stake, and effective control of the Indian operation. The phones are marketed under the Vodafone brand. It immediately gives Vodafone the fourth-largest position in the market, as well as the mobile phone licenses for some important cities. This was Vodafone's third attempt on the Indian market.

SPI Technologies, a content outsourcing company of Philippine origin, has announced its agreement to acquire the medical transcription business of KG Information Services and Technologies Pvt. Ltd. This would provide them with ready-built facilities in India, and a capacity of 800 employees.

Mylan Laboratories, the US pharmaceuticals generics company, acquired control of the Indian company Matrix Laboratories from

Temasek Holdings of Singapore and Newbridge Capital, which held 40 percent of the company; and also acquired all but 5 percent of the holdings of Matrix chairman, N. Prasad. This not only give Mylan relatively inexpensive manufacture in India, but also—through prior acquisitions by Matrix—market access to India, China, and South Africa.

☐ **The acquirer also inherits all problems of the acquired company:** Labor, in particular, may be a problem. Under India law, it may be difficult to retrench unwanted labor after an acquisition. Mergers and acquisitions are notoriously fragile, and bringing an existing company under your own corporate umbrella may require considerable expertise.

According to R. Balakrishnan of the Centrum group, the labor issue can be overblown. "This should not really worry companies. In most cases, it is the factory staff or the lowly paid clerical jobs which cannot be cut. At the end of the day, these costs may not be a large sum and the company has to wait till they retire or die. There is no law stopping you from sacking managers. So the problem is not as big as it is being made out to be." He suggests that the problem is far worse in Europe, and points out that Tata has accepted quite onerous conditions in the Land Rover acquisition.

☐ **Indian tax law tends to favor acquisition of stock and not of assets:** At present, stamp duties on the acquisition of assets from a company—a popular acquisition method in the US, because it allows the acquirer to avoid any unwanted liabilities in the acquired company—are considerably higher than the transaction tax on acquiring shares of a company. However, if the target company is publicly traded, then an acquiring company may be required to make a public tender offer to all shareholders in that company once its holding goes over 15 percent.

☐ **Regulations require fair valuation of Indian shares for sale:** If an Indian entity is selling shares to a non-Indian entity, the government may require a fair value to be used. These regulations may be changing, but you may wish to check.

A startup may be easier to bring into a corporate culture: Starting a subsidiary and building it from scratch may align it more closely with the parent company. Changing an established corporate culture is more difficult than inculcating one in a new company. Staff of existing companies may also have objectives and agendas that are not exactly the same as those of the acquiring company.

When Recaero, a French aeroparts company, decided to manufacture in India, it decided to start a subsidiary. According to reports, it has 75 percent in Recaero India Pvt. Ltd., with the other 25 percent split between the Indian chairman and one of the Indian directors of the company. Recaero is planning to build a 65,000-square foot factory in Bidadi near Bangalore.

No existing company may meet requirements: Startups may also be the best option if no company in India really matches the desired profile.

Smith Dornan Dehn, a US law firm, founded SDD Global in Mysore to handle legal services. While the Indian company is managed by the US firm, the investment came from outside investors and banks. The Indian company does not claim to be a law firm or practice law, but positions itself as a legal services company.

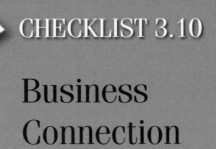

CHECKLIST 3.10

Business Connection

☐ **A "business connection" allows India to tax income offshore:** Recognize that the "business connection" doctrine allows tax authorities in India to tax income from India, even if it is offshore.

Under Section 9 of the Indian Income Tax Act, income includes "income accruing or arising out of business connection in India." This is especially meant for foreign parties: it is intended to cover diversion of income offshore, thus evading tax.

Certain incomes earned in India by foreign companies are clearly subject to tax: dividends, interest, profits on projects in India, royalties, consulting fees, and so on. But income earned by a "business connection" is specifically intended to cover earnings that are obliquely—not directly—taxable in India.

The tax authorities, from time to time, attempt to define business connection, but the gray area remains.

In India's best-known recent case, Indian revenue authorities have sought to tax Vodafone Essar on the basis that it represents the erstwhile parent company, Hutchison. (See "The Vodafone Story.")

☐ **Agents for Indian exports are generally exempt:** The foreign agents of India exporters, and the Indian agents of firms sourcing from India are usually exempt from "business connection" considerations. But an agent who buys goods for processing before exporting to a foreign principal is not exempt: unless it books a reasonable profit on the processing, the government may assume profit is being concealed, and invoke "business connection." It is also possible that a change in the tax law proposed in the 2008 budget will make payments to foreign agents subject to a withholding tax.

For importers to India, agents' commissions may be enough: In the case of agents of exporters to India, the commissions usually represents the taxable value of the business.

The government will usually consider the commission paid to an importing agent as representing the value of the profit earned in India. If the agent proffers this commission for taxation, that extinguishes the liability. But companies should seek advice to ensure that the relationship is not construed to be closer, and the agent is not seen to be providing more services than those for which he or she is fully remunerated.

This is still an evolving area of the law: All rulings still leave revenue officers of the government of India considerable scope in interpretation.

We advise abundant caution and reference to legal and tax experts; owing to the gray areas, even this may not be sufficient. Also, the government may make retroactive changes: in the 2008 budget, a proposed withholding tax on payments to non-resident entities for services performed overseas was to be made retroactive to 1976.

"The tax authorities are like ghosts," commented a business executive, only half jokingly. "They can haunt you on an issue long after you have filed and forgotten!"

3.10.1 The Vodafone Story

India's mobile phone market started out as a highly fragmented one, as the government auctioned many separate licenses for major cities and areas. After the initial rush into the market, a period of consolidation led to a few major players dominating the field.

Hutchison, a diversified Hong Kong company, was an early entrant into India's mobile market: in 1995, Hutchison Max started as a cellular provider in Mumbai. Meanwhile, Essar Cellphone started up in Delhi. A year later, Hutchison acquired a 49 percent stake in Essar Cellphone from shareholder, Swisscom, giving it access to the Delhi market as well. In 1998, Hutchison bought out a 41 percent stake in Hutchison Max from the Indian partner.

By 2006, Hutchison had a 67 percent stake in Hutchison Essar, which was the fourth-largest provider in India. At this point, Hutchison was ready to exit, and buyers were invited. The deal attracted considerable interest, and also controversy; but in the end, Vodafone bought Hutchison's stake for US$11 billion, and rebranded the company as Vodafone.

The actual stake was apparently 52 percent, with options to increase the share to 74 percent. Indian law requires a minimum of 26 percent Indian shareholding in cellular phone companies. Essar, the Indian partner, holds 22 percent of its stake through a company in Mauritius, which means that it is classified as non-India; this limits the remaining foreign stake to 52 percent. The complex shareholding structure also included two individuals: Analjit Singh of Max, one of Hutchinson's early partners, and Asim Ghosh, the CEO of Hutchison Essar. (Hutchison had loaned them funds needed to acquire the stakes. These loans were acquired by Vodafone.)

According to reports, a Netherlands company owned by Vodafone bought a Cayman Islands company from another Cayman Islands company owned by Hutchison. The company Vodafone purchased indirectly held a controlling interest in Hutchison Essar. The Indian tax authorities have held that Vodafone Essar, the Indian company, acted as an agent of Hutchison, and have withheld capital gains taxes on its behalf; this would amount to about US$2 billion, according to reports. Vodafone believes that no capital gains taxes are due on the transaction since it took place entirely overseas, and involved the sale and purchase of overseas assets.

The Indian revenue authorities claimed that there was a business connection through the Indian entity, and therefore the transaction is taxable. They seek to "lift the corporate veil" to look at the beneficial effect of the transaction—the sale of shares in an Indian company by a Hong Kong company. Since there is no double-taxation avoidance treaty between India and Hong Kong, they consider the capital gains deriving from Indian assets to be taxable in India.

As of September 2008, the matter was still in court. Meanwhile, the Indian government amended the *Income Tax Act* retroactively, to make the buyer of shares responsible for Indian taxes if the seller does not pay them—and will impose a penalty in case of failure to do so.

India's Supreme Court has ruled that retrospective changes to the law are permitted, so long as the change is not discriminatory.

CHECKLIST 3.11

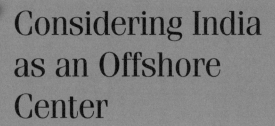

Considering India as an Offshore Center

☐ **India has the fastest-growing offshoring business:** India has become known, in the past few years, as a source hub for such operations as call centers, and for IT services of all kinds. According to a 2005 report from consultants, McKinsey & Co., India had the world's largest and fastest-growing offshoring sector.

☐ **It offers lower costs, a flexible workforce, and time zone advantages:** Companies that have outsourced such operations to India look for lower costs, higher efficiency, and the ability to grow their businesses without taking on extra headcount or infrastructure. Since the primary reason for outsourcing or offshoring is cost, most offices for these companies are located somewhat outside the main city centers.

The availability of an abundance of relatively inexpensive, quite well-educated people, many of whom speak English, was a major draw. The time zone difference with most Western countries allowed for some tasks to be performed overnight, a concept sometimes referred to as "follow the sun."

According to a manager at outsourcing company, Corbus: "India's advantage is that it's cheaper—the gap is closing, but there's still an advantage; the work ethic is good; and the people have a great desire to learn."

Some companies base their data and research centers in India: the executive search firm Heidrick is an example. (See "Heidrick's Knowledge Center.")

The scope of possible services goes beyond call centers and IT: India has burst onto the global scene as a supplier of services—call centers, business process outsourcing, and IT back offices.

In recent years, this has expanded in scope; companies now use India for medical transcription, personal assistance, architectural drawings, in fact, any work that can be performed offsite through electronic communications or with computers. "Medical tourism" is also becoming a notable market sector as Indian hospitals improve, and are now able to offer care equivalent to Western facilities at significantly lower costs. Indian companies are becoming more flexible and responsive to clients' needs as they gain experience, and are very interested in opportunities.

India is an interesting center for R&D: India has a strong knowledge base, and substantial intellectual capital. Managers tend to be culturally flexible, having in practice had to adapt to cultural differences within India. Most Indians are multilingual. This may make it an interesting place for research and innovation. According to one report, there are more than a 100 foreign companies doing R&D in India.

Google has facilities in Bangalore and Hyderabad, with smaller offices in Mumbai and Delhi, and more than 1,100 employees, and managers have explicitly stated that the diversity of the Indian workforce is expected to contribute to innovation.

Pfizer has a clinical research group in India, conducting clinical trials. Canon, the Japanese digital imaging company, announced in April 2008 that it intended to add R&D to its software outsourcing operation in NOIDA, and was looking to add perhaps 30–40 more engineering staff. Tandberg, the telepresence company, announced that it had set up an R&D center in Bangalore, one of its four worldwide. (The others are in Oslo, Norway; London, UK; and Hamilton, New Zealand.)

3.11.1 Heidrick's Knowledge Center

Heidrick & Struggles International, Inc. set up its global knowledge management center (KMC) in New Delhi in 2002 as a subsidiary incorporated in India. The KMC supports Heidrick & Struggles' operations worldwide, with database support, and corporate and business development research responsibilities. (The company also has two fully staffed business offices in India—located in New Delhi and Mumbai—representing Heidrick & Struggles' core executive search and leadership development business.)

Heidrick & Struggles' KMC is registered as a Software Technology Parks of India (STPI) company, an export-oriented structure that may have certain tax advantages. The KMC has approximately 160 full-time and part-time employees. According to Rajiv Inamdar, the KMC's managing director, the company faces fewer employee turnover problems than some of the larger firms: attrition rates are in the neighborhood of 25 percent, rather than the 40–50 percent large companies have been known to encounter. He attributes this to the less impersonal atmosphere in a smaller firm.

Cost, quality, and logistical issues have been deal breakers: The corporate experience has not been an unmitigated success. Cost, quality, or logistical issues have sometimes forced companies into other arrangements.

A few companies that had used had Indian call centers initially eventually pulled out: Delta Airlines, for instance, did not renew its contract with IBM Daksh in April 2007. In early 2008, TCS, IBM, and Yahoo! all laid people off.

In some cases, the issue was quality: as the call centers proliferated, staffing quality fell. Other places—the Philippines, in particular, for voice work—may have offered better costs for the acceptable quality.

Comments an observer: "Here, I feel that the work ethic of the Indians has a lot to do [with it]. With the focus on price to penetrate markets, quality is being compromised... It doesn't help either that Indian companies are deigned to spend on quality and research due to the paucity of capital and competition of market."

For some companies, the logistical issues of managing an offshore operation demand too many internal resources for the solution to be viable.

Currency movements can affect cost structures: If the US dollar remains weak, India's cost advantage in the business process outsourcing (BPO) space will come under pressure for American companies. This sector requires a high level of skill, and better English-language capabilities than many others, and wages are rising under competition.

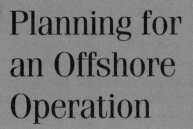

CHECKLIST 3.12

Planning for an Offshore Operation

☐ **Is the role of an outsourcing or offshoring center suitable for India?:** Indian operations arbitrage the cost and availability of "knowledge workers." The function or operation must also be self-contained enough that the Indian operation can function with some autonomy, and distance is not an issue.

The operations should also be fairly well specified and defined. If too many gray areas exist, the outsource workers are unlikely to fill in gaps independently.

If you want the Indian operation to work with open-ended problems, it can be successfully achieved by giving the Indian operation considerable autonomy. This means, though, that it will need high-level and experienced people on the ground, a resource that is in ever-shorter supply. The operation may also become more difficult to manage, since as the metrics become increasingly vague.

☐ **Outsourcing, offshoring, or something in between?:** Outsourcing to India is finding an Indian company to take over some part of an operation that would normally be done within your company. Offshoring is setting up a captive unit, usually wholly owned or an offshore branch, to perform corporate functions for units based in other countries.

Companies seeking to outsource an operation must determine whether it is actually outsourcing or offshoring they want. Some options are available:

◆ Set up your own Indian operations to supply various services to the rest of the organization. This is offshoring without outsourcing.

◆ Use an Indian provider who can give you a dedicated team.

◆ Outsource to experienced Indian providers on the basis of volume of business.

◆ Select a provider in your home country that has an associate company in India.

Corbus, an outsourcing company based in Dayton, Ohio, with its Indian associate company in NOIDA, provides various services to clients, particularly procurement outsourcing. It has teams both in the US—usually Indian IT people—and in India, thus providing a seamless interface for clients.

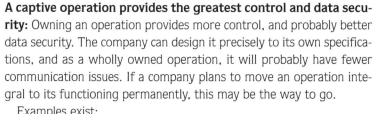

A captive operation provides the greatest control and data security: Owning an operation provides more control, and probably better data security. The company can design it precisely to its own specifications, and as a wholly owned operation, it will probably have fewer communication issues. If a company plans to move an operation integral to its functioning permanently, this may be the way to go.

Examples exist:

◆ GE has its Indian Innovation Center in Bangalore.

◆ Oracle also has a major operation there.

◆ IBM reportedly employs more than 50,000 people in India, while it has reduced headcount elsewhere by about 30,000 from 1992.

◆ Cisco Systems plans for 20 percent of its top talent to be in India in five years, according to an April 2007 report in the *International Herald Tribune.*

◆ VMWare, based in Palo Alto, California, announced in 2008 that it plans to invest US$100 million in the next two years in various projects, including an 82,000 square foot R&D center in Bangalore. It expects to double its team size to 1,000. The company, which entered India in 2004, already has 700 employees there, and has more than 300 customers in India.

◆ Heidrick & Struggles has a knowledge management center in the NCR.

◆ Deloitte has a large center in Hyderabad.

Companies that have set up their own operations in India have usually done so in expectation of a high volume of work. It also involves the company in all the operations, and requires a major fixed investment. In the end, it may not lower the costs for the parent company, substantially particularly if currency movements wipe out cost advantages, as they can rapidly do. Since the subsidiary usually follows some of the parent company's policies, its costs may be higher than that of purely Indian firms. It is much more difficult to unwind in adverse circumstances.

Simply outsourcing an operation has many benefits: Companies that do not have the critical mass, or the resources, or the desire to invest in their own operation can find a host of potential suppliers in India, ranging from tiny operations that will staff up for each new project, to major BPO firms with thousands of employees. For example, US retailers such as Best Buy, Albertsons, and Nike use the Indian company Wipro for IT support.

The trick here is selecting the right firm. Reputation is important. We also recommend inspecting the firm's facilities to get a sense of how it functions. Allow for some months of parallel operation before discontinuing the home-country process.

The pseudo-captive operation has many positives: An interesting via media that has evolved as Indian companies meet client demands more flexibly is the "pseudo-captive" company. Foreign firms have an annual contract, specifying the number of dedicated staff they require. Payment is made based on the number of individuals engaged each month, and the employees are paid to work solely on the projects of the contracted client. The Indian company provides the infrastructure, the governance, and the management.

"A virtual office is a good way for small and medium-sized companied to test the waters," said an Indian BPO executive. He points out that the resource commitment for the foreign company is minimal, and very flexible. However, even large companies have found it a worthwhile approach.

A few examples:

◆ The UK company, Pace Micro, for instance, had had 75 software engineers working at Tata Elxsi in a dedicated design center in Bangalore.

◆ In April 2007, UK pharmaceutical firm, GlaxoSmithKline (GSK), announced that it would outsource data management, and medical trial and regulatory reporting functions to India, with a new operation established by Tata Consulting Services at an existing GSK site. GSK has about 2,500 employees in Mumbai and Bangalore.

◆ In 2007, Robert Bird Group, an Australia-based international structural engineering company, established an eight-person office in Hyderabad, through the Indian company Ramtech, and brought in an Australian expatriate manager.

Sometimes a simple joint venture works best: If both partners expect to benefit equally, and bring equivalent values to the table, a joint venture may be the solution. However, it may have some of the same issues as joint venturing for market entry—control of the venture going forward can become a point of contention.

R&D is one possible area for partnership, especially if both partners are to share equally in the results. In March 2008, Yahoo! announced a joint effort with Computational Research Laboratories of Pune, India—a wholly owned subsidiary of Tata Sons—for research into "cloud computing." This is the use of giant data centers in remote applications. The draw here was CRL's supercomputer, the EKA, which is the fourth-fastest in the world, and the only one of the top 10 that is privately funded and available for commercial use.

CHECKLIST 3.13

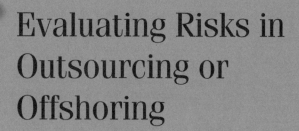

Evaluating Risks in Outsourcing or Offshoring

☐ **Selecting a company based largely on the quoted price is a risky strategy:** Damaging competitive pressure can erode provider service. Companies in this space face intense competitive pressure. "Demanding clients, demanding employees, and tough infrastructure," noted one BPO manager. "I'd guess of all the thousands in India, perhaps about 100 companies are seriously profitable. The others are marginal and lack scale."

The implication of this for their clients is that while this tough competition may lower prices, the resulting pressure on revenues and costs may impact service—and staying power.

☐ **Scale is getting difficult to achieve with infrastructural constraints:** In all the large cities, the infrastructure—mainly office space, roads, and residential accommodation—are seriously under pressure. Companies employing tens of thousands of people tend to overload facilities, and it is becoming harder to achieve that size.

This means that companies looking to outsource must either go with the existing big ones, or recognize that the small partners they have is unlikely to become major players. A shakeout is possible. "I doubt that Bangalore can sustain another Infosys," he commented, referring to India's big outsourcing success story.

Locations in smaller cities may be cost-effective: Infrastructure and real estate costs are forcing companies to consider cities other than Delhi, Mumbai, Chennai, and Bangalore: some choices are Kolkata, Pune, Bhubhaneswar, and Mangalore.

ASIC Architect Inc., a US based IT company, set up its Indian operation in Bhubhaneswar in 2006, and expanded it at a new location near the airport in 2007.

For some niche players that have identified a source of talent, even smaller cities can work well. Robosoft Technologies is based in Udipi (population of about 115,000), 35 miles from Mangalore. It started out as a Mac OS specialist, before diversifying into other platforms and activities, employing graduates from local technical colleges.

Moving to small towns may make access and hiring difficult: For larger companies, though, moving to small towns is difficult. They want to be located near an international airport, and they fear that staffing problems will only be worse in distant locations. The size of the talent pool favors large cities, and few people choose to relocate to small places. Senior managers also prefer to remain in large cities.

There may be difficulties in finding and retaining enough people: The single largest problem is a shortage of people with relevant skills. The rapid expansion of the Indian economy and the influx of foreign businesses have mopped up a large part of the skilled labor pool. The churn rate is high, so a good operation can deteriorate if trained employees are replaced by new ones faster than they can be retrained.

Projections should build in rising costs due to higher demand: Salaries are rising sharply, as are expectations.

Real estate costs are another critical issue. Acceptable office space is becoming tight, and rentals have increased 20–50 percent annually in recent years. Quality office space remains expensive and difficult to get, though a building boom has added millions of square feet of space on the outskirts of major cities.

Travel costs—particularly the cost of hotel rooms—have also gone up substantially, following the widespread shortage of high-quality hotels. Distances in India can be surprisingly large, so even domestic travel can be expensive.

Budgets and forecasts may need to include currency fluctuations: Currency movements can play a surprisingly large role in cost increases. The rupee has historically been a weak currency, tending to depreciate against the US dollar more or less in line with relative inflation. In 2007 and early 2008, the dollar had actually weakened so much that the rupee's value rose by about 20 percent—with a concomitant increase in costs.

With the fall of the US dollar, other countries are becoming target markets for outsourcing companies. Although India still provides major opportunities in this regard, constraints are beginning to appear.

India's cost advantage may need periodic review: With growing competition for space, infrastructure, and people, costs are rising, and India's cost advantage can no longer be accepted as a given.

One expatriate manager noted: "If you're in India as for cost reduction, you may need to frequently review the situation to see if you're still getting value. Costs are rising fast—salaries are up; rents are up; travel costs are up. 'Cheap' is not necessarily the best quality, or a permanent condition."

However, as another person pointed out: "With over a billion people, the labor costs at the relatively unskilled end of the market are bound to remain lower than most Western countries. With good management, India will be a low-cost source for years to come."

Another, the head of a major BPO company said: "Costs are rising, but not spiraling. Our salary costs go up 10–12 percent per year, but our wage bill is only 40 percent of total cost. Other costs are not rising as fast. Out telecommunication costs are actually falling."

3.13.1 Case Study—A Captive IT Center for a Healthcare Company

"It's all about getting butts in seats fast," said an executive of Company A, which set up an IT center to support its healthcare business in 2006. "It's expensive to be here, so it's important to start up as soon as possible." It took Company A about a year. "Delays are inevitable, so 12–15 months is reasonable."

The most important thing, he suggested, was to establish the leadership team up front, and get local help for legal issues. "Lawyers here can cost as much as in New York—but you really need them."

The next challenge was space, which was in short supply. Company A was able to find a company that was downsizing, and willing to sublet part of its space. It started with two temporary offices: one in a business center, the other in the premises of the downsizing company.

With that, it was ready to start hiring. In three months, it moved from 0 to 300 employees; in another nine months, it was at 1,500; and now, 18 months on, it has a headcount of nearly 2,000. "It's a very emotional process, building a company. The structure and decision-making procedures change. Some people perceive it as a demotion because they have less control than when the company was small. They get emotionally attached to what was."

CHECKLIST 3.14

Selecting an Outsourcing Provider

☐ **Define what to outsource quite specifically:** Until there is a clear definition of what functions are to be outsourced, it is difficult to select a provider. All specifications of selection criteria start here.

☐ **Decide whether to have one provider or several:** Some companies prefer to go with one vendor for all their needs. It has the advantage of being easier to manage, providing a deeper ongoing relationship, which may build commitment, and simplify the communications process. On the other hand, one supplier may not be enough. It may not have the size or the capacity for all of a large company's outsourced work. Meanwhile, having multiple suppliers spreads the risk should anything go wrong (it may also raise the risk that something may go wrong).

Some large companies have a separate department managing outsourcing; they typically pre-qualify several companies, and provide the business departments with a shortlist of qualified candidates to choose from.

☐ **Major providers may work best for large jobs:** If the job is large and routine, a major provider from among India's best-known outsourcing companies may be the best match.

These companies have strong processes, good controls for confidentiality and data security, and considerable experience working with foreign clients. They also more robust hardware, including power and connectivity backups.

Innovative and non-routine work may fit better with a smaller company: If the work being outsourced is more innovative and less routine, and changes quite rapidly, a smaller company may be a better fit.

Smaller companies, particularly those that specialize in the same or related fields, can be more flexible and accommodating than large ones. If your company is a relatively important client, they may make special efforts.

Matching company sizes may work best: Some managers recommend seeking partner that matches your company in size. If your company is a large multinational, it will probably need a large Indian provider. If your own outfit is a relatively small company, you may get more attention from a provider with, perhaps, a couple of hundred people.

Allow for potential growth: A company that is perfectly matched now may not be able to meet your company's needs in two or three years, unless it has the potential to expand as the business grows. This may force a change or an addition.

Consider contacts and reputation as ways to find a good vendor: Some of the companies happiest with their outsourcing providers discovered them by word of mouth from other companies in their industry or related industries. It is usually no secret who the clients of outsource vendors are.

Robert Bird Group, the Australian international structural engineering company, found its Indian provider Ramtech through TAE Group, an Australia-based agent for Ramtech.

Check out the company: Visit potential suppliers, talk to key personnel, and ask for references among existing clients. Talk to its bank—unless it is publicly listed, in which case, it can share its financials—to ensure it is financially stable. Of course, run an Internet search on the company.

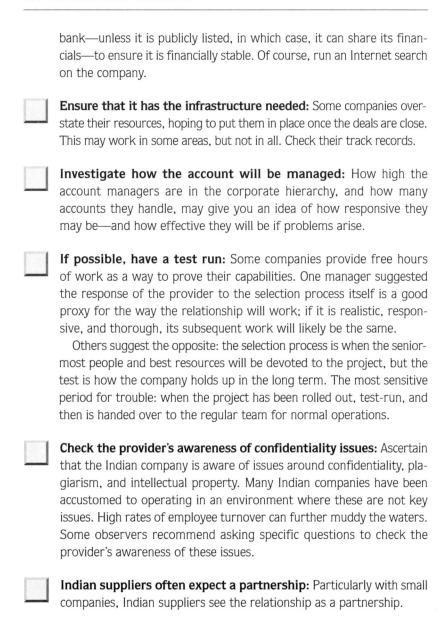

Ensure that it has the infrastructure needed: Some companies overstate their resources, hoping to put them in place once the deals are close. This may work in some areas, but not in all. Check their track records.

Investigate how the account will be managed: How high the account managers are in the corporate hierarchy, and how many accounts they handle, may give you an idea of how responsive they may be—and how effective they will be if problems arise.

If possible, have a test run: Some companies provide free hours of work as a way to prove their capabilities. One manager suggested the response of the provider to the selection process itself is a good proxy for the way the relationship will work; if it is realistic, responsive, and thorough, its subsequent work will likely be the same.

Others suggest the opposite: the selection process is when the seniormost people and best resources will be devoted to the project, but the test is how the company holds up in the long term. The most sensitive period for trouble: when the project has been rolled out, test-run, and then is handed over to the regular team for normal operations.

Check the provider's awareness of confidentiality issues: Ascertain that the Indian company is aware of issues around confidentiality, plagiarism, and intellectual property. Many Indian companies have been accustomed to operating in an environment where these are not key issues. High rates of employee turnover can further muddy the waters. Some observers recommend asking specific questions to check the provider's awareness of these issues.

Indian suppliers often expect a partnership: Particularly with small companies, Indian suppliers see the relationship as a partnership.

Western companies that keep bargaining for the best price, particularly if they drive down the prices each year, may force compromises on quality as well as hard feelings that result in problems in the long term. Indian managers expect foreign companies to make an effort to understand their points of view. Initial negotiations may be hard, but over time, they expect the relationship to grow.

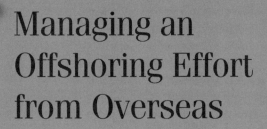

CHECKLIST 3.15

Managing an Offshoring Effort from Overseas

☐ **It may not work simply to hand over the process:** Companies may expect to simply move the specified processes to an offshore entity, but this is a best-case scenario.

Often, when companies think about offshoring, they visualize handing over a set of specified processes to the Indian company, whether outsourced or inhouse, and then wait for results. They expect that after an initial burning-in period, the offshore operation will run as smoothly as though the distances did not exist. In some cases, this is exactly how it works.

In many others, it is not. Instead, companies find that keeping the offshore operation running smoothly and with proper coordination requires hands-on active management. Cost calculations should include this ongoing management.

☐ **Communication problems can exist owing to language barriers:** Outsourcing companies all offer business conducted in English. However, spoken English ability varies widely, especially as the shortage of people makes this a lesser consideration than before. To add to the problem, accents can be varied and quite heavy. If the communication is between technical people on the Indian side and people on the business end in the client company, that may result in confusion. Some outsourcing companies combat this by placing liaison people at or near their clients' headquarters.

Your company may have to train the provider's Indian employees: Although outsourcing companies can train their staff in the basics, the client company may need to provide inhouse training and guidance. Without it, the provider is unlikely to meet internal standards. United Airlines, for instance, had two outsourced call center operations, in Mumbai and Pune. They sent teams from their US operations for months at a time to do the training.

Indian liaison people in the US are likely to keep changing: Although having Indian liaison people is, perhaps, the best option for facilitating communication and smoother management, it is not necessarily easy. The incumbents keep rotating for a variety of reasons. "It's a huge hidden cost that is seldom factored in," said an observer. "Each time we send one back, find someone else, get a visa, bring them over, train them... it easily runs into thousands of dollars."

It also demands managerial attention. One manager said, "I have learned more about their personal lives than I ever expected. We worked with one guy, brought him up to speed, and everything went well for a while. Then he was sent back to Bangalore because his parents wanted him to get married. In another case, the man wanted a US assignment, and was given one; but then his wife could not get a visa, so he returned to India. Another man had a motorcycle accident in India, and couldn't come back."

Getting US visas for liaison people may be problematic: The US government strictly limits the visas available to Indians to work in the US on a temporary basis. As a result, each time a rotation is required, visas are an issue. According to one manager: "You need visa-enabled people on standby."

One possible solution is to look for US citizens or permanent residents. They are generally able to commute easily once they get Overseas Citizen of India status.

3.15.1 Case Study—Robert Bird Group's Arrangement with Ramtech

Robert Bird Group (RBG) is an international consulting structural engineers head office in Brisbane, Australia, with operations throughout Australia, UK, and the Middle East. It had decided on outsourcing as a way to expand their resources while mitigating risk. "There's a worldwide shortage of engineers and draughtspersons," said Paul Moreton, who was involved in setting up its operation in India in 2007.

RBG had clearly defined criteria in selecting a country for outsourcing:

◆ very little sovereign risk

◆ an educated population with good communication skills

◆ preferably with English as the business language.

India met its specifications, and also had relatively low labor costs.

"You need commitment and will on both sides," said Moreton. Establishing a relationship was easy: the people at Ramtech were professional, and the initial contact positive. Even the legal side of it was simplified because everything was in English; there were no language barriers. It went more smoothly than they had expected, and took only three or four months. "Ramtech eased the way for us. It's very important to get a robust and credible partner."

RBG currently has a pseudo-captive office in Hyderabad with 12 employees. It is legally part of Ramtech, but in every other way, it is managed as a RBG office. "We treat it as an extension of our facilities," Moreton said.

An Australian expatriate from Brisbane has been brought in to manage it in the initial stage. He will be there for a total of a year, and then will be replaced by another engineer from RBG. The plan is generally to have an expatriate present on site, to supervise and ensure quality control. There was no difficulty in getting a business visa; Ramtech provided local sponsorship, and it only took 10 days.

The only issue it had was that it had underestimated the training required. "But that is a matter of time," Moreton said.

Retention has not been an issue so far, and in any case, it is Ramtech's responsibility to supply the contracted staff. Costs have risen only about 5 percent per year, which is just a little higher than inflation.

Another is to subcontract. "With the shortage of H1B visas," said a manager of an outsourcing entity that has operations in the US, "some companies decided to capitalize on it. They get the visas and the people, and hire them out."

Management across time zones can be complicated and expensive: Several managers spoke about the cost and effort of managing a distant operation. "The lack of face-to-face contact does matter," said one, who gets out to India twice or three times annually for a couple of weeks at a time.

Another spoke of the costs. "You don't necessarily build in the costs of all the visits that are necessary," said another. "Whether it's your going there or bringing them here. Airlines, hotels, other travel costs. It adds up."

"Conference calls happen at strange hours," warned a US executive. "Managing an overseas operation can't be done on a US schedule."

3.15.2 Case Study—An American Outsourcer Speaks Off the Record

Company C has two separate offshoring initiatives going on. One is outsourced to four separate, well-known outsourcing providers in India. The second is a wholly owned unit based in NCR.

For company C, the objectives of outsourcing were the usual ones: Cost reduction since the Indian technical people would cost a fraction of its US employees; a large resource pool available at short notice to deal with a spiky workload without becoming a permanent cost to the company; and in the long term, building up resources to "follow the sun"—work round clock.

Company C has a separate department that managed all the contractual requirements: security, connectivity, and legalities. All the outsourcing companies qualified by the department had a CMM Level 5 rating.

(The Capability Maturity Model—CMM—rating system was developed by the Software Engineering Institute based at Carnegie Mellon University. It set down guidelines to institutionalize the development process. From December 31, 2007, it has been superseded by a new model, Capability Maturity Model Integration—CMMI.)

CMMI has been an important tool in allowing clients to assess the capacity of an outsourcing provider. Moreover, the imperfections of individual employees are compensated for by a strong process. Theoretically, it enables relatively inexperienced employees to perform within the guidelines, leading to an interchangeable pool of labor. It emphasizes procedures and documentation, reducing the need for rework months or years down the line.

In this process, Company C was reasonably successful. It has a portfolio of applications to be handed off to the outsourcers. The Indian companies provided liaison people who were based near Company C.

The situation was not quite as envisioned though. The Indian company's liaison people in the US—technical staff who were quite experienced, and were supposed to hand off the work to less experienced employees in India—often found it easier to fix problems themselves rather than spend hours explaining it to people in India. For company C, much of the cost-saving came from the very process of reviewing the portfolio, and deciding not to perform some functions, or redesigning them to be easier to outsource. Specifications and metrics were both altered as the effort proceeded.

The second effort was more complicated. Here, the offshoring was from a business group, not a technology group; the unit would perform the functions that were earlier provided by embedded technologists. This group dealt with small systems with a high level of change, rather than large systems that were quite stable. The business group staff were not technical, and not specially good at defining specifications. There was a need for the technical people to try to understand the uses of what they were building.

Part of the incentive for offshoring was from the political processes of Company C; while the business group believed it needed dedicated technical staff, it always faced pressure to move them into the technology group and off its budget. The second was cost saving, with the potential for the Indian unit to become a profit-making entity.

This unit required a different paradigm: rather than process-driven software production, it needed to be nimble and responsive to the needs of the business group—for instance, building models based on the data provided. This unit was not CMM Level 5. As a subsidiary, there was a perception of stronger security, both at Company C and among its clients: their data was kept inhouse.

Several problems arose. First, many of the applications to be transferred were poorly documented for various reasons, chief of which was that it had not been a priority, so Company C had not provided the staff with the necessary capacity.

The second was the extreme inexperience of most of the Indian staff. While Indian pay scales are one-third or one-fourth those in the US, they yield relatively inexperienced people. With the talent wars and competition, companies in India are hiring entry-level people, a situation one observer compared with the dotcom boom in the US. Even 18 months of experience makes an employee an old hand.

"We're convincing ourselves it doesn't matter," said a manager dealing with the results. "What we've done is to reduce the intellectual content to the point where they just press buttons."

"How does a programmer in India stay aligned with a company headquartered halfway round the world?" The answer for the outsourcing companies was to provide US-based liaison people.

Company C's India unit found this problematic for several reasons. Since it was not part of the original game plan, they did not have visas in hand, and getting visas was a major problem. Many of the employees, hired locally, had family responsibilities that prevented them from taking extended trips. After all the expense and effort, they don't necessarily transfer the technology back; many of them move on to other jobs. Expense was another factor. "Once we start doing that inhouse, it really drives up expenses," a manager said. "It's treated like a business trip, since they're our employees. They stay in hotels and need a daily allowance. At US$200 a day, these costs add up quickly."

The whole thing was complicated because at Company C's end, there was a continually changing cast of characters. The company reorganized a couple of times. Each time, there was uncertainty over the appropriate role of the India unit.

So far, Company C's own offshore effort cannot be considered a success. "They're sweet and nice to work with," a manager said. "They just don't get anything done. The results are spotty and censored for public consumption."

Manufacturing in India

Manufacturing in India is worthwhile for some firms: Manufacturing a product in India may be worthwhile, particularly for companies operating in an industry where the regulatory frameworks—for instance, customs duties—favor local goods. India probably has a competitive advantage in knowledge-based production, which would include not just software and IT services, but also such things as medical research and development. It also has advantages in some manufactures, such as textiles.

Teva, the Israeli pharmaceutical generics company, announced in 2008 that it would invest some US$250–300 million in building a generics manufacturing facility in India as part of an ambitious US$1 billion expansion scheme, which might include buying out some Indian companies. India has a well-established generics production capacity, with Indian companies such as Dr. Reddy's Laboratory, Ranbaxy and Cipla having established themselves in the market under an earlier, favorable patent regime. Teva is experienced in India, with an R&D operation in Delhi, and a presence in India through a subsidiary company.

Nokia instituted manufacture of mobile phones and base stations in India (in Chennai) in 2006, and now employs about 8,000 people there. (The company's India headcount has grown from about 450 in 2004 to more than 9,500 by March 2008.) It ships products from India to more than 50 different countries.

But before deciding to manufacture in India, there are several considerations. It is not an easy venue for production.

3.16.1 One Company's Decision Against Local Manufacture

For the present, international shoe company Crocs does not expect to manufacture its products in India, both because of cost and supply chain issues. It investigated the possibility, but on analysis, concluded there was no advantage in doing so.

"India is not a high-cost manufacturing site," said regional sales manager Mark Langhammer, "but it does not have as efficient a supply chain to be internationally competitive for our types of products. Also, duties are low (10 percent), but the add-on costs drive up the imported product costs. These same costs would apply if we manufactured in India, so there is little cost advantage to manufacture in India versus our large-scale and highly efficient overseas factories.

"Major global athletic footwear brands do not export from India due primarily to quality issues. They manufacture in India for the India market only, and generally for lower-price-point products.

"India is very good at textiles, and at traditional leather products, but not so good at sports footwear, rubber and synthetics, and a number of other products. Even the steel racks we use in our stores are 40–50 percent cheaper to import than to fabricate locally—and the quality is better."

Is there enough volume to manufacture in India? For some products, the market—even though it is growing rapidly—is just not large enough to justify local manufacture. Many companies have found that even with the logistical problems and expense of shipping, it is cheaper to make their products in China or other locations and export them to India.

Would the product lose its cachet if made in India? Some products have brand images dependent on manufacture at particular locations—for example, Scotch whisky, or French perfumes. While the "craze for foreign" products that was lampooned for decades is abating as imports become freely available, some products may lose value in the consumers' eyes if they are made locally. Nevertheless, some companies are producing in India, usually if they get a duty or tax benefit from doing so.

Audi, the German luxury car company, started assembling cars in India in 2007. Even though it started with a capacity of only 300–400 cars annually, it had an incentive in the relatively high customs duties on automotive imports. It also had the benefit of an existing factory, owned by a sister company, Skoda, with spare capacity. Finally, its major competitors, Mercedes and BMW, had already started production in India.

Are there supply chain issues? If your raw materials are not easily available in India, manufacture there may be more trouble than it is worth. By the time the materials have been imported, transported, and processed, costs may have exceeded has initial projections.

Crocs, the American shoe company, decided against local manufacture. For the present, it can import its China-made product more cost-effectively, and with fewer logistical problems. It is concentrating its efforts on marketing.

Do cost projections allow for escalation? With rising competition for all resources, manufacturing costs in India may rise more quickly than in more stable economies, and possibly faster than inflation. Production that seems economic now may be less so in a few years. Companies that require dedicated assets—such as specialized machinery—may need to be cautious.

What about infrastructure problems? Infrastructure bottlenecks are a key problem for any company that plans to manufacture in India. The planned new special economic zones (SEZs) may be a limited answer, since they are expected to secure water supply, power, and transportation. Manufacturing in India does bypass the bottleneck of the ports—unless imports of raw materials or components are required. Very often, the "last mile" is a problem. Comments an observer: "Getting from 'almost there' to 'there' can be very frustrating and expensive."

Where should the facility be located? Most companies prefer to locate somewhere near a large city with an international airport. These locations not only make communications and logistics simpler, but also make it easier to recruit good employees. However, more remote locations may have a cost advantage, primarily because of lower real estate prices. All major cities now have problems with power shortages.

Nokia set up the 210-acre Nokia Telecom Industry Park in Chennai because it found skilled labor was available, the state government supportive, and the logistical connections good. The mission of the Park is "is to create a network of co-located and co-dependent partners that operate at world class standards, and manufacture high-quality products." Seven suppliers had signed up by May 2008. It provides, the company notes, "the benefits of a pollution free environment, inhouse customs clearance, and uninterrupted power supply."

Sourcing Products from India

☐ **India has a competitive advantage in certain products:** Even though India is best known as a source of services, whether call centers, architectural drawings, or medical transcription, it is also a competitive supplier of some goods, including some manufactures. It also exports some agricultural products such as rice, meat, sugar, and spices.

☐ **There is a huge range of textiles and handcrafted products:** Indian textiles fall into two broad categories: those that are handmade or made on a cottage scale, and those manufactured in textile mills. The handmade products are breathtaking in their variety and creativity. Most of this work tends to be in cotton or silk. Mill-made textiles are more modern and Westernized in their designs. Special orders are possible. Pricing is competitive. The Swedish home furnishings company, IKEA, is a major buyer of Indian textiles. The country exported around US$6.5 billion of textiles and garments in the first six months of fiscal 2007–2008.

Some apparel manufacturers also source garments from India. Other handcrafted products including metal work, leather, wood furniture, glassware are also exported. Gems and jewelry are also an major exports; India is a cutting center for tiny diamonds.

☐ **Indian metallic castings and automotive parts are competitive in price and quality:** Another general area in which Indian manufacturing is competitive is in castings. The country exported about US$17 billion of "metal manufactures" in the first half of fiscal 2007–2008, accounting for more than 23 percent of its total exports.

Several automotive manufacturers are sourcing components from India. According to Singapore-based international consultant PC Abraham, these exports are growing fast:

"[They're] expected (by the Automotive Components Manufacturers Association) to rise to US$20 billion by 2016. Auto companies—including Ford, Fiat, DaimlerChrysler, Renault, and Volvo—source components from India. General Motors plans to source US$1 billion worth of auto components from India annually within five years. International auto component manufacturers—such as Arvin Meritor, Bosch, Magna and Valeo—are ramping up activities in India as are major local players such as Bharat Forge and Amtek Auto."

BMW is reportedly planning to increase its purchase of motorcycle parts. Volkswagen is also said to be looking for suppliers of engine parts to supply its Indian operation and global manufacturing. India also makes quality machined parts. Some sources claim cost savings of up to 30 percent.

India may be developing a special competence in small-car manufacturing. Suzuki, which has been in India since the early 1980s, is considering using it as an export base. Tata Motors is also reported to have export plans for the next generation of its new inexpensive small car, the Nano.

Agents can help match companies with suppliers: Potential importers can get help from their embassies (if they have an active commercial section); from business and industry associations; and from agents who specialize in intermediation.

Quality and reliability vary considerably: As in most things, Indian suppliers vary hugely in their ability and reliability. The best ones are world class in quality control and in assuring supply. The worst are incompetent and perhaps dishonest. Selecting a good supplier is critical.

Infrastructure issues may delay even the best suppliers: All exporters from India must cope with the stretched infrastructure of the roads, rail, ports, and airports. If timely delivery is critical, work with the India supplier to allow extra lead times. If feasible, it may be worthwhile to maintain larger stocks of a routinely used product to cushion delays in supply.

Establishing long-term supply relationships is useful: Buyers that can establish a long-term relationship with their suppliers are likely to get better and more personalized service. Indian companies will often go out of their way for clients in such cases. Information flows are also likely to be better, including early warnings regarding problems.

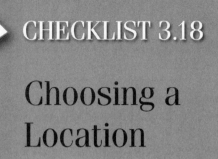

CHECKLIST 3.18

Choosing a Location

☐ **In which state do you want to locate?** For a company that has decided to have a presence in India, location may be the next big decision. With deregulation at the federal level, the states have become far more important. They vary considerably in available resources, attitude toward business, and regulatory environment. "Some states have started to compete for attention," said a manager. "Himachal dropped sales tax and gave incentives, and got significant interest." (See "Ranking the States.")

☐ **Do you need to be in a city?** The best strategy is probably to find a suitable city to locate in, and then to ensure that it is in a business-friendly state. Mumbai is commonly regarded as the financial capital; Delhi is important for any company doing business with the government, and its suburbs of NOIDA (in the state of Uttar Pradesh) and Gurgaon (in Haryana) have become centers for the IT and other industries. Bangalore in Karnataka is known as an IT hub, and Hyderabad (Andhra Pradesh) for IT and biotechnology. Chennai (Tamil Nadu) is also an important new business area.

    The choice depends largely on the nature of the business. A liaison office will need to be in the Delhi NCR, or perhaps in Mumbai to be effective. An offshoring facility has more flexibility.

Said R. Balakrishnan from Mumbai: "Each city has its ethos. Bombay brings the best brains, due to migration. Delhi and Bangalore are like that [too]. Pune is emerging hot. Chennai is also emerging as a good manufacturing base for auto ancillaries, auto and so on."

The Delhi NCR is a favorite choice: The NCR may be the best choice for a company that needs to interact with the government, especially as a client, and may be appropriate for others as well.

New Delhi—or rather, the National Capital Region, which includes Gurgaon and NOIDA—is a sprawling area, with a population of 13.8 million people (2001 census). The capital of India, it is the only suitable location for any company that wishes to do business with the government. Hindi is the local language.

Many companies have set up in the area; while the infrastructure is stressed, it still functions; there is an international airport; and it is a large city with all the opportunities and problems implied. On the whole, it is considered business friendly.

On the negative side, it is extremely polluted, especially in winter, when an inversion frequently costs grimy air over the city, and open fires are often lit for warmth. It also has a higher rate of crimes against people than other large cities in India.

Mumbai is important for any financial services company or bank: Mumbai (formerly Bombay) is the financial capital of India, and also the heart of the "Bollywood" show business. It is one of India's most cosmopolitan cities. The climate is less extreme than in Delhi. The major local language is Marathi, but English is used extensively. A local form of Hindi serves as a lingua franca.

The monsoons can cause spectacular flooding, since large parts of the city are low-lying areas of reclaimed land. Maharashtra generally—and especially Mumbai—have attracted huge amounts of migrant labor, which have become critical to the economy. Recently, it has been a battleground for political parties that used local pride as a platform to rally for support, and caused some social and business disruption.

3.18.1 Ranking the States

Surveys have come up with varying assessments of the attractiveness of the major states.

The best known, perhaps, because of its controversial 2004 results, is a survey by Bibek Debroy and Laveesh Bhandari, ranking 20 states in India on "economic freedom." In 2005 (based on data variously drawn from 2002, 2003, and 2004, as available), it gave the following results for the top 10:

State	2005 Rank	2004 Rank	2005 Index
Tamil Nadu	1	5	0.515
Gujarat	2	1	0.450
Kerala	3	3	0.447
Andhra Pradesh	4	2	0.381
Madhya Pradesh	5	9	0.374
Haryana	6	8	0.366
Jharkhand	7	16	0.354
Uttar Pradesh	8	13	0.347
Karnataka	9	12	0.337
Maharashtra	10	6	0.335

The study used three groups of variables in this assessment: size of government: legal structure and security of property rights, and regulation of credit, labor, and business.

The study is widely quoted by businesspeople in India. However, as is evident from the table, where the rankings have shifted quite noticeably between 2004 and 2005, it does not yield a very robust assessment, and may not be a suitable basis for location decisions.

A World Bank/CII study in 2003, surveying businesspeople in 12 industries, came up with subjective rankings that were rather different:

State	2003 Ratings	2000 Ratings
	percent saying best minus percent saying worst	
THE Best		
Maharashtra	29.1 percent	38.6 percent
Delhi	16.7 percent	1.6 percent
Gujarat	9.6 percent	23.1 percent
Andhra Pradesh	8.6 percent	6.6 percent
Karnataka	6.8 percent	7.8 percent
Punjab	4.9 percent	–0.7 percent
Tamil Nadu	3.7 percent	8.6 percent
Haryana	1.1 percent	
THE Worst		
Madhya Pradesh	–6.8 percent	
West Bengal	–30.6 percent	–21.9 percent
Kerala	–15.0 percent	–16.1 percent
Uttar Pradesh	–30.6 percent	–32.6 percent

Although these results are also not very robust, they seem to reflect specific factors: the rise of Gurgaon (in Haryana, on the outskirts of Delhi) probably influenced Haryana's arrival in the rankings, while the awful riots and killings in Gujarat may have downshifted its rating.

Bangalore has become the center of the IT industry: As India's third-largest city, with a population of about 6.5 million, Bangalore is India's "silicon city."

Bangalore has a brand new airport some 38 miles from town, a reasonably equable climate, and a reputation for greater safety than northern cities. Slums are not as evident as in some cities; only 10 percent of the population are slum dwellers. The local language is Kannada; Tamil is also fairly widely spoken.

Hyderabad is known for IT and biotechnology: Hyderabad in Andhra Pradesh is a center for IT, and also for biotechnology and pharmaceuticals. With a population of 5.5 million in the 2001 census, estimated at 6.5–6.7 million in 2007, it is a significant tier II city, and has attracted a number of international companies seeking less expensive cities.

Microsoft has its largest development center outside Redmond in Hyderabad; GE has about 5,000 of its 22,000 Indian employees in its centers there; IBM, Samsung, Deloitte, Oracle, Yahoo, Dell, Franklin Templeton, Qualcomm, Agilent, ADP, Bank of America, CSC, Verizon, and Convergys are some of the *Fortune* 500 companies that have a significant presence in this city.

The main languages spoken are Telugu, a south Indian language, and Urdu, essentially similar to Hindi but written in an Arabic script.

Chennai has back-office functions and manufacturing: Chennai is the city formerly known as Madras. Located in the southern state of Tamil Nadu, it has become another major IT industry hub.

It has an international airport and rail, road, and sea access. A seaside city with a chronic water shortage problem, Chennai is trying to tackle that with such methods as rainwater harvesting. Its population in 2007 was estimated at 7.5 million (6.4 million at the 2001 census).

"[It's] also in manufacturing," comments R. Balakrishnan. "Ford, Nokia, Hyundai, World Bank, British Airways, Infy, Sify, Wipro and Satyam all have a large presence. One of the largest unlisted BPO companies, Sutherland, is at Chennai."

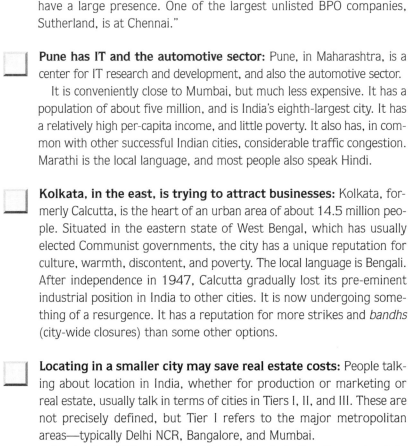

Pune has IT and the automotive sector: Pune, in Maharashtra, is a center for IT research and development, and also the automotive sector.

It is conveniently close to Mumbai, but much less expensive. It has a population of about five million, and is India's eighth-largest city. It has a relatively high per-capita income, and little poverty. It also has, in common with other successful Indian cities, considerable traffic congestion. Marathi is the local language, and most people also speak Hindi.

Kolkata, in the east, is trying to attract businesses: Kolkata, formerly Calcutta, is the heart of an urban area of about 14.5 million people. Situated in the eastern state of West Bengal, which has usually elected Communist governments, the city has a unique reputation for culture, warmth, discontent, and poverty. The local language is Bengali. After independence in 1947, Calcutta gradually lost its pre-eminent industrial position in India to other cities. It is now undergoing something of a resurgence. It has a reputation for more strikes and *bandhs* (city-wide closures) than some other options.

Locating in a smaller city may save real estate costs: People talking about location in India, whether for production or marketing or real estate, usually talk in terms of cities in Tiers I, II, and III. These are not precisely defined, but Tier I refers to the major metropolitan areas—typically Delhi NCR, Bangalore, and Mumbai.

An April 2007 article by Knight Frank India, the real estate company, defines the Tier II cities as Chennai, Hyderabad, Kolkata and Pune.

Places banded under Tier III are Chandigarh, Ludhiana, Lucknow, Guwahati, Bhubaneswar, Jaipur, Ahmedabad, Surat, Nagpur, Indore, Goa, Visakhapatnam, Mysore, Coimbatore, Kochi, Vijaywada, Mangalore, Trivandrum and Baroda.

☐ **Tier III cities may be possible future locations:** Companies looking for new locations for offshoring, or for additional offices, are looking at smaller cities.

The Knight Ridder study also analyzed the Tier III cities for attractiveness, using five parameters: real estate cost, population (growth, purchasing power, literacy), physical infrastructure, social infrastructure (educational institutions, urban amenities such as entertainment), and business environment (attitudes of the local government, general economic activity). On this basis, it rated Chandigarh and Nagpur as the top two; Goa and Kochi tied for third place; and Visakhapatnam and Ahmedabad came in fourth and fifth.

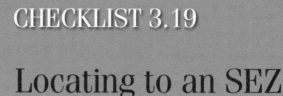

CHECKLIST 3.19

Locating to an SEZ

☐ **An exporter may consider SEZs:** For a company planning to export from India, an SEZ location has advantages.

India's SEZs started out as small export-processing zones—areas where companies seeking to manufacture for export could operate more efficiently, free of the complexity of taxes and duties applicable in the rest of the country. Their limited scope made a relaxation of many of India's restrictive regulations, and the provision of efficient infrastructure, more practical. Companies in SEZs are required to have net positive exports. Regulations have become much less stringent, and with the *Special Economic Zone Act 2005*, this concept has become extremely popular.

The plan is to have defined areas in which superior infrastructure, tax holidays for the developers of an SEZ as well as the companies in production there, and relief from many regulations to permit companies to operate in a business-friendly environment. The government thereby hopes to attract foreign companies to invest in India, and generate jobs, and economic growth.

☐ **Offshoring companies as well as manufacturers may apply:** Individual companies (or other entities) are permitted to set up SEZs. These zones can be single-company (that is, a company can have its factory in an SEZ); single-industry but multiproduct; or multi-industry. Some of those approved have been in the IT and IT-enabled services sector.

3.19.1 Controversies Around SEZs

Although the SEZ concept has been gaining traction with businesspeople, it is surrounded by growing controversies over whether the social cost is worth it. How these are resolved could affect the success of SEZs in India. The main problems, from a policy standpoint are:

◆ Displacement of agricultural employment. Most SEZs require the acquisition of agricultural land, with deep social impact. Land titles in India are notoriously hazy, so the de facto owners of the land might not be able to prove ownership. Even where they can, the amount of the compensation is not necessarily sufficient, and furthermore, is often spent quite rapidly on consumption expenditure. Agricultural workers, who have no ownership in the land, lose their jobs. These farmers and workers do not necessarily have the skills to find employment opportunities in the SEZs, and as a result, fall into even worse poverty than before. Clashes between agriculturalists loath to be displaced and authorities trying to acquire land have led to several deaths.

◆ Displacement of crop production. India is short of water, and land with good water access is highly valued. Unfortunately, industry needs water too, and land that is suitable for SEZs is often prime agricultural land.

◆ Loss of taxes. When production that would have taken place outside is shifted into an SEZ, the tax holidays offered reduce revenues. Under the current regulations, every company has an incentive to move its production into an SEZ.

◆ Pollution. SEZs have sometimes been sources of environmental degradation and pollution.

◆ Lax labor laws. SEZs have also developed a reputation for providing competitive jobs but harsh working conditions, with no reasonable grievance procedures for workers.

◆ Land grab. The situation of SEZs makes them attractive not just as manufacturing sites, but as residential areas; and they provide a vehicle by which developers can get agricultural land converted to urban residential land and profit from it. Essentially, it allows a developer to set up tax-spared company towns.

According to the government of India, by March 2008, some 439 SEZs had been approved, of which 202 were notified, that is, had leased or bought the land, and defined their site.

SEZs are controversial, and carry risks: SEZs have become extremely controversial on three counts. First of all, the land acquisition from farmers has been questioned from a rights perspective, as well as from a social perspective. Opponents argue that the government has procured land at below its economic value, and displaced not just farmers but also agricultural workers who are not qualified for employment in the new zones. Secondly, there has been concern over the environmental impact of these new zones. Finally, the finance ministry has suggested that it provides a legal loophole that allows almost every company to avoid taxes, and thus adversely affect revenue at just the time India needs it most. (See "Controversies Around SEZs.")

Companies operating in these zones may become vulnerable if these issues become nationally and internationally salient.

Evaluate the potential benefits of tax holidays: Companies in the SEZs will get substantial tax holidays spread out over 15 years: 100 percent tax exemption for the first five years; 50 percent for the next five; and 50 percent of the regular tax on export profits for a further five years. Developers of the SEZs will get a complete income tax exemption for 15 years. The developers and the SEZ companies would also be exempt from numerous indirect taxes: customs duties, central excise duties, central sales tax, service tax, and securities transaction tax. In essence, the SEZs will be an area of complete deregulation, and treated as foreign areas.

Companies in SEZs need to be export surplus: Since an SEZ is essentially treated as foreign territory, imports are easier, and customs duties need not be paid on these imports, since it is assumed they are for exportable goods. If a company in an SEZ wants to sell its products into India's domestic market, it can do so paying by the customs duties.

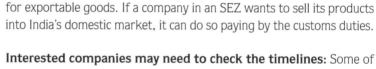

Interested companies may need to check the timelines: Some of the SEZs planned are massive, and it may be some years before they are fully functional. In selecting an appropriate location, it is best to visit the site to get a sense of the probable completion. Multinationals interested in locating at an SEZ should probably check on these ambitious projects, and assess whether probable completion dates will gel with the company's plans.

"The one near Bombay will be a city half the size of Bombay as we know it," said an Indian business executive. "The Reliance SEZ in Haryana will be a new city. In the next five-to-10 years, there will be about six town-size SEZs."

Companies should look at infrastructure benefits carefully. The intent is for about half of the land in an SEZ to be used to provide infrastructure that will allow it to function as a self-contained corporate township. Said a manager of a company involved with developing an SEZ: "It's the only way to deal with the issue of broken infrastructure in the existing cities. Governments haven't provided the basic infrastructure."

However, how far these plans will be realized is undetermined at present.

Land acquisition: Land acquisition is the key issue, and one that is gradually being resolved. Initially, all SEZs—and many new industrial activities—relied on government acquisition of land by eminent domain, usually with nominal compensation.

"It's the only way, and it's tough," said one consultant who is not sanguine about the problems being resolved. "If you try to buy in the open market, prices will go up the minute it's known. And you have to deal with hundreds or thousands of farmers holding tiny plots of land. What do you do if someone refuses to sell?"

"You have to work with the farmers and all the stakeholders," said an executive who has been involved in an SEZ. "You have to consider the politics. The key is to buy the land at market prices. There's no shortcut."

Government response: The government's stance is that SEZs do provide jobs, possibly with greater density than agriculture does. This makes them politically attractive to many states, which have been competing to establish them. They may also lead economic growth, so they have spillover benefits greater than what the SEZs may bring.

In response to the criticisms, the *SEZs Act* requires SEZs to follow local laws regarding environmental controls and labor, and also prohibits the acquisition of land from farmers who do not wish to sell. However, most of this is left to state governments, and implementation is likely to be variable.

The October 2007 legislation also specified that multiproduct SEZs should be of a certain size: 1,000-50,000 hectares (approximately 2,500–125,000 acres), except in some states, where these sizes would be impracticably large, and smaller 200-hectare (500-acre) SEZs would be permitted. It also provided for the "processing area" (that is, the productive area) to be at least half the total area.

PART 4

Managing in India

This section's checklists deal with the issues that arise on the ground in India. Some of them are about understanding and adapting to the market, others are about personnel hiring, retention and management; the high costs of premises; protecting intellectual properties; and corruption.

CHECKLIST 4.1

Understanding the Indian Market

India's market is growing of vast and not yet saturated: For many products and services, India offers a market that is quite large, growing fast, and not yet saturated.

India provides a steadily growing market still somewhat insulated from the world economy. Although the country remains poor overall, pockets of prosperity exist, and these pockets may be the size of small nations. Conservatively, about 50–100 million people constitute India's middle class, a group with purchasing power for modest luxuries. A small group of wealthy individuals are in the market for luxuries (but many of these have access to international markets, and may choose to shop overseas).

The Indian industry is substantial if not yet of global scale, and buys machines and raw materials. Imports, though still hindered by tariffs and other restrictions, are much more accessible than before, and merely exporting to India can now be a viable strategy.

The Indian market, fast growing, youth driven, and in the process of rapid change, is still quite different than Western markets. Companies that assume a parallel with Western markets of a few decades ago may find themselves mistaken.

Despite its huge size, India still provides a concentrated market: For most products offered by foreign companies, the major markets would be in the three largest cities: New Delhi NCR, Mumbai, and Bangalore. It is likely that some 50–80 percent of their sales will come from major cities, unless they sell specifically rural products such as pesticides, seed, or tractors.

India only has about 200 cities and towns. The eight largest cities probably account for some 70 million people. These cities and their 2001 census populations in millions are: Mumbai (formerly Bombay)—16.4; Kolkata (Calcutta)—13.2; New Delhi (including Delhi)—12.8; Chennai (Madras)—6.4; Bangalore—5.7; Hyderabad—5.5; Ahmedabad—5; and Pune—4. All these numbers can be assumed to be at least 5–10 percent higher in 2008.

However, smaller towns are of growing importance: As wealth trickles down to the smaller cities, and the media—particularly TV—raises consumer awareness and aspirations, these markets, too, are growing. These cities are small only by Indian standards; their populations are 5–10 million in size. Many companies are now factoring the so-called Tier II cities into their marketing plans.

Reebok, the shoe company, has a sales strategy that includes Tier II cities; and in 2007, had about 40 percent of its sales outlets in them. However, Tier I cities accounted for about 85 percent of their turnover.

The rural market is growing rapidly, and is of increasing interest: About 70 percent of India's population still live in the villages. Television access and some increase in purchasing power are changing consumption patterns. Even though only 39 percent of rural homes had TVs in 2006, shared viewing would probably mean the actual number of viewers was higher. Accessibility is limited mainly by infrastructural constraints.

India is a cash market, not a consumer credit market: A report by the US consulate estimates that only 10 percent of sales in India are credit sales.

Debt collection from individuals by legal means is extremely difficult, owing to a dilatory legal system. Even well-known organizations have been known to resort to using strong-arm tactics, largely through collection agencies.

These have a poor reputation; the means they use are usually associated with illegal trade in the US, including physical threats against not only the defaulter but also family, friends and associates, and in one case, reportedly—alleged kidnapping and homicide. (ICICI Bank's collection agency, Elite Financial Services, was accused of illegally confining an individual who owed Rs15,000—about US$350—causing his death. The Andhra Pradesh Human Rights Commission has ordered an investigation.) The Reserve bank has stated that banks are responsible for the actions of their collection agencies.

Credit scoring agencies for consumers are in their infancy: Although there is currently no widespread means of checking credit records in India, banks and financial institutions have started to share consumers' records informally.

Although this may reduce some of the risks, consumers have been annoyed by the lack of recourse if they are blacklisted. For the present, it is probably prudent to assume that credit card penetration will be limited to large cities, and to deal on a cash basis where possible.

This is an area where further development is needed, and it is now a high priority with the RBI. A new organization, Credit Information Bureau India Ltd. (CIBIL), associated with Dun and Bradstreet, aims to provide these services.

Indian markets tend to be price-sensitive except at the highest end: Most foreign goods face local competition. Some of the large distributors—for instance, Pantaloon, a chain of department stores—have introduced house brands that compete favorably with imported products. One executive noted, "Creativity is needed to get to the right price points. There is very fine segmentation. Pricing may be the most critical factor in the marketing mix."

4.1.1 Amway India—Adjusting to the Market

(Note: This example is derived from published materials.)

Amway, a US multilayer marketing company specializing in personal care products, launched in 1998 with only six products. It used its characteristic multilevel marketing model with home delivery, and initially established offices in five major cities.

In 2007, it had sales of about US$170 million, and more than 50 offices. It was the first major company to introduce multilevel marketing in India, and it is strongly identified with that strategy.

The Amway model overseas largely involved home delivery. Clients would order the products by phone or the Internet, and these would be delivered to their homes. Amway did not sell its products through the normal retail outlets.

In India, though, they found that consumers wanted to see the products before buying them. In an environment where mom-and-pop shops offered free home delivery to neighboring homes, this was not in itself a draw. Amway established pickup centers to function as de-facto sales outlets.

Moreover, Amway globally kept its costs down by offering a range of products, but only one package size. Indian consumers prefer smaller pack sizes at least for trial purposes, and also because for price-sensitive consumers, large packs require a larger immediate outlay. Amway responded by introducing multiple pack sizes for the Indian market.

It also needed a broader range of offerings. In 2007, it offered 80 products in four categories.

Amway in India also pursues a more aggressive promotional strategy than in other countries, using TV and print media.

Through an arrangement with other companies, it is also using its channels to sell life insurance and co-branded credit cards (with ICICI Bank).

It has also introduced products for the rural market, including a surfactant to increase the effectiveness of pesticides.

Warns R. Balakrishnan: "I think the main issue is that in many cases, it is 'dollar' costs and 'rupee' revenues. This makes the road to profitability a very long one."

Indian consumers often favor smaller pack sizes: Limited storage space and a reluctance to make a large outlay make smaller pack sizes popular in India. A range of pack sizes is important for most consumer goods.

Limited purchasing power and low consumption levels encourage people to buy smaller amounts than what is practiced abroad—cigarettes, for instance, sell as sticks as well as packs, and very seldom by the carton. Colgate has introduced the foil-tube pack of toothpaste. Cosmetics companies offer products such as shampoo in small bottles or even as sachets. Companies may also consider small pack sizes as a way to improve margins.

The analogy can be extended to industrial goods, where smaller machines, if priced lower, may sell more readily than extremely fast, sophisticated ones that require a major capital investment or substantial expensive maintenance.

Local tastes will almost certainly require customizing of products: Most companies find that consumer products need modification for the Indian market.

However, products that are commonplace in the West may have novelty value in India. Adapting to Indian markets is often a critical success factor; merely replicating strategies that are successful elsewhere may very well be suboptimal.

The marketing plan will probably need to be locally developed: It is worthwhile to hire a good local advertising agency. A product will probably need a different marketing approach in India than in the West. Many foreign advertising agencies have a local presence and local capabilities.

The market is becoming increasingly segmented: The Indian market requires increasingly sophisticated targeting. Marketing separately to men, women, and children; to metro, small town, and rural populations; and to different socio-economic strata pays off. Many markets are quite regional in character, and a message or method that succeeds in the south may fail in the north, or the west. Different channels and messages may be necessary; in some cases, products may need to be tweaked for the different segments.

India is also a brand-conscious and status-conscious market: According to a study conducted by global market research company Nielsen in November 2007, India is the world's third most brand-conscious market, after Greece and Hong Kong. If price were no object, Gucci, for instance, would find its products more popular there than in any other surveyed country, with 41 percent of the Indian respondents interested in purchasing the branded goods.

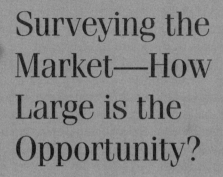

CHECKLIST 4.2

Surveying the Market—How Large is the Opportunity?

☐ **Talking to the trade "insiders" can give "quick and dirty" estimates:** Companies can get a very rough estimate of market dimensions by talking to stockists, dealers, and others in the trade. In general, Indians are not very secretive about market data, and merely having discussions with people involved in it can give one some sense of market size and characteristics. Sales of related products can also be a useful starting point for analysis.

☐ **Demographic data can provide a rough guesstimate of market size:** For many consumer products, a guesstimate can be arrived at by considering demographic data.

Data on income levels, age structure, urbanization, and Westernization can provide a broad estimate of the market. Government statistics can be the raw data, but these are often old; market research firms and similar organizations often have their own surveys that are both more recent and more relevant, and cost only a few hundred dollars.

However, R. Balakrishnan, currently with the Centrum group, warns: "One thing all businessmen should keep in mind while doing their sums on the Indian consumer market, is the fact that the per capita income is under US$1,000 per annum. So while the customer base is large, the spending power is limited by this. Added to that, there is tremendous disparity in wages, so the market size has to be estimated with caution."

A good market research company may serve consumer goods well: Companies in the consumer products sector should seriously consider hiring a good market research firm to do a thorough industry survey.

It should cover the present size of the market; significant local producers with their capacity and their production levels; imports, if any; the small-scale sector, if it is an important source; major users of your products; and growth projections.

It should also include government policy toward this industry and the user industries, the main regulations, and the applicable indirect taxes and levies.

Good market research companies—many with international affiliations—operate in India, and their reports are reliable. But not all companies are good; it is worthwhile to choose carefully and check their methodology.

For some industrial products, the best research is inhouse: Market research companies are not necessarily the only—or the best—solution, particularly for industrial products.

"They are not very useful in the nonretail sector," said a British manager at an industrial goods company. "It takes too long to educate them about your product and its market." He recommends observing the market, and asking your customers as a way of building a competitive profile.

Keep stratification in mind for market estimates: India's many social, cultural, economic, and geographical stratifications affect any product that is to be sold nationally.

Extrapolating from a limited survey is unlikely to give reliable data. Representative towns are not easy to find. For urban consumer markets, test marketing is best done in some segments of the major markets.

Most market research companies now offer Simulated Test Market (STM) programs. These are quantitative models that, based on some survey data, provide a reasonably reliable estimate of first year market share and volumes in the first year of introduction. STMs provide a less expensive alternative to a full test-marketing effort.

It is critically important that the STM be tailored to Indian conditions, and updated as they change. IMRB, for instance, offers a model called "PROBIT" that is, according to its website, fitted to "Indian response conditions, and extensively tested subsequently." Nielsen's product, BASES, is also used in India.

Check others' plans to enter the same field: Although this will increase competition in fairly predictable ways, it could also help to build markets, especially for new products. Some markets in India are still nascent, and having multiple entrants increases the overall awareness of the products.

Watch out for wide but shallow unsaturated markets: An apparently large market with considerable unsatisfied demand may turn out to be very shallow—specially in durables, which have long replacement cycles in India. Some companies have found that after an initial surge from pent-up demand, business tapers off. "It's easy to get carried away," said a marketing professional, "There's sometimes a herd mentality. Some people wear rose-tinted glasses."

High running costs can detract from popularity: Initially, attractive products may fall out of favor if purchasers find that running costs are high. This has been known to happen with printers needing expensive cartridges, copying machines requiring costly paper and toner, pricey repairs to cars, and so on. Indian consumers are price-sensitive.

☐ **It may be possible to develop a market where none exists:** Making products available at affordable prices, bringing in a new technology, or even just positioning the products differently may create a market where none was apparent. Some companies have found market surveys pessimistic because they obscured these options.

☐ **The small-scale sector usually has a price advantage:** Small-scale companies usually have lower overheads and some tax breaks. This sector competes aggressively on prices. Some industries are reserved for the small-scale sector, and although larger companies may be allowed to make those products, they should expect price competition.

If they are very active in your field, consider variations in strategy to tackle them. The easiest option is to outsource some of your manufacturing to this sector if possible, with enough oversight to maintain quality control. Many consumer product companies have small-scale firms making products for them.

☐ **Check that your product really provides a perceived benefit:** Indian technology is a mix of old and new. This sometimes suits customers who may find the older products cheaper, more durable, and easier to repair. This is especially true of machinery of all kinds.

At the same time, Indian consumers are more demanding than before. Indian consumers now have access to imported products, and will not always accept older products that do not have specific benefits.

Mitsubishi Electric closed an air-conditioner subsidiary in Tamil Nadu: consumers were opting for newer split unit air-conditioners rather than the old-fashioned window models.

☐ **If manufacturing in India, consider exporting some products:** This will supplement the home market, and also lend your products local prestige. If the export component exceeds the imports, you may be able to locate the plant in an SEZ, with all the tax and infrastructure benefits.

CHECKLIST 4.3

Accessing India's Rural Market

☐ **The rural market is changing and growing:** India's rural market may be of growing interest as it becomes more accessible and tastes change.

Most of India's population is in its 600 thousand villages—accounting for some 70 percent, or about 700 million of its people. India's rural market has grown more affluent over the past 10 years. For some products—particularly less expensive consumer goods—the rural market is now about the same size as the urban market.

Access is the single largest problem. At present, some villages are not connected by surfaced road, and lack electricity. The government is trying to expand the infrastructure, and when it succeeds, these areas may also become interesting markets.

☐ **Some already find a potential payoff to a rural marketing strategy:** If the product is appropriate, this market could grow faster than urban markets. LG Electronics reported, in a 2007 FICCI speech, that after such an effort, 60 percent of its color TV sales were to rural areas, and the rural market was growing at 25 percent, compared to 15 percent in urban areas.

☐ **Is it possible to piggyback a product on existing channels?** Although distribution is the single largest problem in accessing rural markets, some companies are putting in appropriate channels, that may be available for other companies' products to piggyback.

Access through nearby towns is the easiest option: Some rural markets can be accessed by proxy, by providing distribution to towns that function as district centers. Not only do people from the villages come to these places to shop, some micro-retailers purchase their stocks for sale in the villages.

As with the urban market, rural markets are also concentrated: Although India has about 600,000 villages, about half of the 700 million or more rural inhabitants live in maybe 100,000 of them. This is the easiest rural target market to access.

Regional differences are more marked in rural areas: Indian markets are all regional, and this difference is more marked in the rural areas than in the cities. Not only would the languages be different, there would also be differences in the festivals celebrated, seasonality in incomes, apparel choices, and food preferences.

Rural consumers are even more price-sensitive: Even more than urban markets, sales to rural markets depend on affordability. Rural consumers are on the average not as wealthy as urban consumers, and are more likely to buy inexpensive goods in smaller packages. Coca-Cola has introduced a smaller 200 ml (6.7 oz.) pack, and several consumer-product companies have introduced small foil packs or sachets of products such as shampoo. Companies that provide a good price proposition are more likely to succeed.

Rural markets may demand innovative promotional methods: For durables, the weekly, monthly, or annual village fairs—which usually attract visitors from villages in a radius of a day's travel—may offer an opportunity to showcase products. Maruti-Suzuki, the automobile company, used this method to popularize its vans in rural areas.

Visual and sound media are better than print for rural marketing: Illiteracy is more widespread in villages than in towns. Most villages with electricity have some TV access, even though rural penetration of TV—averaging 39 percent of households—is still a lot lower than in urban areas.

CHECKLIST 4.4

Advertising and Promotion

India has many channels: Television is the single largest medium in India, with channels in English, Hindi, and other languages. For consumer products, it offers the most cost-effective way to reach the consumer. An estimated 78 percent of urban homes had television in 2006, and 77 percent had cable TV. (In the largest cities, these numbers were 83 percent and 78 percent respectively.)

In addition, India also has a vibrant print media industry in English and in many Indian languages, billboards (hoardings), flyers, point-of-purchase advertising, and direct selling. Mobile phone advertising has started with the spread of mobile phones, and trade fairs are held in major cities.

Internet is still a nascent medium in India. Computer penetration figures are low. It may be useful as an additional element in a plan for specific products.

However, being heard above the "noise" is not necessarily easy: A lot of advertising takes place, and consumers are bombarded with messages. The field is only growing more cluttered. Meanwhile, fragmentation is an issue as channels proliferate. According to TAM Media Research, in 2006, 36 channels accounted for 80 percent of the viewership in the six largest cities, up from 20 only six years earlier.

Advertising in India is largely TV-based, and celebrity endorsements are important. Many companies pick spokespersons from the fields of cricket—by far India's most popular sport—or Hindi films. There is some concern now that this is shifting as celebrities become over-exposed and less credible because of the range of products they endorse.

Niche markets may be difficult to target specifically: As most of these media are broad based, companies with specific niche markets may find it more difficult to reach their target consumers. Although India has a lot of print media, few of them are closely targeted to specific niches. The Internet is not a major channel yet.

India is no longer a seller's market: For decades, the Indian market was starved for goods, and almost anything that was reasonably priced sold well. Since liberalization, this is no longer true. Sellers must compete for consumers, for distribution channels, and for shelf space—and for consumer mindshare.

Select a strong advertising firm in India: The local market demands local expertise. Some advertising agencies—many of the major global agencies are represented, and often allied with firms originally of Indian origin—can help companies develop their promotional plans for India. Foreign companies tend to choose agencies used by their parent companies. Most of the large agencies have a broad competency in the Indian market.

Depending on the products, local advertising may be more or less important to their marketing mix. In addition to understanding local tastes and media, the local agencies are aware of conventions and regulations. For instance, prescription pharmaceutical products are not advertised, but over-the-counter products are. Medical equipment may be advertised in trade journals.

A product may need a different promotional strategy in India:
The kind of campaign needed in India may be quite different than the
approach used elsewhere.

But the differences can go further, right down to the marketing
strategy. Amway, for instance, has found that local advertising was
useful in building sales in India, even though in its US market, it relied
entirely on direct selling.

Crocs, which globally relies on public relations and event
participation, is considering media advertising.

Reebok, the shoe company, gave away 10,000 pairs of shoes in
2007 to launch a promotion entitled "Run Easy."

The Indian market may demand modifications to a product:
Products may need modifications to make them more relevant to the
market, and companies that have the flexibility to do this have an
advantage.

Nokia, the mobile phone company, entered the Indian market in
1995. It introduced an Indian ring tone in 1998, and Hindi menu in
2000. In 2003, it introduced a "made for India" phone. In 2005, it
added eight additional Indian languages to appeal to a broader audience, as well as a vernacular news portal. In 2007, the BBC reported
that India was the second-largest market for Nokia.

Another example is Maruti, the Suzuki company in India. Its
Maruti-Suzuki Swift that came out in 2005 had a suspension modi-
fied for India road conditions: it had greater clearance and could take
the potholes.

Plan a budget accordingly, and build in an inflation factor: One
experienced manager suggested that a consumer product advertised
nationally and mainly in the urban market would require a budget in
the ballpark of Rs150 million–180 million (about US$4–5 million) in

the first year. Including the semi-urban and rural markets might cost an additional 20–25 percent.

He estimated that a similar level of expenditure would probably be needed for about four or five years at least. Allowing for media inflation, he did not think that the spend could be reduced, and it might need increasing.

CHECKLIST 4.5

The Special Case of Retail

☐ **Foreign multiproduct retailers are not currently allowed:** The Indian government does not permit foreign-owned retailers to sell to consumers. This restriction is intended to protect the 12 million or so shopkeepers operating small businesses. However, exceptions are being made, and further liberalization is possible.

☐ **Single-brand companies can have joint ventures:** At present, the government does allow foreign companies that have a single brand to have joint ventures in India with up to 51 percent ownership.

In December 2007, Italian fashion company Dolce & Gabbana announced a plan to set up a 51 percent-owned joint venture with DLF, a major real estate company. (DLF plans to take a 49 percent share.) Initially, D&G plans two retail outlets, in Mumbai and Delhi. The choice of a real estate company underlines a key issue for business in India— the limited availability and high cost of real estate, even for rental. (Foreign companies are not permitted to own real estate in India without governmental permission.)

Crocs, the shoe company, has a joint venture with one of its distributors as a partner.

☐ **Cash-and-carry subsidiaries targeting businesses are allowed:** A second exception is that foreign retail companies are permitted to set up wholly owned "cash-and-carry" subsidiaries targeting businesses.

The cash-and-carry business, as defined in India, is essentially a wholesale market targeted at small businesses, including microretailers. It usually works on a membership basis. This area has attracted several foreign companies in the past few years. However, they are currently not permitted to source agricultural produce directly from farmers without an Agricultural Produce Marketing Committee (APMC) license.

Metro, a German company, has been operating in India since 2003.

Wal-Mart has an arrangement with Bharti Industries, a company better known for mobile phones, and plans to open its first store by December 2008.

Franchising remains a possibility: Many foreign companies—especially those in the consumer goods area—have found franchising an interesting entry strategy.

Although it is particularly suitable as a low-investment way to expand, many companies with substantial resources are also using it as an entry route. It is a nascent market, and huge opportunities remain. The US Commercial Service estimated that the country had 40,000 franchisees in 2007, and the growth rate was 40 percent per year. It claimed there were more than 700 franchise systems operating in India.

Companies choosing this route find it gives them enormous reach, compared to relying solely on owned outlets. The key is selecting franchisees whose goals are closely aligned with yours.

Planet Retail, an Indian company of the Future Group, has franchise arrangements with several global brands, including Debenhams and Marks & Spencer.

Starbucks, the US coffeehouse chain, decided on franchising in India after its attempt to invest was not permitted. It announced in April 2007 that it would go through its Indonesian franchisee V.P. Sharma (who is of Indian origin) and Kishore Biyani (of the Pantaloon Group). Starbucks had earlier sought an 18 percent share in a retail company Sharma and Biyani owned, but the government of India did not permit it.

Carrefour, the French retailer, is also planning to franchise. It has set up two separate entities in India. Carrefour WC&C India Pvt. Ltd. will set up company-owned stores that cater to businesses. Carrefour India Master Franchise Co. Pvt. Ltd. will manage the franchise operations and seek suitable franchisees. The franchise agreement will include a clause that Carrefour may take a majority stake when and if the government permits foreign companies to enter consumer retail.

McDonald's, the US fast-food chain, currently operates through joint ventures in India, but is reportedly considering franchising as a route to faster growth.

Adidas, the shoe company, has been present in India since 1996. Its distribution strategy is driven by a mix of franchisees and owned stores.

Purchasing an Indian company is one route: If a company has the resources and can find a suitable opportunity, acquisition or buying into an Indian brand or company may give access.

Lavazza of Italy reportedly acquired the Indian coffee shop chain Barista in March 2007, and paid US$125 million for that and another company in the coffee vending machine business.

Direct selling may be an option: The government seems predisposed to permitting direct selling through multilevel marketing. This model, introduced to India in the past decade, has been quite successful. Amway, which was launched in India in 1998, achieved sales estimated to be about US$170 million by 2007.

However, there is a risk of early market saturation. Although India seems to be a huge market, social circles tend to be closed, so multilevel marketing may have fewer attractions than seems apparent at first.

Distribution Channels

India's distribution system is under pressure from competition: One of the main issues for companies that are interested in selling in India is distribution. Rapid growth and increased competition has put pressure on India's traditional multilayered open distribution system, which channeled goods from factories to stockists, to wholesalers, to retailers, and even to tiny shops in remote villages. Companies now must compete for attention and shelf space; and some firms are building their own networks. Others still rely on distributors, but are increasingly careful about selection.

India has a complex and relatively efficient multitier open distribution system for consumer products, providing a rural reach despite the poor infrastructure. However, an unprecedented quantity of products is now being pushed through these channels. The system comprises stockists, who in turn distribute the products to wholesalers, who distribute to retailers. In some cases, the wholesalers sell to other (smaller) wholesalers, who then distribute to retailers. A US Commercial Service report (June 2007) noted that there were an estimated 12 million retail outlets in India.

Large modern malls after prestigious venues: Although Indian retail is dominated by small stores, large modern malls have opened in all large towns to provide a prestigious venue for upmarket retail. Most of India's retailing is still performed by small individually owned and family-managed entities. But in big cities, glittering malls and modern stores have opened and some are now publicly listed organizations. These malls are attractive to companies trying to establish upper-scale brand identities.

Consider establishing single-brand stores or showrooms to build your brand: Companies as diverse as Crocs, the shoe manufacturer, and Audi, the luxury car company, are putting in stores and showrooms in critical locations.

In February 2008, Hong Kong-based clothing manufacturer, Giordano, announced an aggressive retail strategy, opening stores in Delhi, Mumbai, Chennai, and Ahmedabad. It also planned to establish stores-in-stores in leading department stores, and outlets in duty-free areas.

However, single-brand stores, which must be located in prime areas to have the desired brand-building effect, are expensive. One consumer goods executive estimated the cost to be about US$250,000 annually.

Corporate retailing has spread despite reservations: The government is cautious about corporate retailing, but many chains have opened anyway. Some Indian businesses hope to transform retailing in India.

◆ Bharti Retail has an association with Wal-Mart.

◆ Reliance Fresh has opened a number of stores.

◆ The south Indian retail chain, Subhiksha, has nearly 1,000 stores.

◆ The all-India group retail giant, Pantaloon, has established several chains, including "e-zone" for electrical and electronic goods, and Big Bazaar for groceries.

◆ The Tata group has the Westside chain of stores, which focuses on clothing and gifts; and the Landmark stores, which sell books, music, and stationery.

◆ The Aditya Birla group has started the More supermarkets, and also acquired the Trinethra chain, based in Hyderabad.

- Videocon has the NEXT retail chain, specializing in consumer electronics.
- Vishal Retail has 108 outlets in 73 cities, selling garments, home furnishings, food, and household goods. "One of the best models," comments R. Balakrishnan. "[It's] focused on the 'real' middle-class consumers, and is the most profitable retail chain."

There is policy-level concern about the impact of corporate retailing, since the old family-run concerns are labor intensive, and provide, the livelihood of millions of tiny shopkeepers, and their families. However, big businesses hope to make the process more efficient, provide higher prices to the producers, and create millions of jobs in the supply chain. Until these issues are resolved, the government's policy on retail liberalization is likely to be uncertain.

Corporate retailing faces several challenges: In addition to the growing competition as major players in Indian industry rush into retail, these chains also face other issues. These stores require more electricity, and more space—and of higher quality—than traditional outlets. They also require trained employees, while the small stores rely more on family members and unskilled employees they train on the job. All three resources are in short supply: quality real estate, power, and trained staff. This may drive up costs.

R. Balakrishnan comments: "Staff turnover in retail [is] extremely high. This pushes costs up dramatically, in terms of hiring and training. Anybody with one year's experience becomes a wanted guy for the next new startup [seeking] a trained hand who can be up and running quickly."

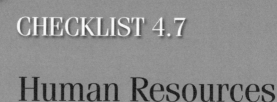

Human Resources

☐ **The "abundance of inexpensive labor" is not so abundant now:** While many companies were attracted to India in the past decade by its apparent abundance of inexpensive labor, the situation has changed.

A survey of Japanese companies operating in India by JETRO, published in 2006, quotes two companies that make automobiles and home appliances respectively as estimating wage increases at between 7 percent and 10 percent annually, and perhaps 15 percent in the IT sector.

In a survey of 61 firms, the same study noted: "increase of employee wages" as the main labor issue in India (from 72 percent of the respondents), followed by "low rate of worker retention" (36 percent), restrictions of staff dismissal and reduction (33 percent), and labor disputes (31 percent).

☐ **Shortages exist in every skill-set:** One of India's biggest attractions is the large pool of educated labor, and for many decades, companies could expect to be flooded with applicants whenever a position became available. This is still true, but with the rapid economic growth of recent years, not as true as it was before. While it is still possible to get excellent Indian staff, the market is much more competitive.

"From a situation of excess labor, in the last few years, every skill-set is in deficit..." said a senior manager at an international bank.

The natural effect of this is that wages are going up; the rate of increase varies from about 7 percent annually to about 15 percent annually, depending on the industry.

Western compensation practices—such as bonuses—are spreading. It is still possible to get low-cost labor—for example, you can find an engineer for US$6,000 annually. At the other end of the scale, some MBAs get a starting salary of US$100,000.

Advertised openings draw floods of resumes, some of them fake: Paradoxically, advertised openings still draw a great deal of attention.

"We advertised two positions and received 3,000 resumes—almost all of them entirely useless to us," said the head of a legal firm. "People send resumes even if they don't meet the advertised criteria. Or, they interpret them loosely. We asked for five years of experience; we got applicants who had worked for five years, but not in anything relevant."

A fairly recent phenomenon is a rash of fake qualifications on resumes. There are small businesses that will fabricate an entire background for a fee, complete with certificates for schools the person never attended, and degrees he or she didn't earn. So far, these are not of very high quality, and alert HR personnel can spot them easily, but it is only a matter of time before the quality improves.

"Many CVs are...exaggerated," said a British expatriate manager delicately. "It does happen everywhere, but it's become more common here. In fact, it's more usual than not."

Most companies can expect high staff turnover: Rising competition in certain industries—particularly call centers—has made for a very mobile workforce, with little loyalty to the organizations. Some companies have complained of turnover rates of up to nearly 50 percent annually.

"We're seeing staff turnover of 10–15 percent or more," said the manager of an IT company in Bangalore. "There's a talent war, no doubt about it. For mundane applied work, the turnover is 20–25 percent. At the lowest end, it can go as high as 50 percent."

This means companies need to be proactive to retain key people. "I had some very talented people," said one manager with some regret.

"In retrospect, I didn't value them enough. I didn't realize it until after they left, but I should have given them raises faster."

"Hiring is no problem, it's retention that's very difficult," said a manager who has had to replace people half a dozen times in under three years.

☐ **Employee noncompete clauses are illegal under Indian law:** In employment contracts, companies cannot build in clauses that extend beyond the contract period. Indian law does not permit companies to enforce contracts that, for instance, prohibit employees who leave from joining competitors, or from setting up their own competitive operations.

☐ **Entry-level staff tend to be very inexperienced:** Most entry-level employees have no work experience, even in summer jobs.

Campus recruitment is becoming popular—not just at the Institutes of Management or at the Institutes of Technology, where it has been routine for decades, but down to the level of undergraduates. These hires will be very inexperienced—few Indian students work in summer jobs or internships before or during college—so extra training may be necessary, depending on the positions they will fill.

"Large numbers of Indian graduates are unprepared for real-world jobs," said one entrepreneur. "Additional training is always required. Some 'finishing schools' have been set up to do this."

"Millions of graduates are being churned out who are utterly unemployable," said a consultant. "They don't even have basic useable skills."

Another executive spoke of the sense of entitlement among young employees; he finds them very materialistic, and not realistic. "They want to decide what kind of chairs we should provide, and what colors to paint the walls. And they're big spenders. Their buying patterns are based on the probable increase in salary—they expect 20–30 percent per year. They want a new role and a new title every 18 months. It's rather dangerous. There's bound to be a correction."

An influx of immature workers can warp a corporate culture:
The impact of the massive influx of younger workers on the corporate culture can also be an issue. "In some areas, there's no one over 35; no one who can act as a sounding board; no one who's seen hard times," one manager said. This can lead to decisions based on the assumption that things can only improve.

He recommends that startups first grow to 400–500 experienced employees before they start hiring junior people. Of course, this ideal situation may be difficult to achieve, but the principle holds: try to get the corporate culture established, and put in place a layer of experienced people who can provide a sense of perspective.

Flexibility about timings is needed for business across time zones: Managers and staff interfacing with the US and other Western countries will need to be flexible about timings. Companies will need to be flexible too, perhaps providing for in-home teleconferencing.

Especially for companies that are in the area of BPO, flexible timings are a critical factor in smooth operation. Managers especially, but even more junior staff, may need to operate on a global timetable, working at night when offices around the world are open, or participating in international conference calls by phone or videoconference. Most Indian staff are comfortable with this, but it should be discussed before they join.

These timings may be particularly problematic for female employees on two levels. First, there is the issue of safety. Conditions vary considerably, but few places in India are entirely safe for a woman to be alone late at night. Secondly, women may have more familial responsibilities after work than men.

One executive in the IT area participates in a weekly teleconference that involves Bangalore, the San Francisco Bay area, and the UK. Finding a time that works for all three locations is an ongoing challenge, and the teleconference is held at odd times—including between 10 p.m. and 11 p.m. in India. It is generally accepted.

"In a global economy, the services sector requires a constant two-way flow of information. Once you have a Blackberry or PDA, you're on call all the time. The work–life divide is blurred. You just fit everything in where you can."

"What with calls to the UK and US," said an American expatriate, "you end up working 60-hour weeks."

Moving people can be problematic: With such a shortage of good people, companies may be tempted to move them around to operations in various cities, if needed. They should be aware of some problems peculiar to India in such moves. While it can be done, a cautious approach is best.

Housing is always an issue, being both scarce and expensive in most big cities. Usually, a move involves some assurance of reasonable housing parity being maintained. A second—less tractable—issue is children's schooling. India has no equivalent of good government-funded schools, that exist in most developed countries, so parents seeking a good education for their children put them in private schools. The best schools have limited enrollment, and parents will not move their children unless they are assured of school admission in the new city.

Workarounds are many: some companies agree not to move the family, but instead to fly the executive home every weekend at least. In some cases, the children are placed with other relatives while they complete their schooling. Some executives find places in boarding schools for their children to leave them freer to move.

Managers may resist moves to smaller towns, primarily because of schooling issues, but also because the smaller cities are a lot less cosmopolitan than the large ones.

Even those without families may be reluctant to move; Indians often have responsibilities to their extended family. However, this is also a cushion: extended family can take on responsibilities, thus freeing a manager to move.

CHECKLIST 4.8

Labor Trouble, Retrenchment and Dismissal

☐ **Firing managers is fairly easy, but dismissing workers is not:** Retrenching or dismissing worker can be difficult, though reducing managerial staff is less so.

Hiring is extremely easy; firing is difficult. In the World Bank 2008 benchmarking ratings, India scored 70 on a 0–100 scale, where 100 was the most difficult, and 0 the easiest. Firing costs were an estimated 56 weeks of salary.

Employers are lobbying for changes to the legislation that restricts laying off or firing workers. These changes are opposed by advocates for organized labor, which has considerable political clout, although it constitutes only about 7 percent of the total labor force of nearly 500 million.

(A major problem has been the complete absence of any kind of social safety net—unemployment benefits or social security—which can make job loss catastrophic. However, instituting such safety nets would be extremely expensive, and the government has not yet tackled this because of owing resource constraints.)

☐ **Two workarounds: outsourcing; and employing only managers:** Many companies seek to get around restrictions on dismissing workers by hiring labor on contract, often for long periods. Outsourcing every-thing that can be outsourced also makes the payroll more flexible. Some outsourcing companies now provide human resources that are carried on their payrolls, but are actually hired, trained, and controlled by the client company.

TeamLease, for instance, started in 2002, and now, according to its website, has 70,000 employees, and more than 450 locations. It claims to provide temporary and permanent manpower solutions to 650 clients. In a media interview, a company executive said that clients sought "labor liquidity" and "flexibility of headcount."

There are fewer restrictions on laying off or firing "managerial" employees, and so, some firms use this classification for many addi-tional levels in the organization. "The trick is to be above the minimum wages law, and have only 'officers' on the payroll," says an experienced observer, who has seen companies do just that.

Planning an exit is even more difficult: If a project should fail, for whatever reason, a company may decide to close down its Indian oper-ation and exit. However, it is not so easy as that. The government of India, in the interests of preserving employment, generally restricts a company's right to go out of business. A High Court order is required to wind up a company. The main concern, then, are the employees and debtors.

The World Bank 2007 report estimated a period of 10 years to close down a company, and ranked India 135th of 178 countries. In 2008, it ranked it 137th.

A Voluntary Retirement Scheme can trim headcount: Some companies use Voluntary Retirement Schemes (VRS) to reduce headcount.

However, bear in mind that the government specifies many of the terms of a VRS through the income tax rules (see "VRS Conditions"), and it must be offered to all employees. This may result in the departure of those most easily re-employed, while less productive employees opt not to volunteer.

Nevertheless, they can be useful. Says R. Balakrishnan: "A VRS may not get you tax write-offs, but if generous, can solve all your problems. Many financial services firms used it in India in the 1996–1999 period."

India has a history of strikes and disruption to work: According to the statistics from India's Labor Bureau, the labor situation is mixed. Organized labor has historically been powerful in India, partly because of the political ties that the unions have with various parties.

Between 1991 and 2006, the number of reported industrial disputes (that is, actions leading to either a strike or a lockout) halved from 927 to 460. However, the disputes involved more people: the number of affected workers started at 1.3 million in 1991, reached a peak of 2.9 million in 2005, and then fell to 1.8 million in 2006. The total workdays lost seem to be less predictable, varying between 26.8 million (1999) and 22.2 million (2006), but they were as high as 30.3 million in 2003.

A changing work culture and more business-friendly legislation may reduce these numbers further. The government—and the courts—are attempting to head off strikes that occur primarily for political reasons. The Supreme Court ruled in 2004 that there was no "fundamental right" to strike.

Some labor troubles originate outside the organization: Companies may be unable to avoid labor troubles that originate outside the organization.

Many of the major strikes are not individual disputes between workers and a company, but broader actions that may have political bases. India's five major trade unions all have historical ties to political parties. This led to a considerable amount of disruption not for labor issues, but

4.8.1 Voluntary Retirement Scheme Conditions

A company can have different Voluntary Retirement Scheme (VRS) for different types of employees, but they must all follow the regulations given in the income tax rules:

◆ VRS can be offered to employees who are at least 40 years old, or have worked for 10 or more years at the company.

◆ It must be offered to all employees, although not to directors of the company.

◆ It must result in a reduction in headcount (that is, the places of the retiring employees should not be filled with new hires).

◆ The retiring employee must not be re-employed in the same company, or another company with the same ownership.

◆ The maximum that can be offered is the lesser of 1.5 months' salary for each year of service, or total pay until the employee reaches normal retirement age, with a ceiling of Rs500,000.

◆ Employees are only eligible for a VRS if they have not, in the past, used one.

as a result of politics. Popular discontent with this situation is pushing the unions toward more independent positions. The five leading trade unions are:

◆ Bharatiya Mazdoor Sangh

◆ Indian National Trade Union Congress

◆ Center of Indian Trade Unions

◆ Hind Mazdoor Sabha

◆ The All India Trade Union Congress

These are less of a threat to private-sector and foreign companies: Although these unions are relatively strong in the public sector (that is, government-owned entities), they are less important to newer companies in the private sector, which largely have inhouse unions. They can disrupt the infrastructure though, making work impossible on strike days.

Although usually less affected, foreign companies should not consider themselves immune to labor disputes. They have sometimes turned violent; the Indian CEO of an Italian-affiliated company was killed in September 2008 in NOIDA. Local managers with a sense of how to negotiate should be able to manage the situation.

☐ **Competition for talent is rising:** Companies are becoming flexible to find the people they need, since in this environment, the competition for good people is increasing.

"There's a dearth of good people at the middle and senior levels," said the head of a major BPO company, "and people at the top get international-level salaries. At lower levels, people are available, but staff turnover is very high."

A rigid approach to hiring is unlikely to yield results. If the parent company needs to provide policy waivers, it is best to procure them in advance.

☐ **Networking is probably the best way to fill a senior position:** Urban India is still small enough that most people know most others at the senior levels. The flipside of this is that new companies that do not have a high profile in India may find it more difficult to get good candidates than companies that have established reputations.

☐ **Provide sufficient time to find the right people for key positions:** "Allow a lot of time for the interview process," recommends the country head of a new Indian operation. Companies that do not have a high profile may find it tougher. "And you may need to pay above market rates and offer particularly good working conditions."

☐ **Head hunters have become increasingly active:** Recruitment companies, both local and multinational, are active in India. They can help find candidates at all levels of the company.

☐ **Advertisements work but generate masses of useless applications:** Advertising openings is still a good idea, but going this route will probably mean that some prescreening will be required to deal with the patently unsuitable applications.

☐ **An expatriate may be the best solution:** In some cases, companies are looking abroad for talent and experience, and hopefully, knowledge of the best practices in the industry.

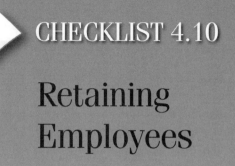

CHECKLIST 4.10

Retaining Employees

☐ **Retention is important; employee turnover tends to be high:** Employee turnover is one of the major operating challenges for companies. Companies have sought ways to manage this turnover, which can be very costly for firms, especially small, training-intensive operations.

Wipro, a major IT company, reportedly had an attrition rate of 48 percent in 2006–2007, and it is considered one of the best companies in the field. Others face rates that are similar or worse.

☐ **Consider retention bonuses at every level:** "We can't afford to lose people every few months," said a manager of a BPO company in NOIDA. "When I hire someone, I ask them their expectations. Then I offer them 20 percent more, with the last 20 percent to be paid as a retention bonus on the completion of a one-year contract. My boss asked why I was changing the compensation structure. I explained, and we tried it out. It's worked very well: our turnover is much lower than our competitors'."

If you are using this structure, make sure it is competitive. "Some year-end bonus is standard in the industry," commented a manager. "That's why the maximum turnover takes place in April, after people get their bonuses."

☐ **Create a positive work environment with a sense of involvement:** The head of a medical equipment company that is just setting up its

Indian subsidiary said, "We weren't known in India, so it wasn't easy getting good people. We invest a lot in training. We don't want them to leave. I work to create a positive atmosphere that makes them want to stay; we involve the top team in everything. We just took the whole management team, 14 people, to Davos." So far, one year in, they have had no departures.

Minimize the need for staffing by outsourcing: "We outsource all the routine work," a manager said. "Accounting. Tax advice. Legal services. We don't have company cars and drivers; we leave it to individuals to hire those." By distributing the problem down to smaller units, it can make the best use of people with all levels of expertise.

Offer benefits beyond the compensation structure: "Use shortages to your advantage," recommended a consultant. "Housing in big cities is always a problem. So is schooling. Companies that provide good housing to their key people, and have arrangements with schools so that their children will get admission, are more likely to retain them." (However, note that fringe benefits are subject to the fringe benefits tax, payable by the company, on benefits that are not taxable in the hands of the employee.)

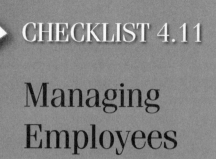

CHECKLIST 4.11

Managing Employees

☐ **India's work culture is more personal and group-oriented:** Foreigners may need to adjust to the culture. Typically more group-focused and personal than in the West, it is not as detached or task-oriented.

"India needs a different management style," noted one executive who has worked in the US before returning to Bangalore. "It's a group culture. An effective manager has to be a people person, participate in the group, and be much more visible, larger than life. It's not suitable for introverts."

"If you work for a company that's data and metrics driven," said an American who worked in Delhi for some years, "you have to learn to manage the emotions. It's an emotional society." He finds it positive, because it sets up a friendly environment at work, but also problematic in that responses to problems tend to be emotional first.

"You have to have different management techniques," he said. "Here's a small example: in our company, if someone is late for a meeting, they have to pay a forfeit. Sing a song, usually. In the US, they'll be embarrassed, and if they'll sing, it's something like *Happy Birthday*. Here, it becomes an occasion for entertainment..."

☐ **Allow for expectations of a paternalistic employer:** Indian employees often expect employers to be somewhat paternalistic; flexible over absenteeism for family reasons, or with extending personal loans.

From the employee's standpoint, sometimes the employer is the only possible source of emergency funds. "We had a medical emergency," one young woman said. "My mother-in-law collapsed with a heart problem. The hospital to which we took her said she needed a pacemaker immediately, but they would only operate if we paid them Rs2 lakh (about US$5,000). We don't have that kind of money. We didn't know what to do. Luckily, my husband was able to get a loan from his company, and it saved her life."

Get comfortable with micromanagement: "Managing people here takes an adjustment," an American said. "Micromanagement is more common, and people expect their managers to be involved with their work. They feel ignored if they're left alone."

"They wait for instructions," said an outsourcing client at a US company. "Programmers just aren't proactive."

Work on defining deliverables: Some staffers tend to measure input rather than output. When coupled with a reluctance to act without instructions, the result can be a lot of spinning of wheels. Especially when working with less experienced staff, it is important to ensure that the output is defined, processes understood, and managers check back with employees to make sure there is no confusion about what is required.

Expect overt deference to authority: Managers have commented on a lack of willingness to question, especially among junior staff.

"They are still quite timid," said the manager of a construction outsourcing company, who has been trying to change this. "They would go ahead and do something wrong rather than ask."

Cultural consultants point out that companies may need to work on making questioning a positive within the corporate culture.

"Some people here don't like to think for themselves," said Nigel Marsh, an Australian expatriate manager. "We're trying to teach them to ask questions."

Do not rely on workers to take the initiative: "In some of the outsourcing companies, the whole thing has become very process-driven and responsibilities closely specified," said a US manager. "No one seems to take any initiative or have any flexibility or innovation. But sometimes, that's what you need."

Expect that you will need to probe to discover problems: "No one wants to tell you the bad news," said a manager with considerable experience in India. "I tell them that if we don't know, we can't take steps to solve it. But they would rather pretend it's all fine."

This is not an easy problem to deal with, since it requires changing how people instinctively wish to work. Employees may fear that mentioning bad news indicates a bad attitude. Sometimes, a "shoot the messenger" element may exist in the corporate culture without the senior management being aware of it.

Group praise should be done publicly: Praising the workgroup helps to build a positive environment, and encourage the group to provide the results needed. Praising individuals publicly is also good, but remain aware of any tension and jealously that might build as a result, and be ready to defuse it by being even-handed. Perceptions of favoritism can be awkward.

Any criticism should be made in private: Indian culture is sensitive to criticism, as well as to "face" and respect. If it is necessary to criticize an employee, it should be done in private, and with tact. Public criticism is considered insulting to the employee, and demoralizing to the group.

Work around a certain lack of rigor on timings: It is preferable to allow some leeway in appointments and meetings; sticking to the calendar too closely can be problematic. This applies to deadlines as well: a slippage of a few days is seldom considered serious.

"Lack of respect for time can be a challenge," said a manager. "We've had conference calls delayed because some people were late. No one thinks anything of it."

4.11.1 Case Study—Training Call Center Employees

Ms. Gita was a service director at Company B, a US company that out-sourced its customer service operations to two Indian companies, one in Mumbai and the other in Pune. Ms. Gita visited India to help train the call center employees to Company B standards. The employees she was working with had already undergone voice and accent training. Her six-month assignment was to instill Company B norms, procedures, and attitudes.

Her observations

◆ The employees were very bright, smarter than she had expected, but also more immature.

◆ Their main problem was unfamiliarity with the geography of the US, so they could not understand local conditions, or visualize alternatives if problems occurred.

◆ Loyalty to the company was negligible, and staff turnover was high because it was very easy to hire them away. "They were shocked when I told them I'd worked for the same company for 11 years."

◆ However, their loyalty to individuals was considerable, and many of the trainees remained in contact with her years later.

◆ Some employees worked elsewhere, and then returned.

◆ Many of the employees did not understand the concept of customer service, and did not make human contact with customers. However, employees of one company were noticeably different from the other, so it may have been a local corporate culture issue.

◆ There was a surprising amount of illness, given that most employees were in their mid-20s.

◆ She also heard about a considerable amount of favoritism and internal politics.

CHECKLIST 4.12

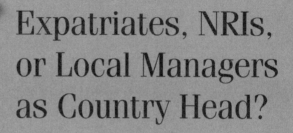

Expatriates, NRIs, or Local Managers as Country Head?

☐ **Selecting the first head of the in-country operation is critical:** Once a company has decided to set up an Indian operation, the decision as to who should head it comes up. This is a critical decision, since a poor start can delay a company's success or prevent it altogether.

Some companies prefer to depute an expatriate from the headquarters or elsewhere in the company; others hire someone new, either from overseas or in India. There are pros and cons to each option.

☐ **An expatriate may communicate better with the head office:** Consider bringing in an expatriate if communications with the head office are critically important, as they may be in a startup situation.

A company that brings in a manager from elsewhere within the company at least know it is dealing with a known quality. The manager in India will be familiar with the company and its objectives, and is likely to be committed to those objectives. Fewer communication problems with the head office are likely.

☐ **Choose someone with the right overseas experience:** If you decide to take the expatriate option, consider an individual with Asian or third-world experience.

"Most of the time," noted an observer, "We see expats being brought in from Asia. Places like Malaysia. India's less of a shock to them."

"It's an easy place to get along," said an Australian expat about India, "but I think it would be daunting for people who had no Asia experience. Especially the poverty, the extremes. The government is trying to do something about it, but with a billion people, it's tough."

Ensure the person being brought in has the right attitude: "We didn't have trouble finding someone to come here," said an Australian manager whose company brings expatriates in on one-year assignments. "But it can be quite a culture shock, and it's difficult to move around. You need to have someone with an adventurous spirit to make a go of it."

"Attitude is extremely important for an expatriate," said a local manager who has worked with several. "India is tough, but optimistic realists succeed."

If selecting an expatriate, take extra care to provide local support: The downside is that the expatriate manager will likely have little knowledge of India. Executives who have been in this position say that it depends on local alliances and advisors—legal firms, consultants, local employees, even the personal chauffeur.

"You need an Indian partner to interpret nuances and give wise counsel," said the country head of a UK firm in India. Another recommendation: "Make embassies and high commissions part of your team. They're knowledgeable and connected."

"I couldn't have done it without my driver," said one young executive of a health care firm. "He not only takes care of the usual stuff like recommending where to shop, he helped me find my apartment and negotiate for it, he helps me to understand what is really being said when I talk to shopkeepers, he helps me to understand the country."

Factor in appropriate costs for expatriates: The cost of an expatriate country head to a company can be approximately twice to four times that of a local manager.

It is usual to provide not only housing, but also home leave once or twice annually, school fees for the children, if any, and all relocation costs, in addition to normal remuneration. Some companies treat India as a hardship post, and provide an extra allowance. "We have a 'living away from home' allowance, said a manager from Australian construction company Robert Bird. "Compared with say, England, the cost of living component would be lower, but the hardship component would be higher."

Locally hired managers can work within the Indian system: Experienced local managers bring a lot of benefits: their social and professional networks, and their knowledge of the business environment. They are familiar with the regulatory and cultural terrains, understand the problems, and know where to seek solutions. They have realistic views both of opportunities and problems. They usually cost less than expatriate managers (though compensation for top managers is getting close to international levels).

"The ideal country manager," said one country head, "is someone who's done it before, preferably in the same industry. A local person knows his way around, and is well connected. The trick is to find such a person, and then look after him so he is not hired away."

Deliberately integrate local managers into the company: Companies selecting local managers may need to make extra efforts to integrate them into the company.

The flipside of the local knowledge is that the Indian manager may not completely understand the company, its culture, or what top management wants. Their perspective may be skewed by their commitment to the country operation. They may also have less credibility with top management than a known person.

Companies following this route are advised to ensure plenty of interaction at the early stages, to make both sides comfortable with shared assumptions. This may mean involving the Indian manager in decision making that is not strictly local in nature, and providing a hotline to the senior management.

Companies whose management is uncomfortable with people they do not know well, or cultures that they do not understand are particularly in need of local country managers—but may also find it more difficult to integrate them into the company.

Consider the option of a returning NRI: NRIs can be extremely effective, but companies should note that being of Indian origin is not a sufficient condition for success. The attitude and circumstances of the individual are critical.

For some companies, finding an NRI either from inside the company, or as an outside hire from the same industry promises the best of both worlds. Sometimes, it delivers: the NRI is familiar enough both with India and with the world of the foreign company to bridge the gap, while being effective locally, and quickly forming social and professional networks. Visa issues are minimal or nonexistent, easing the logistics associated with the move.

Sometimes, though, such a manager faces an uphill battle. India has changed considerably in the past five years, and a returnee may presume more familiarity than is warranted. Professional networks may be more difficult to build than before, because others can sometimes be suspicious of the returning NRI.

Some NRIs find it difficult to reconcile the logistical and regulatory problems they face with the expectations they had before returning, and with the convenience to which they have become accustomed. They may feel more free to openly criticize than foreigners do, and it is not always well received. If the NRI also assumes that foreign experience is a substitute for local competence, it can lead to multiple problems.

"Do not get an Indian who has stayed away from India for more than 10 years," advises an experienced observer. "The India they knew has changed. The landscape has changed, their contacts are [gone], and the locals will have a problem dealing with them."

On the other hand, open-minded and flexible NRIs can be extremely effective, because of the ability to bridge communication gaps, and understand both cultures.

Adjusting to India as an Expatriate

☐ **India can be a fascinating but problematic expatriate assignment:** For Western expatriates, India can be exciting and frustrating at the same time. It is relatively accessible for someone who speaks English, and those who are interested can make Indian friends, get involved in local activities, and travel to fascinating places. Indians are quite open to foreigners, especially Westerners.

"It's amazing," said a young American. "I never know what I'll see outside. A troop of camels. A street protest. Women workers in colorful saris carrying bricks on their heads. A new building coming up or something being knocked down. It's always changing. India's often annoying but it's never boring, never mundane."

He felt the same way about the work situation. "It's always changing. You never know what'll happen. It's like project work, nonstop."

A British expatriate had a different take on it. "India is an easy country to visit, but a tough one to live in. Even routine matters like doing the family shopping are very time consuming; there's no single place to get everything." In addition, there are problems like power and water shortages. His company still treats India as a hardship post.

It may be easier on singles living in big cities. "It's almost like being in college again," said one young executive. "Go into any big bar or disco at 1 a.m.—there are a lot of foreigners. It's very different from life at home.

"The best thing about India is the hospitality. People *want* you to have a wonderful experience. But you need somebody to help you navigate the culture."

"It's been a good experience," said an Australian. "Our Indian partner bent over backward to make sure I had everything I needed. Maybe even too much. I had to convince them I was safe and comfortable walking around, and could take care of myself." He took the opportunity to see more of the country than most Indians do, traveling by train all across it.

Provide resources to the expatriate and family while they adjust: Easing the transition may mean the difference between a successful assignment and a failed one.

Companies may need to make special efforts to help the expatriate (and the family, if there is one) make the transition. The price of failure is often an assignment cut short, or even a resignation. Among other suggestions: bring the assignee, together with spouse, to visit India before the move is made.

Accept that the logistics of the move are seldom easy: Especially for people from countries where most of the conveniences of living are taken for granted, moving to India brings a host of problems. Not only are the logistics an issue, they may be unaware of workarounds that most people employ, or how to manage the difficulties.

"Setting up in India is very frustrating," said an expatriate of Indian origin who had lived overseas for a decade. "People often have no sense of time. A workman says he'll come, and you wait for him—and he shows up the next day, or the next, at a completely different time. It takes effort to get things done."

"Running a household is complicated," observed another. "There's a waiting list for gas. You have to find the cable company and Internet provider, and where to shop for groceries. Some people just stay in a hotel if they're only here six-to-12 months."

"Depends on which city," says an observer. "In Mumbai, cable and the Internet [connections take] less than a day. One-stop groceries are many. The key problem [for] the expats is language. If they can get a local colleague to help, life becomes easier."

Consider using an expatriate relocation company: Relocation companies that offer transition support are now available in India. Smoothing the transition for their expatriates by getting agents specializing in expatriate relocation can be valuable.

"Use a professional firm if you can," suggested someone who moved recently. "They can not only move you but also help you get settled. You may not know how to start getting cooking gas or the Internet. They do."

Chennai-based Global Adjustments—with offices in Bangalore, Gurgaon, Pune, and Hyderabad—is one of these. Its CEO, Ranjini Manian, has quite literally written the book on adjusting to India: *Doing Business in India for Dummies* (Wiley, 2007).

Get the appropriate visas: It is important to ensure that expatriates get the right visas, and ideally, for a sufficiently long period. Extending visas in-country is a tedious and annoying process, and normally, the expatriate will have to go in person, and wait around in offices with inadequate climate control. People who overstay their visas even by a few days risk being hassled at the airport, and being barred from leaving, until they have gone through the formalities.

Expatriates should register with the police: Note that all foreigners who have visas permitting a stay of more than six months must register with the police within two weeks of arrival.

Five cities—Delhi, Mumbai, Kolkata, Chennai, and Amritsar—have a Foreigners' Regional Registration Office (FRRO). The one in Mumbai (located in South Bombay, Times of India Lane) is reportedly quite user-friendly; the Delhi office less so. In other locations, foreigners must register with the district superintendent of police.

Housing of Western standards is difficult to find: It is harder to find expat quality housing than regular housing, and it costs considerably more. (see "Checklist 4.16: The Problem of Premises" for more detail.) It may be particularly difficult in smaller cities or towns, where the quality may be an issue. In some cases, companies may need to allow for considerable work on a rental unit to bring it up to the standard required.

Real estate agents, relocation agents, or the local Indian partner can all assist in finding suitable accommodation.

A dependent's visa does not provide permission to work in India: Spouses, particularly those with careers, may have problems with moving to India.

When a married couple moves to India, the transferee's spouse typically has a dependent's visa. In cases where a spouse can find work locally, salary disparities are so great as to make the remuneration a very minor factor. However, most cities provide huge opportunities for community contributions of all kinds, for cultural activities, and opportunities at the embassy or high commission of the country. English-speaking spouses will find India easier to live in than many other Asian locations, where language barriers hamper communication.

In some cases, the spouse may choose not to move, but to visit frequently instead.

"My wife would love to live in India," said one expat, "but she's got a career to look after. She visits when she can, and I go back every six months or so."

CHECKLIST 4.14

Schooling for Expatriate Children

☐ **Expatriates may need assistance locating schools:** If the expatriate being moved has school-going children, the company should consider helping him to find and contact schools.

Although many more schools now exist, choices are still limited outside the major cities, particularly for American children who need to stay within a US curriculum. The school year may differ from that in the expatriate's home country. The company's help can be very useful in dealing with schooling issues.

☐ **Parents should start the school admission process early:** Families should allow themselves enough time to find a school. Some of the schools for expatriate children fill up very quickly, and may have long waiting lists.

More than 20 international schools exist in India, mostly in Delhi, Bangalore, Mumbai, Chennai, Kolkata, and a few other locations. Some are residential, particularly those located in "hill stations." Some are run by Christian organizations, others by various foundations and groups. Most prepare students for the International Baccalaureate exams, or for the GCSE, and the A-level examinations.

☐ **Children who plan to go to school in India will need student visas:** Student visas are issued once the students have gained admission to recognized schools. If a child has not yet been admitted, it is possible to get a provisional student visa, that is valid for six months. Student visas are valid for five years, and are single-entry visas, but additional entries can be applied for.

Only a handful of schools offer a US-style education: American parents face a particular problem, with a paucity of American-style schools. American parents need not restrict their choices only to these schools. However, it can cause problems for students attempting to switch from one system to the other at any point after eight grade.

Three schools are run by the US embassy: The American Embassy School in Delhi, The American School of Bombay, and The American International School of Chennai. Kolkata will soon have a school operating from the US consulate. In addition, two Christian schools, Kodaikanal International School and Woodstock School in Mussoorie, offer US curricula as an option.

The main difference between the US system and the others occurs in grades nine to 12. US education provides for subjects to be done in a modular fashion; for instance, students will do chemistry one year, biology another, and so on. Most other systems allow students to pick a group of subjects in the ninth grade, which may be further narrowed in the 11th grade; these are all studied simultaneously in preparation for a school-leaving examination.

Most other international schools will enroll American students, and US colleges are very aware of other curricula and accepting of school leaving results.

International schools charge high fees: In planning for expatriate costs, bear in mind that school fees can be quite substantial—and more so if a child must go to a residential school.

Most expatriate compensation packages include school fees for the children. These can be quite high.

For the 2008–2009 school year, for instance, the American School of Bombay charged fees of US$15,000–32,000, a registration fee of US$1,000, and a one-time capital levy of US$25,000 per head. (Other schools charge less.)

Residential schools, which may become essential if the parent is based in a city that has no international schools, would of course cost even more.

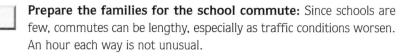

Prepare the families for the school commute: Since schools are few, commutes can be lengthy, especially as traffic conditions worsen. An hour each way is not unusual.

Many schools have buses, but this lengthens the commute still further.

In many cases, the family keeps a car and a driver for family use, separate from the official car used by the expatriate.

Often though, the parents object more than the children do: the school bus ride can be a social occasion.

CHECKLIST 4.15

Living in India–
Logistical Issues

☐ **Workarounds exist for many logistical issues:** Expatriates in India face many logistical problems. In most cases, workarounds exist, ranging from barely adequate to absolutely seamless.

"Live near a senior politician, a minister, if you can," said one expat, only half jokingly. "You'll get better power supply and better security. Or near a large company headquarters."

☐ **Power is in short supply and outages are common:** India is perennially short of power, and outages, planned and otherwise, occur fairly frequently in most cities. Most residents who can afford it have backup.

The most common is a battery of lead-acid cells (similar to car batteries), which is charged when the power is flowing, and discharged through an inverter (which converts the current back to AC) when the power goes out. They take little maintenance besides topping up the battery water from time to time, and usually provide enough power to run lights, the refrigerator, and some fans for a couple of hours. They cannot provide for most machinery: air-conditioners, washing machines, and electric heaters, which tend to require too much power.

Some households (and many modern apartment blocks) also have diesel generators. These are noisy and polluting, but provide a larger output than the battery–inverter setup. They can be used during extended outages when the batteries of the inverter systems run down.

Some people have begun experimenting with solar panels, but on the whole, they are not yet an effective backup. Solar lanterns can be useful in an emergency.

Most cities in India are unable to provide 24-hour running water: Residents have responded by setting up their own little reservoirs. These take the form of 1,000-liter (264-gallon) plastic tanks, usually placed on the roof, behind the house, or in some corner of an apartment. These store water when the supply comes in, and provide a supply sufficient for most domestic purposes. It is rare for a household that is properly equipped with tanks to run out of water.

A car and chauffeur are common amenities: Assume that it will be necessary for the expatriate to have at least one car and a chauffeur, possibly two.

Indian cities have very limited public transport. Taxis can be hired, but drivers often speak very little English, so giving complicated directions may be problematic. Even after the planned metro lines are completed, automobiles will remain essential. Most expatriates employ one or two full-time drivers, since driving in Indian cities is complicated both by chaotic traffic and unfamiliarity. In some cases, a driver does more than just drive: he can be a source of local information.

"Give your driver a mobile phone, if he does not have one," advises an executive. It is an invaluable tool for contacting the driver if he must park far from the drop-off point, which is usual, or to communicate errands, or change instructions.

Some schools provide school buses to pick up and drop off children home. For families with children in a broad age range, this may be complicated by differing school timings for elementary, middle, and senior grades and after-school activities.

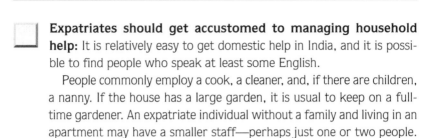

Expatriates should get accustomed to managing household help: It is relatively easy to get domestic help in India, and it is possible to find people who speak at least some English.

People commonly employ a cook, a cleaner, and, if there are children, a nanny. If the house has a large garden, it is usual to keep on a full-time gardener. An expatriate individual without a family and living in an apartment may have a smaller staff—perhaps just one or two people.

While sincere, these workers may be less sophisticated than their developed-country equivalents, and expats have reported communication issues. Nevertheless, domestic help remains extremely useful in coping with India's difficult living conditions.

Shipping in large quantities of consumables is less necessary: There is less need than before for families to ship large quantities of consumables into India. With the recent liberalization and economic growth, a broad range of products from overseas is available, at least in the larger cities.

Even a few years ago, foreigners living in India found it difficult to get the products to which they were accustomed, and the shopping experience was often tiring and confusing. Now, a much broader range of products from overseas is available, and in major cities, modern shopping malls are quite similar to their counterparts in the US or Dubai.

India still provides opportunities for customized furnishings, custom-tailored clothing, and other individually created items that would be prohibitively expensive in the West.

Urban pollution may be unavoidable: Expatriates living in large cities such as Mumbai and Delhi may need to become accustomed to pollution. Foreigners coming to India for the first time, and staying in cities may be surprised at the level of it. Mumbai and Delhi (especially in winter) are the worst. Dust and grime get into even climate-controlled homes.

Some expatriates run their air-conditioners year round, and change the filters often; others accept it as a cost of living in India.

Factor in noise: Noise is another disturbing factor for new expatriates, especially for those accustomed to large homes in quiet neighborhoods. Street noise, machinery, dogs, birds, and human voices are all ubiquitous in India; there is no cultural awareness of noise pollution. Double glazing is almost unknown. Again, keeping windows closed and using air-conditioners does reduce the ambient noise.

Even the nights are not necessarily quiet: "The noise can get on your nerves," said an Australian expat, who otherwise enjoys living in India. "They don't seem to consider other people at all at night. There's someone who was using power tools at 2 a.m. the other day. There's a car that usually comes to pick someone up at 5.30 a.m., and the driver always honks loudly to indicate he's arrived."

In some places, night watchmen are employed for security—and to indicate that they are awake and on patrol, they walk around thumping their staves, and whistling or calling out. Other night-time disturbances can include trucking traffic with airhorns, and packs of barking dogs.

Although all this takes some acclimatization, most expatriates do adjust after a few months.

The traffic can be tedious and frightening, even for passengers: Even though few expatriates drive themselves, dealing with the traffic is still uncomfortable. It is not merely a matter of delays and jams; it is the chaos on the roads. Few Indian drivers receive any kind of driving education, and most remain unaware of the concept of road rules. Traffic tends to be competitive and Darwinian.

"It's each man for himself," said an Australian expat who has traveled widely in Asia. "It's the worst I've seen anywhere. People will do anything on the road, so a driver has to look out for cars where they're supposed to be, and also where they aren't. Like coming the wrong way on a one-way street. Motorcycles will ride on the sidewalk, sometimes in the wrong direction. I was nearly hit once. When they widen the roads, they take away the sidewalks, and people spill onto the road. It's scary."

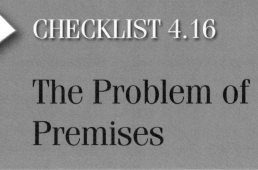

The Problem of Premises

☐ **Real estate costs in India are high and escalating:** Foreign companies need approval to purchase their own premises, and this is not usually available. (A wholly owned subsidiary, though, would be allowed to buy.) Most companies lease their offices. Unfortunately, the imbalance of demand and supply has led to an escalation in costs, particularly in Mumbai, always one of the most expensive real estate markets in the world.

"Comparisons with the US are useless," said N. Madhavan, the former Reuters correspondent, "Tokyo is a better comparison."

The costs of business premises vary hugely, depending on the location. In Gurgaon, on the outskirts of New Delhi, a company recently rented 1,000 square feet in a smart new building for about US$5,000 per month. Similar offices in the heart of New Delhi might cost six times as much. It is also normal to pay a deposit (equivalent to around six to nine months rent in Delhi) and some rent in advance (three months in Gurgaon).

The problem is not limited to business premises. The high costs of real estate relative to salaries means that companies will have to take housing costs into account in their compensation packages.

In property transactions, the problem of unaccounted payments still exists, though it is now sometimes possible to buy directly from builders with no "black money" payments.

☐ **Expect creative legal formats in renting residential housing:** India's rent control laws strongly favor the tenant, and it can take years to evict someone. To avoid the restrictions of tenancy laws, apartments are usually offered under a "lease and license agreement" for 11 months at a time. Since rent control laws apply to leases of 12 months or more, this provides something of a loophole. Nevertheless, it can take a long time to evict an unwanted tenant; GlobalPropertyGuide.com estimates, in a June 2006 article, that it takes seven or eight months.

Expect to pay a substantial deposit when renting: This is particularly true of Delhi and Mumbai, but may apply to any city. Owing to inflation and housing shortages, market rent rises very rapidly. In Mumbai, rents went up 50 percent in 2005–2006. Landlords try to manage this situation by demanding a deposit more or less equivalent to the value of the apartment they are renting—as much as two years' rent.

Rental costs may rise faster than inflation: Although the problem is worst in Mumbai, which like New York, is a major commercial center with limited land mass and stringent rent controls, prices have shot up in every major city—Delhi, Bangalore, and Chennai—as well as some of the smaller cities, such as Pune.

Consider renting housing for employees on company lease: In Mumbai particularly, landlords are often reluctant to rent to individuals, preferring companies as tenants. One young executive found that house hunting as an individual, he was shown extremely inferior apartments. Eventually, when his company agreed to lease a place for him—and pay the deposit—he was able to find a tiny one-bedroom place. Then he discovered it was infested with bedbugs...

Be sanguine about pests and other problems: Despite the high rents, the quality of the accommodations tends to be inferior to what would be available in other high-rent cities internationally. Maintenance may be poor, and problems with water and electricity shortages may occur. One ongoing problem is insect infestation—cockroaches are found even in the best buildings. Part of the issue is that if the apartments are individually owned—and most are—no common approach to pest control is possible. This means that the pests move around the buildings, but are never completely eradicated.

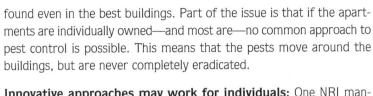 **Innovative approaches may work for individuals:** One NRI manager relocating to Bangalore found an apartment in Bangalore owned by another NRI, and signed the contract in New Jersey. This will theoretically permit recourse to the New Jersey court, should the contract be broken—doubtless a comfort to the landlord.

Property transactions may require unaccounted payments: The real estate sector has become less crooked and more transparent, but black money and bribery still exist.

Gains on real estate sales are taxable, and since most real estate is sold only after being held for long periods, these taxes can be substantial. As a result, a "black money" system has developed: sellers demand (or buyers insist on) unaccounted cash payments. The stated value of the property is likely to be only 50–60 percent of the actual price.

There have been some breakthroughs. A few reputable builders offer new apartments for "all white" or "100 percent check" payments, that is, there is no "black money" component. However, this is still the exception and not the rule.

Companies may offer employee housing loans: Although few foreign companies buy real estate, they may offer loans to their employees to buy housing. Employee loans to buy housing is a significant perquisite. In an arm's-length transaction, the issue of "black money" is dealt with by the borrower.

Companies have a few options to reduce their costs, beyond the usual economies and cost controls. Some do acquire properties so that they can avoid escalating rents. In this situation, the company will benefit from rising property values. However, this can tie up a significant amount of capital, and it may reduce the flexibility to move as needed.

☐ **Moving offices out of the city center may lower costs:** Some companies choose to move to the outskirts of cities, or move some part of the operations there.

Rents in Gurgaon, for instance, are perhaps one-sixth of the rents at the center of New Delhi. Navi Mumbai is much cheaper than Bandra-Kurla or Nariman Point in Mumbai. The downside is the travel time required if visits to government offices or centrally located clients are necessary. One option that some companies use is to maintain a small city office, so that someone who needs to go into town has a base to work at for the remainder of the day.

☐ **Some companies locate in smaller towns:** This rent-reducing tactic can work for companies that do not require highly skilled staffing. So far, Tier III cities are substantially less expensive than the metros.

However, the availability of suitable employees becomes an issue, and getting senior managers to relocate there may be even harder—especially if schooling for their children is problematic.

Operating Against the Odds

Companies should institute business continuity plans: Operations in India face a series of challenges from power outages, strikes, political unrest, to natural problems such as floods. Most of these problems can be managed through appropriate planning and anticipation.

Companies need business continuity plans in case one site needs to close for hours or days. Those that have multiple locations often keep a little excess capacity at each location so that work can be moved smoothly from one site to another.

"Business continuity plans are crucial in a situation of localized unrest," said a BPO manager. "We had a bomb blast in Hyderabad. Raj Thackeray shut down Mumbai. This is really critical for outsourced operations. You need multiple sites. We're doing a major project for a client, and it involves a lot of resources—450 people, a million drawings. What if something goes wrong? We have a center in NOIDA and Hyderabad; each can take over from the other."

IBM announced in January 2008 that it was launching a 2,500-seat "work recovery center" in Navi Mumbai (near Mumbai), "to help clients minimize the effects of disruptions to existing workplace."

Consider local conditions when planning premises: In some locations, flooding can occur during the monsoon season. If a building has been occupied during the dry season, this can come as a surprise— particularly if a very wet year follows several dry ones.

Leaks can also be an issue, and are difficult to see in the dry season. If in doubt, select interior designs for the offices that have fairly readily accessible walls and ceilings. That way, the leaks can be seen and mended—or at least, will not cause much damage.

In some areas, fire is a hazard: Generally, this is less true than it is in some Western countries that use wood-frame construction, since most buildings in India are constructed of concrete, and are less inflammable. However, as interior decoration grows more elaborate, the fuel load also rises, and fires occasionally occur. Prewar buildings in Mumbai and elsewhere that use wooden rafters can be a major risk, especially since fire codes are often inadequate or violated.

Multiunit industrial *galas* (a type of warehousing) and multiunit industrial estates may also be problematic if another tenant is working with explosive materials; not all factories take safety precautions.

Power supply will inevitably need to be backed up: Depending on the quantity and reliability of your company's power needs, arrange for appropriate backup power. Most big cities have outages fairly frequently—sometimes daily. When the demand for power exceeds supply, the utilities respond with load shedding: outages for between one and four hours per day. Some rural areas lose power for nine or 10 hours.

In Mumbai, some shopping malls face regular cuts, which is very bad for business because the air-conditioning and lighting—both major draws for customers—are immediately affected. (Companies seeking retail space may want to check on this before signing leases.)

Consider generators if your power needs are heavy: Diesel-powered generators can be used as backup power for everything, from a household to a manufacturing plant. However, the two problems with generators are noise and emissions. They cannot be used in an enclosed space. It is also important to ensure a regular supply of fuel.

Batteries and inverters work for moderate power requirements: For most purposes, and in areas where individual outages are not lengthy, consider a system of rechargeable batteries and inverters. Batteries typically can supply enough power for a couple of hours of light use. They cannot support air-conditioners, heaters, or heavy machinery. They must be safely sequestered and disposed of, because both lead and the acid used are somewhat toxic.

Computers can be fitted with an uninterrupted power supply. An uninterrupted power supply has limited power, but can prevent data loss. Laptops, of course, come with their own batteries.

India has been substantially reforming its tax levels: India's process of liberalization has also included some major tax reforms. Most tax reform has benefited companies. Indirect taxes form about half of the country's funding, and reform has been most useful in this area. The tax structure remains important to most companies doing business in India. (See "Tax Structure.")

Watch for the budget and the import–export policy: Both the budget and the import–export policy are announced in February for the following fiscal year (starting April 1). They make important changes to taxes and duties, and indicate the direction in which the government is likely to take legislation.

The tax authorities have been increasingly active in assessing tax: In recent years, the tax authorities have become increasingly active in their efforts to bring foreign companies into the tax net. Two areas of special focus have been "business connection" and "transfer pricing." Companies should seek expert advice on this matter.

The 2008 budget, for instance, specified that when Indian companies employ nonresidents to provide services overseas (for instance, marketing services), payments to that nonresident entities would be subject to Indian withholding taxes. This was made retroactive to April 1, 1976, and overturned an important Supreme Court decision.

Does India have a double-taxation treaty with your country? Many countries—some 79 as of September 2008—have double-taxation avoidance treaties with India; check whether yours is one of them. (There is a government website with this information.) Australia, the UK, the US, China, and Singapore are among those with the arrangements.

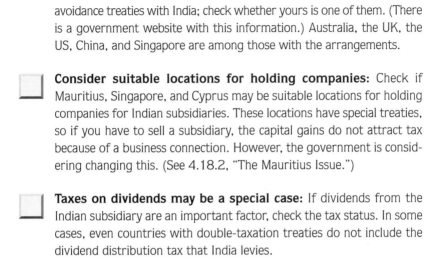 **Consider suitable locations for holding companies:** Check if Mauritius, Singapore, and Cyprus may be suitable locations for holding companies for Indian subsidiaries. These locations have special treaties, so if you have to sell a subsidiary, the capital gains do not attract tax because of a business connection. However, the government is considering changing this. (See 4.18.2, "The Mauritius Issue.")

Taxes on dividends may be a special case: If dividends from the Indian subsidiary are an important factor, check the tax status. In some cases, even countries with double-taxation treaties do not include the dividend distribution tax that India levies.

4.18.1 Tax Structure

Indirect taxes

A range of indirect taxes is levied by cities, states, and the central government. All taxes are subject to an education cess (special levy) of 2 percent of the amount of the tax.

Central government taxes

Customs duties are levied on most imports; in some cases, a further "anti-dumping duty" is levied.

Excise duty is imposed at manufacture on the price at the initial sale from the producer to the first buyer, and is payable upon the removal of goods from the factory. For most products, the rate is about 16 percent, although some products may incur an additional 2 percent of special excise duty. A few products are liable for excise duties of 30–32 percent—these are central government levies.

The equivalent of excise for services, the service tax, is 10 percent of the value of the services provided. (It is also subject to the education cess.) Services paid for in foreign exchange are not subject to service tax.

State-level taxes

Most states used to levy a sales tax, but the different levels of taxation encouraged interstate smuggling and tax evasion. From 2005, the government sought to introduce a value-added tax (VAT) as a substitute. Most Indian states now use VAT instead of sales tax; for most products, the rate is about 12.5 percent (lower for mass consumption goods and industrial inputs, and zero for essentials—mainly food). The central government, however, imposes a sales tax of 2 percent on interstate sales.

States also levy a stamp duty on transfer of assets. Some also tax luxuries, and income from plantations.

Local taxes

Some cities levy *octroi*, a city tax on the entry of goods. There may also be taxes on properties and buildings, which are also imposed by the local authorities.

Direct taxes

Indian companies pay a basic tax rate of 35 percent, with a 2.5 percent surcharge and the education cess, totaling 38.25 percent, on their global income. Foreign companies pay taxes of 40 percent on their Indian income (43.85 percent with surcharge and education cess).

The government offers tax incentives to encourage companies into socially beneficial activities; with good tax planning, the rate can be substantially reduced. However, a minimum alternate tax (10.2 percent) applies even to companies whose taxable income would otherwise be lower (7.5 percent + 2.5 percent + education cess).

Tax incentives take the form of tax holidays, accelerated depreciation, or tax breaks on certain activities. The main corporate incentives are for: new investment in infrastructure; power distribution; operations in SEZs; research and development; housing construction; foodgrain handling; food processing; investments in certain areas that need economic assistance; production and refining of mineral oil.

Corporations with net assets exceeding Rs1.5 million also pay a wealth tax of 1 percent.

Long-term capital gains (more than three years for most assets; more than one year for securities listed on a recognized stock exchange, and for mutual funds) are taxed at 20 percent (or 10 percent without indexation). The calculated capital gain is adjusted for inflation, using index numbers published by the government. Short-term capital gains are treated as ordinary income.

However, effective from October 2004, long-term capital gains from equity (or funds with at least 50 percent equity investments) are not taxable, and short-term gains are taxed at 10 percent.

Dividends are taxed at 12.5 percent, but are not taxed as income for the recipient.

Withholding tax

The government requires the following taxes to be withheld on payments to nonresident companies or individuals:

◆ on royalties and technical service fees: 10 percent

◆ on interest payments: 10 percent

◆ on dividends: 0 percent (since it is taxed at the time of distribution)

◆ on all other services: 30 percent of income for individuals, 40 percent for companies.

However, India has double-taxation avoidance agreements with several countries, and as such, the rates may be decided by the agreement.

Securities transaction tax

Transactions in securities listed on a recognized stock exchange attract taxes of between 0.017 percent and 0.25 percent. With the rise in the values of Indian stocks, the government is reportedly considering raising these rates.

4.18.2 The Mauritius Issue

Nearly half of the foreign direct investment in India is reportedly routed through Mauritius, a country with which India has a double-taxation avoidance treaty. Mauritius has no capital gains taxes, so companies legally incorporated there pay no taxes on capital gains on their Indian investments. The Indian government is concerned about the loss in revenues, and also fears that it may be a conduit for illegal transfers of funds.

India and Mauritius signed an avoidance of double-taxation agreement in 1983. In fiscal 1992–1993, Mauritius made capital gains non-taxable for its residents—which included companies legally incorporated in Mauritius. This made it attractive for companies to route their investments in India through that country.

Financial institutions, in particular, found that by setting up a legal entity in Mauritius, they could save the capital gains taxes of between 10 percent and 40 percent on their profits from India. It is estimated that between 2002 and mid-2007, about US$20 billion of India's incoming investment came through Mauritius—from a total of US$51 billion in that period.

The setting up and management of "global business companies" is fairly simple: management companies in Mauritius provide all the necessary documentation, and will set up and manage a company. They are generally not permitted to do business within Mauritius, or invest in its stockmarket; they must keep their bank accounts in foreign currencies. They pay a small tax on profits in Mauritius.

This makes it attractive to several types of businesses. However, it has allegedly also been used by Indian companies to evade taxes, send the money overseas, and bring it back into India as an apparent "investment."

The Indian government has made several attempts to change the terms of the treaty, making taxation based on the source of the profit, rather than on the residence of the company.

For Mauritius, though, its financial services industry is extremely important, and it strongly resists any efforts to change this. It is probable that if the treaty were change, a substantial percentage of the global business companies would depart, with a depressing effect on its economy.

India's finance ministry has been talking with the relevant authorities in Port Louis, and had hoped to institute changes in 2008. With the volatility in world financial markets, and Mauritian opposition, it looks like the issue will be pushed back for a year or two.

CHECKLIST 4.19

Overview of India's Financial System

☐ **The BSE and the NSE are India's main stock exchanges:** Although India has some regional stock exchanges, the main ones are the Bombay Stock Exchange (BSE) and the National Stock Exchange (NSE). Many major companies are listed on both stock exchanges.

The BSE is the oldest stock exchange in India; it was founded in 1875. Based in Mumbai, it changed its structure from an association of persons to a corporate entity in 2005. It has strategic partnerships with the Deutsche Borse, and the Singapore Exchange. According to its website, it had US$1.79 trillion in market capitalization as of December 31, 2007. More than 4,700 companies are listed on the BSE, perhaps the largest number on any bourse in the world.

The NSE was founded in 1993, and started operations as a wholesale debt market in June 1994. It is also based in Mumbai. It started trading equities in November that year, and derivatives in June 2000. As of January 7, 2008, it had a market capitalization of about US$1.72 trillion.

☐ **The key indices are the BSE Sensex and the NSE's Nifty:** The Sensex (Sensitive Index) is a basket of 30 key stocks, and is tracked internationally. The index is value weighted, based on market capitalization of the stocks.

The NSE's Nifty—or the Standard & Poor's CRISIL NSE Index 50, or S&P CNX Nifty—is an index of 50 major stocks in 21 sectors, and is considered a good proxy for the market. It is also weighted by market capitalization.

SEBI is the regulatory body: The regulatory body for the stock exchanges is the Securities and Exchange Board of India (SEBI). It is intended to protect the interests of investors, and to regulate the securities market.

Both the BSE and the NSE trade debt as well as equity: The NSE started trading debt in its wholesale debt market even before it started trading stocks. Government debt completely dominates the Indian debt market. The debt instruments of public sector companies are technically corporate debt, but most investors treat them as sovereign debt.

State-owned banks dominate the banking sector: The government-owned State Bank of India is the single largest bank in India. State-owned banks own more than 70 percent of the assets of the sector, according to the February 2008 *Economic Survey*. This is a legacy of the time when all major private sector banks—except the foreign-owned ones—were nationalized in 1969, and in 1980. Nationalized banks have a widespread branch network, reaching right into small towns.

Nearly 30 foreign banks—including such majors as Citibank and Bank of America—operate in India, mostly in large cities. In addition, there are a few non-nationalized Indian banks, as well as some small rural banks.

Nonbank financial institutions also exist: Nonbank financial institutions—mostly in the public sector—play a role in India's financial system. Their main role is to provide long-term finance, such as the Export-Import Bank, which renders trade finance.

The RBI regulates banks and makes monetary policy: The Reserve Bank of India is the Central bank of the government. Just like the US

Federal Reserve, or the UK's Bank of England, it authorizes the expansion of banks' branch networks, typically through an annual approval for the number of branches, and regulates credit.

Reforms are under way: The banking sector is in the midst of a reform. The first phase has required Indian banks to conform to Basel II norms. The second phase will allow increased foreign ownership, and will aim toward a consolidation in the sector, so that instead of the hundreds of banks that exist currently, six or seven major banks will dominate the market.

Corporates prefer private placements for debt: Corporate debt reportedly accounted for less than 2 percent of total issued debt as of 2007. Although companies do issue debt, most debts are placed privately, rather than through public issues. Private placements have several advantages: they have lower issue costs; require less disclosure and no listing, therefore have no listing requirements; and can be tailored to the mutual preferences of the company and the lender.

The secondary market for debt is very thin: India's debt markets are underdeveloped compared to the equity markets. In the main, there is little secondary trading. Purchasers of corporate debt usually hold it to expiry. Efforts are now under way to improve the trading activity.

Corporate five-year debt cost about 9–11 percent per annum in 2007: Triple-A rated five-year bonds were issued at between 9 percent and 11 percent in 2007, up from 8.5–9.5 percent the previous year, and 7.3–8.5 percent in fiscal 2005. At December-end 2007, corporate bonds had a market capitalization of Rs680 billion (about US$17.4 billion).

Many companies consider raising debt overseas: Large Indian companies, as well as others that have access to foreign markets, sometimes prefer raising money overseas. The typical instruments are bonds. Foreign currency convertible bonds are growing in popularity; they provide for a conversion at a premium to the current market price of the stock.

Equity can be issued to the public or privately placed: Companies in India have the option of issuing stocks on local exchanges, or tapping international markets through American depository receipts or global depository receipts. Qualified institutional placements—private placements with domestic institutional buyers—offer a relatively inexpensive way of raising funds.

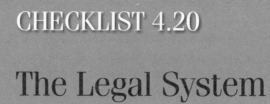

CHECKLIST 4.20

The Legal System

India's legal system is based on British jurisprudence: In the 60 years since independence in 1947, India's jurisprudence has diverged somewhat, but still follows the same essential tenets. Modeled on the British legal system, India's judiciary is broadly considered fair and impartial (although there has been mention of corruption at lower levels, and the *Global Integrity* report of 2007 gives India a poor score for judicial accountability). The judiciary is quite independent. English is the language of law and of the courts.

The main complaint is usually about delays: The main issue with India's legal system, from a business viewpoint, is the time required. Cases typically drag on for months or years. In certain areas, enforcement may be difficult. The World Bank 2008 report ranked India 177th of 178 countries in enforcing contracts, with an average of 1,420 days required.

One huge problem area is debt recovery from individuals, an issue that has given rise to extreme and extralegal tactics by collection agencies.

Consider choosing other jurisdictions when writing contracts: Foreign companies can specify in their contracts that disputes will be subject to the laws of another country. Referred to as "proper law of contract", Indian courts have generally upheld such terms even when the parties have chosen laws that are not Indian. Contracts can also specify international arbitration. These options are probably useful for foreign companies.

What does a foreign company do if the contract specifies foreign law, and it wins a judgment against an Indian company? It depends on whether the country whose laws were used has a reciprocal arrangement with India on the subject. (The UK, Singapore, the UAE, Malaysia, and Hong Kong are among the reciprocating territories; the US is not.)

If it does, the judgment can be executed as though it was an Indian judgment. If not, the foreign company can file a suit in India to have it enforced, which is of course another legal procedure.

Implementation and enforcement of the law is another issue: Although India's laws are generally considered reasonable and equitable, enforcement depends on mechanisms that may not be as strong as the legal system. According to George W. Russell, the India correspondent for *Asialaw*, the international legal monthly based in Hong Kong: "The implementation (or no implementation) of laws—and their supporting rules and regulations—is often more significant than the laws themselves."

The *2007 Global Integrity* report rates India as "moderate" on rule of law, but "weak" on law enforcement.

Foreign companies may have concerns about specific areas: The *Competition Act 2007* replaces the former *Monopolies and Restrictive Trade Practices Act*. Any company with sales of more than Rs30 billion or assets of more than Rs10 billion requires approval from the Competition Commission of India (CCI) for any merger or acquisition. The CCI has 210 days (with a possible 60-day extension) to respond. It also requires Indian companies to seek permission for mergers and acquisitions overseas. This act thus concerns any foreign company trying to acquire an Indian company.

The act also defines predatory pricing as selling below cost. Observers suggest that this could lead to lengthy disputes as to how "cost" is to be calculated.

Russell mentions some of the other concerns of foreign companies:

♦ ... anything from tax to merger rules, repatriation of profits, and current and future laws covering investment in major sectors such as retailing.

♦ The *Finance Act 2007*—effects on fringe benefits and venture capital investment—and the *Companies Act 2007* are also key changes.

♦ It remains to be seen whether the tax relationship with Mauritius will change.

♦ *SEZs Act 2005* is still controversial

♦ "Introduction of Phase 1 clinical trials will have a major impact on pharmaceutical industry, while the Novartis challenge to the amended *Patents Act 1970* was a landmark case."

(*The Finance Act* made certain fringe benefits taxable to companies. Changes are expected to the *Companies Act*, which may be amended to include tougher disclosure norms, and possibly also to make mergers and acquisitions easier. The use of Mauritius as a tax haven is under pressure. SEZs remain a concern. Novartis lost its case to retain a patent on "Glivec" in the Chennai High Court.)

♦ **India permits retroactive changes to the law:** In 1975, and again in 1997, India's Supreme Court has affirmed that retrospective changes to the law are legal. However, the changes can be challenged if they are discriminatory. Most recently, such changes were made to the tax law in the context of the case against Vodafone (see 3.10.1, The Vodafone Story).

Intellectual Property Protection

☐ **India conforms to international protocols:** India has changed its intellectual property rights (IPR) protection laws to conform with international norms.

India became more determined to protect IPR as its global position in the software industry strengthened. It is a member of the Paris Convention, protecting patents, trademarks, and designs; and of the Berne Convention, covering literary and artistic work. India belongs to the World Trade Organization, and is therefore bound by *TRIPS (Agreement on Trade Related Aspects of Intellectual Property)*.

In recent years—starting in 1995—India has updated its laws on copyrights, patents, trademarks, designs, and geographical indications. The government of India's department of industrial policy and promotion is responsible for matters pertaining to IPR through the office of the Controller General of Patents, Designs, and Trademarks.

India permits the registration of service marks (excluded earlier) but, under the *Foreign Exchange Management Act*, allows foreign companies to register trademarks only if they are doing business in India, at the very least by licensing technology. However, in 2008, it decided to accede to the Madrid protocol concerning international registration of trademarks, and it would amend the India's *Trademarks Act 1999* to do so.

IPR protection in India is an issue of enforcement: Despite the favorable changes, some issues remain:

◆ piracy of entertainment content—video and music. Movies are often available on DVDs ahead of their release in cinemas

◆ cable television piracy

◆ counterfeiting of popular goods

◆ trademarks that strongly resemble well-known marks, so that the consumer might be deceived.

Companies may have to act to protect intellectual properties: Low awareness of the issue of counterfeiting at the street level means that even though the intent is good, implementation of the protection really relies on companies protecting their intellectual properties. On a recent trip, fake Gucci and Armani wallets were displayed at a state government outlet at the airport, and fake brand-name goods such as Coach bags were openly available in Janpath in New Delhi.

Pharmaceutical companies may have special concerns: An area that remains contentious is the common one of pharmaceuticals, particularly companies seeking to extend patents on existing drugs. Novartis had attempted to do so with the leukemia drug Glivec, available in generic form from Indian manufacturers, but lost the case in the Chennai High Court.

Sometimes judicial action can help: When one US ultrasound imaging company started up in India, it found a cyber squatter using its name on a fraudulent website. It took the cyber squatter to court and won. India's trademark laws that prohibit "passing off"—the use of trademarks similar enough to an existing one to be confusing—has been a useful tool against the registration of domain names similar to major brands names. Maruti-Suzuki won a similar case in 2000, as did Yahoo in 1999.

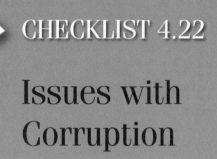

India has a problem with corruption: In a 2007 survey of corruption perceptions by Transparency International (TI), India ranked 72nd (on par with China and Mexico) out of 180 countries. India's rank was down from 70th in 2006.

For comparison: Denmark, Finland, and New Zealand tied for the first place, followed by Sweden and Singapore. The UK ranked 12th and the US 20th. On the other hand, Pakistan's rank was 138, and Indonesia's, 143, as was Russia's. Myanmar tied for last place with Somalia.

The TI survey links corruption with poverty. Others have theorized that cultural and political factors are also extremely important. Whatever the genesis of the problem, what it will mean for anyone trying to do business in India is that it is an issue that must be worked around. The *Right to Information Act* (see "The *Right to Information Act 2005*") may help to reduce corruption, but for the present it continues to exist.

The Global Integrity organization rated integrity in India in 2007 as moderate (scoring 75 on a 100-point scale), highlighting implementation of the law as a particular area of weakness. It also mentions poor judicial accountability, nepotism in the civil service, and harassment of investigative journalists as weak points.

"Corruption is endemic," one business executive said. "If any company says they never pay bribes, they're lying. They've probably outsourced it."

The flipside is corporate willingness to pay bribes: In 2006, TI also made a survey of corporate propensity to bribe overseas, and found a high correlation between the corruption environment of companies' home countries, and their willingness to pay bribes when doing business abroad. Indian companies were among the most willing, particularly in other low-income countries and Africa.

However, TI pointed out that they were not alone, and companies from all major countries have been perceived as paying bribes. According to its website, "The BPI looks at the propensity of companies from 30 leading exporting countries to bribe abroad. Companies from the wealthiest countries generally rank in the top half of the index, but still routinely pay bribes, particularly in developing economies. Companies from emerging export powers India, China, and Russia rank among the worst."

Corporate Switzerland topped these rankings; US companies ranked ninth; Italy's were 20th; and India's 30th.

Large firms in India reportedly find it relatively easy to escape making the minor payments—but small companies may find the "dog's bite" inescapable, and they do not have the power to refuse. According to TI, in its *Bribe Payers Survey*, small companies (less than 100 employees) reported more corruption than large ones (more than 500 employees).

Foreign firms try to stay away from bribery, but do not always succeed: TI's *Bribe Payers Survey* (2006) notes that on a 10-point scale, no country's companies did better than 7.8 (Switzerland's score) or worse than 4.62 (India's). British companies scored 7.39, and US companies 7.22. Bribery was the worst in low-income countries. Foreign companies reported seeing less corruption than did the local companies.

This would indicate that while companies may pay bribes with greater or less reluctance, many will do so if it becomes a requirement for business success. US companies usually try to comply with the *Prohibition of Corrupt Practices Act.* Companies from elsewhere also prefer to achieve their objective in a straightforward manner.

"Or so they say," said a cynical observer. "Their Indian associates take care of it, and they turn a blind eye."

Careful preparation and anticipating problems may allow companies to minimize payoffs. Many bribes are given by those seeking shortcuts. Business people report corruption of varying degrees of seriousness; at the lower end, it is more like gratuities than payments for favors.

Workers request tips (*baksheesh*) for services performed: This is often called "tea money," and is usually considered acceptable, in part because amounts are small, and the requests are not very different than gratuities that are customary in many other countries, where tipping is the norm. Unfortunately, this kind of corruption can sometimes progress to refusal to perform the service without a tip, and then, depending on how crucial it is, the size of the tip may become a negotiating point.

Gifts may be used to influence decisions: In India, it is customary to send gifts to business associates at festive times, which can include anyone influential (including government officials). Often, they take the form of foodstuffs and perishables—typically sweets or dried fruit and nuts at festivals such as Diwali—and are part of the fabric of relationship building.

However, sometimes gifts can become quite substantial, and then, there may be a hint of reciprocal obligations.

According to one executive who has worked in several different companies, "At one company I worked for, we'd get a wishlist for Diwali gifts from the functionaries we dealt with. And if we tried to substitute something else, we'd get a phone call..." Someone else was asked to import medicines for a government employee's sick mother—but without payment.

"It's a matter of what you accept," said another. "Our company never responds to these requests."

Businesspeople report petty corruption in many areas. "Anywhere where there is repetitive contact with an organization at a junior governmental level," said one analyst, and gave examples: any registration required; minor licensing activity; factory inspections of any sort.

"Large firms can avoid these payments," said the manager of a small firm, "But they want to ensure a good relationship, and save management time on trivia."

Major corruption is reported to occur: According to observers, areas where they are likely to face demands include: getting licenses in those areas where they are still required; large purchase contracts, especially from the government; matters relating to land and land use; any area requiring special permissions. Unscrupulous companies may have a competitive edge.

Contacts and exchanges of favors can help: "It is still important to build relationships, and knowing the right people and having a good reputation certainly helps," said one manager.

Another disagreed. "This is changing," an executive said, rather bitterly. "Most of the time, it's straight cash."

Not all corruption is in the official sector: While official corruption gets the most attention, it also occurs in the private sector. "You may want to think about corruption in a nongovernment context... it's there between two private parties too," said a manager. According to other reports, these kinds of payoffs may be made in such areas as procurement or even banking. Transactions relating to real estate are particularly vulnerable.

4.22.1 Is Corruption Getting Better or Worse?

Opinion is divided over whether corruption is getting better or worse.

"It's getting better," one executive argued. "There are fewer approvals required, so fewer opportunities."

"The number of payments is smaller, but the level of payments has gone up," said an entrepreneur.

"It's about the same," said a manager. "Of course it exists, but you can manage without it."

"I think it's improving," said an expatriate manager. "The government is serious about controlling it."

"It's better," said an observer. "The *Right To Information (RTI) Act* has really helped transparency."

Another businessman agreed. "The *RTI* has been a huge success and a very effective tool. There's more transparency and access to bureaucrats has improved."

"Corruption has become worse," said a small business owner. "With liberalization, there are fewer opportunities for corruption, so everyone is loading onto the points that do exist—or making up problems where there isn't any. India has moved beyond the corruption regime where you paid to facilitate the clearances you needed, to an extortion regime where problems are created expressly to extort money. Big companies are not very vulnerable, especially foreign companies because all this is taken care of by their Indian partners. Small and medium companies may have problems."

Another executive referred to bribes as a "nonharassment fee."

"It's there, but it's mainly grease money," said a Bangalore executive. "At least in Bangalore. Delhi is notorious."

Corruption inside the government has reportedly been increasing. One senior bureaucrat who wanted an assignment in a different city for personal reasons was told it would cost Rs15 lakhs (about US$37,500).

"It's worse," said another executive. "Government salaries have not kept pace with the private sector, but aspirations have risen the same way. And since there are few approvals required, the burden on the existing choke points is much more."

"It's the worst I've ever seen," said a senior manager who has worked both in India and internationally." Liberalization has made it worse, he suggests. Earlier, most controls were at the center. Now all the power is with the states, and everything has to be "paid" for. This doesn't necessarily mean it's inefficient; if it's paid for, it gets done.

4.22.2 The *Right to Information Act 2005*

This act, similar to the *Freedom of Information Act* in the US, allows any citizen to demand information from the government or governmental entities, and also to access information that the government can access from private entities. It covers all of India except for the state of Jammu and Kashmir, and is specifically intended to increase transparency for better functioning of India's democracy, and to reduce corruption.

Overseeing the process is the Central Information Commission, headed by a commissioner who is chosen by the prime minister, a selected minister of the ruling party, and the leader of the opposition. Every effort has been made to ensure the independence of this individual, who is considered to be on a par with the election commissioner.

The act requires the central government, and the state governments, to institute a public information officer (PIO), who would respond to these requests for information. He or she would give the information to the requester within a period of 30 days for most matters; 48 hours if it involves the life and liberty of a person; and a maximum of 40 days if it involves a third party who may need to make a representation about the information.

If a request is not answered, the PIO must inform the person of the outcome; whom to appeal to; and by when such an appeal must be made.

APPENDICES

Acronyms You May Encounter

ASSOCHAM	The Associated Chambers of Commerce and Industry of India
APMC	Agricultural Produce Marketing Committee
BOT	build–operate–transfer—a process by which a company builds something (usually an IT system or project), starts the operation, and then transfer ownership to the commissioning organization
BSE	Bombay Stock Exchange (based in Mumbai)
CCI	Competition Commission of India (a body dealing with mergers and acquisitions; or Cricket Club of India
CII	Confederation of Indian Industry
CPI	Consumer Price Index; or Communist Party of India
CPI-UNME	Consumer Price Index for Urban Non-Manual Employees
DEA	Department of Economic Affairs (in the Ministry of Finance)
ECB	external commercial borrowing (that is, foreign loans or debt)
EOU	export-oriented units (often refer to companies that export 100 percent of their Indian products)
FBT	fringe benefits tax

FDI	foreign direct investment
FEMA	*Foreign Exchange Management Act.* A significant landmark in the process of liberalization, the *Foreign Exchange Management Act 1999* (FEMA) replaced the highly restrictive *Foreign Exchange Regulation Act 1973.* FEMA is administered by the RBI, and covers issues of foreign exchange flows and foreign investment.
FICCI (usually pronounced "feeky")	Federation of Indian Chambers of Commerce and Industry
FIPB	Foreign Investment Promotion Board
FMCG	fast-moving consumer goods. Distinguishes these consumable products from consumer goods bought less often, such as clothing.
FRRO	Foreigner's Regional Registration Office
GDP	gross domestic product
GMT	Greenwich Mean Time
GNP	gross national product
ISV	independent software vendor—a company that makes and sells customized software
IPR	intellectual property rights
IRS	*Indian Readership Survey*
MoF	Ministry of Finance
MLA	member of the legislative assembly
MMTC	Minerals and Metals Trading Corporation (a government-owned company)

MP	member of parliament; or the state of Madhya Pradesh
NASSCOM	National Association of Software and Services Companies
NSE	National Stock Exchange
NCR	National Capital Region. The greater Delhi area, including New Delhi, Old Delhi, Gurgaon, and NOIDA
NNP	net national product (GNP less depreciation)
NOIDA	New Okhla Industrial Development Authority; a part of the NCR that lies in the state of Uttar Pradesh
NRI	nonresident Indian
NRS	*National Readership Survey* (an annual media survey)
OCI	overseas citizen of India
PIO	person of Indian origin—a status used before the OCI was introduced to give certain rights to ethnic Indians overseas. Also, public information officer—person who responds to requests under the *Right to Information Act*
PSUs	public sector units (that is, state-owned companies)
PVC	polyvinyl chloride—an inexpensive flexible plastic
QIP	qualified institutional placements (private placements of equity to qualified institutional buyers)
RBI	Reserve Bank of India
RTI	*Right to Information Act 2005.* An act giving Indian citizens the right to demand certain information from the government
SEBI	Securities and Exchange Board of India
SEM	search engine marketing. Using Internet search engines as a way to publicize a product or service

SEO   search engine optimization-a process to make websites more easily noticed by search engines. Professionals who do this, search engine optimizers, may also be called SEOs.

SEZ   special economic zones

SME   small and medium enterprises (that is, small and medium-sized companies)

SPC   Sports Performance Center—Adidas' name for its own-product store

STC   state trading corporation (a government-owned company)

STP   software technology park (also STPI, software technology parks of India)

TDS   tax deduction at source

TRIPS *Agreement on Trade Related Aspects of Intellectual Property*

UP   Uttar Pradesh (name of a state)

UPS: uninterrupted power supply—backup power, usually for computers

VRS   Voluntary Retirement Scheme—a way of reducing headcount, subject to government regulations

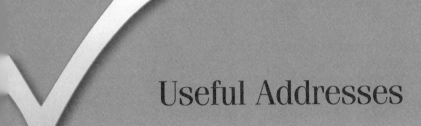

Useful Addresses

US embassy

US Embassy, New Delhi
Shantipath, Chanakyapuri
New Delhi 110021
Tel: 011-2419-8000
Fax: 011-24198407
Email: nivnd@state.gov
Homepage address: http://newdelhi.usembassy.gov/

American Consulate General, Chennai
No. 220 Anna Salai
Chennai 600006
Tel: 044-2857-4242
Fax: 044-2811-2027
Email: chennainiv@state.gov
Homepage address: http://chennai.usconsulate.gov

American Consulate General, Mumbai
Lincoln House, 78 Bhulabhai Desai Road
Mumbai 400026
Tel: 022-2363-3611–18
Fax: 022-2363-0350
Email: mumbainiv@state.gov
Homepage address: http://mumbai.usconsulate.gov

American Consulate General, Kolkata
5/1 Ho Chi Minh Sarani
Kolkata 700071
Tel: 033-3984-2400
Fax: 033-2282-2335
Email: ConsularKolkata@state.gov
Homepage address: http://kolkata.usconsulate.gov

UK embassy

Homepage address: www.ukinindia.com

British High Commission
Shantipath, Chanakyapuri
New Delhi 110021
Tel: 011-2687-2161
Fax: 011-2687-0065
After-office hours: 011-2687-2161
Email: postmaster.nedel@fco.gov.uk

British Deputy High Commission
1A Ho Chi Minh Sarani
Kolkata 700071
Office hours: 0830–1600 hrs
Tel: 033-2288-5172; 2288-5173–76
Fax: 033-2288-3435
After-office hours: 033-2288-6536
After-office hours emergency helpline: 98-3107-5663
Email: Kolkata@fco.gov.uk

British Deputy High Commission
Maker Chambers IV, Second Floor
222 Jamnalal Bajaj Road, Nariman Point
Mumbai 400021

Tel: 022-6650-2222
Fax: 022-6650-2324
Emergency duty officer: 98-2000-0343
Email: postmaster.bomba@fco.gov.uk

British Deputy High Commission
20 Anderson Road
Chennai 600006
Tel: 044-4219-2151
Fax: 044-4219-2322
Duty officer: 98-4008-2731
Email: bdhcchen@airtelmail.in

Singapore High Commission (Embassy)
E-6 Chandragupta Marg
Chanakyapuri
New Delhi 110021
Tel: 011-4600-0915 (visa and consular); 011-4600-0800 (administration)
Fax: 011-4601-6413 (general); 011-4601-6412 (visa); 011-3042 0393
    (administration)
Email: singhc_del@sgmfa.gov.sg
Homepage address: http://www.mfa.gov.sg/newdelhi/

Government offices

Reserve Bank of India
Central Office
Shaheed Bhagat Singh Road
Mumbai 400001

Central Board of Direct Taxes
North Block
Delhi 110001
Homepage address: http://incometaxindia.gov.in

Foreigners Regional Registration Office (FRRO)

Foreigners' Registration (F&R) Branch (Delhi)
East Block-VIII, Level-II
Sector-1, R.K. Puram
New Delhi 110066
Tel: 011-2671-1443; 011-2619-5530; 011-2617-1944
    extn.142/302/141;
    011-2619-2634 extn.142/302/141
Fax:011-2671-1348
Email: boihq@mha.nic.in; frrodelhi@hotmail.com; frrodli@nic.in
Contact person at airport: AFRRO (departure/arrival); Tel: 011-2565-2389

Foreigners Registration Office (Mumbai)
3rd Floor, Special Branch Bldg., Badruddin Tayabji Lane
Behind St. Xavier's College
Mumbai 400001
Tel: 022-2262-1169 (O)
Fax: 022-2262-0721
Email: frromum@nic.in; dcpsb2.frro@indiatimes.com
Contact person at airport: AFRRO (departure/arrival); Tel: 022-2682-8098

FRRO Kolkata
237 Acharya Jagdish Chandra Bose Road
Kolkata 700020
Tel:033-2247-0549 (O)
Fax: 033-2247-0549
Email: frrokol@nic.in
Contact person at airport: AFRRO (departure/arrival); Tel: 033-2520-8100

FRRO Chennai
Shastri Bhawan
26 Haddows Road
Chennai 600006

Tel: 044-2345-4970 (O)
Fax: 044-2345-4971
Email: frrochn@nic.in
Contact person at airport: SIO (departure/arrival); Tel: 044-2345-4976 (O);
    Fax: 044-2345-4977
Contact person at harbor: SIOI; Tel and Fax: 044-2345-4975

FRRO Amritsar
123-D Ranjit Avenue
Amritsar 143001
Tel: 0183-2508250 (O)
Email: frroasr@nic.in
Contact person at airport: AFRRO (departure/arrival); Tel: 0183-2592986

Ministry of Commerce and Industry

Department of industrial policy and promotion
Udyog Bhawan
New Delhi 110011
EPABX: 011-2306-1222
Fax: 011-2306-2626

Confederation of Indian Industry (CII)

Confederation of Indian Industry (CII)
The Mantosh Sondhi Center
23 Institutional Area, Lodi Road
New Delhi 110003
Tel: 011-2462-9994–7
Fax: 011-2462-6149/24633168
Email: ciico@ciionline.org
Homepage address: http://www.cii.in

Confederation of Indian Industry (CII)
India Habitat Center
Core 4A, 4th Floor, Lodi Road
New Delhi 110 003
Tel: 011-2468-2230–35; 01-4150-4514–19
Fax: 011-2468-2229; 2468-2228
Email : ciico@ciionline.org
Homepage address: http://www.cii.in

Confederation of Indian Industry (CII)
Plot No. 249-F, Udyog Vihar, Sector 18
Gurgaon 122015
Tel: 0124-401-4060–67
Fax: 0124-401-4080
Email: ciico@ciionline.org
Homepage address: http://www.cii.in

Confederation of Indian Industry (CII)
6 Netaji Subhas Road
Kolkata 700001
Tel: 033-2231-5571; 2231-0574
Fax: 033-2231-0577
Email : subrata.niyogi@ciionline.org; ciicocal@ciionline.org
Homepage address: http://www.cii.in

FICCI Head Office
Federation House
Tansen Marg
New Delhi 110001
Tel: 011-2373-8760–70
Fax: 011-2372-1504; 2332-0714
E-mail: ficci@ficci.com
Homepage address: http://www.ficci.com

The Associated Chambers of Commerce and Industry of India
ASSOCHAM Corporate Office, 1 Community Center Zamrudpur
Kailash Colony
New Delhi 110048
Tel: 46550555 (hunting line)
Fax: 4653-6481–82; 4653-6497–98
Email: assocham@nic.in
Homepage address: http://www.assocham.org/

Schools

American Embassy School
Chandragupta Marg, Chanakyapuri
New Delhi 110 021
Tel: 011-2688-8854
Fax: 011-2687-3320
Homepage address: http://www.aes.ac.in/web/AES/index.htm

American School of Bombay
SF 2, G-Block
Bandra-Kurla Complex Rd, Bandra (E)
Mumbai 400098

American International School—Chennai
100 Feet Road, Taramani
Chennai 600113
Tel: 044-2254-9000
Fax: 044-2254-9001
Email: HeadofSchool@aisch.org
Homepage address: http://www.aisch.org/

Woodstock School
Mussoorie 248179
Homepage address: http://www.woodstock.ac.in/

Kodaikanal International School
PO Box 25
Kodaikanal 624101
Tel: 04542-247-500
Fax: 04542-241-109
Email: contact@kis.in
Homepage address: http://www.kis.in/

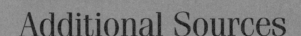

Additional Sources

Rama Bijapurkar 2007, *We Are Like That Only: Understanding the Logic of Consumer India*, Penguin.

Hiru Bijlani 2005, *Succeed in Business: India*, Marshall Cavendish Business.

Central Board of Direct Taxes, circulars of July 23, 1969 and May 29, 1975; ITA 2003.

Paul Davies 2004, *What's this India Business?*, Nicholas Brealey Publishing.

Doing Business Project, World Bank Group, *Doing Business 2008/ India/ Comparing Regulations in 178 Economies*.

Ernst & Young 2006, *Tax and Business Guide; Doing Business in India*.

Nicki Grihault 2003, rev. 2006, *Culture Smart! India*, Kuperard.

HLB India 2005, *Doing Business in India*.

India Brand Equity Foundation, various publications (IBEF is a partnership of the Ministry of Commerce, Government of India, and the Confederation of Indian Industry).

Gitanjali Kolanad 1994, *Culture Shock India*, Times Books International.

Rajesh Kumar and Anand Kumar Sethi 2005, *Doing Business in India*, Palgrave MacMillan.

Eugene M. Makar 2008, *An American's Guide to Doing Business in India*, Adams Business.

Ranjini Manian 2007, *Doing Business with India For Dummies*, John Wiley & Sons.

Roderick Millar 2007, *Doing Business with India*, Global Market Briefings.

US Government, *Country Commercial Guide*.

URLs

http://indiabudget.nic.in/

Indian government's *Economic Survey* and Indian budget

http://india.gov.in/business/taxation/agents.php

Indian government's article on taxation of agents

http://business.gov.in/outerwin.htm?id=http://incometaxindia.gov.in/mappop.htm

Indian government website with double taxation avoidance treaties

http://finmin.nic.in/fipbweb/fipb/webpage.asp

The Foreign Investment Promotion Board webpages

http://mha.gov.in/fore_division.htm

The website of the foreigner's division of the Ministry of Home Affairs

http://dipp.gov.in/cgpdtm/cgpdtm.htm

Controller General of Patents, Designs and Trademarks

http://www.immigrationindia.nic.in/

The government website for immigration issues, including visa matters

http://www.dni.gov/nic/NIC_2020_project.html

Forecasts for the year 2020 by the National Intelligence Council (US) http://persmin.nic.in/RTI/WelcomeRTI.htm

About the *Right to Information Act*

http://www.transparency.org/news_room/in_focus/2007/cpi2007/cpi_2007_ table

Transparency International's corruption league tables

http://report.globalintegrity.org/India/2007

Country reports on several measures of integrity by Global Integrity

http://www.nasscom.in/Nasscom/templates/NormalPage.aspx?id=6216

Opening a branch

http://adaniel.tripod.com/politics.htm

Notes on Indian politics

http://www.nseindia.com/

Website of the National Stock Exchange

http://www.bseindia.com/

Website of the Bombay Stock Exchange

http://www.sebi.gov.in/

The website of the Securities and Exchange Board of India

Index

Companies Index